Tequila Shooters

Al Daniels

Published in 2011 by New Generation Publishing

First Edition

To Jenny, Raggy and the Immortal Johnny Cash…
'One piece at a time'

Prologue

Dan Paige sat back, digesting a stringy beef enchilada. His partner, Brenda, was attempting to relax in the passenger seat of their tired black and white. They were parked by a Taco Bell a stone's throw above San Diego's renowned Mission Bay. The lunch had been filling, if not exactly scrumptious – and it certainly hadn't been enhanced by the unpleasant odor radiating from the back seat. They'd just delivered a notorious local bag lady to the Christian Fellowship Shelter in nearby Linda Vista and the old hag had left behind her unmistakable calling card – excruciating BO. The stink barely registered with an old hand like Dan, but near-novice Brenda hung her head out of the window, sucking in fresh air.

It was a typical early summer afternoon. The tourists were undoubtedly trying to convince each other that the irritating mist would soon burn off, so that they could enjoy the beach or a visit to Sea World. But the natives knew that clearing skies weren't really a good bet. June, as usual, was turning out to be 'America's Finest City's' dreariest month.

Dan lifted a half-full plastic cup off the dash. It clipped the steering wheel, spilling the remains of the black tar that was attempting to pass as coffee on his unpressed uniform trousers. "Shit! Why can't they equip these units with the fuckin' basics, like a damned cup holder? Is that asking too much?"

His striking partner could barely conceal a smile. "Perhaps they've decided reliable radios and handy shotgun racks are more useful accessories for street cops?" She may have been a rookie, but Brenda was no longer wet behind those lovely ears. She knew she'd been fortunate to be partnered up with Dan – and she'd already discovered in their brief time together that he could *take*, as well as dish, the crap.

As Dan was about to toss a witty rejoinder Brenda's way, a message blared from central dispatch. *"All Sector B units... 459 in progress at 4106 Mt Bigelow Drive. Who can respond?"* Dan tossed his empty cup on the floor and turned the engine over as Brenda grabbed the mike and responded. "Two-ten on our way."

A bold daylight break-in seemed to be going down... up the hill and a bit further inland. No siren – a 'silent response' – was SOP for a neighborhood crime in progress.

In a couple of minutes Dan was cruising up to the 60's ranch-style dwelling. He parked directly in front. On this typical San Diego street, the house number was painted on the curb in black numerals in a white background. The house was weather-beaten pale green, complemented by peeling, brown faux-shutters affixed next to the windows. The sunburned lawn was more weeds than grass and badly needed a cut.

They leapt out of the car and Dan quickly surveyed the scene. Brenda ran around to his side of the car, putting its bulk between her and any curious perp watching from a window. She rested her hand on her holstered gun. The only activity Dan could detect was some old lady across the street peeking through her curtains. No time to waste... there was every chance the burglar was still hard at it inside. "Stay low and go around back Bren. Cut him off if he ducks out your way, OK?" Protocol dictated holstered weapons... no need to alarm the neighbors or ratchet things up with an already jumpy perp.

Brenda stood around five-nine and was exceptionally fit. She'd look after herself round back. Dan trusted her instincts and skills more than most rookies he'd broken in. As he heard no sound emanating from the house, he paced stealthily to the front door, looking for signs of a forced entry. His partner had already disappeared behind the side gate. She'd be in position, behind decent cover, in a moment or two.

No broken panes or doorframe damage – and the garage door also appeared to be undisturbed. The lack of signs of a break-in on the *street side* was no surprise. Perps typically jimmied the sliding doors around back and left that way as well. Brenda was more likely to face a fleeing intruder (or, God forbid, *intruders*) from her position. Hopefully, if it came to this, it would be an easy collar for her. A week before, he'd have covered the back himself, instructing her to knock on the front door and back off. But, if the shit hit the fan, he'd rather be the one entering an enclosed, hostile environment – and a shout at the front door gave the burglar the option of a presumably safer exit out the back. In the back yard, a perp could be taken down in the open. Dan was comfortable with his decision... Brenda was capable of covering a primary exit on her own.

After allowing Brenda a few extra seconds to set up, Dan pounded on the door. *"Police! Open up!"* He expected no response; and the burglar might be long gone by now. If he heard anything, it would likely be the perp running through the house and out the back. But hold on, the front door actually opened a crack. Dan instinctively relaxed, surmising that the householder was in and the neighbor's call had been a false alarm. He prepared to identify himself to a startled occupant.

The door opened another inch and a bright flash exploded in his face. A searing heat scorched his left jawbone – and he immediately found himself on all fours. Temporarily blinded and deafened from the blast, his first instinct was to yell a warning to Brenda... and then it was all he could do to concentrate on maintaining consciousness. Later, he remembered thinking as he slumped on the front steps, "I hope to hell another shot's not on its way." Then, all went black.

He came around in the ambulance; its siren wailing a dissonant back-up track to an incessant ringing in his head. He felt like some prankster had set off a cheap alarm clock in his skull. A paramedic was shouting in his right ear, "Officer Paige, Officer Paige!" His hand crept up and he felt the loose bandaging on the left side of his face. He prayed that the dampness running down his body was sweat, and not blood.

In the weeks that followed the constant, irritating ringing (the doctors diagnosed it as post-trauma tinnitus) had become a personal alarm call... in more ways than one.

Brenda visited him in hospital nearly every day. She looked extremely tidy on her initial visit, admirably filling out a burgundy wrap-around dress and sporting rather fetching off-duty makeup. She tiptoed to his bed, placing a leafy plant and some car magazines on the side table. Dan remembered thinking, "Why hasn't this fantastic broad attracted a guy?" He reminded himself that she'd chosen to be a cop, a vocation that required suitors to deal with the unsocial hours and stress her work generated. Dan and Bren didn't really hang out off the clock, so the true story underlying her social choices hadn't yet surfaced. He knew that, as usual, he'd been a better *talker* than listener with his captive audience in the squad car.

A few visits later, Brenda told Dan what he already suspected... the lone punk behind the door at 4106 Mt Bigelow had *unquestionably* been high on PCP. As any seasoned cop knew, a 'wired' intruder wouldn't even concede the threat posed by a black and white pulling up. After greeting Dan and squeezing off a single round from a Saturday Night Special, the kid had run out the back, just as Dan had suspected he would. Apparently, he was over the fence and gone before any backup arrived.

Dan didn't bother asking Brenda how the perp had managed to elude her. There was little point. It was over. Looking ashen and distraught, Brenda volunteered the low-down on her behavior during the fiasco anyway. She'd run around front when she heard the shot, more concerned with Dan's condition than with covering the perpetrator's exit. Brenda seldom cursed, but she earnestly added, "Fuck it. I'd do *exactly* the same thing again if it came down to it! Your life is worth far more to me than collaring some lit-up punk."

Later, a woman who lived on the next street over told the follow-up team that she'd seen an agitated boy leap over the back fence and run through her yard. She was able to give the cops a pretty decent description... *White, late teens, slim build, long blondish hair and a wispy beard – wearing a retro Padres cap, baggy jeans and a gold Lakers jersey.* This narrowed the hunt down to about ten thousand street-smart punks in the Clairemont/Linda Vista area. The little shit was never apprehended.

After a brief hospital stint, Dan went home for some well-earned R&R. His wife, Melinda, tried her hardest to be an attentive nursemaid. In fact, she seemed more caring and thoughtful than she'd been in ages. She'd actually stayed home from the office for *two* whole days, but her fidgety bedside manner had been more distraction than aid in his recovery.

Melinda assured him that the thin wound along his jawbone was healing nicely... "That little old scar will barely show, honey – and besides, I think it's kind of sexy." While she didn't mention the idea specifically, Dan realized she was hoping his injury would be their ticket to his long-deserved promotion.

His eventual return to duty was, however, less than enthralling. Dan had risked his butt, yet again, in a losing battle against a growing army of drug-addled punks and sociopathic gang-bangers. And, as usual, he'd proved that the odds of prevailing against these dipshits were less than even-money. He was beginning to see the bigger picture... this shitty job just wasn't worth the price that he and his overmatched associates were being asked to pay.

Dan accepted his colleagues' backslaps and hoped, mostly for Melinda's sake, that an overdue promotion would be forthcoming. But, it didn't happen. Three months later, he began reading the Union-Trib's *'Help Wanted'* classifieds... in earnest. Not long thereafter, he said adios to Brenda and a few buddies over lunch and quietly resigned from the force.

Five years on...

The surgeons had worked wonders on Dan's wound. The recovery nurses repeatedly reminded him he'd been very lucky. The crease on his jaw line was superficial and it had healed nicely. Nowadays, the scar was hardly noticeable to anyone but Dan himself. And even *he* had to concentrate to make it out when he looked in the mirror. When he thought about the scar at all, Dan kidded himself that the pale seam along his jaw lent an 'air of mystery'. Maybe Melinda's "It's so sexy, hon!" verdict was a bit over the top, but the crease did serve as a daily reminder of a life he'd well and truly left behind.

He kept in touch with a few pals on the force – particularly Brenda, one of the few cops he'd ever bothered to draw into his tight circle of 'civilian pals'. These days he preferred to keep his head down. Younger, more single-minded devotees of law enforcement could 'protect and serve' an oblivious, and increasingly apathetic, public.

Chapter 1

San Diego County hugs the magnificent California coastline. Beginning at Imperial Beach, Otay Mesa and San Ysidro – small communities adjoining the border with Mexico to the south – Greater San Diego's landmass stretches fifty-five miles northwards. It finishes beyond Oceanside, butting onto the Marine Corps' massive Camp Pendleton. The shoreline is dotted with traditional beach towns, many in situ before the turn of the last century. Today, the county is an urban strand... a megalopolis, gradually spreading inland to accommodate the dreamers and Snowbirds continually flocking to this Promised Land.

Tijuana squats below San Diego's border with Mexico. 'TJ' is more populous than the incorporated city of San Diego itself. And, the two areas' economies are irrefutably linked. San Diegans rely on their Mexican neighbors for cheap labor, as well as a growing demand for goods and services unavailable in Baja. Tijuana looks to San Diego for decent regular wages... and for the vital flow of tourista dollars into a fragile economy.

The US Interstate 5 Freeway stretches north some fourteen hundred miles – from the Mexican border all the way to Canada, at her boundary with Washington State. In San Diego County, this straight ribbon of highway creates an identifiable dividing line, separating two distinct Southern California lifestyles. In the narrow strip west of I-5 to the ocean, two socio-economic groups peacefully coexist. A dying breed of beach bums and aging hippies reside cheek-by-jowl with many of the county's wealthiest residents. To the east of the freeway, 'Inland San Diego' provides more affordable housing for the county's middle classes and hard working blue-collar families.

For each mile traversed inland, the county's ambient temperature rises dramatically. Green coastal topography morphs into mesas, sagebrush and desert. A significant number of the elderly and wealthy actually prefer the heat and clear skies inland, opting for the suburban, brush fire-threatened 'Rancho' communities scattered throughout the rolling hills north of the city proper. While many younger inland dwellers declare a preference for the year-round warmth and mall-based lifestyle, most would unhesitatingly trade up to the coastline and La Jolla – Spanish for 'The Jewel' – a buttoned up, golf and tennis-obsessed beach community, long known as a major haven for the county's movers and shakers.

The Scots have a word for pesky coastal hazes that only warming temperatures and ocean breezes eventually dissipate. They call their

9

mists *'morning haar'*. *This guttural term would no doubt sound apropos to those eager tourists who arrive in San Diego for early summer vacations and disappointedly discover that the coastline remains overcast well into the long afternoon.*

Unchecked population growth has been an abiding theme for San Diego over the past thirty years. The historic city of distinct districts – 'villages' coalescing to make up an agreeable whole – has disappeared. Hectares of inland scrub (wasteland that no sane person would have deemed suitable for development) are nowadays covered in nondescript tracts of 'cookie cutter' houses and condos.

Dan Paige was San Diego born and bred. He'd traveled a bit in his younger days, but never yearned to move to greener pastures. He'd witnessed change – good and bad – and like most people approaching middle age, he preferred the more livable city of his youth. But, he knew that no one could turn back the clock... so he tried to focus on the things he loved about his city, assiduously ignoring the liberal doses of odious 'progress' he couldn't abide or alter.

Friday, late-March, 2009

Hey, surf's up!

Dan was on top of a monster. He was riding the biggest wave he'd ever caught off Ocean Beach, working it for all it was worth. On shore, a couple of stray mutts appeared to be his sole spectators. The dogs stood motionless, showing apparent interest in his attempt to master this awesome twenty-five footer. Then he caught sight of his dad, standing further down the beach. Dressed in the very suit he'd been buried in years before, Paige Senior was beckoning his son to join him ashore. But in that instant, the wave broke, sending Dan tumbling. Both surfer and board were thrown like flotsam into the murky gray-green depths. Holding his breath and looking beyond the brine's distant surface, he could just make out a faint patch of blue sky and sunlight. But for some reason he was now stuck fast in the sandy ocean bottom, buried up to his elbows and calves in something very much like quicksand!

Lungs exploding, Dan struggled to break free. But he was simply sinking deeper into his underwater death trap, fighting a losing battle for his very life! His mouth opened involuntarily and he drew in... *air?* He awoke with a gasp and inhaled deeply. Shit! Another morning was commencing with this absurd recurring dream. It occurred to him, yet again, that he was losing his marbles, big-time.

10

Dan lay sweating, reconnecting with reality. He attempted for the hundredth time to unravel the twisted messages emanating from his subconscious. Growing up in OB, he'd earned a reputation as one of the Southland's most venerated surfers. Years on, the dudes who currently ruled OB's precious piece of oceanfront were still in awe of him. But this fantastic trip on a monster wave bore little resemblance to the reality of his past... undeniably; he'd never been the mythical, cool 'lone surfer' of his disturbing dream.

Dan reckoned, not for the first time, that his beckoning old man was going to caution him to leave San Diego – to seek a fresh start. If it weren't for his resurgent love life, this well-meaning message could no doubt comprise the nucleus of a very solid plan.

As he dangled his legs over the edge of his sagging single bed, Dan decided that a short, intense run would restore some equilibrium to his morning. He threw on jogging shorts, an old *Grateful Dead* tee shirt and his scuffed running shoes before heading quietly out of his apartment into an overcast Southern California morning.

Thirty minutes later he was back in his bedroom. He stripped off his sweaty clothes, threw them into an overstuffed hamper and staggered to the bathroom. Bleary-eyed, he peered at the face staring from the mirror as he hacked at it with a cheap disposable blade. The thin scar along his jaw line was certainly more noticeable when he sported stubble. His new love, Sophie, described Dan's unshaved visage as his 'villainous look'. But while he felt (or at least *hoped*) that she wasn't serious, he did hedge his bets. If he couldn't swing by home before heading up to her place in Del Mar, a battery-powered shaver was charged and ready in his Chevy's glove compartment.

An increasingly craggy countenance made Dan ponder, not for the first time, if a more rigorous skincare regime might be in order. That sassy Colin – the grooming guru of the self-described 'Fairy Godfathers' on TV's *Gay Guys Put You Wise* – could no doubt offer up some timely tips to resurrect his still not unsalvageable mug. Oh well, Dan knew an array of costly goop would only gather dust in his medicine cabinet. On the other hand, he'd continue to slap on the pricey aftershave Sophie had given him... it couldn't hurt! He was just ten pounds over his high school defensive back's weight; still minus the spare tire so many of his old chums were sporting. Some women he'd known since his high school days actually told him he'd matured into a passably attractive guy.

Dan jumped into what passed for a shower. In truth, he had to make do with a rusting, lime scale-encrusted showerhead poised over his grubby tub. Years of pummeling by San Diego's mineral-laden

Colorado River water had deposited white scum all over the tub's surface, as well as staining his torn shower curtain. The bathroom lacked a working extractor fan... the grubby grill in the ceiling was there for effect; never connected, at least since he'd moved in. An opaque sliding window provided the room's only ventilation. Even with the window and the door to the hallway wide open, the atmosphere reminded him of a cheap Turkish bath. A sexy, leisurely shower in the company of a luscious partner was a scenario that this bathroom's mildew, dirty tiles and cracked tub couldn't readily support.

He padded into the bedroom, patting down his light brown hair. Cut short, the style was a hangover from his years on the force. His efforts to stay trim, neat and in shape kept him ready for most contingencies. But, these days, he had to admit that it was more for self-esteem than as a prerequisite for his duties as a commercial insurance claims adjustor.

He threw on navy slacks, a tan shirt and a slightly frayed navy silk tie, adorned with powder blue horses. Grabbing a brown tweed sportscoat and the last clean socks in his drawer, Dan headed barefoot to the kitchen. A breakfast bar divided the compact cooking area from the apartment's minuscule living room. The Formica countertop and a pair of old chrome barstools were functional, but not particularly apropos for chic dinner parties.

Dan's oxblood loafers still lay where he'd left them; under an overstuffed armchair sitting in front of his tiny old television. He put on his socks and shoes, shining the toes on his trouser legs as he headed through to the kitchen.

This one bedroom, upper-level box was definitely a single man's haven. 'Worn around the edges' and 'lived in' were two of his favorite descriptions. Outside, a concrete walkway served the building's upstairs units. A rear landing led to ground level. Four identical apartments hovered below Dan's floor – and a mirror-image building faced his own block across a badly landscaped common area. He joked to his friends that this Normal Heights neighborhood possessed "a nearly-lost San Diego charm – in spades"... implying it still oozed an ambiance that the newer, outlying neighborhoods could only pine for.

He filled his *Lost in Space* cereal bowl with off-brand corn flakes and microwaved a mug of water for instant coffee while listening to the *Doobie's Greatest* on a tinny mini-CD player. There was no decent music on morning radio... and he wasn't in the mood for the news. Although he'd been a teenager in what many considered a fallow decade for rock – *the Uninspiring 80's* – Dan's own musical tastes stretched towards an earlier era. He venerated basic, 'in your face' guys

12

like Bob Seger and ZZ Top – top live performers who'd done their utmost to keep 'that old-time rock and roll' alive and kicking.

A few minutes later, Dan stealthily headed out into another morning. Not quietly enough however. His aged neighbor opened her adjoining door and graced him with a beaming smile, enhanced by a prolonged flash of tea and cigarette-stained dentures. He knew the drill. Mrs Getz's request for a 'small favor' would unquestionably be forthcoming. Oh well, he didn't always keep his music that low and she never complained (probably down to *deafness* rather than any inherent neighborliness). Honestly, running the occasional errand for this eccentric old woman was a small price to pay for tranquility on the home front.

Probably the lady was no more than seventy-five, but her wrinkled, rice paper skin gave Mrs Getz a look that could best be described as 'fresh off the coroner's slab'. As Dan passed, he foolishly paused and glanced into her rheumy eyes, aiming for a friendly, if noncommittal, "Hello!" as he attempted to breeze by.

Mrs Getz was having none of it. "Sweetheart, could you drop this tiny bundle in the bin on your way?" She was already handing him a brimming plastic garbage bag. Dan couldn't spot any major leaks, but normal 'Getz odors' – over-ripe cat food remains, bacon grease and Pooky excrement – wafted from the unsecured top.

So, he'd been caught again – flat outfoxed! "Sure, no problem Mrs Getz." He gripped the top of the bag gingerly between forefinger and thumb, having spotted an apparently unsoiled handhold. "See you later."

He slung the odious bag into one of the overfull bins at the rear of his stucco-spackled building. A fading sign posted on the wall identified the mini-complex as the *'Sunset Hills Apartments'* – and warned that trespassers were subject to prosecution. Both apartment buildings badly required fresh paint and their rusting gutters clung tenuously to the overhangs on the cracked tile roofs. He headed out front and walked down an uneven sidewalk towards his uninspiring Chevy Malibu – a classic 'company car'. He reflected on the dearth of bicycles and skateboards scattered around his street these days. Young kids, primarily the children of Chicanos who'd migrated from Southeast San Diego, lived in similar apartments further to the east, but Dan's immediate neighborhood remained blue collar, white and emphatically *elderly*.

The Eagles' *New Kid in Town* accompanied his drive down the hill into Mission Valley. This three-mile freeway commute used to take fifteen minutes tops, even in rush hours. Nowadays, he was quicker taking side streets… forsaking the so-called 'direct' route. In the past decade, San Diego's roadways were beginning to match LA's renowned gridlock.

Fridays could be tedious, enlivened only when an unusual claim came in prior to the weekend. Many of TriState's larger insureds encouraged their Risk Managers to clear paperwork on work-related accidents or petty pilfering before heading out for the weekend. It would probably be a desk day for Dan, with no major breaks, logging in the normal pre-weekend crap. Walt Crozier, his Regional Manager from LA, would be down next week to review Dan's 'Open' and 'Closed' Claims Logs… *exciting stuff!* What the hell, Dan reflected; at least I'm no longer a sitting target for Angel Dust-addled perps since quitting my old gig.

Chapter 2

Paying the price

As Dan was driving into his underground parking garage in Mission Valley, a stone's throw away a purported 'importer/exporter' named Manny Tejada was about to begin his first meeting of the day. Manny rented a small office suite in a nondescript glass and steel 'cake box' a quarter of a mile east of TriState, on Camino del Rio North. Tejada's location and furnishings weren't luxurious, but the office was freshly decorated – and imposing enough for his requirements.

Manny was wearing his notion of a snappy business suit... electric blue sharkskin, three-button and 'Western Cut'. A faux brass plaque in the outside corridor advertised Manuel Tejada as: *'Sole Proprietor, SoCal Import and Export'*. With a curvaceous blonde receptionist/secretary as his sole supporting player, his aura of legitimacy was nearly credible.

Most bottom-rung importers staked out cheaper office space in unfashionable locations nearer the border, but that wasn't for Manny. He intended to go legitimate in the not too distant future and it was time to act the part. He felt that his taupe silk shirt set off his intended 'businesslike and refined' look. He'd explained to his receptionist that his dress shirts would cost a *fortune* in top shops in the States, but he bought them in bulk down in TJ at a knockdown price... "Straight from the fuckin' wholesaler, in five distinguished business shades." His Italian silk ties were the real deal, no third-rate 'faux-designer' labels for him – and *certainly* no polyester knock-offs.

Today's meeting wouldn't concern his legitimate trading interests. In point of fact, longtime associates, men he couldn't ignore, had allocated him a crucial task... a job requiring the talents of a couple of trustworthy, street-hardened soldiers. He'd already decided that this delicate mission called for a pair of hombres who flew under the radar in San Diego.

His buxom assistant buzzed the intercom, announcing the arrival of his intended henchmen. "Two gentlemen out here say they have an appointment, Mr Tejada." She lowered her voice to a whisper and added, "They don't look like your average businessmen, sir. The hefty one just let loose a thunderous fart on our new leather couch and the whole room reeks! Should I send these morons through or instruct them to vacate the premises?"

Manny considered, yet again, if the undeniably attractive, but achingly dim, *puta* in reception required upgrading. The answer was

15

obviously in the affirmative, if he was being honest with himself. It was not her place to comment on the demeanor of potential business associates – in either a positive or negative way. Sure, she was great for copping a quick feel or as a target for his lewd remarks, but she wouldn't last if she couldn't zip her mouth!

A minute later, Jesus and Flaco slouched opposite his desk, cigarettes dangling from their mouths. They seemed unperturbed, as if they hadn't overheard his secretary's comments; smiling and whispering together in Spanish. Purportedly street-smart, hardened *vatos*, these two still managed to give off that distinct 'dumber than tree stumps' vibe. Their obvious lack of sophistication niggled at Manny, but this job simply required "point and fire hit men" – as the instructions from his superiors had *specifically* indicated. These guys could do that type of dirty work... delivering promptly and on the cheap.

Manny's valet (and valued *Executive Assistant*), Enrique, had been using Flaco and Jesus as local muscle for the past couple of months. Manny remembered them delivering a few packages and a message or two to his house. He valued his valet's judgment, and Enrique indicated they'd proved dependable enough for 'uncomplicated' tasks. He'd described the pair as "smart enough to do as they're told, but not clever enough to get any bright ideas."

Manny sat uncomfortably behind his desk and eyed the two keyed up henchmen. Legitimate customers shouldn't see these types in his office. But, he convinced himself he could relax. He had no appointments scheduled for the rest of the day – and 'Miss Eye Candy' out front wouldn't enquire too inquisitively about why thugs like these had turned up on their doorstep. Right now she'd be sitting on her fine ass, filing her nails and perusing that issue of *Celebrity Gossip* that he wasn't supposed to have spotted on her desk. (In fact, he was mistaken about the blonde's present activities. At that moment, she was circling the reception area, misting it with a bottle of her overpowering cologne.)

Jesus and Flaco had no idea why their *jefe grande* had summoned them. Flaco, the undisputed 'brains' of the partnership, was pretty certain they hadn't fucked up in a major way. So it probably meant the boss had some important new assignment for them!

The more reticent *Mejicano*, the bear-like Jesus, stood well over six feet and was going to lard. Ultra-snug, grimy leather trousers no doubt exacerbated his high-pitched voice... a contralto noticed by everyone when he rarely spoke. His long-sleeved cowboy shirt hid the multitude of tattoos covering his arms, torso and neck. Born and raised in Central

Mexico, he'd moved up to the border towns as a teenager, seeking his fortune. In fact, an obviously pregnant thirteen-year-old orphan had also influenced his decision to leave. Well over a dozen years later, Jesus had risen to a low-level crime post down in Ensenada – and he'd kept his nose fairly clean with his bosses and the *policia*. (Mercifully, to his benefit, most Mexican cops were paid to steer clear of cartel soldiers and drug dealers.) Today, he was content to make eye contact with Mr Tejada, letting his pal Flaco do the talking. He could feel it... this meeting could lead to a *permanent* move up to Tijuana from the backwaters of Ensenada. *El Norte* assignments would become routine; promising both of them a precious shot at better, more lucrative working lives.

The corpulent Jesus preferred slapping on powerful layers of Brut to regular washes... he believed that such a fine men's cologne was manufactured *specifically* to mask any hint of unsocial manly odors. This habit had been an obstacle to his career prospects, although he wasn't aware of it. At this very moment, his malodorous stench permeated Manny's office. The boss man was, in fact, wishing that the building's architect had incorporated opening windows in the structure's exterior design.

The smaller man, Flaco, sat forward, fidgeting on the edge of his padded chair. Short and wiry, he deemed himself to be not only the physical, but also the *mental* antithesis of his burly *campanero*. His clothes were clean and tidy – pressed jeans and shirt, dark boots shined to perfection. In his late thirties, he felt that the few years he had on his partner made him the natural leader... along with the mental superiority he so obviously possessed.

More weather-beaten than most men of his age, Flaco's mahogany skin and prominent Indian nose gave him the look of a sly, Aztec-bred Ron Wood. One ear sported a gold earring, but Flaco bore no other piercings or tattoos. He'd explained to Jesus on many occasions, "I'm maintaining a *clean* look; the ladies don't dig ink." In fact, while Flaco feigned a certain machismo, his oft-described dalliances with 'the ladies' were really a closet gay's fantasies.

As a street kid in Jaurez, he'd been recruited as an errand boy and lookout by local troublemakers. He taught himself to be handy with a flick knife, affecting slicked-down hair, tight jeans and black tank tops. But, even at fourteen, he'd been aware that other *vatos* who dressed and behaved in this menacing manner were sexually attractive to him. He knew better, however, than to act on such feelings with his brutal companions.

Even a dim bulb like Jesus knew the score on Flaco's 'social preferences'. But, they avoided the subject of homosexuality like the plague; such talk could lead to serious misunderstandings with some of their less enlightened associates.

Flaco had relocated to Tijuana from Jaurez a year earlier, fleeing troubles that he didn't care to share with his new crowd. A top quality counterfeit green card made him a convincing 'legal alien' in the US... he could hang out in San Diego when he liked. A 'quick study', with a near-photographic memory, he already knew his way around the backwaters of Northern Baja *and* San Diego County. He'd earned himself a lucrative role as a trusted mid-level soldier in his powerful cartel of linked Tijuana and Ensenada families.

The dim, but loyal Jesus latched onto Flaco's coat-tails soon after they'd met in Tijuana; elated when the diminutive man had eventually selected him for assignments over the border. In fact, what had attracted Flaco to his burly sidekick was the big dude's '84 Firebird low-rider. Flaco, probably against his better judgment, had succumbed to the fundamental appeal of *cheap transportation*, with an obedient chauffeur at his beck and call.

Manny Tejada took a moment to contemplate his odious new assignment. He'd put the fear of God into these *pachucos* – it was crucial to command their strictest attention right off the bat. They had to believe he could be *ruthless* – and that there were even crueler people behind him if they failed in this important task.

A disloyal foot soldier – a San Diego-based *pocho* of little importance – had become very greedy. This bastard would have to disappear... and it needed doing quickly. Manny understood that Flaco and Jesus were better off ignorant of the gory details. He started right in... "Take off your hats and put out those smokes! Don't you assholes know there's no smoking in public buildings up here? And speak *English* in this office, okay? You're in San Diego today, so get used to fitting in. *Now listen up...* A certain person has his head stuck so far up his ass he's no longer sure if it's day or night! He'll soon be taught a serious lesson. We're holding up this *hijo de puta* as a crystal clear example for everyone. No one rips us off or gets too clever! Unquestioning obedience is rewarded in our organization – and disloyalty invites an all-encompassing *shitstorm*. Are you with me?"

Both men pinched out their cigarettes and stashed the butts in a trouser pocket. Flaco was certainly taking it all in. He earnestly replied, "I'm with you. You want him seriously fucked up, damaged for life, right boss?"

"On the contrary boys, we want this fucker *dead* and his bloody corpse left somewhere in the open, so the cops discover it pronto. This particular hombre bounces between *Méjico* and up here – a bit like yourselves, in a way. But he must be found in the US and his death *must* be investigated by the San Diego *policia*. Then, his untimely demise will be well covered in the California press, instead of his worthless carcass disappearing virtually unnoticed, as often happens in *Méjico*. It will be clearly understood – on both sides of the fuckin' border – how we deal unmercifully with greedy fuckers."

Manny took an index card from his desk drawer and handed it to Flaco. "Here's the background on the worthless turd. His name's Benito Rosado. He lives legally in the US, I guess; but he was born in Tijuana and many of his relatives are still there. His *mama grande* heads the Rosado clan and many of her offspring remain near her, in adjoining *casas* on Avenida Aguila. The Rosado men hang out at Cantina Gaudalupe, smack in the middle of her street."

Tejada handed Flaco a second card, containing a hand-drawn map of the bar's location. "You'll get a lead on this asshole from the cantina's daytime bartender, a guy named Jorge. He owes us a favor or two for getting his brother out of a tight spot... but he's not on our payroll. He won't be working until Monday, so drop by that afternoon, after you finish up your regular TJ business. Benito's been extremely hard to find lately – maybe he knows we're onto him. Remember, you must take him out *up here*... in San Diego. Our message must be loud and clear: No one who dares to double-cross us is safe, north or south of the border. If you fuck us over, you pay! Got it?"

Flaco reviewed Manny's index card description of their intended victim...

Benito Rosado - *5 feet, 8 inches. Around 45. Lean, but muscular. No facial hair, visible scars or tattoos. Medium length full head of black hair. Likes the ladies and throws money around (when he has any). Likes titty bars. A sharp dresser – often wears Western shirts with silver collar tabs and belts with silver buckles. Dressy outfit would be slacks, loafers and a turtleneck or silk shirt.*

Flaco glanced up and asked, "Have a photo?"

Manny replied, "No, but you shouldn't need one. That barman Jorge – and practically everyone in the neighborhood – knows Benito real well. Someone will put you on his trail pronto. And, you can use the weekend to nose around up here in San Diego. You never know, you might get a head start before Monday."

For the first time, the taciturn Jesus chimed in. "How much does this job pay?"

Manny extracted an envelope from his breast pocket and handed it to Flaco. "$500 each now and $500 more when it's done – and done properly. I want him found quick and then fucked up *terminally*... with high visibility, somewhere in *this city*. I repeat – it has to be done *very, very soon*. Understood?"

Flaco momentarily hesitated, but caught himself, sat up straight and reached deep within himself to summon up the courage for a bit of bargaining. "No offence, but a grand each doesn't sound like much for a job like this. I think we deserve three."

Manny immediately shook his head. In a way, however, he was pleased to see that Flaco was showing real *cajones*. "The money ain't negotiable. You should consider this as an audition for bigger and better things to come. For starters, Rosado's old territory will be up for grabs after you whack him. And, with our business interests expanding, there'll be plenty of fresh opportunities in the pipeline. Any other questions, or is this assignment too much for you two?"

Flaco discreetly decided to back off. "No sir. You can consider this here job as good as done. We'll be in touch when we get a lead on Benito. I assume you'll expect regular updates?"

"Right, but be discreet for Christ's sake! Now, get to work on your regular duties as well... and be sure to sort out Rosado as your top priority. If you don't fuck up, you'll soon be rolling in clover. That's a promise!"

The two *vatos* pulled their frayed straw cowboy hats low on their foreheads and headed back into the reception area. Manny asked them to close the door after themselves and retrieved a can of pine scent air freshener from his bottom drawer. He sincerely hoped that the building's feeble air conditioning would quickly and effectively deal with the lingering pong.

Chapter 3

Monday

Dressing for success?

So, the new week began with Dan closing down the final of a slew of routine 'Signed-off Claims' files on his PC. He leaned back, closing his eyes. He was already ravenous and his screen-weary brain needed a break. He'd never warm to the monotony of deskwork. It was the pits. Workdays only moved at a tolerable pace when he could escape into the field.

A multitude of 'Open Claims' still rattled around in the system. Many simply required a final review and sign-off – others demanded more attention. And as his boss, Walt, would be down from LA in the morning for their routine case review, today's lunch break would be short and sweet.

Of course, Dan had anticipated an office-bound day, so he'd headed to the front entrance at 10:30 to buy some provisions from that old stand-by... the 'roach coach'. (To put it more succinctly, he'd visited the convenient, if unappetizing, mobile snack truck when it hit the parking lot's entrance.) He'd been tempted by a chili beef wrap and sour cream kettle chips, but settled for a 'Healthy Bite' tuna on whole wheat and a diet cola. Dan patronized this 'greasy spoon on wheels' often enough to know that most of their plastic-wrapped entrees tasted like cardboard anyway, and repeated on him like an M-60.

By noon, Dan had polished off the tuna sandwich, taken the last sip of his soda and opened another e-file. From his desk, he could just make out Trini, TriState's cute and loopy receptionist, chatting into her telephone headset. Her desk was situated just over his cubicle's dividing partition, in close enough proximity for Dan to pick up the latest tittle-tattle as it wafted over the thin barrier. Today she was gossiping with her pal Flo, blithely putting any number of incoming business calls on hold. Apparently, the kittenish Trini had turned up for work today straight from a riotous weekend at a guy named Tommy's place... and she'd been unable to find her new push-up bra and black silk thong in her stud-puppet's messy bedroom before she'd run out the door.

Trini was in full flow with her obviously sympathetic pal. "Thank God I wore decent designer jeans and a clean linen blouse for Sunday Brunch in Balboa Park. If I'd worn one of my bitchin' 'pussy pelmet' minis and that halter-top that complements my nipples, I'd be screwed, blued and tattooed right now. Yours truly would either be arriving late after swinging by home or spending the entire day slouching down below desktop level! Tommy left for the machine shop before I rolled out of the sack, Flo. I'll give you ten to one he's taken my undies into work, so he can brag about another conquest to his pathetic pals." Trini giggled before adding, "He'll just have to fork up for 'em. He'll try to return said unmentionables – and, of course, I'll make an almighty fuss before consenting to take back my pawed-over property. I'll assure Toe-suckin' Tommy that I'll *never* wear those lacies again after they've been ogled in the boy's bog by his pathetic buddies. *Appropriate* replacements – and by that, I mean shockingly expensive designer items, I can assure you – will be mandatory if he's serious about seein' this foxy lady again."

Dan laughed to himself, attempting to tune out Trini's inane conversation and return to his boring work. Unsurprisingly, his mind turned instead to a vision of Trini playing beach volleyball at a recent office picnic. Her ample bosom had practically erupted out of her skimpy halter-top; delighting male admirers, while eliciting the visible disgust of their less amply endowed girlfriends and wives. And then, suddenly, Dan's mental slideshow clicked back to an even earlier image... his ex-wife Melinda curled up naked and contented on their conjugal bed. He found himself wondering if her glorious rack still stood proudly of its own accord. But, these days, he wasn't prepared to satisfy his curiosity, even if she might be amenable to 'green lighting' a harmless fling with a willing ex-husband. Her current partner, Gene – and even more significantly, Dan's own love, Sophie – made this tempting scenario a distinct non-starter. Dan was *learning...* he knew that any fleeting pleasure he'd undoubtedly enjoy with the still enticing Melinda would come at a truly disastrous cost.

Where the elite meet...

As Dan returned to his work, his lovely ex-wife was sitting down to lunch in one of La Jolla's most exclusive bistros. The place was all bamboo furniture, outsized plants and exotic paintings – with a main dining room overlooking the village's glorious cove. The haze was just burning off along the coastline and the view through the massive picture windows was stunning. Corby's was a long-time 'beanery of choice' for both local businessmen and the blue-rinsed women's club set. Their longtime hostess was expert in ignoring (and often deflecting) tourists in jeans and shorts... those unwelcome intruders

22

who'd strayed onto forbidden territory. Ernest Kincaid, an 'A-List' member in good standing of San Diego's old money crowd, sat opposite Melinda. She usually chose this venue for their tête-à-têtes. The chef created, in her oft-repeated words, "salads to die for, unspoiled by those glutinous and calorific dressings." She'd also figured out long ago that Corby's window tables were a terrific setting for attracting the notice of La Jolla's 'great and good'.

Having recently 'officially' celebrated her thirtieth birthday (her oldest friends knew she was at least thirty-two), Melinda's still-slim body attracted admiring glances from hordes of breathing, straight males in the room. Tall, with light auburn hair falling just below her shoulders, she religiously avoided prolonged exposure to the sun (having learned in her youth that it did her flawless complexion no favors). Initially, Dan had unreservedly adored her fair skin and barely discernable freckles... until he'd discovered what a whopping dent her creamy complexion created in their outdoor activities. Even in her teens, she'd never gone out in daylight without practically bathing in Factor 50 – and she never lingered in direct sunlight without wearing a sunhat the size of a beach umbrella.

When they'd met, Dan had almost immediately aimed for 'exclusivity' with Melinda, content to leave his roving behind. Of course, this conversion was down to those perky tits, slender hips and her stunning beauty – and certainly not to a surplus of brains or personality. His first lingering view of her perfect breasts had reminded him of those iconic chrome nosecones on his step-dad's '57 Eldorado. By the time she'd condescended to becoming his exclusive squeeze, she'd already set the wedding date.

Occasionally, friends and admirers told Melinda that she bore an uncanny resemblance to the luminous Julianne Moore. Hearing this, she'd 'reflexively' tilt her head to the side ever so *slightly*, so that her shiny hair cascaded over one shoulder. Smiling (thus 'unconsciously' flashing her perfect white enamels), she'd take the opportunity to murmur in her sexiest voice, "You're so kind. Do you really think so?" These ego-stroking complements assured her that all of the demanding maintenance work she so stoically bore still paid dividends.

Melinda's lunch partner was in his mid-sixties; tall, distinguished and attractively graying. Today, Ernest wore an expensive charcoal pinstripe suit, in keeping with the 'Ivy League aura' he so carefully nurtured. His attire was in sharp contrast to the open-neck shirts and linen blazers favored by most of the 'dapper, but casual' businessmen in the room.

An only child, Ernest's father had been San Diego's mayor for three terms just after the war. Thus, his 'old money' credentials were impeccable. His business card identified him as an 'Investment Analyst'. In reality, years before, back from a brief stint in college, he'd turned up at his father's accountancy firm, Kincaid & Partners. He soon installed himself in the space next to the old man's, relocating a respected Senior Partner to an office one floor below. Young Ernest dabbled in hazy and somewhat offbeat business deals, using a bit of the firm's spare change – and managed to just about hang on to his shirt. When Old Man Kincaid died, Ernest slid into pater's corner office. He promptly renegotiated the contracts of two of the firm's second-tier (and, at this juncture, *stunned*) CPAs, proclaiming them 'Managing Partner' and 'Chief Financial Officer' respectively. His father's loyal first-line deputies soon resigned or quietly retired. Mercifully, his new appointees managed to keep the core business ticking over, although a few lucrative long-term clients chose to leave.

Ernest never married. The 'great and good' assumed that he was simply too preoccupied with turning the Kincaid family fortune into an even more impressive sum. In the early years, some of his less dubious deals had even turned into winners. (In the last quarter of the twentieth century, one didn't have to be a rocket scientist to make a fair turn in San Diego real estate, even if one neglected his homework.) He courted his fair share of lady friends; thus the infrequent gay rumors never stuck. He'd recently opened a small branch office in La Jolla, on the top floor of the flashy four-story complex that commanded the trendy intersection at Ivanhoe and Silverado. The ever-helpful Melinda had scouted out the space for him.

Clearly preoccupied throughout lunch, Melinda's companion barely touched his sea bass; only toying with his rocket lettuce and spinach leaves. When his cell beeped, Ernest grimaced and cooed, "Sorry my dear, I've got to take this."

Although this interruption was a serious social gaffe, Melinda could hardly object. Ernest was simply too important a contact... showing dismay would be a blunder. Instead, she retrieved her phone from her Prada bag and speed-dialed Metro Police Headquarters. She asked for hubby Gene, but just as the desk officer was putting her on hold, Ernest finished his own call, saying as he disconnected, "Fine then, Mr. Tejada, please inform me when the consignment goes out."

Ernest tucked his phone away; so Melinda immediately disconnected and followed suit. Hubby Gene could wait. Anyway, she'd only phoned at that particular moment to trump Ernest's rudeness – and, if she'd gotten through to Gene, to remind her forgetful husband to pick up a few items at the QFC's fabulous deli counter on his way home. She smiled at her luncheon companion and they returned to their conversation about a glitzy charity gala they'd both be attending.

Thirty minutes later, Melinda was saying her goodbyes to Ernest in the restaurant's crowded foyer. She had to drive inland to the La Jolla Mall office to meet with a prospective client and still had five or six condo brochures to print off. Her coastal La Jolla office averaged close to three million per sale, while the mall office, up near Interstate 5, focused on 'executive' condos and townhouses in the $650- to $900,000 range. Melinda was hoping to soon extricate herself from these journeys up the hill to the 'minor leagues'.

Melinda's boss, Ed Marks, established Coastal Estates Realty in 1980. At the time, he and his wife Sissy were rich, bored and childless – and already in their late forties. Starting out as their receptionist, Melinda quickly became one of Coastal's biggest producers. Nowadays, she virtually ran the La Jolla Mall office, with the help of a couple of sharp young sales associates. She figured she'd be offered a sweetheart buy-out deal when Ed and Sissy finally, *mercifully*, retired. She'd earned it... having made her so-called 'bosses' piles of cash. But she knew she'd have to be patient. After all, as she'd often told each of her husbands in turn, "LA's *'Three B's'* – Beverly Hills, Bel Air and Brentwood – weren't built in a day... and my new 'Coastal Realty, Phase II' won't transform into a 'Top Three' agency overnight either!"

Extricating herself from Ernest's company was sometimes tricky. His persistent wooing was becoming evermore irksome. She'd made the mistake a few months ago of telling her attentive mentor what a sorry loser second hubby Gene was turning out to be. Ernest mistook her slip as an invitation to rev up his oily charm.

As they parted on the sidewalk, he clinched Melinda too tightly, giving her a wet peck on the earlobe before turning towards his Silverado Avenue office. Truthfully however, as attractive as Melinda was, at that moment Ernest's mind was mulling over his recent telephone conversation. He prayed that Tejada could be trusted to sort out their current difficulties – and to resolve their problem in a relatively low-key and civilized fashion.

As she strolled to her car, Melinda redialed hubby Gene – and this time she got straight through. His unmistakable, nasal voice came on the line, irritating as always... "Pussycat, I'm about to dash. What can I do for my princess on this fine day?" (All that cooing and prattling... obviously some dim cop, who was quite understandably in awe of Gene's ultra-fine wife, was in the room with him!)

"Get out your Blackberry, detective. As I told you this morning – and I didn't see you jot it down – we'll need sun-dried tomatoes, a fresh baguette and some Parma ham from the QFC. Remember, not their own-brand insipid thin ham; get the *real Parma*! And, before I forget it, another bottle of Tuscan virgin olive oil wouldn't go astray. If you get home first, toss a salad and do a couple of ham rolls. Open a bottle of that Chianti Classico Reserva you bought last week. I may be late, so you can wait for me or eat when you please. Bye."

Gene hadn't managed to shoehorn in another word. Melinda slid into her Sebring convertible and shot out of her office's parking lot, heading inland towards the mall office. Hopefully, another productive afternoon was on the horizon!

Mighty Mouse Eddie

Quitting time at TriState... Dan sat back, flexed his shoulders and stared out of the plate glass window to his right. Across the nearly deserted rear parking lot, beyond Mission Valley's perpetually dry riverbed, stood that old San Diego white elephant – 'Jack Murphy Stadium'. Some brain-dead entrepreneurs and politicians (in Dan's words, "a consortium of soulless bastards") pawned the memory of San Diego's greatest sportswriter for a pile of sponsorship loot. So, the stadium was now officially 'Qualcomm Stadium'. But this hideous name would soon be history as well, if the Chargers had their way. They were negotiating for a new site somewhere downtown or outside the city limits, where a 'modern' stadium (i.e., an edifice with significantly greater numbers of high-profit luxury boxes) could be erected with minimal interference from penny-pinching city officials. Bankruptcy was still not out of the question for America's Finest City... and some spoilsports even felt that 'inessentials' like the Chargers could leave town to help make way for fiscal sanity.

Today, there were no signs of life across the riverbed. Sometimes Dan forgot that the Padres had decamped to (God protect us!) 'Petco Park' to play their baseball. Located downtown, the new ballpark was supposedly an 'instantly vintage' edifice... a major city-center redevelopment that came to fruition just before the leaner times kicked in. Anyway, it was currently spring training over in Arizona for baseball, so even if the Pads were still using the archaic Jack Murphy, there'd be no one around today but the odd caretaker.

His last e-file updated, Dan felt adequately prepared for Walt's visit. He was certain that one client, a small partnership called 'Right Conduit PCs', was attempting to swindle TriState out of $4500 by

26

concocting a bogus burglary claim. One of their sleazy partners thought he'd discovered an easy way to turn a profit on obsolete stock. No doubt their 'earlier generation' wholesale gear was being put to good use somewhere over the border, having been sold on for a song. Of course, Dan would mention this transparent scam to his boss, having already earmarked Right Conduit's file: *DO NOT RENEW COVER*. Commercial insurers have access to an industry-wide claims database. So, even if they got away with it, it was pretty certain that Right Conduit would sacrifice more in bottom-line profit – due to inflated premiums down the line – than the value of the bogus payout. Of course, this would hold true only if the partners stuck together and were silly enough to carry on using the same business name.

At 5:15, Dan's office was empty... no go-getters or 'late-night candle burners' at TriState. He locked the front door behind him and decided to pop into The Web Surfer Deli on his way home. It was only five minutes from his apartment, on El Cajon Boulevard. He needed to touch base with Eddie Kane, an invaluable business contact.

A prime hangout for computer geeks and SDSU techno-nerds – this internet cafe was young Eddie's home away from home. Dan hadn't been surprised to learn that the boy had added a few key modifications to the PC at his favored workstation, which was located in the café's darkest corner, away from the service counter.

Just sixteen, Eddie stubbornly clung to his 'cross-cultural throwback' dress sense. The boy was very dark, extremely handsome and sported a shortish Afro. His taste in clothing ran to heavy metal tee shirts (touting long-forgotten bands) and torn Levis 501's. Without a doubt, this teenager would lack even an ounce of street cred with his fellow African-Americans... and his communication skills and ready display of general knowledge were certainly foreign in the present-day street culture being foisted upon Southeast San Diego.

Dan pulled into the dated strip mall and parked the Chevy. Approaching the cafe, he spotted Eddie, deep in thought in front of his screen. The boy couldn't afford his own decent hardware or even a second-hand laptop. It was safer to use the deli's stuff anyway; personal gear might get ripped off in his neighborhood. He did odd jobs and upgrades around the cafe to pay for his Internet time and was pretty much left alone by an appreciative owner who knew he was getting first-class maintenance on the cheap.

Approaching the boy, Dan got straight down to business. "Any luck on Ortiz, Eddie?" Fred Ortiz operated a shady body shop down in National City. A TriState underwriter had demonstrated a pathetic lack of smarts by taking on the shabby garage's property and liability

27

insurance, ignoring Dan's extremely negative risk survey, completed just a month before. Like anyone with a police background, Dan recognized a chop shop when he saw one. Last week he'd gotten around to asking Eddie to run some clandestine business and criminal searches on the shifty proprietor. Dan presumed that public records (and perhaps some more esoteric data that only a first-rate mole like Eddie could access) would connect Ortiz to a few dodgy used car dealers; some crooked wrecking yards or a disreputable parts shop or two in Southeast San Diego or Tijuana.

If an e-trail of dirty dealings existed, Eddie would find it. The boy charged Dan $15 to $25 per assignment... just enough to generate walking-around money. He loved Dan's assignments. The work was edgy enough to stretch even his capabilities. Besides, Dan didn't patronize him or ask too many questions about his unique advanced search techniques.

Eddie was already downloading his still-meager results on Ortiz as Dan approached. "Sorry man, no luck so far," he replied. "The guy's pretty slick. I've got a couple more leads to run down, so you can check back tomorrow if you like. So far, I can't track any dealings into Mexico, but he doesn't seem to sell parts to any genuine dealers up here either. Unsurprisingly, there's little evidence of Ortiz carrying out legit repairs – and few conventional customers seem to be paying any money into the shop's account. It appears that most of his traceable 'repairs' are made to vehicles that eventually get sold on as scrap. I'm checking the DMV's files to locate any kosher buyers for the few drivable vehicles he's flogged in California."

Dan nodded, quickly thanked Eddie and turned to leave. As he headed out, an unfortunately all too rare bout of scruples overcame him. He turned and added, "Eddie, let me know if I need to kick up the retainer on this one. It sounds like a lot of hassle." Eddie was already back to his keyboard, but he nodded and waved a hand in Dan's direction.

Dan stopped at the counter and paid for two jumbo bags of popcorn. It was the favored snack item in this establishment and thus tended to be pretty fresh. He took a bag to Eddie and laid it on the corner of his workstation before heading out to his Malibu. He was happy to be heading home for a quiet night, with an NBA game or baseball's spring training on the tube.

Chapter 4

Sometimes, you get what you need

Minutes later, tiptoeing past Mrs. Getz's door, Dan slipped into his apartment. He microwaved some frozen macaroni, broke out his popcorn and uncapped a Henry's, settling in to watch the end of a Padres spring game from Arizona's Cactus League.

The Pads lost on a game-ending double play, so Dan switched to the local news, featuring star anchor, Matt Burlington… a jovial mannequin billed as *'San Diego's Favorite Ear to the Ground'*. It was obviously a slow news day. Matt *himself* was in the field, charming viewers with a 'local color story' from that old standby – The San Diego Zoo. Matt was trying to convince his loyal following that he was falling head over heels for a newborn koala. In fact, the tiny animal looked like a wizened, hairless gargoyle and the newsman's smile was of the 'pasted on' variety. Frankly, Dan had to side with 'Mr Oily' on this one… he didn't give much of a crap about zoo babies either.

Losing interest in the 'news', Dan's mind wandered back to the ancient history he'd been revisiting earlier in the day. Not unusually, his musings conveyed him to the same end-game: a sense of *utter relief* at his relatively painless escape from Melinda's social-climbing clutches. Sure, he'd paid some serious alimony for a time (though she'd been the bigger earner in their marriage). But his nemesis, Gene Jeffries, rode boldly to the rescue. The little geek had been sniffing around Melinda, even while she and Dan were still supposedly happily hitched. For her part, Melinda seemed to enjoy and encourage his old adversary's clumsy advances. And, after two years with Officer Dan, it was abundantly clear to her that her young hubby wasn't on the force's 'Detective Lieutenant Fast Track'. She couldn't help comparing his future career path to Gene's… clearly to Dan's detriment.

Dan and Gene Jeffries graduated in the same Academy class. Small, dark and perpetually over-tanned, Gene was a workout fanatic, but *not* a natural athlete. Even now, he maintained a teenager's 30-inch waistline… often admiring his flat abs in the mirror when he assumed no one was looking. A fanatical networker, he'd wangled a coveted Downtown Precinct motorcycle assignment early in his career, quickly adopting the role's de rigueur trimmed moustache and tightly tailored tan uniform.

At the Academy, instructors and fellow cadets enjoyed throwing these misfits together – forever pairing up the laid-back Dan and the unsubtle, provocative Gene. *'Dan and Gene'* became the class's favorite sparring duo. The reference was meant to bring to mind that sixties partnership, 'Jan and Dean', who sang sweet harmonies (and were actually known to *hit the surf...* unlike the Beach Boys, excepting Dennis). But the cadets' rocky relationship was more *'Dead Man's Curve'* than *'Surf City'...* each repeatedly refused to extend the slightest courtesy or respect to the other. From the beginning, they had assumed the mantle of leadership for opposing cliques; Dan attracting the 'Dudes' and Gene fronting a group quickly nicknamed the 'Neo-Nazis'.

When Dan and Melinda had mercifully separated, Gene immediately laid his most serious moves on her. After initially playing coy, Melinda pragmatically reeled in her standby suitor eighteen months later... when it became abundantly clear to her that more promising prey had avoided the bait. When she'd first dated the cocky little bastard, Dan was certain it was just a shoddy ploy to piss him off. He chose not to react, expecting that Gene would soon get the bum's rush. But, miraculously, things seemed to grow more serious between the unlikely pair. If Detective Gene genuinely floated Melinda's boat, Dan found the prospect perplexing; but he was basically down with it.

For his part, Gene considered marriage to Melinda a great victory over his adversary and took every opportunity to inform Dan that, "I satisfy her in so many ways that you never could." So, on a petty and personal level, Dan couldn't help but continue to hate the little weasel. But, keeping his distance, he bit his tongue and moved on. Now, he and Melinda only spoke every couple of months, when she'd call him out of the blue on some fairly tenuous pretext and flirt down the line.

When they'd initially dated, Gene had been dispassionately assessed as "second-tier promising" in Melinda's meticulous scoring system... especially as the determined little shit seemed more than willing to buckle to her tutelage. So, eventually, she'd simply settled on him. Then she began to earnestly drill him in the subtleties of ascending that slippery, yet attainable, law enforcement career ladder.

But, the news wasn't good... it soon dawned on Melinda that Gene had reached his innate level of competence long before she hitched herself to his unstable wagon. In one late night call to Dan, she'd let slip that unless she took a hands-on approach to Gene's career, her lot would be that of an uncomplaining wife to a low-grade detective... supporting his delusions of grandeur until he retired to fishing trips and golf outings with his puerile buddies. These days, she was encouraging Gene to chuck it all for a relatively lucrative Security Director's

30

position with an IT conglomerate. But, she seemed to be fighting a losing battle.

Melinda couldn't help herself... she loved basking in her glory days. She'd often reminded Dan that in her prime she'd been head cheerleader *and* a sorority president at San Diego's prestigious UCSD. Charm and drive, harnessed to some shameless flirting with a couple of pathetic teachers, got Melinda on her High School Honor Roll. Then, her dad's best friend put in a word for her with some influential alumni at the university. Upon arriving at the Torrey Pines campus, she advised her pals optimistically, "UCSD's smack in the middle of *Grade-A Territory* for snagging a successful husband."

She attended her business classes with relative regularity. (Dan was certain it had been more to scout potential partners than to acquire an education.) In her spare time, she frequented upscale restaurants and cocktail lounges in nearby La Jolla. After all, an *already* successful (but not yet decrepit) businessman would also make a fantastic catch.

Dan met Melinda when she was a couple of years out of college – and, frankly, harboring real concerns about her ongoing quest to land 'Mr Right'. Dan later learned that she'd wasted the previous three years on a married dentist. The experience had obviously given her a more 'grounded' view on the must-have attributes of a suitable long-term partner.

One night she'd been slumming with two old classmates in the fabled Quad Tavern in Ocean Beach and the roguish Dan Paige caught her eye. Obviously a hero to the bar's scruffy patrons, that night he appeared to be the ringleader of a gang of fun-loving cops and retired Charger studs. While these guys weren't San Diego's movers and shakers, they certainly seemed to have cash to burn and they knew how to show a girl a good time.

She and Dan hit it off. And, to the surprise of many, they married two months later. Almost straight away, Melinda began to regret her hasty decision. She decided to salvage the situation by ragging Dan about every police promotion she got wind of. "Go for it birdbrain!" and "It could have been you!" were her all too familiar refrains.

Dan, in turn, quickly discovered his bride was more into 'labels, lunching and posing' than in being a supportive wife. Initially, the bills piled up, while her budding (but, at that time, still not overly successful) real estate career demanded her time and attention. Between Dan's shift work and Melinda's odd hours, their battling began in earnest.

"Water under the bridge," Dan thought as he turned his attention back to the TV. Matt Burlington was still 'on the scene' at the zoo,

31

flirting disgracefully by the grizzly bear enclosure with the perky Carla Sands. The station's new weathergirl had obviously wangled a featured spot in today's creampuff field assignment – and she was milking it!

Dan certainly didn't regret the time he'd spent as one of 'San Diego's Finest' – or cry over his short-lived marriage to the gorgeous, overly ambitious Melinda. Anyway, tomorrow he'd be in a much better place, spending an evening with the unimaginably lovely Sophie. She was extraordinary... and surely the best thing that had ever come into his chaotic life.

Serendipity

Dan's news program ended just as a dilapidated '84 Firebird low-rider pulled up in front of Cantina Guadalupe, the Rosado's local Tijuana hangout. The modest bar was in a residential area, a few blocks east of the scruffy city's main drag. The old Pontiac was metal-flake purple, 'enhanced' by emerald green racing stripes and a reverberating exhaust. Belching blue smoke, it trumpeted its arrival well before turning onto Avenida Aquila. Gold lettering on the rear panels told onlookers that they were in the presence of *'The Purple People Eater'*. Tattered Naugahyde seat covers and a fading gold dash and headliner set off the 'custom' interior. This was some distinctive ride, even by *Mejicano* standards.

Jesus had rolled up his sleeves while driving down from San Diego, exposing innumerable tattoos. The motifs on his lower arms were primitive – prison-style, forearm-covering 'shirtsleeve' efforts. The artwork on his upper arms and torso was more flamboyant – inked by so-called professionals, but tacky nonetheless. On the drive, he outlined his desire to have a single teardrop inked below his left eyelid. His partner, Flaco, insisted this would take things too far... "The ladies hate that shit man. You'll look like a fuckin', gang-bangin' loser! And, besides, who have you killed in the line of duty? That's what each teardrop signifies, you *tonto*!"

Jesus' grimy denim shirt was covered in sweat stains; many still damp, others dry. His ample belly hung precipitously over a wide, studded black leather belt. This evening, he sported his favorite bling – a heavy gold neck chain and matching chunky bracelets. He thought this look was an enormous boost to his 'street cred'.

Flaco stepped out onto the crumbling sidewalk and shook his head in disgust as he glanced across at his corpulent 'chauffeur', still exiting the car. "Man, I don't know what's worse, your *oloroso* BO or those greasy farts you been cuttin' all day. Try to let them off in the open... they're too potent for this car's confined space!"

"You've just been gettin' a heavy whiff of my Brut, man," replied Jesus as he stifled a yawn. "The ladies love it." The big man uncouthly juggled and scratched his balls – and passed another dose of deadly gas as he hitched up his belt. His grubby leather trousers were tight, ruling out rapid movements; so he adopted a casual stroll as he sauntered over to Flaco.

As usual, Jesus sported a dog-eared, fingerless leather glove on his right hand. "A fighter's grippin' and swingin' hand needs protectin'," was his justification for this affectation. Flaco, on the other hand, said the ridiculous glove was useful for just one thing... unscrewing jar lids or bottle caps. But the little man's taunts didn't deter Jesus. He knew this distinctive accessory enhanced his machismo, creating an aura that had finessed him out of more than a few tight spots.

As they walked up to the small cantina, Flaco returned to business. "Remember, I'll do the talking. If we stay cool, we'll get what we need and leave without causing a ruckus. Shut up and don't give anything away, got it?"

Jesus nodded, but he was already focused on more urgent concerns. "Play it your way man, but however it goes down, I'm takin' a piss right away, okay?"

Nearly empty in the early evening, this simple cantina bore little resemblance to Tijuana's tourist traps, where unscrupulous bartenders poured cheap and copious rounds of rotgut tequila down adolescent gringos' gullets. In the wee hours, local toughs hanging around those *tourista* bars could fleece drunken kids, while the cops looked away or joined in the easy pickings. Cantina Guadalupe was a respectable local watering hole. As they entered, Flaco picked up tantalizing aromas, as well as the laughter of a busy female cook emanating from a tiny kitchen behind the bar.

Grabbing the last stool at the end of the long wooden counter, Flaco caught the bartender's eye. "*Dos grande* tequila shooters... your best stuff. By the way, would you happen to be Jorge?" Jesus stood behind his partner momentarily, poised to head off for that urgent piss.

The bartender poured clear liquid from an opaque bottle into two double shot glasses. "Yeah, I'm Jorge. What can I do for you?" The bottle had some indistinct wording inked in flowery script on a plain white label. Jorge neither salted the glasses' rims nor offered the men a slice of lime... these flourishes were pure tourist shit.

The lure of the freshly poured booze got to Jesus... he settled an elbow on the bar and downed his glass, momentarily ignoring his pressing need to urinate. Flaco drank his tequila, wiped the corners of his mouth with the back of his hand and nodded for refills, asking, "Do you know how we can catch up with Benito Rosado? A friend of mine, Manny Tejada, told me he grew up around here. We're into a nice little business deal and there could be a fair few pesos in it for him."

Jorge hesitated and stared at the strangers. This pair obviously weren't smart enough – in either appearance or brainpower – to be involved in any significant business deals. And, while he did indeed owe their 'friend' Tejada a favor, ratting out one of the Rosados, even the devious Benito, seemed like a big ask. Besides, even if these strangers knew his brother's benefactor's name and could, therefore, have been sent by Tejada, he could see no reason to trust them.

As he refilled their glasses, he warily replied, "A lot of Rosados come in here, man. The family lives around here, okay? I'll tell you what I'll do. I'll tell his kin you're looking for Benito when they come around. Leave me your names and a telephone number."

Jorge avoided making eye contact with his other customer, a dapper looking guy in his mid-forties. Obviously not a manual worker, this lone patron was studiously eyeing his Aqua Caliente Racing Form at the far end of the bar. Outwardly, this hombre showed little interest in the newcomers, but, obviously, he *was* taking everything in. It seemed clear to Jorge that the strangers hadn't taken the time to give this man the once over... at least not yet.

Imagine the odds! There sat *Benito Rosado* – the living image of the description Tejada had so recently provided to Flaco and Jesus. The man folded his paper, slipped off his stool and headed towards the back of the cantina. This was clearly an opportune time to take that dump he'd been contemplating. These strangers didn't look like people he'd wish to know – or get involved with *in any way*. He was thankful that Jorge was a trusted family friend.

Benito headed to the men's room, located next to a handy back exit. He slid into the lone cubicle and locked the door. As usual, he tore wide strips from his racing form to cover the cigarette-burned toilet seat. Then he lowered the waistband of his pressed sharkskin slacks to just above his calves and gingerly sat down. He was practiced in keeping his trouser cuffs suspended above a damp or soiled floor – and he took great care not to wrinkle his immaculate outfit. His dark tan lizard loafers and fine silk stockings added the finishing touches to what Benito considered a suave, 'understated' look.

The dapper man settled in for the duration... contemplating, as always, that while his crap gave off a distinct odor, it certainly didn't smell unpleasant. Probably this was down to his diet. He avoided greasy foods and ate only the better cuts of meat and chicken. He knew inferior ingredients nailed your insides, but pronto... creating havoc in your gut. His ladies invariably told him he looked to be in his late twenties or early thirties. Benito had always looked after himself – and these days it was really paying off. And, as luck would have it, he was currently being presented with yet another stellar opportunity to look out for his interests. He'd avoid these *vatos* – surely a sound strategy for insuring his continued good health.

He heard heavy footsteps clomping down the corridor. And moments later, peering under the cubicle's door, Benito recognized the scuffed boots belonging to the larger stranger entering the room. The guy was heading towards the urinals, farting loudly as he went.

Benito Rosado sat quietly while the big man finished a long, slow pee, reflecting on his good fortune. He decided he'd try a pretty underhanded tactic... but he was fairly certain that no real harm would come of it. He'd need to throw these men off of his scent – and there was a pretty simple way to do it. He leaned back to contemplate and refine his next move.

Sorry, cousin!

Both *Benito* Rosado and his first cousin *Benny* had grown up in this very neighborhood. Their *mama grande*, Hortensia, still lived two doors up from Cantina Guadalupe and she'd looked after countless local kids – some relatives, some not – while their mothers scraped out paltry livings on both sides of the border.

Benny Rosado was a year older than his cousin Benito. Their fathers, brothers Rafael and Victor, both named their first-born sons after their *own* beloved father, the *senior* Benito Rosado. The sainted man had uncomplainingly toiled to an early grave. So, the grandsons had always been "Benny and Benito" to family and friends... the slight name difference giving each boy a clear identity. And, their grandfather's devoted partner, Hortensia, had been the key authority figure in both boys' upbringing.

Benny's parents, Rafael and Inez, remained close to the entire Rosado clan. They bought a house near Hortensia – and Rafael found steady work as a gardener at Tijuana's famed Aqua Caliente Racetrack. They worked hard and set money aside, planning to add to their little family. But their planning was cut short. One weekend, while on a rare shopping trip in San Diego, their car was T-boned at an intersection by a drunk in an ancient pick-up. The truck sped through a red light, killing Rafael and Inez instantly. The offender was convicted for DUI –

more than twice over the limit – and his license was suspended. But, as he was uninsured, penniless and his victims were 'only Mexicans', no one even attempted to extract compensation for the orphaned Benny. Hortensia received the meager proceeds from the sale of Rafael and Inez's house and her grandson moved in with her.

Cousin *Benito's* father, Rafael's brother Victor, was a black sheep. He invariably went after the easy money – with little regard for legalities. While still a callow youth, he foolishly impregnated Katia, an older and very streetwise Tijuana prostitute. When Hortensia heard of the pregnancy, she approached Katia with a proposition. She offered the apathetic *puta* a significant portion of her meager life's savings to take a 'work rest' and carry the baby to term. Then, all Katia had to do was give up the child and move to Ensenada. Victor *finally* acknowledged his probable paternity and attended the boy's christening before heading up to Arizona, to disappear forever. So, when Rafael and Inez died, Hortensia began, in effect, raising *two* orphans.

It seemed that 'nature', rather than 'nurture', played a significant role in the boys' characters... the young apples didn't fall far from their respective trees. Benny grew up to be a dedicated husband and father. Truth be told, Benito, a misfit and loner, was always more than a bit jealous of his cousin. He scraped by, making ends meet through one dicey deal or another; but he almost eagerly nurtured his 'black sheep' role. So, Cousin Benny naturally earned everyone's love and respect... something the younger Benito could never hope to achieve.

Benny started his landscaping business with one ancient truck, tending residential gardens, mostly in South San Diego County. Soon after their marriage, he and Consuela decided to move up to San Diego permanently. They did it the right way, earning green cards with the support of US-based family members and the glowing references of his American customers. He visited his *mama grande* in Tijuana on a weekly basis, invariably purchasing premium-quality plants and flowers at competitive prices from a few trusted Mexican suppliers when he came down.

These days, his business was thriving. Benny could run a crew with the best of them, but this had become a rare activity for him. His two older sons, along with Gunnar, his trusted foreman, ran the three crews that were in constant demand from a lengthening list of county contractors and a number of first-rate property managers.

But, Benny's reliability could have its downside. Still settled in his toilet cubicle, Cousin Benito's budding plan was quickly coming together. That very afternoon he'd dropped by his *mama grande's* and she mentioned Benny would be down from San Diego around eight the next morning, if Benito wanted to catch up with him. Then Benny would be heading out, as usual, to buy supplies at his favorite gardening depot.

This morsel of information would now pay dividends for the crafty Benito. He could deflect these strangers in their sinister mission... at least for a few precious days. With these hombres off his scent, he could sneak up to San Diego to discover exactly *why* they were after him – and then make sure that Manny Tejada, almost assuredly the instigator of this current dilemma, could be diverted from a miscarriage of justice.

So, it was time to make his move. Benito cleared his throat and hunched forward on the stained toilet seat. He spoke in low tones, trying to attract the attention of the beefy guy, still hovering over at the urinal at the far wall, without alarming him. The dude was farting again and already zipping up his fly. "Hey man, I couldn't help overhearing your conversation out in the bar. You lookin' for Benito Rosado? I live around here and I can put you in touch with him if you're lookin' to put some business his way."

Benito awaited an answer, which wasn't forthcoming, and then continued to speak towards the scuffed boots, still visible under the cubicle door. They were now pointing in his direction. "I know for a fact that Benito will be around tomorrow morning, man. He's up in San Diego tonight, but he'll be picking up supplies at that big garden center over on Pio Pico around nine or nine-thirty tomorrow morning. *You can't miss him!* It'll say 'Rosado & Sons Landscaping' in big green letters on the doors of his white pick-up. He'll almost for sure be wearing jeans and a flannel shirt – and he'll probably be heading right back up to San Diego."

Jesus strode to the sink, turned on the tap and pretended to wash as he listened to the stranger. He couldn't believe his luck! Tejada hadn't even mentioned that their target owned a landscaping business, but it made perfect sense. It was a fantastic cover for traveling to and from TJ – and for carting drugs and large quantities of weed around San Diego. He turned towards the cubicle door and politely enquired, "Why, exactly, are you telling me this man?"

Benito was ready with a quick answer. "I overheard you saying that there'd be a bit of money in it for my friend Benito. That's the case isn't it?"

Jesus paused, attempting to instill just the right note of sincerity in his reply. "Oh, that's *for sure* man."

A sly smile crossed Benito's face. He'd be back in San Diego the next morning. By the time these idiots figured out that they were tailing the wrong Rosado, he'd have a solid lead on which of his menacing associates was coming after him this time – and why his tit was, yet again, in that proverbial wringer. This had been a close scrape – too close for comfort. He attempted his most ingratiating tone in his final words to the gorilla by the sink. "Man, I wouldn't help you if I wasn't sure you were on the level about doing right by my dear friend Benito Rosado. Give my best to him when you see him. Tell him his old pal *Raul* says hello."

Jesus smiled to himself. "I'll surely do that, Raul. And, *gracias* for the heads up."

The big man dashed out front, hands still unwashed of course, just as Flaco rose from his barstool. Jesus tossed back the second tequila awaiting him on the counter and caught up with the little man near the door. He whispered, "Hey amigo, we just got real fuckin' lucky. An hombre who's takin' a shit out back is tight with Benito Rosado and he's put us onto him. Our mark'll be down here from San Diego in the morning – and this guy Raul was kind enough to tell me when and where we can find him!"

Flaco stopped in his tracks and looked incredulously at Jesus. "This sounds too good to be true. Let me talk to this 'Raul' guy. Where is he now?"

It dawned on Jesus that he shouldn't have left his new friend alone in the back. He could have waited for him to finish his shit and accompanied him back to the front of the bar. Oh well, no fixing that now. "He's still back there on the shitter I suppose. I haven't seen anyone come out. Have you? Believe me, he seems to be on the level. He didn't have no axe to grind... he was just trying to help out a pal. He bought our story about an attractive business deal for Benito and he's willing to do him a good turn."

Moments later, when they pushed their way through the door in back marked *'Hombres'*, the washroom was empty. They retreated back into the corridor and spotted a door, still open, leading onto a deserted alley. The shy, but helpful Raul had obviously beaten a hasty retreat. When they returned to the front of the bar, Jorge could tell them little about their mysterious 'Raul'. He claimed the man sitting at the end of the bar was not a regular.

Flaco had a decision to make. Should they trust the mysterious dude who'd beat a hasty retreat? The clincher had to be the lack of a real downside – they probably had very little to lose. Time was marching on and Manny Tejada expected a *result*, so they'd just have to chase this half-assed lead and hope for the best.

Chapter 5

Tuesday

Putting the world right

Dan awoke famished. The previous evening's macaroni, with the popcorn chaser, obviously hadn't sufficed. A substantial breakfast was on the cards. In twenty minutes he was pulling into Lenny's, an *'Always Open'* greasy spoon west of his apartment on El Cajon Boulevard. Unsurprisingly, the fading façade and cheesy interior décor remained unchanged from an earlier *Denny's* period. It was amazing what a cash-poor entrepreneur achieved by simply changing a single letter on the external yellow sign... and trimming back the former chain's extensive menu! The interior was now a bit shabby. But Dan knew that the Mexican cooks – ably assisted by veteran waitresses like the unflappable Rosie – delivered the goods. The fare was nourishing and downright flavorsome, if a tad greasy.

Dan sat at the counter, next to two Lenny's stalwarts – Stan Crawford and Jerry Stein. Both were retired, but definitely not resigned to the tranquil (in Jerry's words: *'brain dead'*) existences lived out in 'nineteenth hole' clubhouses and cocktail lounges by many of their peers. This Formica counter was their venue of choice for endless two-man debates.

In his early sixties, Jerry was as dapper as ever in his dark suit and tie. He'd been a 'Senior Creative' at Menlo & Duggan, a highly respected advertising agency. Truthfully, he'd look more at home in an upmarket La Jolla deli or smart Coronado coffee shop than in this greasy spoon. But, Jerry was that rare sort... a born and bred San Diegan who still resided in the neighborhood where he'd grown up. And, serendipitously, his Hillcrest stomping grounds were on the up again (if now a tad more 'camp') after a prolonged period of decline. Lenny's was still his spot.

Jerry prided himself on the generous slice of inherited 'New York savvy' he brought to his vocation. In his heyday, his ad pitches had been razor sharp and 'in your face'. His work contrasted – unequivocally to its *merit* – with the bland, safe copy and clichéd visuals favored by the up and comers in his old agency.

He'd inherited his mindset from his parents. They'd moved west, to the 'Land of Opportunity', just before the Big War, but still clung stubbornly to their Gotham roots. Jerry attended downtown's ancient San Diego High in the fifties, hanging out with the sons and daughters of many of the city's movers and shakers. In those days, scores of the great and good lived just north of downtown, in a tight, safe radius of affluent neighborhoods scattered around San Diego's still-glorious Balboa Park.

As his agency years approached their natural, if unceremonious, conclusion, Jerry began to mentor the more amenable young bucks in the firm – including two bright sparks who were now the Managing Partners. As he approached his forced early retirement, he introduced some young colleagues to his best clients, explaining to his 'go-getter' bosses: "These kids have *career tracks*... I sure as hell can't locate mine anymore."

A few years previously, Ty Phillips, a 'Senior Account Director' (i.e., a prize-winning 'winer and diner', lacking in creative talent), had sidled up to Jerry. Ty had just delivered a successful pitch (which benefited *immeasurably* from the old warhorse's input) and Jerry expected a heartfelt "Well done!" Instead, the insufferable asshole suggested that Jerry might want to "pick up the pace". Jerry shifted up a gear or two all right... walking out the door, never to return. These days, now of legitimate retirement age, he freelanced and made a few bucks, mainly because a couple of old clients preferred Jerry's punchy copy and resourcefulness to the 'group think' crap his old firm continuously churned out.

Menlo & Duggan's hotshots hadn't comprehended that they could have tapped into Jerry's creativity – and solid business contacts – on the cheap. Unfortunately for them, his sometimes irascible attitude and unvarnished observations didn't always dovetail with those shiny new 'Career Path Signposts' in the firm's training modules. The glossy DVDs, cobbled together from an "Extensive and Incisive Field Study" carried out by a trendy LA-based consultancy, had become the firm's new Bible.

So, Jerry Stein was a semi-retired lone wolf... and all the happier for it. He had the time and inclination to keep a hand firmly in the advertising business, while turning up regularly at Lenny's counter and arguing interminably with a worthy adversary – Stan Crawford.

Stan was pushing seventy. A former aerospace worker, he'd been the most gifted machinist in his company's hand-picked 'Test Assemblies Unit'. He took pleasure in hanging out at Lenny's, primarily for the mental sparring provided by his resourceful pal. He favored faded jeans, denim shirts with pearl snaps and thick-soled black engineer's boots... steel-toed, of course! This was the gear he'd worn for forty years – no need to 'smarten up' now.

He enjoyed contributing snappy strap lines or odd bits of punchy copy to Jerry's projects. Occasionally, his offerings were even decent enough to use. Jerry referred to Stan as "my one-man Gray Market Focus Group", often running ideas past him for 'quick and dirty' target audience responses.

On this particular morning, a ravenous Dan walked in and waved to Rosie just as Jerry was tucking into his onion bagel and black coffee. Stan was polishing off the remains of his 'Senior's Special'… one large egg (*"Any way you'd like it!"*), hash browns, three crispy bacon strips and two slices of toast (*"White, brown or rye – your choice!"*) – All for $3.99.

The aroma of Stan's fried breakfast was simply too alluring. Dan decided to forego Lenny's 'Cholesterol Beaters', ordering two *real* eggs over easy, rye toast and hash browns. Rosie had already plunked down a steaming mug of black tar. When his toast arrived, Dan spread on genuine butter, not margarine, and opted for two mini-tubs of sweet grape jelly.

It only took seconds to plug into the boys' discussion. Stan asked, "Jerry, you're a professional pitchman. So, what kind of assholes voted us *'America's Finest City'* this time around? We're winnin' it for the umpteenth time – as proudly reported by that dimwit Hal Gorham on the fuckin' radio. Is this dippy 'civic honor' really a tourist scam, or what?"

Jerry chuckled and replied, "Our city's publicists can't single-handedly invent and spread around this crapola Stan. This time, it's right out of a *New York Times* Survey, based on God Almighty knows what."

Stan used a grubby thumbnail to scrape a smidgen of dried egg from the corner of his mouth. "I know these asinine surveys aren't plucked out of thin air Jerry. Generally, the fuckers rate on such 'essential' criteria as a city's *'kosher bakeries per capita'*, numbers of *'progressive schools for attention deficit scholars'* or the *'year-round costs of Jacuzzi maintenance'*. In other words, we've scored *big*, based on happy horseshit no one gives a flyin' fuck about! I'd say if San Diego's so shit-hot, *why don't we just keep it to ourselves?* Too many asswipes have flocked here already. Mass migration by mindless zombies tends to turn these surveys and ratings into dogshit as soon as they're published anyway!"

Jerry smiled and nodded. "San Diego may already be sliding down next year's pop charts for that very reason Stan. Overpopulation is indeed killing us. I used to tell my out of town visitors they'd soon discover San Diego resembled their 'Imaginary Los Angeles' – but LA

41

itself hasn't lived up to that image of Shangri La since the fifties. These days, we're no longer many Midwesterners' dream destination either. Seekers of a 'Western Paradise' are opting for art enclaves and ranches in Utah and New Mexico for Christ's sake! And, more power to them."

Dan, against his better judgment, found himself chiming in. "I remember when the mist cleared off by noon. Now, what's charitably referred to as 'mist' is more likely *smog* – and it won't clear until the next Santa Ana winds eventually blow all the gray-brown crap out to sea. If we lose much more ground on the 'best climate' rating, we'll probably topple from the overall charts."

Jerry had obviously heard enough. "Read my lips... it's demographics. Baby Boomers retire to the sun and expect to catch a few ballgames, go out for cheap eats and live in condos that discourage late-night parties. Up to the eighties, the gray brigade gravitated here for that lifestyle. But now, we're just like LA. Midwesterners and Canucks on fixed incomes look at our relatively overpriced housing and congestion and shell out that bit extra for air conditioning in a cheaper home in the desert. Maybe our house prices will tail off even more as our old-timers die off or leave. Then we'll have come full circle and be affordable again. I think I'll wait it out."

Stan, ever the pragmatist, pointed out a prospective silver lining in Jerry's 'full circle' scenario. "Maybe we can exploit your boomerang demographics in a timely way! How about we open up a slew of *'Old Farts' Membership Warehouses'*, stacked floor to ceiling with cheap laxatives, giant tubs of pile cream and bulk-packaged incontinence pads? Or, we could create a wrinklies-only dating agency – *'Silver Fantasies'... your dream partner is CPR-qualified and our escorts are fully trained to give you a pre-date blue rinse and set; it's guaranteed!*"

Dan left the boys lamenting the decline of California's lone utopian city – 'lone' that is, if you were willing to ignore the bullshit being circulated by those boastful wishful thinkers up in the Bay Area. He left a decent tip for Rosie, paid his bill and headed to his car. He still had a job to get to.

Just when you think you've seen it all...

Dan opened a couple of e-mails, one with a new claim file attached. All claims were routinely routed from TriState's central Customer Services Center. One attraction of the job was the sheer diversity in his workload. No two workdays were alike, even if some *were* actually boring. And, occasionally, an oddball claim turned out to be even more amusing than the sporadic funny shit he'd dealt with on the force.

Recently, he'd settled a claim involving a small client's delivery van. On the accident report the office supply company's creative (and apparently unremorseful) driver reported that his truck had, *in his exact words*: "... inadvertently reversed itself through our customer's plate windows as I attempted to leave after making a delivery." Apparently, the guy recovered quickly in the ensuing pandemonium... hastening to remove the van from the reception area by driving it back through the lone *unbroken* pane in the shattered frontage. Perhaps the driver had learned his lesson though. He claimed to have judiciously come to a full stop and carefully signaled for his left turn before leaving the strip mall's lot.

But even that fiasco could be topped. Dan's favorite all-timer had to be the celebrated Robert Crossley matter. Tall and muscular, with dark good looks, the charming Bob had "inadvertently slipped" at work – while standing on bone-dry and debris-free new carpeting by the photocopier. Six months into a long-term disability (and continuing to receive generous payouts from TriState's Workers' Compensation coverage), Big Bob's injured right arm, which had taken the brunt of the fall, still remained in a cumbersome sling.

One morning, upon opening his only piece of 'snail mail', Dan discovered a neatly clipped feature article from the Oceanside Weekly Gazette. The headline read: *"Popular Local Actor Opens New Shamu Show at Sea World"*. No note accompanied the clipping. The article pictured the aforementioned Big Bob, poised on a platform extending fifteen feet over a gigantic water tank. He held a sturdy white pole, arms outstretched and clearly using both hands. Shamu the Killer Whale was captured mid-leap, touching his smooth black snout to a large red ball attached to the pole. The picture's caption read: *"Looks like Shamu is reserving a front row seat for the new production of 'Our Town' – starring Oceanside's own Bob Crossley. Catch it next week at the North County Dinner Theater!"*

Budding thespian Bob was soon to discover the true meaning of sacrificing for his art. TriState, with the rock-solid support of his embarrassed employer, sued him for his false claim and won a substantial settlement. He couldn't repay much of what he'd swindled, but he most assuredly lost that all-important day job, which covered the bills while he wowed his adoring dinner theater fans. Unfortunately, barring a miraculous talent infusion, his dramatic skills weren't going to take him to the big time. Big Bob was well and truly screwed!

Eventually, they discovered who'd sent in the Sea World clipping. At Bob's day in court, his ex-wife testified, "I felt like I had to do the right thing. Besides, he's way behind on my alimony, so to hell with him!" It just hadn't paid to get too greedy... Bob should have prioritized his ex's alimony when TriState's manna began falling from the skies.

As Dan returned to logging his files, he overheard Trini and her pal Ada, TriState's part-time data processor, chattering beyond the partition. There was no practical solution to TriState's 'open plan' din. Dan wondered if the directors in their big offices had ever factored in the financial impact of the unproductive chitchat generated by a lack of personal space... or cared about the widespread discontent that open plan overcrowding created.

Trini was confiding to her pal, "Girl, I'm goin' ape with a colossal case of crotch itch – and, sure as shit, I'll be breaking into a hellish rash! I popped out for a bikini wax a couple of days ago and the bitch conned me into spending an extra five bucks on a sexy Brazilian 'landing strip'. *Mistake!* Let's just say that the short-cropped scrubland next to my little runway is already pure torture! And I know it'll be agonizing until my bush grows out."

The ever-supportive Ada commiserated with her friend, offering some homespun medical advice. "Have you tried slapping on some of that 'Mother Nature's Tea Tree Balm'? It seems to do wonders for Lloyd's razor burn."

Dan heard Trini audibly sucking in her breath. "But Ada, won't tea tree extract sting like crazy? Besides, I doubt if the antiseptic aroma will work wonders for my sex life." Trini hesitated for a second and giggled, "If I do try it, don't accuse your Lloyd of nuzzling around my nether regions next time you catch the scent wafting off him."

Ada sniggered and wandered off as Trini flipped a switch near her desk, closing every blind on the office's north-facing windows. Dan had to remind her, yet again, to forego the master switch and to simply close her own blinds – manually. He preferred *daylight*, even with an accompanying morning glare. Trini reset the blinds and replied apologetically, "Sorry Dan, I've been a bit preoccupied this morning."

Dan couldn't resist a dreadful pun: "Yeah Trini, I gathered that. Well, I guess we'll both be *itching* to get back to work now."

A run of fortune

Dan sat at his desk and let his mind wander to the highly anticipated coming evening. He'd be seeing Sophie, the *only* woman in his life for the past eighteen months. He truly savored their dates – he couldn't spend enough time with this fascinating woman. He prayed he wouldn't slip up, so that this relationship could last a lifetime. Dating Sophie coincided with (no... it had undoubtedly *initiated*) a late blooming maturity in Dan. In rowdier days, he routinely referred to his wife Melinda as "the old ball and chain". Sadly, that flippant moniker actually reflected his true feelings. When his pals eyeballed the gorgeous Melinda, they thought he'd lost it when he moaned about going home to her! How could a guy not pinch himself when such a goddess awaited his return to the old conjugal sack? Marriages, however, are built on more than attractive partners who qualify as 'Grade-A Arm Candy'. And, Dan had learned this bitter lesson the hard way.

Nowadays, he enjoyed nothing more than his mellow evenings with Sophie. Naturally, he was in awe of her grace, intelligence and beauty. More remarkably though, he'd come to value Sophie's innate consideration and sensitivity. He felt he could share his every thought with her.

Raised in a township in upstate Massachusetts, Sophie exuded the practicality and common sense attributed to grounded New Englanders. No one would describe her as particularly 'outgoing' – but, her inner spark shone in private moments with close friends. Small and dark, she looked years younger than her actual mid-thirties. Sophie's simple hairstyle was what Dan anachronistically called a 'pageboy'. Her generous brown eyes sparkled in any conversation that caught her imagination. When they'd first met, Dan's gaze had lingered on those dark eyes for an eternity... long before he'd taken any notice of her stunning figure. She was more Salma Hayek than catwalk model, but she didn't dress to flaunt her natural curves. Sophie possessed true elegance... she didn't have to *work* to attract a multitude of male admirers. On a rare day at the beach, Dan noticed old geezers and callow youths alike surreptitiously ogling her firm derrière. In her white one-piece, she could have passed for a teenager from behind as she sauntered towards the car. Dan recalled that on that late-spring day, lost in wonder, his mind had inexplicably wandered to a long buried and emphatically contrasting image... the startling sight of his mom in her bedroom, door slightly ajar, squirming into a 'waist to thigh' Spandex girdle. Unbelievably, she hadn't been much older on that unforgettably grim occasion than his lovely Sophie was now. Neither a workout fanatic nor a particularly judicious dieter, his new love was simply blessed with fantastic genes, aided by her participation in a relatively sedate weekly yoga class.

Ten years ago, Sophie relocated from Boston to San Diego. She'd been the Deputy Administrator for a small cancer charity in Massachusetts and moved straight into similar work at the Salk Institute in Torrey Pines. Her reason for moving west was straightforward. Her job had taken her to a San Diego conference and she'd met Gus Durden, a respected local businessman and involved charity supporter. Some years before, already in his early forties, he'd married a quiet young woman who'd worked closely under him. The local 'ladies who lunch' gossiped, "Well, he's finally been hooked! Who'd have thought that a serious gal like Nancy Sims would reel in Gus Durden?"

His charming Nancy passed away two years before Sophie met Gus, having lost her tough battle with breast cancer. Bereft, he'd been left with their two children, who he worshipped – ten year-old Alicia and Jason, nearly eight. Over a delegate's dinner after a tiring day of conference workshops, Gus admitted to Sophie that while his children meant everything to him, Nancy had been his anchor – and, regardless of the many community projects he valued and actively supported, he'd begun to drift through life.

Despite the obvious age difference, Sophie immediately formed a bond of friendship with Gus. She quickly saw why his Nancy had been so captivated by this unassuming man. Sophie, much as Nancy before her, didn't see Gus as a 'father figure' or mentor. As the conference wound down, they'd surprised themselves by becoming lovers. A lifetime partnership was the natural progression... neither was looking for a short-term romance. Sophie tied up loose ends in Boston and returned to San Diego for good ten months later. They married almost immediately. Sophie described the union as "pure bliss" to Dan. She didn't seem to mind fondly referring to her all too brief relationship with Gus as they'd become more intimate.

When Sophie and Gus married, the children were still plainly grieving over Nancy's untimely death. Initially, Sophie had been unsure if she should attempt the role of 'mom', 'friend' or 'big sister'. Fortunately, Jason warmed to her quickly. And Alicia soon realized that Sophie wouldn't dream of usurping her mother's memory, or still vital position, in the Durden family. Before long, Jason took to calling her 'mom'... and while Alicia stuck to 'Sophie', their budding relationship soon knit tightly.

Their own children didn't come along, but Sophie didn't fret. She was already fulfilled; she'd become a lynchpin in a family that clearly required her love and attention. But, one dreadful day, Gus didn't return from a round of golf. He'd suffered a fatal heart attack, with no warning, far too prematurely in their new life together.

Dan initially met Sophie while he was handling TriState's 'Key Man' Life Cover and Director's Beneficiary claims for Gus's firm. At that point, he was still emerging from his own messy divorce. He intuitively knew that comparisons between his problems and Sophie's all-encompassing grief were derisory. He settled the claims quickly and efficiently... and attempted to put the beautiful, grief-stricken widow out of his mind.

He couldn't forget her. Nearly a year later he'd phoned Sophie on some barely credible pretext, arranging to meet her for a very proper and public business lunch. With the 'business' out of the way – a trivial disclosure form he could've mailed for her signature – they lingered at their table. Another hour simply flew by as they shared a very enjoyable and more personal, if still very proper, conversation.

Dan learned that Sophie and her stepkids – now approaching adulthood at twenty and seventeen – still resided in their longtime family home up the coast in Del Mar. A neat ranch-style with a massive wooden deck overlooking the ocean, it was certainly more than adequate... but hardly the flash seaside crib that Gus could have afforded. In all things, Gus – *and* Sophie – avoided ostentation.

After a few more quiet lunches, Dan was convinced they were simply sharing past woes and experiences – as friends tend to do. But over the months their get-togethers became more frequent and Dan realized Sophie was gradually allowing him into her life. In time, a magical candlelit dinner turned into a sleepover. Now, nearly two years on, Dan saw no one else – and he knew Sophie wasn't dating other men. He was the only lover she'd been with since Gus. Of that, he was certain.

The clincher that Dan was *the* man in her life had been Sophie's kind invitation to garage his beloved Fiat two-seater at her place, thereby freeing up his mom's already cluttered Ocean Beach garage. Years before, he'd purchased a ten-year-old '124 Spider 2000cc' with his first – and *only* – Chargers' post-season bonus. Even the lowly equipment managers and physios had been given a little something from that year's playoff kitty. His pride and joy was British Racing Green, with a pristine tan leather interior. "In great shape, one careful owner," the ad had stated and the little car set him back all of $2500. Now, thankfully, his classic Spider rested comfortably in Sophie's double garage, well away from his irrepressible little brother, Marty.

Sophie's kids were used to Dan and tolerated him. Maybe they were even warming to him, as he'd obviously provided their stepmother with the contentment she so richly deserved. He and Sophie had settled into their pleasant routines. Often he'd take her for an early dinner down the

47

hill by the beach, returning to her place for an evening of TV or music. They'd kick back in her living room or relax on the wooden deck, taking in the Pacific sunset and Del Mar's coastal lights – usually with an unassuming bottle of soft red.

Sophie loved Tio Jorge's... a stucco pile just above Del Mar's business strip and sandy beach. The authentic burritos and spicy Mexican salads, served on a tranquil patio, were historic. Their margaritas were potent – lacking the cloying sweetness that spoiled the flavor. An evening at Tio Jorge's reminded Dan why San Diego was still heavenly... *if* you were lucky enough to be tucked away in the proper glorious, half-hidden corner.

The key to their comfortable relationship was undoubtedly Sophie's lack of *neediness*. She didn't require a broad-shouldered male to 'make her complete'. In fact, Dan often wondered why she'd allowed a man as immature as he'd clearly been into her life. She seldom made demands – and initially she hadn't been overanxious to introduce Dan into her kids' lives. Over time, Alicia seemed to accept him as an older (but assuredly *not wiser*) friend. Jason, however, was a harder sell. Dan was an interloper... Jason felt that his father's memory needed no rivals. But Dan persevered. And last year he'd made a small breakthrough, inviting the moody teenager to an early morning surfing session at OB.

Ocean Beach remained Dan's favorite haunt – he'd defend it to his last breath as San Diego's finest surfing spot... "miles ahead of La Jolla or Imperial Beach." His mom and half-siblings still lived there, a few streets up from the beach, in the tiny forties bungalow where he'd grown up. Truth be told, Dan was still considered something of a surfing and hellraising legend in this long-established community.

Recently, Jason had dropped out of his freshman year at SDSU – and Sophie was in the midst of her first serious run-in with her moody stepson. He drifted into odd jobs, but like many youngsters, he seemed to lack direction or any desire to apply himself. Sophie reluctantly asked Dan to try to get through to Jason, 'man to man'. She wasn't concerned about *what* the boy chose to do, as long as he took some constructive steps towards securing a happy future for himself.

Of course, Dan made every effort to oblige his beloved. But his initial bonding ploy with Jason – OB surfing excursions – had a wholly unintended side effect. What Dan hadn't anticipated was that Jason would get on so well with his kid brother Marty!

At twenty-three, Marty was striving to become the *second* Paige considered an 'Ocean Beach Legend'... and, at least in his own mind, he was making strong headway. His goal was to attract a more fanatic following among the local dudes than his big brother ever had. If Dan had been a wicked hellraiser, Marty intended to become, in his words, *"OB's All-Time Surfin' Badass"*.

Most of Marty's buddies weren't *that* unruly, but these loafers and lay-abouts would undoubtedly be negative influences on Jason's maturing process. As Jason and Marty grew tighter, Dan knew he'd have to shift into 'damage control'. Otherwise, Sophie could conceivably write *him* off, along with his flaky family. Dan resorted to a stern 'heart to heart' with Marty – and he tried to make it a rule with Jason that the boy would never head down to OB on his own.

An outright *bribe* had actually steered his brother into a more constructive frame of mind concerning his relationship with Jason. Marty accepted two hundred in cash and Dan's most radical 'vintage' board in exchange for barring Jason from his tight-knit clique. When Marty attempted to cool the budding friendship a tad, he was, of course, his usual tactful self. He explained, "I can't hang with you on a regular basis because you're not twenty-one – and your fake ID's been rejected *twice in a row* at the Quad." Amazingly, Jason just nodded in agreement; this lame line of reasoning made perfect sense to him. So, Dan continued to take Sophie's stepson out for a day in the surf now and then... but kept him on a shortish lead.

Recently, Jason's employment prospects seemed to be on the up. He acquired a full-time job at a pottery factory – really an old warehouse and workshop – up the coast in Encinitas. He liked throwing pots... and showed real flair. The work kept him occupied – and even solvent. And the best part was that the workshop was a couple of miles *north* of Del Mar, not fifteen miles to the south and near Ocean Beach. Still, Dan's management of the fragile relationship between Sophie's kids and the unruly Paiges was a definite work in progress.

Dan cut short his daydreaming as Trini's giggles over the cubicle divider brought him back to earth. He refocused on the data on his screen. It was approaching ten and today he hoped to escape for a *real* lunch with his pal Rod Grissom at The Sorrento Steakhouse. He'd have to organize his workload prior to that afternoon meeting with Walt... and he'd only have the balance of this swiftly disappearing morning to achieve it.

Sometimes a plan comes together!

Down in Tijuana, Jesus and Flaco were pulling over on Pio Pico, across from a large and somewhat ramshackle garden supplies depot. Throwing their butt-ends out the window, they settled in for what they hoped would soon turn into a fruitful morning's work. Not ten minutes

49

later, an old long-bed Toyota pickup with California plates came to a stop near the store's commercial loading bay. Jesus glanced at his watch: just as Raul had told them – quarter to ten. The sole occupant got out and walked into the warehouse building's entrance. This man had to be their target... Benito Rosado in the flesh! He fit the description provided by both Manny Tejada and the helpful Raul... driving an old pick-up, in his mid-forties and dressed on this occasion in neat work trousers and flannel shirt. Then Flaco spotted the clincher. The truck's white doors were inscribed in green lettering: *'Rosado & Sons Landscaping'*. If all went to plan, Benito Rosado's truck would head back to San Diego with two unobserved pursuers in tow.

Benny had stopped in for a quick coffee and chat with his *mama grande* and, just as his cousin Benito had predicted, he was picking up supplies before heading up to a couple of jobs back in San Diego. The morning was warm and bright and Benny looked forward to a workday spent predominantly on his own. Digging in the soil and getting his hands dirty were the attractions of the job these days. Gunnar and his older boys, Victor and Omar, managed the crews... he was content to delegate the supervisory drudgery.

The dodgy compadres in the low-rider were attempting to remain discreet and unobserved. Each finished another smoke while a pair of skinny kids loaded the white pickup with a dozen bags of fertilizer and four large flats of bedding plants. Ten minutes later, the laid-back man in the jeans and flannel shirt emerged, waved to the dispatcher and drove away.

Flaco rubbed his clean-shaven chin and spoke sharply to his dozy partner, "Okay, honcho, start 'er up and we'll tail him. Drive safely... and don't get too close. He's surely heading for the border and we should keep a few cars between us when we cross at the checkpoint."

Jesus flushed an even darker shade through his bronzed skin and shot back, "Shit Flaco, save the lecture. I know how to tail a fuckin' pickup!"

Flaco sat up straighter. "I'm sure you do man, but in this shit car, we don't exactly blend in. We don't want Rosado to spot us and get suspicious, okay?"

No fuckin' sweat *vato*," Jesus replied, pulling out into Pio Pico's sparse traffic to follow their oblivious target.

Safe and many miles away, Benito Rosado wouldn't know it, but his misdirection was working to perfection. He'd set up his cousin for a pair of clueless assholes – and, with luck, it would take them some time to figure out their error. In the meantime, his little fib would help him to extricate himself from a sticky 'misunderstanding' with Tejada and the cartel.

As Cousin Benny headed north, he had no reason to be suspicious. If the day went to plan, he'd be working alone, doing a bit of light gardening at a condo complex in Chula Vista. It would be an enjoyable, routine job for a long-time client. Gunnar and the boys would be working their crews elsewhere. Benny knew only too well that both of his sons preferred it when the old man stayed well out of their hair.

He'd break off early. Today's job was a stone's throw from home and Connie wanted to talk about Greg's class load at SDSU. She was thrilled when their youngest had chosen to attend San Diego State, rather than joining the family business out of high school as his brothers had so willingly done. The way the business was growing, Benny agreed that they'd soon need a qualified accountant in the family. He just hoped that Gregorio would stick to his business studies – and not switch to some useless liberal arts major.

Oh well, Benny knew Connie would undoubtedly win out concerning Greg's future career choices. She and *Mama Grande* Hortensia had raised him to be softer than his brothers, but Benny didn't see the harm. Times were changing after all – and Greg was a decent and intelligent kid, who'd make a great addition to the family business if that's what he chose.

As he approached the vast border checkpoint, Benny pulled into a lane reserved for commercial vehicles – a reasonably short line on this weekday morning. He crossed here often, so a fair number of officials on both sides of the border knew him by sight. He expected no hassles. He was unaware of a low-rider fifty yards behind him, in an inconspicuous non-commercial lane. The tail was working perfectly.

Chapter 6

Rubbing elbows with the Mission Valley heavyweights

Dan stepped into the dim interior of one of Mission Valley's most familiar restaurants – the renowned Sorrento Steakhouse. Once the solid oak doors closed behind him, there was no way of knowing if it was daylight or dark outside... hard-drinking patrons soon lost all sense of time. By habit, he hung a left into the crowded cocktail lounge, where he was certain his old buddy Rod Grissom would be perched, elbows on the bar.

Rod was working on his second bourbon on the rocks. He signaled the cocktail waitress to bring his pal a beer, but Dan waved her off. "Let's go straight to our table Rod. I've got a meeting with Walt this afternoon, so lunch will have to remain sane and sober."

"Okay man, but one little beer won't kill you. Lightnin' won't be making it today, by the way. He's busy with some pretty little TV reporter, taping a short puff piece on some new sports field being dedicated to him in South Bay."

Dan grinned and replied, "I'll order one beer when we get to the table okay? I don't want any real booze on my breath when I meet up with Walt."

The steakhouse oozed ersatz 'Italian charm'. The owner endeavored to maintain an East Coast authenticity, as the place had been the San Diego hangout of choice for retired Mafioso since the sixties. Legitimate businessmen *loved* soaking up the vicarious buzz generated by the 'Sopranos-style' atmosphere. In truth, most of the 'connected' patrons had long since passed away... and fewer of the mob's pensioners were supplanting them in the dark corner booths. San Diego's reputation as a relatively safe zone for Mafia geriatrics was still somewhat apropos, but the need for a single 'neutral territory' as a safe haven for retirees was fading. Nowadays, old mobsters opted for the Caribbean or Mexico; or raised a few head of overfed cattle on pretend Montana 'ranches'. One bonus for the taxpayer... San Diego's declining population of retired mob bosses led to a corresponding reduction in head count at San Diego's Downtown Police and FBI Headquarters.

The Sorrento's 'Sicilian' waitresses wore the lowest-cut peasant blouses and skimpiest skirts that Mission Valley's business and tourism industries would tolerate. Occasionally, these buxom ladies had to pass muster with overdressed wives or the young, nubile 'personal assistants' squired in by ill-advised businessmen. Blood-red steaks, accompanied by huge baked potatoes, and overflowing platters of pasta flew out of the kitchen at all hours. Even *breakfast meetings* at the Sorrento called for huge steaks, hash browns and eggs, topped off by large tumblers of fresh-squeezed, pulpy orange juice and steaming coffee mugs.

Rod Grissom was a Sorrento regular. He enjoyed using their 'private dining facilities' for intimate client meetings. He considered himself a vital participant in this macho scene; all but imagining his grinning visage beaming down from the red-flocked wallpaper's gilt-edged frames... schmoozing with the Hollywood stars and retired 'made men' posing shoulder to shoulder in the pictures, cigars in hand.

In the old days, Dan had happily met up with the guys at The Sorrento. And he regularly showed up for Happy Hours at their other favorite watering holes, like Pussies or The Quad. In those simpler times, Rod enjoyed it when Dan turned up in his patrolman's uniform. At The Sorrento, he'd invariably give a broad salute to the walls' celebrity photos and refer to his impending repast to all within earshot as "a clandestine meet with my crooked cop buddy, T J Hooker, Jr."

Jimmy's Sports Bar, known as 'Pussies', was another Valley hangout frequented by the crowd. It acquired its risqué nickname by acclamation from its coarse and fun-loving regulars. Traditionally, it attracted the foxiest (and loosest) young lovelies working in the area. Girls stopped in after work to graze Pussies' free buffets and never, *ever* paid for Happy Hour drinks. Pro athletes – home team guys, as well as clued-in visitors – happily hung out and 'socialized' in the bar's agreeable surroundings. The athletes' fame, bawdy banter and endless cash were surefire lures for each year's fresh batch of lovely bimbettes.

Dan still occasionally met up with his drinking buddies for an hour or two, but those long afternoons and endless evenings were history. First Melinda, and now Sophie, had changed all that – and, obviously in his dotage, he wasn't fretting about it. Dan had originally been the glue for his gang, a natural leader. He'd introduced pals Rod Grissom and Neil Downey to the celebrated Derrick 'Lightnin' Jackson in Pussies years before. Derrick had been the Chargers' go-to receiver in those days – and, even in retirement, he remained a local legend.

Dan had been something of a star cornerback in high school... good enough to attract a 'full ride' scholarship from San Diego State. Eventually slotted in as a no-hope, third-string defender in the competitive world of college football, he spent four years trying to cover the elusive Lightnin' in practice, with little success. But, they became good friends. Lightnin' was the kind of innate team leader who made a point of hanging out with *everyone* – black or white, starter or scrub. He even included the student managers in his wide circle. When Dan graduated with a degree in Sports Physiology, he'd been lucky enough to catch on as an equipment manager with the Chargers. And lo and behold, Derrick, a sure-fire professional, was the team's first draft pick that year. So Dan and Derrick remained tight, hanging out with a few of the unattached (or unfettered) pros after practices and in the off-season.

Eventually Dan moved on from his low-level position with the Chargers, taking on a grown-up's job with the Police Department. By then, Derrick was an All-Star... the showpiece of a potent Charger offense. When he eventually retired, Lightnin' remained a local celebrity. He gravitated to business promotions and real estate deals, earning enough to become one of Rod Grissom's 'A-List' investment clients.

After high school, Rod had headed north for college, bullshitting his way to middling grades and a business degree from Oregon State. He returned to San Diego with a clear ambition: *"I'll be the 'Stockbroker of Choice' to this city's rich and greedy!"* And, to some degree, he'd succeeded. Using his oily charm, he'd become a persuasive (and sometimes lucky) stock churner – making himself a fortune, if not always creating long-term wealth for his less than attentive clients.

When it came to cruising for tail in Mission Valley and the Gaslamp District, Rod's ready wallet, blended with Derrick's superstar status, invariably worked its magic. The pair partied endlessly, with Dan making it a threesome less and less often. Neil, happily married, had seldom joined these evening forays. Dan had enjoyed the bad boys' company – and Rod's well-appointed sailboat was still an attraction. But, these days, he turned down invitations to hang out more often than he joined in their shenanigans.

Over today's Sorrento lunch, Rod was in an expansive mood – even more talkative than usual. The meal passed quickly, with his pal downing three more bourbons while Dan nursed his lone beer.

Rod threw Dan a couple of tired stock tips and then got down to matters of substance. He'd asked Lightnin' and Dan to crew for him in a weekend regatta and Derrick had turned him down with some lame excuse. Neil, as usual, had been cool to his half-hearted invitation as well. Rod leaned in and whispered, "Hey man, what's up with Lightnin'? He's been really preoccupied lately – and it's been two weeks since I've even seen him in Pussies."

Rod seemed to be genuinely upset about Derrick calling off. The question was, was he worried about a friend's frame of mind or merely concerned with his sudden shortage of qualified crew? He considered himself a hell of a skipper, even though he resembled Dennis Conner more in pudgy *appearance* than in sailing ability. Rod had always nursed a strong competitive streak... but, unfortunately, it was tied to negligible athletic talent. He loved winning his local regattas and he knew that Dan, Neil and Lightnin' were dependable, if unspectacular, sailors. Without them, he'd have to struggle with the dregs who hung around the yacht club.

Dan leaned back, smiling to himself at his companion's discomfort. "Even Lightnin' has to ease off a bit now and then Rod. He's been seeing a lot of Joy Lindsey, the Bolts' D-line Coach's daughter. She works in the Chargers' front office. Maybe it's serious, who knows? I'm pretty sure he's not pissed at you or anything. He told me he was looking forward to the sailing this weekend, so I'm certain something important must have come up."

"Okay man," Rod replied. "But you're still on for the race, right? You're great crew. The delightful news is I've lined up some deckhands who work at DataStore Circuits, that big new software outfit. And they're just what the doctor ordered – willing swabbies, with massive hooters and firm asses. They'll be glad to take on the heavy winching – and to tackle a few essential extracurricular duties as well!"

Dan smiled and held both hands up. "I'm there man, but you'll have to entertain these sweet little swabs on your own. I might even bring Sophie along for the day, if that's okay."

Rod's face fell, almost imperceptibly, but he didn't miss a beat. "That's fine, man. You know I love her. Just tell her not to share any of those tired 'Rapid Rodney' stories with my new playmates. I'll be attempting to impress them and I don't need my sordid past nipping at my heels!"

"Sure man, she'll be cool." Dan wondered why Rod would assume that Sophie even remembered any of those well-worn, grossly exaggerated stories Rod recounted repeatedly. He rose to his feet, said his goodbyes and left his pal to gravitate back to the bar. Rod was becoming even more of a 'legend in his own mind' as the years passed. It was becoming harder and harder to salvage a worthwhile friendship out of the little they still had in common. It was easy to understand why Neil saw Rod so infrequently these days. Dan was relieved to be heading back for his session with Walt – on time and in one piece.

A tidy job

Jesus and Flaco crossed into the US without incident and followed the old white pick-up up I-5. They stayed well behind their target as Benny's truck exited west, towards Imperial Beach. Soon their quarry parked on a side street near a new office building, just behind a late model 'Rosado & Sons' van. A small crew was unpacking rolled up sod strips from the van and carrying them twenty yards to the office's unfinished courtyard. A couple of workers hoisted the bags of fertilizer out of the newly arrived pickup as 'Benito Rosado' wandered over to speak with a young dude who was obviously in charge.

Jesus and Flaco stayed put in their Firebird, smoking and feigning disinterest. But the impulsive Jesus was already champing at the bit. "Man, let's amble over to the back of the pickup and see if we can nail our guy when he comes back."

Flaco spat out the window. "Are you loco? There's a half-dozen witnesses hangin' around here – and probably a dozen more inside the building! Drive further down the street and pull over. The fucker has to move on, and sooner or later he'll be on his own... we'll get our opportunity."

Sure enough, ten minutes later, their quarry slid into his pickup and drove away. Flaco punched Jesus on the arm (the big man was already drifting off, mouth hanging open) and ordered, "Follow him, you lazy *puto*... and keep your fuckin' distance."

In another twenty minutes they pulled over across from a smart new condo complex on the outskirts of Chula Vista. Benny's truck was just up the street, near the front entrance. Their intended prey still seemed oblivious to their presence. The dude, obviously clueless, removed two flats of bedding plants and some hand tools from the truckbed and headed around one side of the front-facing of three matching buildings. Flaco smiled. "This looks promising, man. I don't see nobody around. Let's wait five minutes and then take us a little tour of these here premises."

The complex was sizeable; three four-story stucco buildings built in the 'mock-mission' style that Southern Californians favor. The buildings were arranged in a triangle, surrounding a community pool, sauna and barbecues which were all partly visible down the outside passageways. The complex was new; the buildings far from fully occupied. Obviously, 'Benito' would be adding some finishing touches to the landscaping at poolside on this sunny afternoon.

Flaco told Jesus to sit tight. From his vantage point he could observe the balconies of some units overlooking the passageway where their prey had just disappeared. Few possessed chairs or plants – and not many blinds or curtains adorned the interiors behind their sliding doors. And, fortuitously, there was no sign by the front main entrance of a sales office or 'model units'. After finishing his smoke, Flaco exited the car and made a show of stretching his legs while he surreptitiously checked out anything else that might be of interest. He sauntered around to Jesus' open window and murmured, "It looks okay man. I don't see nobody gawking. Let's go 'round back."

Ignoring the front-facing building's grandiose public entrance, they ambled nonchalantly around the side, using the concrete passageway that Benny had navigated a few minutes earlier. As they rounded the back corner, Flaco whispered, "We're in luck. He's over there by the Jacuzzi, planting flowers. See anyone lookin' out?"

Jesus, never a subtle man, stopped in his tracks and peered towards the balconies in the two adjoining buildings. His gloved hand cupped his straw hat's brim to block the sunlight as he gazed upwards in a classic 'Indian Guide' pose. He whispered, "A few blinds are closed man, but most windows are bare. Probably not many people live here yet. There's tables and chairs on a few balconies, but I don't see nobody nowhere."

Jesus basically confirmed his partner's earlier deduction. This was a most auspicious spot for their hit – perfectly suited for a quick 'in and out'. Flaco whispered back to Jesus, not wishing to attract their intended target's attention, "Okay man, keep a fuckin' eye peeled. I'm on this!" The small man crept towards the lone gardener, still facing away from his pursuers, stooped low and digging in the dirt of a pre-prepared flowerbed. Finally Benny Rosado turned, more likely sensing rather than hearing anything, as his stalker pulled a shiny .22 automatic from a trouser pocket.

Not a word passed between shooter and victim. Leaning in from less than three feet away, Flaco aimed his little pistol downwards at a point just above Benny's startled left eye. The older man instinctively raised his arm, as if to ward off a blow.

Jesus, stock-still by the corner of the building, heard a distinct pop; and then a second report. Flaco's surprised prey collapsed face down where he knelt – and a steady stream of blood began to seep slowly into the freshly turned earth.

Jesus tiptoed forward and reached out to the prostrate body. He was going for their victim's wallet, no doubt about it. It was just too inviting... bulging in the back pocket of his trousers. Flaco hissed, "Don't handle him *puto*! We leave him and his wallet untouched, for easy identification – and so it's clear this was a pro hit and not some *tonto* gangbangers takin' out an easy mark. Remember, this here is meant to be a warning message to some tough hombres, not some fuckin' mugging."

"I hear you man," Jesus whispered. Then, he put on his most imploring look and tried to reason with his partner. "But why pass on easy pickings? How about leaving a few dollars on the dude and takin' any real dough? Who'll know the difference?"

"Fuck me! Are you even listenin'? This *must* look like a professional hit, Jesus! The body remains untouched, except for those two little holes in his head. Plenty of people would know how much a hood like Benito usually carries in his wallet – even when he's workin' his shitty day job. Leave him alone and let's get the hell outa' here."

With that, Flaco turned and beat a hasty retreat, with the contrite Jesus in tow. They rounded the front of the main building, strode across the street to the garish Firebird and slipped unhurriedly into the bucket seats. Jesus turned the engine over and they drove sedately up the street, heading back towards the city – and, hopefully, some generous new paydays.

An old woman was peering out of her sliding doors from a studio ground-floor unit facing the pool. She'd been watching that clever scamp Jerry Springer ask his audience to sort the transvestites from the real females on one of his *'Showgirl Lineup Specials'* when she thought she heard a noise like a firecracker in the recreation area. But everything looked okay. All she saw was that cute little Mexican gardener lying on his side near the Jacuzzi. Obviously, he was taking great care with the job, inspecting his handiwork up close.

A quarter-mile to the north, the dull-witted Jesus was actually mulling over one of his rare decent thoughts. "Hey man, you didn't scoop up any casings! Do we need to go back?"

Flaco grinned and leaned back in his seat. "Hell no! The cops sure as shit'll never find this here popgun. It's goin' in the drink off the Bay Drive Bridge tonight. And, I was careful to wipe down every round before sliding it into that little bitty clip... just like the pros do. So, don't worry about a fuckin' thing. If anyone noticed us leaving, we look just like a thousand other wetbacks kickin' around Chula Vista. It's almost for sure that no one'll be able to pick us two *Mejicanos* out of a Latino lineup, even if some fucker did catch a glimpse of us."

To Flaco's surprise, a look of relief crossed Jesus' stolid face. He hadn't believed that the big man possessed the imagination to fear the prospect of their capture. Jesus settled back, farted loudly and contentedly said, "No sweat then man, you covered everything."

Flaco hesitated before adding, "There is one little problem. Let's hope no gawkers noticed this shitheap sitting out front. It sticks out like a sore thumb." He paused and then thought out loud, "But there's no reason for anyone to get suspicious. People wouldn't hear the shots from my popgun out front – or from the streets beyond the two side buildings. And there's no real reason passers-by would take notice as we walked out – or look twice at this piece of crap sittin' in the street."

Jesus grinned. "Fuckin'-A, man. I sure as shit didn't want to go back there to scoop up those casings. Do you think we fucked up Benito enough to spell out Tejada's message?"

"Benito's sportin' fresh holes in his forehead man – and half his blood is already feedin' the daisies. If that ain't message enough, Tejada can go down there and inflict more damage on the fuckin' corpse himself! This hit might even make the news tonight. I think we created just about maximo mayhem, hombre. Doin' this job so good is our ticket to some big paydays, just like Tejada promised."

Jesus stopped at a red light, lifted his left buttock and let loose yet another thunderous fart. "I'm really hungry, *vato*. Let's get us some lunch. How about a pile of fish tacos at El Sombrero? I could've eaten ten of those tasty fuckers when you took me there last week!"

"Okay man, but I did the tough work today, so you'll pick up the check. That's fair."

Jesus punched the steering wheel and grimaced as he whined, "Yeah, I'll pay all right, but I bet we could have been eating *primoroso* meals for weeks to come if we'd lifted his bankroll. What a waste!"

Flaco stared at his partner, his expression indicating that the matter was closed. "You earned five hundred today and you'll have another five hundred in your pocket soon enough, *cabron*. And, miraculously, you didn't fuck it up. Learn to cut your losses and do as you're told... and, in the meantime, point this shitbucket towards El Sombrero and those fish tacos. Believe me, we could end up *lifers* – or dead meat in some back alley – on accounta' that tempting wallet you're pining after. First, it wasn't worth the fuckin' risk; and second, it's not what the boss wanted us to do... *is that clear enough for you?*"

Jesus frowned and eventually nodded; letting loose a loud belch. As he took the slip-road onto I-5 North, Flaco was tuning their ancient radio to a favorite Tex-Mex station.

Chapter 7

Say what?

It was just after four when Dan and Walt completed their routine meeting. As usual, the boss offered more than a few helpful suggestions. His know-how came in handy; invariably helping to tie up the loose ends that sometimes came back to haunt TriState.

On his way out, Walt passed the unnaturally quiet (and hard-at-work?) Trini. His parting ritual included a blatantly transparent, but harmless, sidelong glance at her ample bosom. "So, adios senorita. Sadly, I'm loving and leaving you, but I'm aiming to beat the traffic on my way up to LA. Take it easy, my one and only!"

Trini smiled and blew Walt a parting kiss as Dan slapped him on the shoulder and chuckled, "Thanks for coming down boss. We'll see you in a couple of weeks. Have a great time in Palm Springs. I wish I was joining you guys... on the course and in the bar!"

Walt was eagerly anticipating TriState's annual outing – their only official 'team building exercise'. He loved his family, but this highly anticipated weekend away did them no harm. Never a keen golfer, Walt was liable to pick his ball out of the rough and pocket it long before reaching a green, laughingly instructing his partner to mark him down for a 'charitable ten'. He enjoyed the banter much more than the competition. Walt's true forte was his flawless follow-through on the nineteenth hole... where he traditionally deposited his plastic behind the bar and covered the tab for the entire evening.

As the boss disappeared into the hallway, Trini picked up her ringing phone, exchanged greetings with the caller and signaled Dan that the call was his. He pointed towards his desk, saying, "Put it through Trini." He lifted the phone on the third ring. "Dan Paige, how may I help you?"

A subdued voice replied, "Hey Dan, it's Neil. I take it you haven't been listening to the radio?" Neil was unquestionably Dan's closest friend, but he rarely disturbed Dan at work. Neither had time for chitchat during the day.

Picking up on Neil's somber tone, Dan answered lowly, "It's still afternoon and I'm in my office, so it's unlikely I'm clued up on the latest news, dude. What's up?"

"Are you sitting down? They found a body at some condo site down in Chula Vista – two shots to the head. I'm afraid it's Benny Rosado. Apparently there were no witnesses. I can't believe it! Gunnar phoned us as soon as he got the dreadful news and Annie's already down at their place with Connie and the family. Can you get right over here?"

Thankfully, Dan *was* sitting down. Even hardened ex-cops weren't immune to shocks like this. "I'll run by my mom's, Neil, and then head over." Slipping by habit into policeman's mode, Dan opted for an obvious course of action. "A couple of my pals in Homicide may be able to fill in some background. I'll see what I can find out."

"Thanks Dan. God, it's a lousy world when a mensch like Benny unknowingly wanders into harm's way. It has to be a case of 'wrong place, wrong time'; of that I'm certain. I sure hope that Annie and Father Riordan are providing some tiny bit of comfort to Connie and the boys. See you soon."

"I'll be with you in an hour or so Neil. Try to hang loose." Dan hung up and immediately called Sophie. He got her voicemail and left a quick message. "It's me. I'll need a rain check on tonight. I hate to tell you this way, but you may have already heard. Benny Rosado has been murdered. Annie is with his family – and I'm heading over to Neil's. Call me when you can. Sorry, hon. Bye."

He tried calling a reliable contact in Homicide Division, but could only get through to the Desk Sergeant. Unsurprisingly, he could tell Dan very little; only that no perp was yet in custody. No sense in sticking around the office... Dan headed out.

Twenty minutes later, he walked through the door of his mom's Ocean Beach house. She was relaxing with a coffee, slippered feet resting on the battered coffee table, watching 'San Diego Horizons', a vacuous talk show that was one of her favorites. His sister Mandy was studying in her bedroom and his little bro' was nowhere to be seen. Mandy swiftly came out of her room, as she always did when she heard Dan's voice.

Mandy smiled, but immediately read the grim look on her brother's face. "Sit down with mom for a minute, sis," Dan muttered. He paused to grab the remote and turn down the TV. Annoyed at the interruption – and not adept like her daughter in picking up on his obvious signals – Sally gave him a frosty glance. Dan's stern return look did, however, leave his mom in no doubt that this was serious. She sat back and swept some gray hairs from her eyes.

"Mom, Mandy... Benny Rosado is dead. Neil says he was found at a job site this afternoon– shot twice. As of now, no one can figure a motive. It could be a random gang thing. I wanted you to know before you heard it on the news."

Sally folded her legs under her and began to whimper, resting her head on the arm of the sofa. Clasping her hands in prayer, she began to

61

murmur almost incoherently. She'd never been of any use in a crisis, even when Dan was a kid. As he'd grown up, he'd become as much dad as brother to his half-siblings after their feckless father wandered off.

Mandy ran over and threw her arms around her big brother. "This is awful Dan! Who's looking after Connie and the boys?"

"Annie and a priest are with them, kid – and I'm sure Gunnar's there too. I'm heading down to Neil and Annie's now. Give Marty the news when he gets home, okay?" Dan left the two women slumped on the couch, each lost in private thoughts.

Hangin' in there

Annie had returned from Connie's and was preparing dinner for the three of them when Dan arrived at the Downey's door. Neil was on the kitchen phone, trying to contact friends and parishioners who might not have heard the tragic news.

Both Dan and Neil had been outstanding high school athletes – but Neil was by far the more gifted. In fact, he'd been selected 'First Team, All City' in football and basketball two years on the trot, as well as being blindingly fast on the track. Rod Grissom had appended himself as the unlikely third member in their inseparable high school trio. Chubby and 'athletically challenged', he basked in the glory – and girl-pulling power – of his buddies.

Neil attracted the same football scholarship offer from San Diego State that Dan had gratefully accepted. In fact, many even higher profile schools had recruited him. But he turned them down, opting instead for an entry-level job at the big Chevy dealership in Bay Park. Beginning as an apprentice mechanic, he excelled in his training and quickly worked his way up the ladder. Nowadays, he was the Regional Service Director for a multi-location group of GM and Hyundai dealerships – and highly valued for his hands-on teaching skills with their young mechanics.

Annie and Neil hadn't dated in school. Truth be told, she'd acquired a bit of a 'fast' reputation – and Neil, for all of his popularity, had been painfully shy with girls. Perhaps Annie *had* been around the block a little, but she was no slut. Actively involved in social causes, she was the archetypical free spirit and 'throwback hippie'… gorgeous in her flowered skirts, embroidered blouses and beads. She made friends in all circles, little caring if she ran with the popular crowd.

Neil and Annie had been drawn to each other when he was already working for a salary. The ever-tactful Rod, home for the summer after his sophomore year, told Neil that he should have some laughs with the luscious Annie... but *marriage*? That was out of the question.

Dan, on the other hand, had known the whole story behind this budding relationship. Shortly after Neil began dating her, Annie started 'showing'... single, pregnant and (at least outwardly) unrepentant. She and Neil married just before Julianne was born... but a few people, like Dan, knew that Neil wasn't the newborn's father.

Annie had enjoyed an 'off and on' high school relationship with Steve Flagler, the star running back. They'd even dated occasionally after graduation. She saw something in this loser that others were obviously blind to. Steve couldn't resist wooing Annie, while still availing himself of the silly girls who threw themselves at a handsome jock. Broke and unemployed when he learned his semi-steady girlfriend was knocked up, he managed to escape her clutches by joining the Navy. He made good on his getaway before anyone noticed that staunchly Catholic Annie, now virtually on her own, was pregnant.

Five months later Annie and Neil married in her parish church, their place of worship to this day, with Dan as their best man. Some so-called friends whispered that the couple's lovely and extremely premature daughter was an obvious 'mistake', but Baby Julie was the apple of her dad's eye from the outset. And three years later, their son Rob (the spitting image of his dad) joined the Downey family.

Over the years, Dan's family had become as close to Annie and the kids as they already were to Neil. Annie dragged Neil to Mass in their National City Parish *every* Sunday – and sometimes Dan was coerced into joining them, often with sister Mandy in tow.

Annie introduced the Rosado clan to Neil and her kids, as well as to a few family friends. She and Consuela Rosado had hit it off while serving on various committees; soon becoming firm chums.

Neil's apparently precarious 'shotgun wedding' blossomed into the most splendid partnership that Dan had ever been around. Fifteen years on, their mutual devotion was stronger than ever. Annie grew ever-lovelier as time passed... there was simply no other way to describe her than as a beautiful, slightly maturing 'stone fox'. She could pass for her mid-twenties, shiny sable hair cascading over slender shoulders. Daughter Julie's hair was fairer (she'd inherited her biological dad's coloring), but as the girl approached young womanhood, people often mistook them for sisters. Neil loved it.

The Downey's wedded bliss briefly crossed Dan's mind as he sat in their kitchen, reflecting on the Rosado's tragedy. They were another of the finest families he knew. Still perching on his stool, Neil hung up the phone and greeted Dan. Annie was just serving up the pasta. They all took their plates through the alcove to the family's old wooden dining table. The Downeys ate around this table, often with friends, every evening. It was one of Neil's firm rules. Tonight though, the kids were at their gran's, having gone straight from school when Annie phoned with the tragic news.

First, Dan told them what little he knew. Then, after eating silently for a few minutes, Annie described her visit with Connie. She was obviously still devastated by the dreadful scene at the Rosados. "There were so many neighbors and relatives there that I thought it was best to come home. I left at the same time as Father Riordan. Hortensia is already up from Tijuana, fussing in the kitchen, drying her tears on a towel and ordering everyone around, as grandmothers do."

Neil interjected, "How's Connie holding up?"

"Truthfully, she's totally out of it. The doctor has given her a strong sedative. And the boys were sitting on the porch, talking low, trying to steer clear of their grandmother. They seem to be hell bent on coming up with some kind of 'action plan'. *Action?* There's nothing anyone can do tonight but pray for Benny... and hope that the monster who committed this unspeakable deed is quickly arrested."

Dan gently asked, "Could the family provide any details, Annie? Did you see Gunnar?" Dan hoped the little man would be there, as he knew that the Rosado's oldest friend could keep the boys under control – at least for the time being.

Annie replied, "Gunnar managed to pick up a few details from the police. Benny was lying near a Jacuzzi in the condo's recreational area – shot twice in the head. The Rosados have worked at this complex before. The cops said there must be at least sixty balconies overlooking the pool. But, almost unbelievably, no one seems to have seen a thing! Two girls came out for a swim and found Benny lying there. He'd apparently been dead for at least an hour, maybe more. Most of the condos are unoccupied, so the killer must have walked away unnoticed. No one's aware of unusual gang activity in the area... it isn't gang turf anyway."

Dan still held out a slim hope of witnesses – or at least some evidence that could point to a perp. "Maybe the shooter got away clean, maybe he didn't. Crime scene experts sometimes dig up clues out of apparent thin air. God knows what they may find after a thorough search."

Annie rose from the table, picked up their plates and headed to the kitchen. Neil and Dan followed her with the salad bowls and cutlery, continuing their conversation as she loaded the dishwasher. Neil cracked open a couple of beers as the men sat down at the kitchen counter.

Turning from the sink, Annie said, "There's a family get-together at the house tomorrow, around lunchtime. We're going Dan, and I'm sure that Connie and the boys would like to see you as well. By the way, a memorial service is planned for Saturday, even if the coroner hasn't finished his examination. You know how determined Father Riordan can be though – he'll be on the authorities to release the body for a *proper* Funeral Mass, primarily so that Benny's family and friends can get on with the natural grieving process."

"Of course, I'll turn up tomorrow if you think it'll help Annie. I'm certainly not as close to the family as you and Neil though... I might be an unwelcome outsider."

Annie set down her dishtowel and put an arm around Neil. "I doubt that they'll feel that way, Dan – and besides, you can help put their minds at ease on police procedures. They trust you. Pick up some flowers or fruit and come along, at least for a while. I think the boys could use a bit of calming down and there's no doubt you can help Gunnar on that score."

"Okay Annie. And I'll be checking in with my contacts in Homicide again in the morning. There may be some details they're withholding from the family, although I kinda' doubt it. If the boys are at all typical, the three of them will be antsy to do something... and most likely they'll jump at *anything*, even if it's nonsense! I'll try to help Gunnar keep a lid on unwelcome knee-jerk reactions from the youngsters."

Neil reminded Dan of another matter – one that had faded into insignificance. "You're not still crewing this weekend are you? I wasn't inclined to go before this shit hit the fan, but I haven't given Rod a definite answer. Could you tell him I'm a no-show?"

"Sure Neil, I'll tell him, no problem. Truthfully, I'm not sure if I'll be going. We'll see how things pan out."

Dan knew only too well that Rod and Neil had drifted even further apart in recent years. He didn't bother mentioning that Rod hadn't even implied that Neil was likely to turn up when they'd last spoken. Dan was the only glue cementing a waning relationship between the historical threesome. In spite of his best intentions, Rod still behaved like an adolescent – and his frequent digs about Neil's 'old ball and chain' didn't help matters.

Dan stood and said, "I've got to go guys. I'll see you tomorrow at around one at Connie's." He grabbed his jacket from a chair in the front room as they all walked to the door. "I'll find out what I can, but until an autopsy is released to the DA and next of kin, the cops don't give much away. Thanks for the great meal Annie." He kissed her, slugged Neil on the arm and headed out into the chilly evening.

Heading to his car, Dan glanced at the unpretentious stucco and wood frame houses that dominated Neil's South Bay neighborhood. These working class surroundings were undoubtedly a couple of pegs below what the Downeys could now afford. But Annie saw no advantage in climbing the social ladder. The kids liked their school and they were friendly with all the neighbors. The Downeys were set for the duration.

Inside the Rosado circle

Driving home to Normal Heights, Dan pondered Benny Rosado's potential for involvement, even *inadvertently*, in any nasty goings-on. He doubted this scenario, but if anything was amiss, Gunnar was in the best position to get a whiff of it. He was a helluva lot more than Benny's long-time foreman; he was the deceased's closest friend and confidant.

Gunnar Morales had grown up with the Rosado cousins, virtually as a member of the family. He'd been yet another stray that *Mama Grande* Hortensia had adopted early on. Short and scrawny – with a slightly withered leg and barely perceptible limp – he'd always had to toil to keep up with his adoptive cousins, Benny and Benito.

A couple of years older than Benny, he was fiercely protective of Consuela, Victor, Omar and young Gregorio. Gunnar was the favorite 'uncle' and the boys' confidant. He made it his business to intervene before the overly strict Benny lost his rag and blew up with his rambunctious brood.

Gunnar's mama, Elena Morales, had been a migrant fruit picker. One sweltering summer Elena worked picking berries near Astoria, in Oregon. One evening, she put on her best dress and went into town with her girlfriends. They stopped for a bite in a crowded diner, and there she met a short, muscular man named Lars, the short-order cook. The immigrant Norwegian was instantly pole-axed by Elena's dark beauty... and runty Gunnar was the result. Surprisingly, Lars stuck around when Elena told him of her pregnancy. They moved south to Bakersfield when the berry season ended. They rented a cabin on the edge of town and awaited Gunnar's birth. Lars hoped it would be the first of many children for him and his new love.

Elena managed to catch a night shift waiting tables where Lars was cooking. They pooled their meager earnings to make ends meet – and had a little left over for an occasional movie matinee. Lars adored his son and named him 'Gunnar' after his own father. But their relationship wouldn't endure. In spite of his best efforts, Lars became disenchanted with his dreary life in the dusty farming town. A friend wrote of a promising job in a Reno hotel. The next day Lars packed his cardboard suitcase, promising to send money – and bus tickets – when he'd settled in. Elena sporadically received a few dollars in the mail. The envelopes were postmarked from all over the country. But they never saw Lars again.

By the time he was two, Gunnar was living in Tijuana with Estella, his *mama grande*. Aged and frail, she did her best to raise the boy. Elena sent money religiously as she eked out a living moving from one agricultural job to another. Eventually, Gunnar began to run wild. But his successes on the street were meager, to say the least. By age eleven, the Rosado cousins had drawn Gunnar into their protective circle – and Hortensia naturally took him under her wing. He and Benny became as close as brothers... closer than either boy was to the unruly Benito.

Gunnar's proudest day was when he stood up in church as Benny's best man. He was also Benny's first employee a few years later, when his closest companion started up his business in earnest. He turned down an offer of partnership participation, saying he didn't desire the responsibilities.

When Benny's two older sons finished school, each was assigned to Gunnar – and they supervised their own crews *only* when their uncle felt they were ready. To the youngest, Gregorio, Gunnar was truly a second father. He took immense pride in the boy's ambition and eventually convinced Greg that his father would feel the same way. In fact, Benny told his youngest son that there might just be a manager's job in the company for him after college – "... at least for a while, until something better comes along."

These days, Benny's older boys ran their crews (still under Gunnar's watchful eye) and Gregorio, already a sophomore, studied Accounting and Business Administration at SDSU. Neil and Dan could see that Greg was the apple of Connie's eye – proof positive to a proud mother that the Rosados were moving up in the world.

Thank God for Gunnar, Dan thought, as he drove past Hillcrest's shops heading home. Connie and the boys will be leaning on him even more from now on – and he'll never abandon them.

As he swung onto El Cajon Boulevard, Dan popped Linda Ronstadt's *"Canciones de mi Padre"* into the CD player. Her soulful voice and the wistful Mexican melodies seemed a fitting tribute to a departed father and valued friend.

Arriving home, Dan immediately checked his ancient answering machine (no *voicemail* gizmo for him!). Rod Grissom had phoned, indicating he was "truly bummed" to hear about Benny's murder and enquiring if Dan was still on for crewing that weekend. Dan returned the call, but Rod's mobile was switched off, as usual. He decided to postpone a decision on the regatta for the time being, so he didn't leave a message. He phoned work, leaving Trini the message that he'd drop by in the morning and then probably take a few days off. He knew Walt would forgive the short notice when he heard the reason.

Chapter 8

Wednesday

You can't live with 'em – and...

Awake before the sound of the alarm, Dan was already mulling over the mystery of Benny's senseless murder in his troubled mind. The biggest missing piece of the jigsaw was any hint of a *motive*. Who would wish Benny dead – and why would a family man with no apparent enemies attract this ruthless hit?

After a hot shower, Dan headed out into another gray morning. He'd pop into the office to ensure Walt inherited ordered case files in his absence, in spite of the short notice.

He made a pit stop at Lenny's, just in time to catch Jerry's heartfelt rejoinder to Stan's time-tested approach to 'attracting a fine lady'... "Listen my man, our generation showed a bit of *respect* for women. Remember that strict rule about being able to take a kosher prospect home to mom? Sure, we might hook up with a slut, but the *keepers* deserved their wining and dining. Decent manners – combined with a subtle campaign for wearing down defenses – were the order of the day. And, this approach still pays dividends."

"So true Jerry, for once we agree!" Stan replied. "In our day, *ladies* wouldn't surrender on a first date... and they certainly didn't put out on the cheap. The thrill of the hunt was half the fun! I'm always telling youngsters that persistence pays... and as you truck along in your love life, an occasional slap in the mug can work to your advantage. That temporary setback means you're chasin' a bit of class – and receiving valuable feedback! In our day, rebuffs were the obligatory speed bumps on that well-worn road to paradise. Nowadays, most young guys *give up* at the first sign of rejection and move on to easier targets. But besting bimbos is simplicity itself for one reason... they're not worth a shit!"

Jerry turned to Dan, grimacing. "Don't you just love his classic take on the game of love? In *these* terrifying times, show me a virgin who's over sixteen and I guarantee she'll either be *'Helen Horseface'* or *'Bella Blimp'*. Oh yeah... or, your love object might be some *Bible-thumping Pricktease*, a 'holier than thou' gal, hell-bent on flaunting her demure assets to her unwary victim while sponging meals and drinks, before skulking away. Worse yet, more than a few chicks today tend to disappear and join some dyke commune, attracted by the overpowering scent of frustrated estrogen."

"On the whole, I'd say there's some validity to your assessment Jerry," Dan laughed and replied. "But I think that a few gems are still out there; classy ladies who warrant old-fashioned wining and dining. As Stan says, the hunt *is* half the fun – undoubtedly the more memorable and rewarding half. The secret is to judiciously select that object of your desire."

On that note, Dan sopped up the remains of his runny eggs with his last slice of toast and left a dollar on the counter for Rosie. His parting words to the boys were, "Thanks guys, you've really enlightened me on the mysteries of modern love." As he strode away, Jerry and Stan had already moved on to a new, but indisputably *related*, topic – the telltale attributes of a bona fide *'California Slut'*.

So, what do you know?

Trini was completing her on-line time sheet when Dan arrived in the office. Shifting about in her chair, she was *still* clearly in the clutches of that wicked stubble itch in her nether regions. Dan decided to forego the temptation to lob in an easy zinger about the insalubrious after-effects of her waxing fiasco. On this particular morning, his heart just wasn't into hitting such slow, hanging curveballs out of the park.

Dan quickly closed out a couple of dubious claims and made notations on a few other files for Walt. He could hear TriState's sales team laughing at some puerile joke in the meeting room down the corridor. The field reps were young and modestly ambitious, but obviously making fewer sales calls on TriState agents than their padded field reports avowed. Their ringleader, Sherry Young, swore like a trooper and told more than her share of filthy jokes with real flair. Dwayne and Justin tried to match her... in jokes, innuendo *and* sales figures. The team was in the midst of a weekly conference call to LA... catching up with Charley Chisholm, TriState's Regional Sales Director. Charley imagined he was 'one of the boys' – and a god-like temptation to women between sixteen and sixty. Little did he know that behind his back his team unmercifully referred to him as 'The Gray Gobbler'.

After clearing his desk, Dan phoned Homicide Division and learned that Detectives Knowles and Lopez were working Benny's case. When he was put through to Lopez, the experienced cop told him, not unexpectedly, that nothing earthshaking had as yet been uncovered. The crime scene turned up zilch – Benny's wallet hadn't even been lifted. Benny's truck had been found out front, also apparently untouched.

Before hanging up, Lopez mentioned that he and Knowles would be heading back to the scene to try and flush out any gun-shy witnesses. This was one case they'd work long and hard – heinous murders of solid citizens always remained on the front burner... Chicano victim or not.

As Dan wasn't expected at the Rosado's for at least another hour, he decided to revert to an old routine. He'd jot down what he '*Knew*', what he '*Surmised*' and what was '*Missing Information*'... all on one page in his pristine new casebook. Sometimes – albeit rarely – a pattern emerged. More often, this practice merely created a jumble of so-called 'facts' and near-useless conjecture. He started writing – and in short order his paltry notations included:

KNOW

- .22 cal – two head shots, close range
- No weapon found, casings left at scene
- No signs of struggle – wallet untouched
- No apparent witnesses – yet
- Earmarks of a pro hit – possibly a pair of button men... shooter and lookout?
- Killed almost instantly
- Truck left untouched out front

SURMISE

- Lopez said Benny's office staff didn't know exactly where he'd be that day, so probably no one could have preceded him to the scene. Was he followed – or just in the wrong place?
- Perps desperate? ...reckless? ... or st<u>upid</u>? Shot in broad daylight in a high-density residential area
- Mistaken identity?

MISSING

- <u>Motive</u>!!
- Weapon – likely a throwaway
- Any useful evidence linked to perp(s)

71

- **Links – between Benny and any scam or hidden agenda? (Tenuous!)**
- **Suspects – at least at first pass**

No great insights jumped off the page. Dan hoped he'd have more ideas after touching base with Gunnar and Benny's boys.

He phoned Neil, catching Annie on her way out. Unsurprisingly, she seemed distracted. "I'm off to Connie's, Dan. Show up as soon as you can; I'll see you there. Neil will make his own way down, but he may be a bit late. Connie's aware that you'll be questioning her and Gunnar, and maybe even the boys – and she sounded grateful for your help."

"Does she think that I'm somehow *working* this case for them?"

"I didn't exactly say that to her Dan, but she knows she can turn to you for good advice and maybe even some professional insight. I'm sure she believes you'll do all you can to help the family get to the bottom of this. I didn't make any rash promises about your visit today though, other than to say you'd no doubt help Gunnar to calm her boys down a bit."

"Thanks Annie. I won't make any promises I can't deliver on. I'll pick up some flowers or fruit on the way and see you in an hour or so. I'll think up an excuse to call Homicide again before leaving here, on the off chance that something's turned up in the last hour."

A short time later, when he phoned Downtown Headquarters again, his call was unexpectedly diverted to Detective Lieutenant Gene Jeffries. The self-satisfied geek sounded a bit too chipper to convincingly assure Dan of his heart-felt condolences for the Rosados. "Look pal, I sympathize with the family, I'm sure Rosado was a *mensch*. But who's to say he wasn't just a *teensy* bit dirty? And as you well know, we can't solve every gang hit! Knowles and Lopez are working the case, but in the meantime I'd appreciate it if you'd join the rest of San Diego's well-meaning *civilians* and leave us to get on with our job. Got it?"

Dan bit his tongue and managed to avoid shouting down the phone. But he couldn't screen a sarcastic tone out of his reply. "Judicious advice, pencilneck! However, you may want to chat with Melinda about the integrity and standing in the community of your victim, as well as the worthy reputation of the entire Rosado clan. Once upon a time, Benny's family was on close, first-name terms with Melinda, before you two married and she began to lose touch with the human race. Listen, I'm a citizen and taxpayer with an interest in the case. I'll phone Knowles and Lopez if I damned well feel like it. And, if I come up with anything, they'll be the first to know, 'cause they're *solid* cops.

Now crawl back under your rock, so that you can *'Protect and Serve'* the sea lice that hang out with you there."

Dan paused, enjoying the irritated silence emanating from the other end of the line. Then he gently set down the receiver. He surveyed his desk... tidy for a change. He instructed Trini to forward any important calls to his cell phone and headed for the door. He didn't want to keep Connie, Gunnar and Annie waiting.

Chapter 9

Casseroles, memories – and loosely laid plans

Dan drove into the neighborhood in northeast Chula Vista. The normally quiet street resembled Del Mar's main parking lot on a day with a full racing card. This gathering was no intimate get-together... friends, family and a multitude of parishioners were all closing around Connie and the kids. As he cruised past the Rosado's tidy stucco house he spotted Gunnar on the front lawn, solemnly greeting newcomers. As soon as the little man saw Dan's Chevy, he waved and shuffled into the street. Looking uncomfortable in a white shirt and skinny black tie, he opened Dan's door and slid into the passenger seat. "Pull her up on that lawn across the street man. The neighbor kids will have to look after this heap, 'cause cop cars and 'official' looking rides aren't going down well around here. I'll tell the kids you're tight with the Rosados and it'll be safe as if you parked outside a police station."

"Thanks Gunnar. How's Consuela holding up?"

"Okay I guess, but Omar and Vic are no fuckin' help. Greg isn't home from school yet. Connie wouldn't let him cut classes, even today!"

Dan pulled onto the neat lawn across from the Rosados. Gunnar waved to the kids sitting on the front step and said, "If this here car needs to be moved, get an adult to do it, okay?" He nodded to Dan and motioned him to hand over his keys to the oldest boy. Dan did so after retrieving his sympathy offerings for Connie from the back seat.

Crossing over, they skirted the overflowing house and walked straight into the back yard. Masses of people were overfilling their plastic plates from a long buffet table while downing beers and sodas from a washtub filled with ice. Dan set his own contribution – large baskets of strawberries and apples – near the end of the table, by the desserts.

Annie and Consuela sat under a large umbrella near the bottom of the sloping lawn, their backs to other mourners. Dan decided to join them and get his commiserations over with. He hoped that Annie's presence was a comfort; Connie looked oddly composed as he passed by Annie's chair. He grabbed a recently vacated webbed lawn chair (its occupant was no doubt heading over to the gargantuan buffet) and sat across from the ladies. They were holding hands and although Connie nodded and attempted a smile, it was easy to see that a prolonged conversation would have to wait for another day.

"I can't begin to tell you how sorry Sophie, my family and I are Consuela. Benny was the best. I just hope that it's some small measure of comfort to know that he's surely already with Jesus – and they'll always be looking out for you and your boys."

"I know that's true Dan, but I can't understand why anyone would want to harm a man who did nothing but good for everyone, over his entire life. It's crazy – a terrible mistake! No one would intentionally harm my Benny." Connie Rosado's eyes were bloodshot and her smooth, golden-brown cheeks were tear-stained. Still, she spoke lucidly, without sobbing. Dan was struck, yet again, by the reserves of strength afforded to those with faith in times of gut-wrenching grief. He wished that he could find it in himself to tap into her unquestioning belief in the Almighty, but he knew it was a blessing denied to him.

Dan kept his voice low. "Tell me Connie, did *anything* seem out of the ordinary recently? Did Benny perhaps seem even a little nervous or preoccupied?"

"No Dan. We've been a bit worried about Greg getting on well at college I guess. But Benny always says that worrying about the boys is *my* department, while he and Gunnar look after the business. Everything seemed to be going well – maybe too good? Lately, Benny has been getting back to what he loves... digging, planting and doing the dirty, hands-on jobs. Gunnar and the boys run the crews."

Anyone could see that Connie was exhausted... too tired even for Dan's gentle interrogation. Annie squeezed the grieving widow's hand and her eyes signaled that Benny's widow had endured enough questioning for this terrible day.

Dan rose and looked down at the women. He felt awkward... should he bend down and embrace Connie? Kiss her on the cheek? "That's fine for now. I'll share my condolences with the boys and then leave you alone. But rest assured I'm working on this. And I'll keep you informed of anything I turn up. My friends on the force won't hold back on the information they can share... I've taken care of that. And if anyone hassles you in *any* way, don't hesitate to call me – or Neil and Annie of course."

Connie took his hand and attempted to smile. "Bless you, Dan. Hortensia will be so pleased to know that you're helping us to get to the bottom of this. *Mama Grande's* strong, but at her age, there's no telling how she'll handle the strain in the days to come. I'm trying to talk her into staying up here with us, at least for a few days; but she's intent on heading back home to Tijuana tonight. She insists that the rest of the family expect her to be there... and she *will* be – busy stirring a pot of soup on her old stove."

Dan left the women sitting in their island of grief, surrounded by well-meaning mourners who were congregating and crying together... as *Mejicanos* and Chicanos always have. But Connie was clearly inconsolable. She'd need family and friends – and her rock-solid faith – in the months and years to come. Dan could offer little in the way of relief, but perhaps he could ultimately provide the Rosados with a measure of that overrated healer of wounds... a tiny slice of *'Closure'*.

He headed up the slope towards the large deck, seeking out Victor and Omar. But, halfway up the lawn, he spotted a long-forgotten friend – an old flame he hadn't seen in years. Ellen looked forlorn and out of place; sitting alone in a gauzy green dress – an outfit that even Dan recognized as unsuited to the occasion.

Ellen had been his solitary 'going steady' high school girlfriend, albeit only for a fleeting time. In those days, shoulder-length flame-red hair and a voluptuous body were her all too evident attributes... irresistible temptations for any healthy, breathing teenage boy.

But her teenaged charms soon faded for Dan. He quickly discovered that she took curious pleasure from the agonizing remorse she insisted on sharing after their clumsy attempts at lovemaking. In fact, Dan could see she clearly enjoyed the *guilt* more than their fumbling experimentation. Ellen invariably cut straight to a weepy scene immediately after engaging in (and, in fact, almost invariably *initiating*) their amateurish carnal 'misdeeds'. Her perverse reaction to a bit of tame petting quickly put the nervous and inexperienced Dan off the scent.

He'd been secretly relieved to discover that his pal, Rod Grissom, went behind his back to make a play for the enticing Ellen. Dan backed off, leaving his new girlfriend square in the sights of his brassy chum and the exultant Rod dated the buxom beauty for a few weeks. However, contrary to Rod's schoolboy boasting, Ellen's best pal swore to Dan that Rod never even managed to unfasten Ellen's bra! It was obvious the troubled girl still carried a torch for Dan... ruing the day she'd agreed to go out with his boastful pal. But Dan left Ellen alone. And Rod soon tired of his 'conquest'... for reasons dramatically different to Dan's.

Ellen remained single – and seemed to have experienced few satisfying or lasting adult relationships. A staunch Catholic, she chose to commute from La Mesa down to Father Riordan's mixed ethnicity parish in National City. She was pleased to be among the growing group of ladies who naturally looked to Annie and Connie for leadership.

At first, as Dan ambled up the hill, he barely recognized his old flame, sitting on her own at the buffet table. But that radiant red hair, now a rustier, less natural shade, tweaked his memory. Nowadays, long past voluptuous, she'd be better described as 'fleshy'. Her upper arms nearly burst the short sleeves of her gauzy dress – yet, while seeking obscurity amidst the mourners, she still attempted to surreptitiously skim chocolate icing off the edge of an empty cake plate as Dan approached.

Ellen looked up and her eyes met his. He sensed her discomfort, but he couldn't readily read her thoughts. Was she upset because she'd been caught picking at 'forbidden' frosting – or was she ill at ease at spotting an old friend, while secretly hoping he'd stop to speak to her? There was only one thing to do. They could chat for a few moments about today's sad event. It was important to reassure her that she counted for something in the eyes of the parish, as well as with her old friends.

Dan tried for just the right smile in these precarious circumstances. "It's great to see you here Ellen! I'm blown away by all of the people who've turned up. Connie and the boys are facing some tough times, but they have a great support system, that's for sure."

Ellen also attempted a smile, but managed to only raise one corner of her tight little mouth. "It's great to see you too Dan. Annie mentioned you might stop by. I saw you sitting with Neil and her at Mass a few weeks ago, but I had to run, so I didn't say hello."

"You're sure to see me in church again when Annie and the kids drag Neil and me along. I might even have my little sister in tow. Maybe we can all grab a coffee afterwards one of these days?"

"Sure Dan. Hope to see you again soon." Her unfocused gaze and frozen smile suggested that she was all out of small talk. He'd done his duty and could move on.

Walking away, he wasn't sure if he'd sent out the right signals. Might she imagine he was implying he was available? It was strange how stilted a simple chat with an old flame had become. Sometimes he picked up with a long-lost schoolmate like they'd met up the day before. On other occasions, it could be like talking to a near stranger. He'd experienced a lot since school – much of it pleasant, some bad. And he'd learned to keep on truckin'.

Keeping it cool

As Dan walked further up the lawn to the house, he could see that Benny's boys had abandoned the garden deck. Entering by the back door, he found them in the kitchen, deep in conversation with some workmates and a few neighborhood pals. Dan heard Vic muttering, "We won't pay protection money to some bogus 'security company' – especially after this! We bid for the jobs we want, whenever we want – and we can look after ourselves! No gang-bangers dictate terms to Rosado & Sons! Tomorrow, me and Omar will get straight onto the muscle from that so-called 'security firm' and get to the bottom of this shit. We'll track down the scumbag who killed our dad – and do it *our way*."

"Hold on Vic..." They all turned as Dan entered the room. "If Rosado & Sons has been targeted for a cheap shakedown, tell me about it. I can get these dirtbags rousted and questioned pronto. Let's try that tack before we resort to a personal vendetta."

Omar looked at his older brother before chiming in. "Dan, we know this gang and how they operate. Vic's right – we'll deal with them."

Dan sensed it was time to take things down a notch. "I've been onto my Homicide contacts this morning. Knowles and Lopez are handling the case – they're good cops who know their way around. I can put them onto your punks and they'll get some straight answers. In the meantime, this feels more like experienced button men than some punks' strong-arm tactics gone wrong. When was the last time you heard of gang-bangers opting for a brazen daylight hit? Their style would be a late night, drive-by melee."

Gunnar walked into the room and leaned on the kitchen counter, staring down each of the young men in turn. "Dan's right. We'll sit down tomorrow and establish a viable plan, but we'll base our tactics on logic and hard facts. Remember, your mama will want you nearby, especially in the next few days – and Dan will guide us to an honorable result, with the fewest missteps and least hassle."

Dan could only hope he'd merit Gunnar's faith in him. This wasn't going to play out like some clichéd cop movie... Benny's demise could easily end up a senseless, unsolved murder. There were no guarantees that the good guys would flush out the killers – or that the Rosados would get any measure of justice.

Gunnar grabbed Dan's elbow and herded him out of the kitchen, through the crowded front room and out to the quiet front yard. He obviously wanted a private word. The little man limped to a halt near the curb and let go of Dan's elbow. He leaned in and whispered, "I'm thinkin' man; we haven't even laid eyes on that little douche bag, Cousin Benito, for a week or so. The pitiful turd hasn't even turned up today, to comfort his *mama grande* or Connie. He and Benny were like brothers; it's more than fuckin' weird he's stayed away. I'd like to talk to him – and you would too, believe me. I'll put out some feelers. If I find him, I'll let you know. It smells to me like he could've drifted too close to something nasty – and that's why he's makin' himself scarce. If he turns out to be a blind alley, believe me, that's *excelente*. But he's as good a place to start as any for figuring out why Benny ended up in harm's way. Without doubt, Benito's a much more solid lead than those pathetic lowlifes who've been endlessly hitting up the business for protection money."

Dan's initial reaction was Gunnar's hunch might be a bit of a stretch, but no one had a better theory. He found himself whispering back to the little man, "Why would his cousin allow Benny to come to harm? Was there any bad blood between them?"

"I'm not saying he'd set anything in motion *intentionally*, Dan. But he's so fuckin' loco that he's been known to flap his gums and land the family and his pals in deep crap. Let's just say that when bad shit happens, Benito's exposed rear has a habit of being in the vicinity. I'll get to work on running him down."

"Thanks Gunnar – and take care. Some very nasty people are behind this, so let's watch each other's backs."

Gunnar reached up and put his hand on Dan's shoulder. "I'll be in touch soon, man. Thanks for coming down. By the way, tell your little brother there's still a spot for him on my crew... and he'd better be keeping his nose clean. Later, man."

Dan crossed the street and handed the boys who were conscientiously watching his Chevy a couple of dollars each. He grabbed his keys from the older one, jumped in and was soon heading up the street. He hadn't learned much. But he did know that if he didn't get to the bottom of this disaster *quickly* it could no doubt lead to further troubles, considering the prospective antics of the irrepressible Victor and Omar.

Chapter 10

Winter refuge

As Dan was saying his goodbyes to Gunnar, a rusting green Taurus approached the US border. Benito Rosado felt genuine guilt for the anguish he'd created, but he was also aware there was every chance that Tejada's hit squad would be wise to their slip-up by now. The scumbags might even turn up at Connie's, searching for their *real* prey! He'd phoned *mama grande's* earlier in the day, but she'd left for the wake. A neighbor watching Hortensia's house told him about today's gathering at Connie's and he'd left a message, saying he'd stop by to see his *mama grande* soon. But he knew he'd have to steer clear of Hortensia for now. If they were after him, it would be unsafe... for her and for his own sorry ass.

Fortunately, he had a solid plan. He'd lie low for a while. He was heading up to Winter's place. She and Lila could make room for him in their small Point Loma apartment – he'd be well off the radar until the heat was off. And he wouldn't put a crimp in their nightly routine down at the strip club. Winter was a sweet little gal... and unlikely to get nosey. She'd put him up until he could figure out his next move.

Before his cousin's unfortunate demise, Benito had been confident he was one step ahead of the cartel. Shit, how wrong could he have been? He asked himself, how can I chill this thing out? Are they onto me for cutting product? Did some skankhead complain about the quality of my shit? Or, what if they've discovered that I've indulged in a few side deals with the competition? Shit! If they're onto that, I'm truly fucked.

His mind was reeling. He needed to get it together! He began to flesh out a course of action in his mind, as he drove along. I can phone Tejada and play dumb about Benny's hit. I'll inform him that, not unusually, I'm holding a bit of the organization's current profits. And I'll be paying him a tasty 'windfall bonus' from the added income I generated on a bit of slightly over-cut dope and a couple of inconsequential side deals I was going to tell him about anyway. I'll convince him I was just holding onto his rightful share in *all* our ventures – safe in my hands, until I caught up with him.

Getting this outrageous story to fly was undoubtedly a 'best-case scenario'. Benito knew full well that if 'Plan A' – a clear-cut appeal to Manny's unquestioned greed – didn't work out, he'd have to make himself *very scarce* until things cooled down.

In reality, Benito had recently been trying to pull off a clumsy *triple scam*. Initially, he'd just been cutting his coke supplies by that allowable small drop. Most low-level dealers did so. Then he'd become bolder... not only cutting the goods, but also skimming off a tiny extra slice of the profits. If Tejada, or his single-minded hatchet man, Enrique, discovered any shortfall, he'd simply claim they still had money outstanding with regular vendors and a few trustworthy clients.

In the end though, Benito Rosado had become incredibly reckless. In point of fact, Baja's most formidable crime family was the main competition for Manny Tejada's bosses in the lucrative US heroin trade. And, recently, they'd elected to move into the highly profitable periphery of San Diego's *coke scene* as well. Boldly, they'd recruited Benito Rosado to sell *their* crack and coke to his vendors and contacts. And they'd been extremely persuasive.

The senior generation in Mexico's established cartels seemed to content themselves with the 'classics'... marijuana, heroin, car theft, prostitution and smuggling illegals. Lately though, younger soldiers smelled easy money in the cocaine and methamphetamine trades, predominantly run (badly) by small-timers and amateurs. Independent distributors in San Diego County were natural conduits for flogging Mexico's abundant coke supplies, freshly piped up from Colombia and Bolivia. A second-rater like Benito couldn't resist the easy money. He decided to work *both sides* of the increasingly fierce competition... a risky business decision if ever there was one.

Benito wasn't clever enough to realize that his bosses routinely utilized snitches. Lowlife druggies not only reported on the street activity around them to Tejada's trusted lieutenant, Enrique, but also 'resold' him tiny samples of their recent purchases. These 'tasters' went straight to Mexico, to be tested for quality, chemical profile and origin. In a matter of days, Tejada and his bosses were wise to Benito's latest, unforgivable scam. The quality of his outsourced coke impressed them. It was superior to their product – even after allowing for Benito stamping on his new goods, as he surely did with the stuff they supplied him.

Benito's greed put him squarely in the organization's crosshairs. His unforgivable misbehavior *easily* outstripped the cartel's tolerance for malfeasance. There was only one course of action left to Tejada if he wanted to square things with his bosses... he'd have to swiftly make an example of Benito, giving notice to everyone of the organization's unyielding intention to stamp out disloyalty. Clearly, Benito's plan to square things with an apologetic call to Manny was a pipe dream. He'd overplayed a weak hand – *badly*.

As he drove up the freeway, Benito's mind turned to more pleasurable thoughts. When he'd first glimpsed the new love in his life, the magnificent *'Miss Winter Fox'*, she was spiraling down the shiny pole on The Pink Lady's narrow, backlit runway. He'd flipped out! Her pale skin glowed, nearly translucent under the intense blue-white spotlights. And her long, straight hair, peroxided to a silvery white, fascinated him. Wearing an ice-blue mini-bra and matching thong – accessorized with silver fishnet stockings and pale blue stilettos – she'd been introduced to rapturous applause and loud wolf whistles as *"San Diego's Ice Queen!"* Benito soaked in her beauty and experienced the purest lust he'd ever known, deep in his loins. He – and he *alone* – had to possess this goddess.

Spellbound from that moment onwards, he returned to the seedy club on Sports Arena Boulevard at every opportunity. Finally, he worked up the courage to approach the lovely Winter. He overpaid for a private lap dance and purchased the bottle of 'champagne' required to secure a few precious moments of intimate back room conversation with his radiant angel.

In his finest sharkskin suit, with a generous bankroll warming his breast pocket, he'd begun by dragging out the hackneyed come-on lines the girls routinely deflected from a thousand bored husbands and lonely servicemen. Over the next few weeks however, he began to *listen* as well as talk – and thus managed to hone his repartee. Finally, he felt that he could relax around Winter, boasting about his exploits as a successful exporter and his impressive business connections. She sat on his knee in her skimpy, glistening outfit and feigned fascination... as long as the generous tips and bubbly continued to flow.

But, frustratingly, he wasn't allowed to *really* touch her at the club. In truth, he'd barely cut through her sassy demeanor to connect with the essence of the girl beneath the Lycra and sequins. Things only ascended to another level when he finally convinced her to accept 'a bit of help with the rent' in exchange for the occasional invitation to her place for a drink. In the past few months, snuggling at her pad, they'd gotten to know each other a helluva lot better.

Lately, he believed their relationship was improving dramatically. He wanted her to leave stripping behind... to become his woman *only*. But this was a hard sell. And, the more demanding he was (and the more gifts he plied her with) the more dangerous his addiction to her became. His desire to impress – and *possess* – kindled previously untapped levels of greed in Benito. But just when he feared he might have to recapture control of his senses (and his finances) and forfeit the love of his life, fresh working partners emerged. The new cocaine distributors provided him with very welcome *cash*. He now had ample resources to quench the overwhelming thirst for his Ice Queen.

Winter and her roommate – another popular Pink Lady stripper – lived in a cute little two-bedroom Point Loma apartment. Decorated like Barbie and Ken's fantasy fuck pad, it was all pastels, overstuffed cushions and ruffles. Its proximity to the titty bar – and the complex's gargantuan swimming pool – made the cozy apartment a perfect off-duty haven for these easy living, night-shift ladies.

Winter's roommate, *'Miss Lila Blue'*, was tanned, voluptuous and exotic. She reminded the club's older patrons of a new-generation Raquel Welch. Benito didn't mind that he was actually kicking in for both girls' Point Loma rent. He was pretty confident that the loose-lipped and compliant Lila would inform her new benefactor if other men came sniffing around his lovely Winter during off-duty hours.

What the hell, he thought as he neared the Point Loma exit on the freeway, I can sure as shit stay with these two lovelies for a couple of nights... I'm pretty much paying for the fuckin' place anyway! If Winter and Lila don't like it, they can just grin and bear it.

His mind was racing. Maybe he and his gorgeous Winter would have to skip town for a while, but that could turn into a good thing. It might be the first step in leveraging her ass out of stripping for a living. If he scraped together all of his cash, it came to a tidy sum. It would certainly be more than Winter had ever laid eyes on in her brief life! That cash could be the kicker... she'd probably jump at the chance to blow town with him.

He'd leave the cooperative Lila a few extra bucks, to tide her over until she found a new roommate. And that little turd Marty, the slacker boyfriend who always seemed to be hanging around and pawing at Lila, could start chipping in something towards his girl's upkeep! Winter would miss her roomie... but everyone, especially girls like these, moved on eventually.

Winter and Lila wouldn't be at work yet when he arrived. It was still late afternoon. He'd be on their doorstep in less than half an hour, even at this sedate pace. If they were out shopping or something, he'd use his *own key* for the very first time. (Lila didn't know about it yet. Winter told him to keep that little piece of information quiet, because she didn't want to supply Lila with the ammunition to bestow a similar key on her main squeeze, 'Marty the Maniac'.) Benito Rosado was ready for a cold beer and a little 'R&R'. Maybe this unplanned short vacation would work out okay.

Chapter 11

The 'Chain' gang

Heading north on I-5 from Connie's, Dan made a couple of quick calls as he drove. Typically, he would forego the car's 'hands free' option and pull over to use his cellphone. Talking into thin air while attempting to concentrate on driving was irritating, but today it seemed to be the least of his worries. He missed Detectives Lopez and Knowles, but he did reach Sophie, toiling away in her Salk Institute office. Initially sounding distracted, probably due to her unrelenting workload, she quickly tuned in when he brought up his visit to the Rosados.

Naturally, Sophie was concerned for Connie. She knew only too well how the death of a beloved spouse knocked the stuffing out of you. "Connie will be hazy for quite a while yet, Dan. None of this will really hit home until weeks after the funeral, when she's finally on her own and the well-wishers return to their own lives. Funerals are dismal affairs, but they certainly help many people begin the laborious process of moving on. So, back to the nitty gritty... what's up with the police?"

Dan realized he'd be asked this question repeatedly in the coming days. Everyone, including Sophie, was under the impression that he still had impeccable connections with 'Gossip Central' at police headquarters. In reality, his contacts consisted of a diminishing breed of old-fashioned cops. In answer to Sophie's question, all he could say was, "Nothing to report yet, hon. Any chance of cashing in on last night's rain check for dinner this evening? I'd love to kick back a little."

"That sounds terrific!" A scrap of faintly forced animation seemed to return to Sophie's voice. "Meet me at my place and we'll head down the hill for seafood salads and smoothies. Then, we can curl up and watch the ten o'clock movie on 13... I think it's *Play Misty for Me*. Bring a bottle of that nice Rioja, okay?"

Dan almost smiled to himself. At last, a decent distraction on the horizon! "Sounds like heaven Sophie. I'll see you just before seven."

Sophie, attempting to make supportive noises, tried to filter any anxiety out of her voice. "Stay out of harm's way Dan, and I'll see you tonight."

Dan disconnected, signaled a right turn and took the 'Grand Avenue' exit off the freeway. He headed west towards Pacific Beach. He made a mental note to ask Gunnar to dig out recent photos of *both* Cousin Benito and Benny... they'd come in handy. He'd also have the

Homicide boys pull Cousin Benito's sheet. A solid lead to Benny's killer or killers might be hiding in an old police file – stranger things had happened.

Dan was heading to an old hangout, playing a long shot. 'The Rusty Chain', a notorious biker bar, occupied a rundown shop front near the end of Grand Avenue, just up from the busy beach. Vintage Harley choppers lined the curb during open hours – judiciously left unmolested by passing tourists and surfers. Dan knew many of the bar's regulars; some had been valuable contacts during his time in uniform. In those days, most of The Chain's patrons viewed Dan as a fairly trustworthy pig... a sort of 'best of breed'.

The Chain's owners, Jake and Rattler, ran the bar with steely authority. Truth be told, it was one of the safest beach bars in the city, even for non-bikers. One ironclad rule – written large on the wall – advised... *"Take trouble outside!"* Transgressors were in for a difficult lesson from the no-nonsense Jake. During peak hours, the hard-core owners could be backed up by a couple of massive bouncers, including one butch female, who dealt with the 'ladies'.

The bar remained a useful resource for Dan. The patrons could still provide leads on hot goods or the current whereabouts of a bevy of lowlifes who might be of interest to TriState. Bikers made effective allies – and their enemies could count on a shitload of instant trouble. Benny's mob-style hit in the South Bay might not have registered on their radar; it probably didn't intersect with their scene. But slimmer odds had paid off in the past.

As Dan parked the Malibu across from The Chain, his mind wandered back to a past, most memorable, visit to this hallowed establishment. He'd taken Melinda to the biker bar early in their marriage. She'd been pestering him for a first-hand view of how street cops really operated. He knew that Jake, Rattler and the regulars would be an ideal introduction to the classic snitches and street types typically utilized in investigations.

As they'd entered the bar on that very pleasant afternoon, three biker mamas immediately threw menacing looks Melinda's way... no doubt jealous of her obvious beauty, but also disapproving of some snooty girl poking her turned-up nose into their secure world. Rattler had been the perfect gentleman, meticulously re-washing and polishing a highball glass in anticipation of his new customer's order.

As Dan ordered drinks, Rattler's partner Jake pretended to ignore them, continuing to shoot pool with two hardcore regulars. (Central Casting would have thrown up Alex Karras and Sam Elliott to portray the motley pair.) Moments later, Jake left the table and headed to the bar as their game ended. The two scruffy bikers glanced at the new customers before re-racking the balls. The 'Alex' character wasted no time... giving Melinda a little bow and inviting her to shoot a game or two. She gave the roughnecks her broadest smile and sashayed over to the table. Her lovely ass and stunning cleavage – both displayed to magnificent effect as she bent down to break – mesmerized her playing partners. The biker mamas didn't move a muscle. All eyes, male and female, were glued on Melinda.

An hour later, as they headed back out to their car, Melinda had oh-so-innocently remarked, "How can you describe those loveable bears as nasty or lowdown Dan? Those honeys wouldn't harm a fly!"

Dan had just snickered. "They live by their code, babe. As long as you're the fair damsel, submissively respecting their turf, you'll see their cuddly side. But if you got on your high horse or mocked anyone in that crowd, they'd set their mamas on you in a heartbeat. Today you were a huge hit. Take my advice and quit on a high."

The Rusty Chain hadn't changed one iota from that memorable day to this. Dan walked across Grand and passed by a diminished, yet still formidable, row of weathered hogs on his way to the entrance. Today's visit wasn't social. He knew that on this occasion he could count on the bikers' distinctive take on justice and fair play – they'd help him to find Benny's killers if they could.

Dan entered, eyes gradually adjusting to the gloom. Tinted windows discouraged outsiders from peering in. Inside it seemed like perpetual night time, unless the door was wedged open to catch a bit of the ocean breeze. Jake was tending bar and only one booth was occupied. The pool table was 'resting'. A scattering of patrons bellied up to the bar, nursing beers. Jake's partner, Rattler, was nowhere to be seen.

Jake was in his mid-fifties and balding, with his remaining halo of long hair gathered into a greasy ponytail. He took in Dan with one glance, smiled and continued wiping down the bar. Dan recognized two of the barflies. Bull and Jeter had been regulars since the 80's and their beat-up leather jackets were most likely hand-me-downs from a previous generation of Devil's Disciples. Nowadays, their weathered gear would be admiringly described as "biker vintage" by California's moronic *fashionistas*.

The bar smelled of stale beer – and lingering tobacco odors mostly left over from the good old days, before the Smoking Ban. In truth though, the 'Positively No Smoking' restriction might occasionally be overlooked in this hallowed establishment.

Dan sat down on the stool next to Jeter's and then nodded to both him and Bull. Out of the corner of his mouth, he said, "Hey Jake, how about a pitcher for us? How's business?"

Jake stopped wiping down the bar and began to pull a pitcher from a well-used tap as he replied to his new arrival. "Fuckin' great Officer Dan. But enough of the small talk... let's get down to brass tacks. What can I do for you on this fine day?"

"I'm trying to run down evidence on that daytime hit in South Bay you might have heard about. The victim was a good friend to Neil and me – and we're pretty certain he wasn't into anything illegal. It looks like a pro job... but pulled off by second-raters. An 'in and out' shooting with a small caliber popgun doesn't add up to gang-bangers or some drug deal gone bad. Benny Rosado was a decent family man and a hard working landscaper, not some nut-job asking to be whacked with an unregistered throwaway. I thought I'd just spread the word... if anyone hears anything, I'd be grateful for a call."

Jake nodded as he brought the pitcher over to Dan and filled his glass. "We heard about it on the TV man, but it ain't somethin' our crowd would be mixed up in. I doubt if the Inland County Chapter would know anything either, but I'll check with them." Looking down the counter, Jake asked Jeter, who was more interested in the fresh pitcher of beer than the conversation, "Heard anything?"

Jeter looked at Jake and answered, "No man. Bumping off beaner gardeners ain't exactly our scene." Then he turned to Dan, still eyeing the beer and enquired, "How'd this poor dude get it, Dan?"

"Two .22 rounds above the left eye, Jeter; at close range. As I said, at least superficially it looks pretty professional – but poorly planned and executed, if you know what I mean."

Jeter's pal Bull downed the last of his schooner, leaned down the bar and chimed in, "Any reward on offer man? We could scout around a bit for you."

"There's nothing big on offer yet guys, but I've *personally* got two hundred for anyone who steers me to the scumbags who wasted Benny. And I'm sure his family would show their gratitude too." Nothing seemed to resonate more with this crowd than a reasonably just cause... tied to some ready cash.

With that hook set, Dan drained his beer, slid the nearly full pitcher down the bar to his companions and thanked them as he rose to leave. He left an overly generous $15 on the bar. As he reached the door, he cringed imperceptibly as Jeter shouted after him, "Tell your little bro' it's been too fuckin' long since we seen him, man."

Well, the good news seemed to be that Marty hadn't dropped by The Chain in a while. Maybe the lovely Lila *was* helping the little shit to steer clear of serious trouble. As he walked across the street, Dan decided his visit hadn't been a total waste. Word would spread that Benny's hit wasn't righteous – and there would be a little cash in it for any dude who could provide some useful information.

Dan drove slowly away from the beach and slid Warren Zevon's *'Excitable Boy'* into his CD player. Warren was another of Dan's heroes... a *true mensch*, who'd departed from the scene far too soon. Dan's mind wandered, not for the first time, to an idiotic thought. He pondered if some corner of an Eternal Paradise *really was* held in reserve for the musical giants. If it was, he could visualize Warren there, jamming with Keith Moon, Buddy Holly, The Big O and George Harrison. Elvis and John Lennon would be grooving in their deck chairs. And, who knew... Benny Rosado might already be tending a beautiful flowerbed near that celestial bandstand. Shit, were rosy musings like these even *remotely* comforting for the faithful beloveds left behind? Perhaps. But, Dan felt that such notions were undoubtedly a waste of time... diverting us from creating a better world for ourselves in the present.

He'd head home, grab a shower and later spend some quiet time with Sophie, giving the case a rest for a while. Anyway, Knowles and Lopez probably wouldn't be able to provide any useful updates 'til morning.

Chapter 12

Ice time

Halfway up Grand after leaving The Chain, Dan turned right onto Ingraham Street. He took the Channel Bridge, heading south towards San Diego's ancient and underutilized Sports Arena. He'd promised Mandy a night out at the hockey the following week – and there was no reason to change the plan. He'd pick up the tickets on his way home.

When she was around eight, Dan began taking his little sister to La Mesa's public skating rink most Saturday mornings. Mandy literally had to be pulled off the ice when the free period ended. She wanted to hang around for the PeeWee Hockey League's ice time, which began straight after the mixed-skill skating sessions.

Mandy persisted with her skating, quickly talking Dan into paying for a series of lessons. She was determined to improve – and, as her teacher informed Dan, she was a natural. She soon earned her own blades. (Even Dan could see that the rentals were pretty rank.) He bought her a decent pair of white figure skates and surprised her with them one Saturday morning. But, he had to stop by the sporting goods store on the way to the rink. Mandy insisted on trading the still-boxed, dainty skates for a pair of sturdy black hockey blades. That morning Dan gave in and signed her up for PeeWee Hockey. She was assigned to the 'Tenderfoot League', teams manned by novices and the occasional tomboy – and more than a few no-hopers.

Mandy progressed to a top 'Premier League' team in no time. She despaired of the PeeWee's 'No Checking Policy'... in her words, "A pussy rule for pathetic sissies!" As the quickest – and meanest – skater on the ice, she could literally have had her pick of positions. She chose to be a defenseman, stopping more goals than she scored; although she *was* the highest scoring defenseman in the league. She loved dishing out punishment, a fair bit of it outside the law – invariably concentrating on the opposition's toughest players and most prolific scorers.

Her love of the game never waned. Over the years, she'd whittled the rough edges off of her tomboy exterior (she was now, at least *superficially*, a classic young beauty). But hockey was still a passion. At SDSU she'd been forced to concentrate on other sports, excelling on the tennis team and playing intramural basketball, sometimes making up the numbers at the men's practices. She even acquiesced to throwing on a sundress and strappy sandals, in lieu of her preferred jeans and trainers, if the occasion called for it.

Nowadays, her love for hockey centered on San Diego's minor league *Gulls*. She and Dan were semi-regular members of the Sports Arena's 'Ice Pack'... a noisy gang who gravitated to the Plexiglas barrier in a lower corner of the seating area. These seats' proximity to the action made them perfect for observing *'facials'*... up close and personal. These unforgettable moments resulted when a vicious body check drove an unwary opponent headfirst into the see-through barrier in front of Ice Pack's vantage point. They erupted in raucous cheers when *either* team dished out this classic punishment. Mandy and Dan blithely referred to the most ferocious checks as 'Kodak Moments'.

Mandy's favorite match-up was her Gulls versus the odious Bakersfield Condors. This rivalry was enhanced by the glorious prospect of the brutal LaPont brothers facing off against each other. The Gulls' Barry LaPont was a superhero in Mandy's book. Obviously, it was the stupidity of NHL scouts keeping him penned up in the minor leagues. Dan aptly described him as *"the true goon's goon"* – possessed of meager skating talents, but born with an abundance of grit and heart. Barry was a dirtbag from the old school. He adored his sainted mom, who still raised the younger LaPonts up in Canada. But, on the ice he'd punch her lights out if she broke on goal uncontested. His twin brother Brian, a defenseman for the hated Condors, was inexorably cut from the same bolt of coarse LaPont cloth. Both boys had remained unrepentant hit men and junkyard dogs since their Junior Hockey days in Ontario. They knew of no other way to play the game.

These teams pulled out that bit extra when they competed against each other. But after the final buzzer, players from *both* sides – along with the Ice Pack stalwarts – headed out as one raucous mob for post-game brews. Customarily, everyone trailed behind Barry and Brian. Any festering animosities – well, at any rate, the *worst* of the bad blood – were left on the ice.

One dog-eared LaPont story played out like pure comic book fiction. *But it was verifiably true.* Legend had it that each brother possessed a 'puka shell' necklace... actually made up of his twin's adult teeth strung on dental floss. If one brother was inadvertently absent during an on-ice extraction, the injured party would wrap the incisor in cotton and send it to his twin. Each man's necklace currently contained a *complete* set of gnashers. Barry and Brian were said to wear their unique 'bling' on family occasions, much to the delight of their proud mom, wives and other relatives.

Dan parked in the nearly deserted Sports Arena lot and walked over to the lone open ticket window. He'd be buying tickets for the Gulls versus the Idaho Steelheads... another of Mandy's favorite match-ups.

There was no point in buying brother Marty a ticket. He'd just duck out after the first period and head down the street to the nearby Pink Lady strip club. His love of sport – as a spectator *or* participant – began and ended with surfing. He'd never be a team sports guy.

Great Mex and fine company

Dan managed to arrive a bit early in Del Mar. He and Sophie strolled hand in hand down the hill to Tio Jorge's, enjoying a magnificent sunset. One of the county's best Mexican restaurants, Tio Jorge's had been family run for decades. Fifteen minutes later, they sat in the corner on the peaceful patio, overlooking a calm ocean. Dan inhaled his carne asada and even managed a few bites of Sophie's tasty taco salad. He was onto his second Dos Equis Amber, while Sophie nursed her Corona. He still got a kick out of watching this prim princess drink beer from a longneck bottle.

"Thanks for coming here instead of vegging out at The Sunflower, hon," Dan said gratefully. "I really needed a couple of beers and some rib-sticking Mex; it's been a long day. We'll do the wraps and smoothies next time."

Sophie smiled and rested her head on one hand. "Don't worry, it's okay. You know this is my favorite place anyway. I should have known it would be a night for cold beers and a bit of soft mariachi rather than fruit smoothies and Carole King. Beginning to unwind?"

Indeed he *was* starting to relax. A quick shower at home had put him in a fresher frame of mind. He'd managed to catch up with Lopez, but the methodical detective had little to report. The detective did ask if he'd care to meet up at the crime scene the next day. Lopez suspected that Dan would be anxious to check things out for himself – and he knew that his old colleague still possessed an uncanny eye for crime scene detail. Dan promptly accepted the invitation and said his goodbyes.

He also checked in with Trini at work, called his mom to tell her about the hockey tickets for Mandy and touched base with Gunnar, who remained at Benny's. Connie was resting and the boys were out; God knew where. Dan reminded Gunnar to dig up that recent picture of the two cousins. Gunnar already had a couple of shots to hand.

Now, with the decks clear and melodious mariachi in the background, Dan was poised to concentrate on Sophie's priorities for the rest of the evening. But first, she brought him back to earth with the obvious question. "How's Connie holding up Dan? I'm sure the boys are a comfort. At times like these, there's no substitute for family."

91

Dan realized all too well what his concerned lover was unthinkingly implying. It occurred to him – yet again – that he'd *never* be the top priority for Sophie. Alicia and Jason came equal first, miles ahead of Dan or her love life. He answered, "Connie's still in shock, hon. We may get a better feel on how she's going to rebound after the funeral. The older boys seem to be focusing on *retribution*, rather than dealing with the family's grief. I'd guess young Greg will be more of a comfort to his mother in the coming months. Gunnar will keep Victor and Omar on short leads though, so they don't try anything stupid."

They finished up with tall mugs of Tio Jorge's potent 'Mexican Coffee' (liberally laced with tequila) and then ambled back up the hill. They decided to forego the Clint Eastwood movie, opting instead to relax with the pleasant bottle of red that Dan had brought. He turned the conversation to Sophie's work and the stepkids... any diversion from recent events.

Sophie put on Brian Wilson's *'Smile'* CD. His melancholic voice and the polished musicianship perfectly complemented the soft Rioja... and their eventual unhurried lovemaking came to a gentle finale to the delicious harmonies of *'Good Vibrations'*. A short time later, Dan softly kissed his lover, dressed and prepared to leave. He turned at the living room door to admire her. She was just so oblivious to her stunning beauty! She'd settled back in, curled up like a contented cat on the overstuffed sofa, listening to an old vinyl album of haunting love ballads, sung in lilting Spanish by long-forgotten *mariachis*.

Tomorrow would no doubt be grueling. But Sophie wouldn't have to head into work too early... she could sleep in a bit after her quiet, but relatively late, evening with him. If he stayed over, she'd insist on rising early to make his breakfast and lose out on her beauty sleep.

The drive home was peaceful. In the sparse traffic, drivers seemed to be content to stick to the speed limit. Due to the decent amount he'd imbibed, Dan opted for the back roads. In a pinch, he could attempt to use his ex-cop's patter to talk his way out of a DUI, but his thinning police contacts might no longer cut it. No sense in tempting the gods.

Are we allowed a 'do over'?

Near midnight, just as Dan left Sophie's, the beat-up Pontiac low-rider pulled up near the iron gate of a thirties 'faux-hacienda' in upmarket Mission Hills. The house's entrance was literally midway in a cul de sac. Many of the pricey homes in this district were slightly fading dowagers. Unsurprisingly, the gaudy Firebird stuck out like a painted whore plying her trade in a convent, clashing with the staid vehicles parked in nearby driveways. Manny Tejada's street was lined with art deco lamps and ancient eucalyptus. The trees' funky, almost antiseptic, aroma permeated the night air.

Skulking to the gate, Jesus and Flaco flipped cigarette butts into the spotless gutter. They rang a brass buzzer set in the fence's brickwork and were soon greeted by a feeble female voice in a tinny speaker, "Come in please gentlemen; you're expected."

The iron gate swung open sedately. The men walked up the driveway and shifted onto a stone path leading up to a vaulted oak door. A tiny Latina in a starched maid's uniform stood at the door and motioned them to enter. Without saying a word, she led Jesus and Flaco down the hallway's noisy terra cotta tiles to the rear of the house. They entered a sunken living room, decorated in vintage (many would say 'tacky') 'Classic Mexican' style. The crudely carved furniture supported cowhide leather cushions. Garish oil paintings on black or forest green velvet adorned the rough plastered walls; most depicting fiery Latin dancers or torrid bullfighting scenes. A massive stone fireplace enveloped an immense gas-fed 'log fire'. This working feature required Manny Tejada's air conditioning to belch frigid air at full tilt.

Manny's 'personal valet', Enrique, motioned for the men to perch on two uncomfortable hand-carved straightback chairs in front of a massive desk. His black suit, silk vest and tie were not authentic butler's garb, but the look was a reasonable facsimile. Flaco knew (while Jesus remained ignorant of the fact) that this stern figure had been Manny's indispensable right-hand man, in *all* important matters, for years. Enrique gave the pair a look of utter disdain and said, "The *jefe* will join us momentarily gentlemen. He'll be looking for some lucid answers to his queries on that little job you just completed for him."

Flaco replied, a little too swiftly, "It was done neat and clean man... *neat and clean*. I guess we're due that second installment on our agreed fee – and a quick rundown on those new assignments that Mr Tejada promised us."

As Flaco spoke, Tejada entered through a heavy door next to the fireplace and settled in behind his bulky mahogany desk. His green smoking jacket and fawn linen trousers had been purchased to suggest a casual, yet commanding, demeanor at home. His slippers were supple oxblood leather, with ultra-thin soles. Manny's words emanated in a slow whisper. "Actually boys, you've been summoned to review your last job *only*." His eyes narrowed, fists clenching the carved edging near the desk's inlaid leather top. Even dim-witted Jesus, usually painfully slow at sizing up a situation, knew that something was woefully amiss.

In an instant, Manny's voice shifted to a bark. "You dumb fucks! You whacked the wrong dude." He held up an 8 x 10 mug shot that his two hit men could easily make out; even from the far side of his massive desk. "Is this the guy you hit? Hell no! But the turkey in this picture *is* the esteemed Benito Rosado, you dumb asses! This very *hijo de puta* – the *genuine* Benito Rosado – phoned me this afternoon. And he wasn't calling from a slab at the morgue. Can you guess what he had to say? His *cousin*, Benny Rosado, was the victim of a regrettable, random hit yesterday. So, no surprises here – your target is still vertical… and scared shitless. He tried to cool things down by implying his cousin's death had to be some 'random occurrence' that didn't involve him or any of his colleagues. I agreed and, after offering my condolences, told him things were fine. Then I asked him to pop by my office… just as he hung up on me. So, *fuckin'-A* gentlemen! Benito is very much alive and kicking, if not currently in an overly positive frame of mind!"

The usually taciturn Jesus, mouth open and obviously stunned, softly enquired, "Could I get a closer look at that mug shot Mr Tejada?"

Enrique, standing at near-attention next to the desk, took the 8 x 10 from his boss and handed it to Jesus for inspection. The diminutive Flaco also leaned in for a better look.

After a few seconds, a highly agitated Jesus attempted to whisper an aside to his buddy. "Hey man, that there's *Raul*, the guy I interrupted takin' that smelly dump at the cantina in TJ. We seen him at the bar, remember? When I was drainin' the snake, he told me where we'd find Benito the following morning!"

Manny Tejada couldn't help but overhear. He groaned, "So, you two ran smack into Benito Rosado, in the very cantina where I told you to begin your search – and you let him slip through your fingers? Without a doubt, that asshole's almost as sly as you two are *stupid*… he'll be hard to dig out now that he knows who's on his trail."

Flaco held up a hand, palm open and bravely interjected, "Mr Tejada, don't take no offense, but we visited that cantina to get a fix on our target, just like you ordered. The guy in this picture told Jesus just where we'd find your Benito Rosado. And he even told Jesus the guy's name would be painted, big and bright, on the side of his fuckin' truck. And that's how things went down! That little *puto* scammed us good! It could happen to *anyone* Mr Tejada. Too bad we didn't have a copy of this here picture on us, huh? The important thing now, Mr Tejada, is how do you want us to sort this out?"

Manny shook his head… and, upon reflection, had to admit to himself that there was a more than a grain of truth in Flaco's observation. He looked intently at the little man and said, "Well, you could try using your so-called contacts to get onto the *genuine* Benito pronto. But *now* we can't afford to have the little shit's useless carcass discovered in the US. The local cops might think that back-to-back hits on Rosado cousins signals the beginning of some family feud or gang war – and they'd give a couple of minor crimes too much attention."

Flaco looked slightly bewildered. "So, do you want us to just *locate* the real Benito Rosado, but then get back to you before we take him out, or what?"

"Yes, goddamn it! Find him, keep him under surveillance and don't lose him again! I'll tell you *when and where* to carry out the hit. I'm sure we'll still want to make an example of this little turd, but now it may have to happen somewhere in Baja. Look, you can start your new search at that dead cousin's funeral. Benito might actually be stupid enough to turn up. In the meantime, keep an eye peeled and an ear to the ground, okay?"

Flaco took the photo from Jesus' hand and asked awkwardly, "This time we'll take this picture with us, if that's okay?" They stood up, bowed their heads slightly and turned to leave. As they reached the short stairway leading to the hall, Flaco felt compelled to turn and add, "We won't fuck up again Mr Tejada. The real Benito's loco tale in the shitter turned and kicked us *all* in the cajones, but we're onto the little bastard now!"

Moments later, the boys were outside – and, as they approached the Pontiac, Jesus rubbed his sweaty palms on his greasy leather trousers. "Well man, that meeting sure as shit didn't go to plan did it? Any ideas on how to smoke out that Raul guy again?"

"Listen up, fucknuts. He was *Benito Rosado*, not Raul; you got it? Like Tejada said, we'll go straight to work on it now, but hopefully we can make a real start at that cousin's funeral. Or, maybe we'll catch a break down in TJ. It's back to square one, amigo… but this time we're gonna' find this dude and then bust the real Benito Rosado's *cajones*!"

Tomorrow's another day

Dan rolled over and wished he were still in Del Mar, curled up with Sophie. He knew he'd find a woman like her only once in a lifetime – and that notion made his half-sleeping mind drift to other unions, both more *and* less successful.

Of course, he first considered Neil and Annie. His pal's level-headedness had been apparent, even in their youth. Neil had almost immediately recognized how extraordinary his Annie was. While Dan had always liked her, he didn't initially appreciate her sheer *quality*. While wisdom *supposedly* came with age, Dan felt that real life flew in the face of this old adage. Over the years, he'd come across many *old fools*; himself included. Neil had shown an abundance of wisdom from the beginning. Now, the wonderful Annie was becoming an even more invaluable friend to Connie. The Rosados didn't know his Sophie quite so well, but Dan knew that she too would be a compassionate and caring friend if called upon.

Dan almost laughed to himself as he mulled over the notion that Detective Gene and his *own* ex, Melinda, would never be the idyllic lovebirds that the silly bastard tried to portray at work. He sincerely hoped the wretched meathead would give Melinda a meager taste of whatever success and contentment she so ardently desired. She deserved a little happiness... even though the silly bitch invariably ended up farting in her own bathwater.

And, reflecting on said bathwater, Dan began to drift off, unable to shake off the pleasurable memory of Melinda languishing by candlelight in their apartment's tiny tub. They'd both been so young and, at least in the beginning, he'd considered himself very happily married. Unfortunately, *harsh reality* – even when it's augmented by a matchless sex goddess like Melinda nestling in your tub – can come 'round swiftly and bite many a clueless young dipshit in the ass!

Chapter 13

Thursday

Such a lovely place...

A deafening thunderclap interrupted Dan's fitful slumber. He rolled over, attempting to drift off again with his pillow covering his head. A second ungodly crack summoned him from his bed and over to the window. Southern California's infrequent freak thunderstorms could cause cataclysmic floods in the low-lying areas adjacent to dry riverbeds. Prior to the eighties, Mission Valley's buildings near the San Diego River could find themselves flooded – or sitting atop short-lived, shallow lakes. Since then, a series of enormous (and costly) storm drains had alleviated the worst of the flooding. This long overdue project had been another literal 'drain' on the city's overburdened finances.

As Dan looked out of his window, the neighboring rooftops were bone dry. Any precipitation had passed to the east, probably drenching La Mesa or El Cajon. Dan's alarm was poised to go off, as it was nearing seven. He hoped to get a jump on the case, so he headed for the shower. Hopefully this thunderous wake-up call didn't presage an inauspicious beginning to his new day.

In reality, the odds on an early solution to Benny's mysterious death (and a resultant slam-dunk arrest) were *already* slim. A worst-case scenario loomed... perhaps the button men would simply walk away. In the real world, wicked and even inept perps could simply disappear into thin air... or waltz out of court, 'not guilty' due to inane technicalities. Dan knew only too well that crime busting was a crapshoot.

The steaming water erupting from his aged showerhead helped clear the cobwebs. An Eagles CD emanated from the living room – *Hotel California* was a frequent accompaniment to his ablutions. A run-through of this protracted track was the precise measure of a soak that worked out the kinks without unduly overtaxing San Diego's scarce Colorado River water. Instead of singing along, he stood mutely under the spray.

He was pondering whether any of his 'second-tier' street contacts might be helpful. Probably not, he mused. It would pay to ask Brenda to roust her own snitches... her Vice Squad duties inevitably drew her and her colleagues deep into San Diego's underworld. Brenda had been working Vice for nearly a year. Her sex appeal was an asset in undercover work and her sharp interrogation skills were invaluable for breaking down street-hardened punks and world-weary whores. But this assignment was a meat grinder, chewing up personal relationships as it chipped away at self-esteem. Vice had turned countless young women into hyper-cynical, hardened cops in short order. Dan hoped Brenda would snag a better assignment – and her transfer couldn't come too soon.

As he dressed, Dan considered phoning his old partner again before heading out. But she'd be fresh off shift and catching some Z's... it could wait. She'd be expecting a call though. In fact, she'd be offended if he *didn't* touch base early on.

He was officially off the clock at TriState, so Dan decided it would be okay to beef up his artillery for the investigation. He removed his holstered .38 from his sock drawer, setting it on the dresser. He slid a genuine patrolman's shield, still nestled in its worn leather wallet, into his jacket pocket. (How careless of his old captain... neglecting to follow up on Dan's 'misplaced' shield and ID when he left the force!)

The .38 was wildly inaccurate past ten yards, but it had decent close range stopping power. He hoped that firearms wouldn't feature in the investigation – he fully intended to hand over dangerous work to the police. Dan's fervent hope was that the sidearm would serve only as a *deterrent* in a tight spot – and not be fired in anger.

As he walked to his car, his stomach told him that a brief stop at Lenny's would be most welcome. Who knew if he'd find time for lunch once his day got underway? He stowed his weapon and ID under the spare in his trunk. They'd be there if he needed them.

Non, Je Ne Regrette Rien

Stan and Jerry perched on their habitual stools, looking exceedingly glum. Dan settled in next to them, ordered bacon and eggs, and solemnly stared at his reflection in the surface of the black coffee Rosie instantly placed before him.

After the briefest interlude, Jerry elected to drag their companion into the morose conversation. "You're young Dan, but you remember Harry Chapin, right? He passed on far too soon, but he sure as shit possessed a wise head on those youthful shoulders. His lyrics may have been a tad sentimental, but they sure could focus on life's key regrets and 'what ifs'. I'd say his music – and his fuckin' untimely death, of course – pretty much remind us that we're best off living in the moment."

"I know Chapin's stuff," Dan replied. "Sophie listens to him sometimes... on vinyl, probably from her late husband's collection. She loves his songs, probably because Gus introduced them to her."

Stan, ever the pragmatist, was quickly coming to the conclusion that Jerry had just about exhausted the topics of 'life's lessons learned' and 'chalking up past regrets'. So, he brought the banter around to another proven downer – politics. "My biggest regret is that there've only been certifiable bums in the White House since our *genuine* leaders, solid men like Ford and old Ronnie Ray-gun, rode off into the sunset! Nowadays it seems like people would rather let a rattlesnake loose in the White House than vote for a person of integrity. And, yes, I meant to say 'person'... these days more *women* than men are fit for the job – and that's for certain."

"Hold on Stan! Let's give our sitting guy a chance," Jerry replied. "My dear old dad made those same 'reptilian' references about every president after Truman and Ike, until the day he died. Each succeeding generation believes the vast bulk of their leaders are charlatans."

His partner's tart retort meant that Stan's enthusiasm for the current topic was fast waning. As usual, the quick-witted Jerry seemed intent on trumping his every observation. So, Stan decided to lay down the final word: "I've only got this left to say about the current crop, Jerry... what about 'Dubbya', Sheik Obama and our own state's shining light, 'The Governator'? No politician will *ever* set the bar lower than these turds – so the next guy or gal has a real chance to shine by comparison."

Dan kept his opinions to himself. Whatever their motives or ambitions, he guessed that the majority of men and women who went into public service possessed, at least initially, a few decent aspirations and some desire to enhance the public welfare. He took out his phone and slid to the end of the counter, hoping to get in a couple of quick calls before his food arrived.

"Forgive me Brenda," he reflected as he dialed. It was probably still too early for her to be awake. He got her voicemail; so he said a quick hello and asked his ex-partner to get back to him.

He dialed again. Miraculously, Detective Lopez himself answered on the second ring. He didn't have much to report, but seemed genuinely pleased to share the little he and his partner had discovered. "We'll be down at the crime scene at around two, Dan. You're welcome to join us. It'll be our last shot at scaring up reluctant witnesses or uncovering any evidence we missed. To be honest, we'd appreciate your fresh eye. We're coming up pretty empty."

Dan quickly accepted the invitation. There was probably little new to glean from the now cold crime scene, but he couldn't eliminate this vital line of investigation until he'd at least looked for himself. He took down the address and told Lopez that he'd see them there at two.

As he slipped back down Lenny's counter, his breakfast arrived and the ever-efficient Rosie refilled his empty mug. The 'terrible twins' were rising to leave just as he took a first bite; maybe he'd just about manage to eat in peace. So much for the value of an early start... Dan really didn't know where to head next, now that he wasn't meeting Knowles and Lopez at the crime scene until early afternoon. He decided to drive over to Ocean Beach and catch a few waves. An hour on the surf wasn't wasted time... it generally helped him to clear his head. Besides, early morning was not a great time for chasing down snitches for crumbs of information.

She's got it!

Dan turned out of Lenny's parking lot and merged into the traffic crawling west. Janis Joplin softly crooned an old standard on his CD player – *Summertime*. It reflected his melancholy mood as he headed for his mom's place in OB. He took a few little used side streets and in minutes he'd driven under I-5 at the Old Town underpass. He'd soon be at his beloved beach.

He let himself into his mother's house to change into his gear and grab a board. Not too surprisingly, Marty was the only one home... and still asleep. After taking the requisite five minutes to roust his reluctant surfing partner, Dan downed a glass of grapefruit juice and waited for the lazy good-for-nothing to crawl into his wetsuit.

As they strolled towards the beach, the distant swells looked promising, if not awesome. This stretch of sand would always be Dan's favorite – the mellowest place in the entire world as far as he was concerned. It was nearing ten, but the local citizens in this weather-beaten beach community exhibited few aspirations for rushing headlong into a new day. A mist was rolling in, adding a chill. But the brothers were contented, snug in their wetsuits. A few office workers were setting steaming mugs on their desks, settling in beyond the old shop front windows. A garbage crew emptied the city bins dotting the shoreline. OB's regular surfers still slept, much as Marty had been doing when Dan turned up.

Marty was pouring a half-carton of orange juice down his throat as they walked along, boards under their arms. He was gradually perking up enough to engage in a proper conversation. "Man, I'm truly bummed about Benny. Him and Gunnar have been nothin' but great to me. Without the cash wages they've thrown my way, I'd be screwed. How're Omar and Vic taking it?"

"They're taking it hard Little Bro'. I'm just hoping they'll show the good sense to follow Gunnar's lead and stay cool in the next few days. God, I hope the cops solve this quickly, or the Rosado boys may do something stupid! I've promised to help the family, but my contacts aren't what they used to be. I have to admit it; I'm nearer to being totally out of the action these days rather than immersed in the flow."

Marty nodded and then surprised his brother with his insight. "They'll listen to Gunnar at first, Dan. But Vic's patience will quickly tap out and then him and Omar will start chasing the usual lame suspects. They'll cut a swath through a shitpile of South County gang-bangers and they'll attract some nasty payback for their efforts. It'll all be in a lost cause I'd bet – and they'll just make the cops' job harder. Are there any solid leads?"

"I'm meeting the primaries at the crime scene this afternoon. The trail will have gone a bit cold, but another snoop around could pay dividends, who knows? Gunnar tipped me on one 'iffy' lead that I'll check out... but keep this under your hat, okay? Benny's cousin is a bit shady and this asshole's disappeared into the woodwork. His name's 'Benito Rosado', just like his cousin – they were both named after their granddad. He and Benny grew up like brothers. A load of family and friends gathered at Connie's yesterday and this turd hadn't even bothered to turn up by the time I left. He's probably a dead end, but I'll still try to catch up with the elusive Cousin Benito and see if Gunnar's hunch takes us anywhere."

Marty gave his older brother a knowing look. "You're talking about 'Benito the Oil Slick'. *I know that douche bag Dan!* His ass is always at The Pink Lady – and he's been hanging out with Lila's roommate lately. We shoot the shit and I'd already made the connection between him and Benny. Gunnar even turned up at the club once to try to smooth over some scrape that flared up between Benito and some mean lookin' dude."

Dan rashly decided (not for the first time) to pry into his brother's unfortunate crush on the aforementioned Lila Blue, a flashy stripper who'd plainly earned straight A's in life's school of self-inflicted hard knocks. He decided to lead with the obvious... "So, Marty, you're still courting the lovely Lila?"

"You bet your sweet ass man. She rocks my fuckin' world! When those pathetic goobers scope her sweet action at the club, their eyes literally pop out of their heads. But I've got me a golden ticket to her off-duty world... I'm allowed inside her private space to see the *real* Lila. She's got a genuinely righteous soul, bro' – and she digs me for what I am. For the time being, her dancin' money's too good to give up, so we're kinda' forced to suck up the crap her job sends our way. But, at heart Lila's a one-man woman and I'm that lucky stud!"

Dan smiled. "Sounds like true love kid. I hope she never lets you down and remains the lady of your dreams. Getting back to Cousin Benito's connection to her lovely roommate though... maybe you can do me a small favor? Could you and Lila introduce me to her for a quiet one-to-one chat? Tell Lila I'll keep it low key – I wouldn't put any of her friends in harm's way. And tell her that perhaps we can even help Benito out of a jam, okay? Mention that he isn't suspected of any *serious* wrongdoing, but some bad-assed people may be trying to throw him into the mix. It's all about helping the cops to put away Benny's killers, while Benito Rosado remains safe from harm... a virtual 'win-win' for us all."

"I get the drift Dan. I'm certain Lila can convince Winter that you're only trying to help Benito. The girls get off around two or three a.m. – and then they usually sleep late into the day. If you swing by their place this afternoon around four, Lila and I will have Winter there, primed for that low-key chat. Sound okay?"

"It sounds great, Marty. I'll call around three to confirm. If Winter puts me onto Benito, no doubt I'll quickly strike him off the suspect list... and I'll give him a heads up on what's going down. He's the only lead that I have so far – and, fortunately for him, he doesn't appear to be all that promising."

The brothers approached the beach, sat on a worn bench and removed their tattered Converse low-cuts. Then they slowly walked down the cool sand to the ocean. The tide was retreating, leaving seaweed, flotsam and bits of trash at the water's edge. Marty and Dan ran into the chilly foam carrying their boards and paddled furiously out to the waves.

Two hundred yards out, Marty flattened onto his board and quickly turned the nose towards the shore. Using both arms to burrow deep into the brine, he shouted, "My ride man!" He effortlessly found the crest of a decent breaker and glided away.

Dan proudly watched as his brother easily rode the unassuming wave. He was pleased with Marty's prowess and happy in the knowledge that whatever might come between them, they'd always share their love of surfing. Nowadays, Marty was getting too old to convincingly pull off his 'youthful beach rebel' shtick, but Dan knew that he'd never settle into a boring 'nine to five' existence. In a perverse way, he envied his brother's lack of drive and ambition. It bestowed a true sense of freedom upon one of life's so-called 'losers'.

They spent an hour in the water, enjoying the surfing and each other's company. Dan's outlook was much improved as they headed up to the house. He quickly showered and then dressed in Marty's room, more reconciled to whatever crap the day might bring. Even in this improved state of mind, it occurred to him as he knotted his necktie that this useless accessory was like a noose... a bleak reminder of 'the world of grown-up responsibilities'. The burdens of the past few days returned to his shoulders– and he knew he'd abandoned a simpler place when he'd moved away from OB, exchanging its charms for the crap associated with a host of unwelcome responsibilities.

Sally had returned from her trip to the market by the time Dan finished dressing. As his mother accompanied him to the door, she already looked exhausted. As Dan walked into the yard, he noticed, yet again, that although Marty turned up for occasional shifts with Benny's landscaping crews, he hadn't brought these skills home. His mom did her best, but the yard was primarily crabgrass and withering shrubbery. He'd have to come over and give it a lick or two. Sally grabbed his arm and pulled him close. "Danny, is there anything you can do to help Marty land a *steady* job? He's welcome here, but he's got to start paying his way! Somehow, he thinks he's entitled to Mandy's student's 'room and board' deal – and, in fact, he gives me less money than she does! And he doesn't lift a finger around here."

"I'll work on it mom. I can try Derrick. His *Rocket 88's U-Store-It* out in La Mesa seems to be going great guns. He's mentioned a coupla' times that he's having trouble finding a dependable night manager. If Marty would turn up – reliable and sober – he'd probably fit the bill."

Derrick Jackson had happily blown a bundle since leaving the Chargers, but his astute business manager also managed to set him up in some lucrative deals that even an inattentive retired jock couldn't screw up. The storage units practically managed themselves. It took little of his personal effort – or brains – to run them. The night manager's job could be just the opportunity for the yet-to-blossom Marty; the hours even matched up pretty well with those of his lovely Lila.

Sally visibly cheered upon hearing this encouraging news. "Thanks Danny. It sounds great. The night shift might even mean he couldn't blow so much of his wages in those sleazy clubs he's addicted to. He'd probably bring a few more bucks home."

"I'll chat with Derrick and get back to you mom. I can't promise anything. The job's a cushy number, but it *does* require someone who's willing to turn up and stay focused. If it looks promising, I'll sit Marty down for a serious talk. Frankly, I'm tired of fixing him up with jobs that he just blows off."

"I know what you're saying, Danny. You always do your level best for us. I'm really proud of you. Say hello to Sophie for me – and tell her to pop in when she's down here. We love seeing her. Keep safe now!"

Five minutes later, Dan pulled to the side of the road on his way out of Ocean Beach. He phoned his old pal Derrick, hoping to catch up with him for a quick bite before meeting up with Lopez and Knowles at the South Bay crime scene.

"Hey man, it's Dan. Free for lunch?"

"I'm available if the food and drinks are on you, my man. I'm heading to Pussies soon, so turn up there around twelve. I heard about Benny, man. It's the shits. His boys do some gardening for me. The Rosados are good people. Let me know if I can do anything, okay?"

"I will Derrick. Thanks for offering. See you soon." Dan knew that Lightnin's offer of assistance was sincere. Over the years, Dan had been on first-name terms with a fair share of 'sports legends'. But he'd elected to stay tight with *few* jocks, one being Derrick. The guy had a great heart and a feel for people. Sure, he'd fuck up occasionally, but lately he appeared to be shifting into a smoother gear and arriving at a better place in his life. Maybe he was becoming someone more substantial than a 'local football hero' and assuming the demanding – and more satisfying – mantle of 'community leader'.

There was, however, one remaining fly in Lightnin's ointment. He remained ever-eager to chase easy money – and he was prone to cutting corners if he thought he could get away with it. He could still play the 'dumb jock' when it suited him... and continued to believe that their slippery pal, Rod Grissom, was the epitome of a successful San Diego entrepreneur. On occasion, Dan had warned his old pal about Rod's shadier tendencies. But it was apparent to Dan that 'too good to be true' tax shelters and 'cash on the barrelhead' business ventures still appealed to Derrick's avarice. It probably sprung from the football star's somewhat clichéd and exaggerated 'disadvantaged childhood'... a justification trotted out by generations of jocks when the proverbial shit hit the fan. Good old Rod – the self-described "stockbroker to San Diego's great and good" – possessed an uncanny ability to discover the vital chink in a sucker's armor. Derrick and a few of his former teammates were some of Rod's best clients.

Chapter 14

It's the same old song

Dan could hear the din in Jimmy's Sports Bar from the parking lot. Better known as *Pussies* to Mission Valley's tail stalkers, the place was a famous hangout for the countless baseball and football pros who weren't securely tethered down by their clued-in girlfriends and partners. In fact, the place was officially 'Off Limits' for most opposing players when their teams hit town. The bar's notoriety was down to the customary presence of these fun lovin' jocks – the very celebrities whose photos and jerseys adorned the walls. Professional athletes – both legends and journeymen – attracted hordes of honeys... pliable ladies who in turn attracted loads of the ordinary horndogs working within a ten-mile radius. Distaff bar patrons often took prolonged lunch breaks if the boss was away – and more than a few agreed to join their ardent admirers for languid afternoons in San Diego's Hotel Circle king-sized beds.

Over time, the skimpy outfits, pretty faces and ample bosoms moved on; only to be summarily replenished. But nowadays, the girls all looked the same to Dan. Sometimes, untutored new recruits partook of cocktails or dinner with Pussies regulars without 'putting out'. The scoop on these 'prissy missies' soon got around. Patrons – of both sexes – encouraged these novices to loosen up or move on... 'prick teasers' spoiled the atmosphere.

U2's *Pride (In the Name of Love)* blasted from the bar's Bose speakers... nothing even close to 'cutting-edge' made the bar's play list. Derrick was already settled in a corner booth, happily chatting up the three thrilled bimbettes basking in his presence. Each lady grinned idiotically and frantically vied for her bored host's attention. Lightnin' smiled and waved Dan over.

The platinum blonde bunny was a certifiable Jayne Mansfield look-alike... bright crimson lips and a bodacious rack, probably gifted to her by a boyfriend or her wealthy daddy. She looked up as Dan approached and obviously liked what she saw. She smiled broadly, displaying perfect porcelain veneers. "Hi, handsome! Were you a Charger too?"

Dan grinned and answered, "No hon, but I've washed shitloads of their sweaty jocks with revolting regularity in years past. How you doin' Derrick? Can I have a private word?"

Dan's jockstrap quip left the blonde unfazed. Her smile didn't falter, and she slowly rose to bend forward and slide her drink along so Dan could sit down. As she did so, she treated him to a lingering peek over her unfastened top button – down to her impressive cleavage, cleverly enhanced by a lacy, industrial-strength uplift bra.

Derrick rose to his feet, attempting to shake loose the brunettes who remained steadfastly attached to him. "Sure Dan, we need to chat. Why don't you gals head over to the bar for a coupla' minutes and tell Bob there to whip us up a fresh round, on Dan's tab. I'm sure Dan here'll want a beer – any kind will do."

The women attracted the rapt attention of a bevy of Beta Males as they sashayed to the bar. The regulars knew better than to give Lightnin's action more than a sidelong leer, but a couple of young pretenders, new to the scene, moved off of their barstools and headed towards the trio of lovelies. A glance from the bartender warned the naïve pair to back off. Derrick chuckled, turning his attention back to Dan.

"I don't suppose you'd cut one of these sweeties out of the herd and leave me with the other two? You can take your choice... the blonde seems a safe bet."

Dan held up two hands and slid further down in his seat. "Thanks, but no sale! You'll just have to dial down the charm if you can only handle two at a time these days. The odd one out can latch onto one of those young studs at the bar. Miss Silicone is a generous offer man, but I'll pass if you don't mind."

"What the shit, matching brunettes can be tedious anyway. That lucky little blonde is back in the frame! In the meantime, back to some very disagreeable business. Is there any news on Benny? The TV particulars were scant. Exactly how'd he get it?"

"A pair of .22 slugs in the head – and that sort of popgun is almost always fired from close range. The perp – or perps – left the casings nearby and escaped unseen, taking the gun. Benny was found near the pool, right where he'd been working. I'm meeting a couple of Homicide guys down at the scene later, so hopefully we'll come up with something."

"It's truly fucked man. Who'd do this to a mensch like Benny?"

"Well bro', it has the all the earmarks of a pro hit... small caliber weapon, fired at close range. Perhaps it was a case of mistaken identity or a hurried whack somehow gone wrong... who knows? I need to look into this further, but there's simply no motive leaping out at us. At first glance, Benny and his whole family seem pure as the driven snow."

Derrick had an uncanny ability for tuning out background distractions and focusing on just the *one* thing. He'd done it on the playing field and he was doing it now. He stared intently at Dan and said, "As I said before, if I can do something – *anything* – let me know."

"I will, man. In the meantime, maybe there's another favor you could do for me. Are you still looking for a reasonably reliable night manager for your storage units? I promised my mom I'd ask if Marty could fit the bill. He's getting his act together a bit – and I'd put the fear of God into him if you gave him a shot."

"Sure man. My manager is probably combing through a pile of lame replies to our ad at this very minute. But wouldn't a night job put a cramp in Marty's lifestyle?"

"On the contrary Derrick, it would suit him down to the ground. His new squeeze works nights – so any job that frees him up for a bit of afternoon 'bedspring testing' would be right up his alley."

Derrick handed Dan a business card. The typeface and 'Lightning Bolt' logo bore an uncanny resemblance to those used by the Chargers, but any potential infringement was undoubtedly overlooked by the team, as Lightnin' was still considered family. "In that case, have him phone this number and tell Rick, the day manager, I said to give him an interview. He'll get an offer, unless the veritable 'prince of storage unit managers' responds to the ad. But he'll have to turn up regularly, and *clean*. No promises, but he'll get a shot, okay?"

"That's more than okay man. I owe you one – yet again."

Derrick instantly returned to his laidback demeanor and waved to the cocktail waitress hovering with a tray of food. He said to Dan, "Anything else dickwad, or can we get down to the eats? I've taken the liberty of ordering us chiliburgers – and some daintier finger-food for the ladies." With that, he turned towards the bar and signaled for the girls to return. They waved and wiggled over with the fresh drinks, leaving a trio of newly arrived 'sales executives' slobbering in their wake.

The bolder of the two youngsters at the bar chanced an approach to Lightnin'. "Excuse me, Mr Jackson. You're a hero of mine. I'll never forget that leaping end zone grab that kept us in the '92 Playoffs. I remember my dad telling me that *that reception alone* was worth more than the price of our season tickets."

"Thanks, son. It's great to know that someone your age remembers even one of my catches from the dark ages! Normally I'd invite you to take a load off, but we've got a little business to finish up. Can you excuse us?" The young man nodded and smiled, heading back to his friend at the bar. He'd relished his moment in the sun.

The girls slid in beside them and the shapely blonde snuggled up to Dan, pressing her fake Double-G's into his bicep. Evidently, they'd

107

firmed up their dating preferences at the bar and she was willing to sacrifice sack time with the legendary Rocket '88 to get 'up close and personal' with his hot friend! Dan inched away from her, trying to imply that it wasn't personal, but she'd be better off focusing on her original target.

Small talk flowed, most of it emanating from the girls as Derrick and Dan polished off their burgers. The ladies were content to dig into their popcorn shrimp, potato skins and nachos before they gratefully shifted onto Dan's fries. The smaller brunette, petite and *very* fit, chowed down with astounding gusto. If she worried about her figure, she wasn't showing it. If she screws like she eats, thought Dan, she's a genuine wildcat!

Dan rose to leave, thanked Derrick again and strolled to the bar. He paid the tab – buying another round for Derrick's booth, as well as beers for the two star-struck guys still lingering at the bar. He told the bartender to say that Old Rocket '88 wanted to buy his new pals a round. That would be a cool story for them to share with their workmates.

Benny doesn't work here anymore

Driving to the crime scene, Dan reflected on how unexpectedly a tranquil life could turn a vicious corner. Benny and Connie had suffered and survived their fair share of hardships, but his violent death was something the Rosados would never have anticipated.

Dan's mind drifted to his domestic situation, focusing specifically on how his relationship with Sophie impacted on her step-kids. Unfortunately, progress with the wary Jason created corresponding problems with his *own* brother. Marty had been a willing ally in the Jason 'charm offensive', but this could easily turn and bite Dan in the ass. One offhand remark from Marty could easily jeopardize Dan's hard-won credibility with Sophie. At least he was no longer skating on such thin ice with her stepdaughter. When Alicia recently graduated from UCSD, she decided that a real estate career would suit her capabilities and ambitions. But the flat market made jobs scarce. Dan, against his better judgment, ventured out on a shaky limb. He called his ex and asked if she'd take the girl to lunch... on him, of course. He hoped that Melinda would network with colleagues and point Alicia in the right direction. And Melinda had more than obliged. She laid on the 'intimate lunch for the girls' routine at an expensive La Jolla eatery and finished the meal by offering Alicia the receptionist's job in her mall office while she studied for her agent's license.

In hindsight, Melinda's motives were rather transparent. Without doubt, Alicia *was* intelligent and attractive... she'd easily mastered the receptionist's role. But more importantly, if delicately handled, the girl could provide an insider's access to the down and dirty on Dan and Sophie's budding relationship. Dan's ex had always been singularly adept at 'innocently' wheedling seemingly innocuous information from unwary targets.

So far, Alicia's apprenticeship seemed to be progressing to plan. And, unbeknownst to the overconfident Melinda, the girl's work situation suited Sophie and Dan as well. The youngster was astute enough to recognize when she was being pumped for information. She fed Melinda harmless tidbits cleared for circulation (or even parcels of plausible *misinformation* that Sophie herself invented). Lately, Dan and Sophie had been subtly pulling Melinda's chain, with Alicia acting as a partner in the deception.

Dan checked his watch upon arrival at the condo complex where Benny had *permanently* clocked off. He was a few minutes early. He parked on the street, foregoing the handful of visitors' spaces in the front lot. Placing his sunglasses on the dash, he got out and circled around the side of the front-facing building, looking for the recreation area.

Wandering over to the empty Jacuzzi, he sat on the edge and awaited the arrival of the detectives. Little would be gained by poking around prior to their arrival; fresh discoveries would carry more weight if attributed to Lopez or Knowles. The area was deserted – and few traces remained of crime scene activity. The condos' managers had obviously eradicated any signs of violence as soon as they were permitted to do so. Nothing unusual had occurred here; at least to the untrained eye.

The detectives arrived five minutes later. They strolled to the precise spot where Benny had collapsed and motioned Dan to join them. Lopez, all business, skipped the preliminaries. "He didn't know what hit him Dan. He dropped onto his face right here, exactly where he'd been kneeling by this flowerbed. His arms were flat in front of him."

Dan took a step back, deliberating on the probable trajectory of the diminutive .22 rounds that penetrated the front of Benny's skull – and the fact that the preoccupied gardener apparently hadn't attempted to rise and defend himself. "You think he turned his head up and towards the shooter when he heard him approaching?"

"Apparently so, Dan," Knowles replied. "The coroner said the wound tracks are on a downward slant and there was trace powder on his forehead. Without a doubt, the rounds were fired close in – and they pretty much came from out of the blue as far as Benny was concerned. See the paving stones to your right? You can still make out faint bloodstains."

Lopez added, "Two .22 casings apparently bounced off this stone pathway and into the flowerbed. They're at the lab now. The body appeared to be untouched – wallet, money and credit cards intact. Clearly, robbery wasn't the motive."

Dan paused to look around the closed-in recreational area and asked the obvious question. "Is there any evidence of whether or not this was a lone gunman?"

"We can't tell Dan," Knowles replied. "We've combed the complex for witnesses. All we have are the two teenagers who discovered the body and an old woman who may, or may not, have heard gunshots. As you can undoubtedly see, this has all the earmarks of a piss-poor professional hit. Even a fairly inexperienced button man would use a lookout during a close-range daylight hit, right? That would be my bet anyway."

Dan swept the surroundings, searching for overlooked clues or a promising location that could yield so-far unidentified witnesses. His instincts told him that Knowles was right. "Yeah, it smells like two guys to me... in and out, quick and cool. They were damned lucky to go unseen. But even if they'd been spotted, there's a decent likelihood they'd be well out of town that afternoon anyway." Dan paused and knelt by the faint bloodstains before continuing. "On many levels though, this was sloppy work. There are too many nooks and crannies that could hide witnesses and the escape routes are lengthy and cumbersome. Those things don't point to top-notch shooters. We aren't looking for the elite; we're hunting for cheap muscle. That helps... we could get lucky."

Lopez added a final word. "To me, it has all the earmarks of a drug dealers' turf war, Dan. That's the tack we're taking, even though it might also turn out to be some lame gangbanger vendetta. Rosado drove back and forth across the border regularly. Smuggling could play a part. We'll be looking at the usual suspects, from Los Angeles to Ensenada and as far east as Phoenix."

Dan couldn't deny that drugs could be involved, but he had more than a gut feeling that Benny's hit had simply been a case of mistaken identity. But, he had no reason to share unsubstantiated hunches – presumptions based on little more than personal bias – with detectives who'd been tasked with piecing together an airtight case. He'd keep his lone feeble lead, Cousin Benito, out of the mix for the time being. He wanted first crack at this low-life before the cops grabbed him, read him his rights and he clammed up.

Dan ran his fingers lightly over the dirt in the flowerbed before standing up and dusting off his hands. "Thanks for showing me around guys. I guess I'm outa' here. I'll keep you posted on anything I uncover."

"Thanks, man," said Lopez, as he shook Dan's hand. "We're headed back into these buildings to knock on doors. We might uncover a fresh witness… long shots can pay off. See you later." Knowles gave Dan a short wave as the men headed in separate directions and disappeared into the two side-facing buildings.

Dan strolled unhurriedly back to his Chevy. Probably he was taking the same route – the most direct one to the street – that Benny's assassins had chosen. He glanced up at the windows and balconies overlooking the pathway. He spotted not a single gawker, even though the comings and goings of police should have aroused idle curiosity by now. Did the perps carefully *plan* their entry and exit routes – or had they simply been very fortunate to act quickly and vanish unobserved?

Back in the Chevy, Dan switched on his cell phone. A text had arrived from Brenda. It simply said, "Sorry I missed your call. Phone back." He dialed and she picked up on the first ring. Dan got straight to the point. "Sorry to bother you Bren. I guess you've heard about Benny Rosado?"

"I was really sad to hear about it, Dan. At first I didn't make the connection to your landscaper buddy when it hit the news, but then it struck me."

"It was a shock, Bren. I called earlier to ask if you'd give me a heads up if you run into anything that might tie even remotely into this case. I'm trying to help out the family… *unofficially* of course."

Brenda didn't seem at all surprised. "Sure Dan. I'll run this by a couple of my snitches. Do you think the shooting's drug related?"

"It could be, but only accidentally, as far as Benny's concerned. I'd bet a bundle that he's clean, and the killer – or killers – screwed up and nailed the wrong guy. It looks more like pro button men than gang-bangers, but dim-witted pros at that. Thanks – and stay safe, partner."

"You too, Dan. If you uncover anything, don't act like The Lone Ranger… run it by me. It's never a bad idea to work with an insider, even for a clever dude like you."

"Right, Bren. Fortunately for the Rosados, Lopez and Knowles are working the case. Do you remember them? They can be trusted, so feel free to share with them. But, at least for now, talk only to *those two* or to me, okay? As you know, some of your colleagues care more about their 'career tracks' or easy money than solving cases. I gotta go.... see you soon."

Dan phoned Marty and, sure enough, the girls would be in at four. Lila had to coax her roommate to stick around for a chat with Marty's "ex-cop brother". She calmed Winter's nerves by telling her that Dan was on the level and only needed her help in putting her newest admirer, Benito, in the clear on his cousin's murder. Lila explained that Dan was trying to help out the whole Rosado clan – and that *included* protecting Benito.

Marty gave Dan the girls' address. Dan seemed to recall their well-maintained, seventies-era apartment complex. The units attracted partying singles and less than studious undergrads from USD, a small Catholic college up the hillside in nearby Linda Vista. Before disconnecting, Dan thanked his brother for stepping up and helping the Rosados. "Well done bro', see you at four then. Keep the girls chilled out. I'm not a threat to Winter or her dubious boyfriend... at least not at this point in time."

As he drove north past the airport, Dan pulled off the freeway for a bite at El Charro's, a legendary tin-roofed taco stand at the bottom of University Avenue. He bought a Union-Tribune from the nearby rack and combed the news section for any updates on the murder. Predictably, he found nothing... the killing of an unknown beaner (and a walking cliché at that; a *Chicano landscaper*) wouldn't have legs in the news, unless some sensational drug or gang connection emerged.

El Charro's hadn't changed in thirty years. Renowned for serving up the best and cheapest Mex in the county, this fast-food establishment provided colorful picnic tables for its patrons, set on a square of well-worn gravel next to the take-out windows. Dan's tamales, beans and rice were *real* Mex... steaming hot and gloriously spicy. Some idiots chose to douse their food with extra hot sauce packets. Of course, pre-packaged condiments could never enhance El Charro's perfectly seasoned tamales and tacos. Still, the sachets were available for the foolish or uninitiated.

He sat at a table savoring his food and sipping iced tea while he combed the sports pages. The Pads appeared poised to suck hind tit again as the season approached. There's no substitute for pitching, he thought. And they could use *any* breathing substitute for a couple of the so-called 'starters' in their rotation. It would be another long year for them, even in the mediocre National League West.

Dan polished off his tamales and iced tea and threw the wrappings in a hand-decorated metal bin. He left the newspaper under the condiments bowl on the take-out counter – ready for another customer's repast. Now fulfilled, he headed out to Point Loma to interrogate the divine 'Miss Winter Fox'. He hoped that she would be willing – and able – to lead him to the elusive Benito Rosado.

Chapter 15

The vixens' den

Just before four, Dan parked in the apartment complex's front lot. A prominent sitemap told him their 'Block C' apartment was second story and in the back, overlooking the immense swimming pool. On this sunny afternoon, a profusion of bikini-clad girls and horny studs in colorful baggies hung out by the pool. While certainly not cheap, these apartments were affordable for students who shoehorned three or four roommates into each modest two-bedroom unit.

Dan could imagine the excitement that Lila and Winter would create when they hung out poolside. They'd no doubt try to pass themselves off as actresses or models – and that particular fib might occasionally fly, until a clued-in tenant told his pals about how their sexy neighbors slid down that notorious shiny pole at The Pink Lady.

Dan rang the buzzer and his little bro' immediately opened the door. The living room was minuscule, barely accommodating a cheap two-seater couch and a couple of powder blue director's chairs. A portable TV and iPod player rested on a table in the corner. The kitchenette's breakfast bar was similar to his, minus the bar stools. Instead, a compact dining table and three rickety chairs nearly blocked the tiny balcony's sliding door. The furnishings were dusty rose, powder blue and minty green. In spite of the limited space, throw pillows abounded – enough to kit out a Nevada brothel's vast lounge *and* playroom. Marty flopped back down on the sofa, pressing himself against the brunette vision of pulchritude lounging there. He grinned at Dan and said, "Take a load off man. This here's my lady, Lila."

"Nice to meet you somewhat less 'in the flesh' Lila. Actually, we caught your act a while back when Marty and I were out 'sibling bonding'. You're a great little dancer by the way... very supple, and you interpret your music superbly."

Lila shot Dan a broad smile as she eyed him up and down. "Thanks honey. Marty's told me a lot about you. Is it true you're tight with a lot of the Chargers?"

"Not so much these days, babe. My football buds are mostly *former* Chargers... having been cut long ago or retired to stud. I've a nodding acquaintance with a few of the current crop, but I can't say we hang out. I can still scrape up tickets for you and Marty though, if you'd like to take in a game."

Marty beamed and took the opportunity to chime in. "See Tastycakes, I told you Danny was cooler than shit! And to get back to current business... anything you guys decide to tell him about Benito will stay between us, I guarantee it. He'll pass on *only* the shit that you girls green light, right Dan? And he won't reveal his sources if you don't want him to."

Why didn't Marty ever know when to quit? Dan knew he had to play for a bit of wriggling room on his brother's rash promises. "As Marty undoubtedly told you ladies, we're both close friends of the Rosados – and I'd like a word with their cousin Benito, to give him a heads up on the current situation. Lila, maybe we can go out on the balcony for a chat?"

Marty nodded his assent and got up to move a kitchen chair before opening the sliding door. Lila stepped onto the balcony with Dan and Marty closed the door behind them.

Lila spoke first, getting straight to the point. "If I introduce you to Winter, will you *guarantee* that nothing she tells you will dump us in the deep shit with the cops... or land us on some bad guys' 'most wanted' list?"

"I don't issue guarantees Lila. Life doesn't always work that way. But I can unconditionally assure you that I'll do my level best to protect Winter – and you – from any shitstorm that might erupt. And if Benito is the innocent bystander that we all think he is, I can be his friend as well. I'm in this for the sake of the Rosado family, *Benito included*. Sometimes you have to cooperate with the good guys, so that the bad guys don't take out innocent bystanders like yourselves and skate away scot-free."

Lila gave Dan a long look and waved through the glass. Marty disappeared down the hallway and soon returned, accompanied by a willowy blonde in faded jeans and a halter-top. Her boobs reminded Dan of perfectly crafted porcelain orbs, suspended on high by the halter's taut straps. She'd no doubt possessed a lovely natural figure before surrendering to some surgeon's knife. Now she resembled an overblown Barbie Doll, with a toy-girl face. But she was still prettier than most of the current crop of TV starlets. To Dan, Winter represented the epitome of pinup sexiness. Her 'robot-doll' façade resembled Daryl Hannah's exotic look in *Blade Runner* – thankfully, minus the vacant replicant's black mascara and overcooked eyeliner. She gave Dan a wry smile and walked onto the balcony. Lila returned inside.

"Hi, I'm Carrie... or 'Winter' to you, I guess. That's my stage name, of course."

Dan decided to cut through the bullshit, preferring to connect to the *person* rather than the façade. He looked into her eyes – a gesture most men probably didn't manage at first gaze – and addressed her by her real name. "Carrie, I'm Dan Paige. I understand you've become quite friendly with Benito Rosado. You may have heard that his cousin and longtime friend, Benny, was gunned down the other day. I'm not implying that Benito was involved. In fact, his whole family, including his grandma, is worried sick about him and I'm here to try to protect him – and you – from whatever's going down."

Carrie paused before replying, obviously carefully considering her next move. "Benito has no idea of what's going on, Mr Paige. I've seen him since his cousin's shooting and he's decided it's best to just lie low for a while. He says someone may be after his family for reasons he can't get a handle on just yet."

"If that's the case Carrie, I'm sure I can help."

"Okay Mr Paige, I think I'll have to trust you. But what I'm about to say has to stay *between us*, understand?"

"I'll do my best Carrie. You and Benito can both trust me. I'm a good friend to *all* of the Rosados and I don't want to see any of them harmed."

"Okay then, here goes. Benito's been good to me, but he can be a scary guy. He's possessive – and if he thought I was seeing someone else, he'd blow a gasket. To make a long story short, I may have an idea about why he's being so antsy. Here's the deal. His boss, a pretty dodgy businessman named Manny Tejada, has been sniffing around the club lately. At first he came in with Benito – and threw money around. Now he comes in on his own."

"Had you noticed him before he came in with Benito?"

"No. I had no idea who he was – or that he was actually Benito's boss. The day after his first visit, Mr Tejada sent me flowers and candy at the club. The card attached invited me to join him for the Champagne Sunday Brunch at *Minelli's Harbor View*. It's a family place, you know? And the reservation was for early in the afternoon. I didn't see any harm in it, right?"

Dan smiled and didn't break eye contact – trying to keep things cool. "Sure, he may have just wanted to talk about your relationship with Benito or a give you a heads up on some modeling work, right?" He knew that casting doubt on her intentions or questioning her character wouldn't be a smart move at this point in her all too familiar story.

"Modeling work... yeah, that thought occurred to me. So, one thing led to another – you know how it goes – and I soon realized what a persistent man Mr Tejada can be. He offered me a great-paying job in his office if I'd give up my dancing. I'm no secretary, so I passed on that. But I did succumb a teensy bit to his charms. And, here's the real sensitive bit... I'm sorry to say that he and Benito are now *definitely* 'hole buddies', if they weren't both boffing some other gal before they met me. Benito doesn't know this, of course. And if he finds out, I'll be *very* sorry I spilled this dirt! Whatever goes down from here on out, this little tidbit stays between us, okay?"

Dan felt a little reassurance was called for – and he'd sincerely do his utmost to keep this bombshell under his hat. "I'm sure we can agree on a bit of discretion here, Carrie. You realize, of course, your personal relationships aren't really likely to impact on Benito's current problems."

"That has to be the way this plays out, Dan, even though I can't be certain there's no connection! Manny's phoned me twice in the past week, wanting to know where Benito is – and he can be very insistent. I think Manny's got him running scared. I want to help Benito, but he's got a vile temper and I can't be in the line of fire between him and Manny."

Dan took the troubled Carrie gently by her shoulders and gave her an encouraging nod. "If I talk to Benito, it'll only be to convince him that I can help him – and to assist him in getting a message to his family. We'll undoubtedly unplug him from this murder investigation in short order. The question is, can you get me to him?"

Now it was Carrie's turn to signal through the sliding door. Lila disappeared down the hallway. She soon reappeared, accompanied by a bronze-skinned man who shared more than a passing resemblance to Benny Rosado; but bonier, with a harder edge. His western-cut sharkskin suit would not have been out of place in an old Miami Vice episode. These girls had undoubtedly entertained their fair share of dubious guests, but Benito would almost certainly top the bill. Here stood Dan's quarry, just inside the girls' front room! He'd been easier to track down than anyone could have anticipated.

Carrie/Winter whispered to Dan as Benito approached the sliding door. "He's a bit on the devious side Mr Paige, but he's not evil. He wouldn't have his cousin killed, that I'm sure of. Manny Tejada, on the other hand, is truly messed up. Benito's as scared of him as we are, but he'd never admit it. Tread carefully or you could get us all *very* fucked up."

"Thanks for the advice Carrie. Don't worry; I'll play this hand very close to my chest."

With that, the girl went inside, leaving the balcony to Benito and Dan. The nervous man came out, shut the door behind him and shook

Dan's hand. His palm was sweaty and he seemed anxious to talk. The girls had obviously primed him.

"Marty and Lila say you're okay, Paige. I trust *her* at least. I'm totally in the dark on this mess, but I'll try to help you out. Once I heard about my cousin, it occurred to me that it might involve some vendetta against our family – or even a case of mistaken identity, with Benny unfortunately taken for me. Either way, I have to play this out like I'm a potential target. So, better safe than sorry. I'm holing up here for now. I trust Winter and Lila – and now I'm damned if I don't have to extend that trust to you and Marty."

"There's every reason for you to put your faith in us Benito, but let's start by cutting the crap! Gunnar and the boys are worried about you; but, there's no doubt about it... they also share a not so wild-assed hunch that you can shed some light on Benny's murder. The fact that you're hiding – and you've made no effort to contact them, Connie or Hortensia – smells a bit off to everyone."

"Maybe I'm just being smart Paige. Some unsolicited, very sinister shit appears to be headed my way. I'm only trying to keep my *mama grande* and family out of it. There've been some weird and dirty feuds between *Mejicano* crime families over the years, in case you aren't aware of it. Who can say where this is headed – or if Benny's killing is the end of it?"

Dan was compelled to keep Carrie's dalliance with Tejada out of the frame, but he had to up the ante somehow. He opted for some off the cuff 'creative storytelling'. "Gunnar Morales mentioned a guy named Manny Tejada to me, Benito. He said one of Tejada's boys visited a job site last week, looking for *you*. Any reason these guys might be intent on chasing you or upsetting your family?"

"Look Paige, as far as I know, Manny Tejada is a legitimate importer. I don't know what Gunnar suspects, but I can assure you it's got to be a blind alley. I run errands for Mr Tejada and we're sort of partners on occasion... in some very legit deals. Everything's cool between us – and I hope things stay that way, okay? This line of enquiry could spoil one of my only remaining sources of real income."

Easy money and greed... surely two of Benito's hot buttons! Dan decided to pile on the bullshit and dig a bit deeper. "I've been onto my police buddies and they've told me some interesting tales about Tejada's import businesses. He's walking on thin ice." Dan was really winging it now. He didn't know Tejada from Adam – and had never even run across the name until Carrie mentioned him. "Benito, do you really want to help you and your family out? If so, I can probably help

118

to keep your head above the sewage until the worst of Manny Tejada's shit manages to float downstream."

Benito leaned against the balcony's railing and his shoulders sagged. Dan guessed that the little slimebag was trying to calculate some intricate odds, weighing up his unattractive alternatives. The guy was a stupendously bad liar… there was obviously more going on here than met the eye. But did this dickhead's ducking and dodging tie into Benny's death? Dan's nose told him it did.

Benito finally took a deep breath and straightened up. "Okay Paige, here's the scoop. I may have done a coupla' deals with Mr Tejada that kinda' went sour. Right now, I'm trying to get him to see sense. Honestly, I haven't screwed him over, but he may not see it that way. Obviously, we've got some shit to clear up. But, this is *not* a big deal. Manny wouldn't put out a hit on me – or anyone in my family – over this misunderstanding. Anyway, if he did, he'd never see his cash. This mix-up can't be the fuckin' kick-start for Benny's murder. It don't add up!" Just explaining himself was taking a lot out of Benito. By the end of his little confession, he was sweating and sagging on the rail again.

Benito was trying too hard… Dan detected the pungent whiff of unadulterated bullshit. He knew instinctively the guy was trying to buy time and wriggling room. The little turd would remain vague, because he had so much more to fear from Manny Tejada and his cohorts than he did from Dan, the Rosados or the police. It could be counterproductive to lay another scare on Benito or squeeze him too hard. Better to work with what the little scumbag had already spilled, keeping him on ice at the girls' place in the meantime.

Dan put an arm around Benito's slumping shoulders. "I'm sure you're right Benito. This line of enquiry is undoubtedly a red herring. Your problems with Tejada don't merit a mob hit. You can trust me – and you're no doubt safe here for the time being. I'll tell Gunnar and Hortensia that you're safe, but out of touch for now. Don't mention Tejada's possible involvement to Marty and the girls… if it's a dead end, we wouldn't want to stir up any unnecessary trouble." He hoped that this last admonition, which he'd thrown in as if it were an afterthought, would avert any awkward conversations concerning their 'friend in common' between Benito and his beloved Winter.

The men went in and Dan quickly said his goodbyes, leaving both couples in the living room. Marty and Benito drained Coronas from longneck bottles, while the girls pretended to be busy with their nails. Ricki Lake's voice was grating from their tinny television speaker. The brash chat show doyenne addressed three slutty looking, dubious 'females', rolling her eyes as she said, "It's always those hands and the Adam's apples that give you 'gals' away."

Dan turned on the doorstep and left them with some parting instructions. "Benito, I suggest you stay cool and don't leave the apartment for now. Girls, go to work as normal. No need to worry. And Marty, if I were you, I'd stay away from here for the next week or two. I'll check out what I can and get back to you guys. If things work out okay, the heat will no doubt quickly subside. Stay safe… all of you."

'Getting to know you…'

Back in the car, Dan phoned his old partner and this time he got straight through. "Hey Bren, can you check for an active sheet on a guy named 'Manuel Tejada'? He's a purported 'importer/exporter' here in the city. I could do with his work and home addresses and it would be nice to know about any serious scrapes in the past few years. He's shady without a doubt, so a serious beef with the cops must have popped up at one time or another."

"I assume this connects to Benny's murder? I'll see what I can dig up Dan. I'll phone you tonight. Any known associates?"

"Only one KA I know of Bren, but keep this strictly to yourself. He's been in some dodgy business deals with Benny's loser of a cousin, who's also named 'Benito Rosado'. Their names are similar because Benny and his shifty cousin were both named after their grandfather, although their dads were as unlikely as brothers as you'd ever imagine. This could be a dead end, but I've got to play this one out. Maybe I can shake Benito's and Manny Tejada's nasty tails and some useful shit will topple off."

"I've just made this my top priority Dan. I'll call back before I head out on duty. If we have a jacket on a 'Manuel – or Manny – Tejada', I'll fill you in. If not, I'll rattle the cages of some of my snitches. Of course, hits on this Tejada dude via the grapevine will take a bit longer, but I'll uncover what's out there… bet on it."

"I know I can count on you, Brenda – and thanks. Just make sure that our old pal Gene Jeffries is kept in the dark on this. He'll go out of his way to obstruct anything I undertake on the Rosados behalf, just to spite me. He's a contemptible little asshole."

"No worries there, Dan. My buddies and me don't hang with that dick or his pathetic crew. Jeffries tries to finagle his way into high profile cases that attract the Chief's or DA's attention – and usually fires blanks. In the meantime, the solid cops who know how and where to put in the sweat will find the bastards who did this... count on it."

"Talk to you later Brenda. Thanks again."

Dan dialed San Diego's FBI Headquarters in the downtown Federal Building and asked for Senior Agent Vincent Parelli. The receptionist put him on hold while she paged him.

Dan and Vince had teamed up on a few testing cases over the years, combining intelligence and breaking down jurisdictional barriers whenever they could. Both men realized that the arcane rivalry between local law enforcement and the Feds generated far too much bullshit – and unnecessary legwork – for all concerned.

As trust grew between the pair, they'd eventually turned a professional relationship into a personal one. They had much in common... neither was a glory seeker, each wanted to put the worst of the scumbags away and both were willing to cut a problematic corner or two on occasion to achieve a just outcome.

Vince had been assigned to San Diego from Philly in the mid-eighties. A few years Dan's senior, his rocky marriage was over before he'd headed west. Thickset and swarthy, with pronounced Italian features, he reminded Dan of a burlier and more athletic Joe Pesci. He even seemed to share some of the actor's stock 'street-tough' mannerisms. Vince could be prickly... 'in your face' when it actually hurt his cause. He lacked the tact and diplomacy to win an otherwise deserved senior role in the Bureau, but this meant that one of their best field detectives wasn't buried behind a desk.

A year before, Dan put Brenda and her new partner, Frank Arlen, in touch with Vince when the Bureau was brought in on the gruesome kidnap and murder of a La Jolla socialite. The victim, in her late eighties, had been a minor Hollywood celebrity in her day. She'd married a successful novelist in the fifties and the couple purchased one of La Jolla's prized mansions on a fairway of The La Jolla Golf and Tennis Club. Untidy jurisdictional issues, based on the unlikely prospect of the kidnappers transporting the old gal across state lines, created flak between local cops and the Bureau. Dan was pretty certain that Brenda and Vince could cut through any crap, so he arranged an informal meeting.

Within two minutes of his introduction, Dan remembered thinking, "Shit, there's something more than the beginnings of a healthy working relationship going down here!" He'd never seen Vince so solicitous – or, in fact, acting so goofy! The often assertive, yet socially inept, Italian was clearly falling hard. But, as he'd just come into close contact with the gorgeous Brenda, who could blame him?

In the past, Vince sporadically hung out with Dan and his rowdy pals of an evening – and he'd attracted his fair share of the ladies when they went on the prowl. But Dan had *never* seen Vince stick with one woman. The FBI man was wary of acquiring a new partner; he'd been burned once. And that built-in reticence might explain why Vince made no moves on Dan's lovely ex-partner. He unquestionably lost all semblance of his macho façade on those rare occasions when they connected through work, but Vince seemed to lack the courage to act on his obvious attraction to Brenda.

Brenda, in turn, attempted to act blasé when Dan joked about Vince's obvious crush on her. But, Dan knew she'd secretly be delighted to date a guy who could understand and deal with her peculiar lifestyle. Perhaps Vince was that guy. Bren toned down her customary cop's demeanor around Vince, but an outsider would probably miss the imperceptible softening. Clearly, she was as apprehensive as Vince about shifting their relationship from the professional to the personal.

One evening, Dan mentioned the subtle sparks flying between Vince and Brenda to Sophie. She suggested inviting them out for a low-key dinner and then drinks at her place. Dan warned Sophie about 'cop on cop' matchmaking, explaining: "When lovebirds both work in law enforcement, by and large they don't wind up in *'Happily Ever After-land'*. Usually, they can't even set the ground rules for a long-term relationship." So, the 'Vince and Brenda' match-up remained on Sophie's back burner. Her double-date evening was still a pipedream.

Still on hold with the FBI receptionist, Dan finally heard a click and Vince's voice came on the line, bringing him abruptly back into the present. "What's up Dan? Make it quick, I'm in a supposedly 'essential' meeting, briefing case handovers to our DEA chums."

"Okay man, here's a quick run-down. You heard about Benny Rosado? I'm looking into his murder for the family and I need a hand. Can you dig up anything you've got on a shady importer named Manuel Tejada… T-E-J-A-D-A? He appears to rent office space somewhere in town and trades mostly between here and Baja, I'd guess. I know you're busy, but this is a rush job. Can we meet up tonight at Sal's, with dinner on me – say at eight-thirty?"

"Sure man. I'll poke around and bring along anything I uncover. I realize that Neil and Annie are tight with the Rosado clan. I'll definitely do what I can. Is Brenda helping you out on this one too?"

"Yeah, but she's on duty tonight, so she can't make Sal's. We can probably all get together and compare notes in the next coupla' days though. See you at eight-thirty, dude." Without further ado, Dan switched off his phone, threw it on the passenger seat and fired up the Chevy. It was time to touch base with Eddie at The Surfer Cafe.

Chapter 16

The Baja Connection

Dan hovered over Eddie's workstation at the back of the cafe. You'd be forgiven for believing the boy was a permanent fixture, never going home to change, but Dan noticed that Eddie was wearing a heavy metal tee shirt he hadn't seen before. He hoped that the kid turned up at school once in a while. A high school diploma would probably be a minimal requirement if he wanted to use his rare talents to make some legitimate coin one day.

As usual, Dan spoke quietly... almost in a whisper. The Surfer attracted too many regulars who'd stick their techy noses in if they overheard anything. These hangers-on could almost taste a challenge and were prone to chasing the lure of easy money. Dan decided to begin with Eddie's update on TriState's shady chop-shop policyholder. "So man, come up with anything on our friend Oakridge and his bogus repair shop?"

Eddie hunched his shoulders and peered into his screen. "I've come across a few points of interest Dan. First, the vans that turn up at his joint seem to return to their warehouses with more stock to log *in* than auto parts delivered to Oakridge. And, please don't ask me why dodgy businesses always seem so hot on blatantly logging shady crap into their inventories. Amateurs just don't realize how easy it is to tap into 'password protected' files! By the way, those delivery trucks are often registered to a company called *'Zenith Transport'* – and guess who owns 28% of that venture? Your valued insured... Oakridge."

Dan had to chuckle. It never ceased to amaze him how brazen cheap crooks could be when they smelled easy cash. "I'm impressed Eddie. So, our boy's branched out beyond chops and occasional legit car repairs?"

Eddie turned from his screen and looked at Dan, pride in his successful investigation reflected in his eyes. "His interests certainly go beyond simple repairs, Dan. And there's more. Zenith's delivery sheets show standard routes out of San Diego with maybe a stop or two, ending up as far inland as El Centro – most often at some company over there called 'MexiCo'. Logs indicate one-day turnarounds... 100 miles inland on Interstate 8 and then straight back to base. These manifests show auto parts going to MexiCo, with return shipments of terra cotta and ceramics. The pots and other crap are indeed delivered to tourist shops, mostly in Old Town, and Zenith repeats this cycle with regularity."

Eddie had *easily* hacked into the firm's most sensitive records... extracting vital data that they surely thought was safely hidden from the tax man. As usual, Dan was impressed. "So Eddie, how about this MexiCo operation? Do they just buy and sell in Southern California?"

"No man. They're also pretty big players across the border. They deliver second-hand parts to loads of auto shops in Baja – trading from as far as Mexicali inland, west to Tijuana and Ensenada. Shipments leave that El Centro warehouse like clockwork, going over the border three days a week. MexiCo trucks are logged crossing to the south at Calexico around four in the afternoon, usually on Mondays, Wednesdays and Fridays."

Eddie hesitated and momentarily averted his eyes before continuing. "There's one more thing Dan. And this little crumb of info will no doubt piss you off. It looks like a 'Rodney Grissom' and a 'Derrick Jackson' each hold a 24% interest in Zenith Transport. I'm still looking for the owners of the remaining 24%. Evidently, the silent partner's share, when combined with Oakridge's 28% stake, constitutes a majority interest. Obviously, your friends' participation could be totally on the up and up, Dan. There's nothing *illegal* about hauling ceramics and auto parts between inland California and the coast. And it doesn't appear to be Zenith's trucks that haul shit over the border."

Dan's mind whirled over Eddie's surprising discovery regarding his buddies. "Well, you're sure as shit right Eddie. This does indeed piss me off – royally! If Rod's implicated, it surely involves the lure of easy 'off the books' money. And Derrick will be his stooge... the big dipshit won't grasp the implications. If you uncover the balance of Zenith's ownership, I'll approach Derrick first and see how he reacts. In the meantime, here's another twenty. Keep workin' on this, even though you've already given me more than enough to cancel coverage on Oakridge's chop shop. As usual, you've done a great job. Thanks man."

He could see that Eddie was struggling to keep that hint of self-satisfaction from peeking through. Dan was, yet again, a satisfied customer, but an *unhappy* one at that. Eddie said, "I'll try to have more for you in the next coupla' days Dan. Should I call you at the office?"

"I probably won't be in for the next few days Eddie, but you can reach me on my cell if you dig anything up. And I'll keep popping in here."

Dan hesitated momentarily and shut his eyes. He tried to regain his composure, but Rod's dodgy dealings were creating a knot in his stomach. His pal was a big boy; an avaricious fuck-up who undoubtedly deserved any crap that came his way. Derrick, on the other hand, was greedy but *naive*, with a great deal to lose if this suspect enterprise blew up in his face. Perhaps their clandestine role in Zenith's dodgy dealings could be buried – or, at worst, negotiated into a minor slap on the wrist – if they bowed out *now*. But their shady trading might connect to smuggling into Mexico. And a federal investigation could quickly expand beyond mundane items like auto parts, even linking into the immense drug trafficking over a porous border. Derrick Jackson didn't need this shit in his life! Dan would put a word in his ear – and soon... but only when he had more facts to hand. He'd try to give Old Lightnin', and even the irrepressible Rod, an opportunity to dodge a nasty bullet.

Before turning to leave, Dan considered his alternatives in the Rosado investigation one last time and decided to tap into Eddie's talents for this primary task as well. He drew near and whispered, "Eddie, I have another assignment for you. It involves the import/export world again, but, for obvious reasons, now I'm praying it's unrelated to Oakridge's dirty dealings. Can you see what you can uncover about another dodgy importer here in San Diego? His name is Manuel Tejada – and his office is meant to be somewhere in Mission Valley, I think. He *may* be mixed up in Benny's murder; it's a long shot. Any known associates of this Tejada could be very useful to me Eddie. But, be *very* cool. We can't afford an e-trail leading back to you on this one. Keep your distance, for sure."

Eddie locked eyes with Dan, clearly excited. "No fears there Dan. You're not speaking to an amateur, you know. Do you have an idea of the name of his company or any of his regular customers?"

"Sorry Eddie, I don't. The following bits of information are probably as useless as tits on a bull, but I know he sometimes hangs out at The Pink Lady strip club on Sports Arena Boulevard... and he's done business with Benny's low-life cousin, a guy who's *also* named Benito Rosado. It's not much to go on, but these scraps may help you to pick up his scent."

Eddie grinned and leaned back into his screen. "I've started jobs with less to go on. I'll get right on it Dan. Thanks again for the twenty."

"I owe you a lot more than that, kid. If you uncover anything on Tejada, let me know pronto, okay? It might just break things open on Benny's murder if we luck out. You can reach me on my cell – anytime at all. See you soon, take care!"

Dan felt more than a little uneasy as he left the cafe. He knew better than to drag an innocent kid into an ugly situation, but he had so little to go on! He hoped this was a chance worth taking.

The finest burgers on the beach

Dan was already seated in Sal's cocktail lounge when Vince Parelli
sauntered in. Dan ordered him a Corona without asking and told
Tommy, the bartender, they'd head through to their table when it was
ready. Tommy nodded and set Vince's long-necked bottle, with no beer
glass, in front of the stool next to Dan's. The FBI agent sat down,
smiled and tipped his bottleneck towards Dan in thanks.

"Don't get too comfortable," "Dan said. "Our table awaits, señor."

Sal's was a Mission Beach institution, set a block up from the
waterfront's crowded pedestrian promenade for as long as Dan could
remember. It was a hangout for young professionals, as well as the
scruffier beach crowd. Sal's interior was set off by split redwood
paneling and indirect lighting – and their menu remained firmly
entrenched in the sixties. They didn't do 'trendy'. An ancient storefront
entrance led straight into the cocktail bar, reserved for adults. A short
corridor led to a roomier 'family area'. This dining room had red
leatherette booths running down two sides and wooden tables in the
middle, all dimly lit by fairy lights strung around the low plaster
ceiling. The walls' redwood panels were nearly devoid of
ornamentation, save for a few photos of Mission Beach in the forties
(when the building had housed the local butcher and a neighboring
bakery).

Sal's was still family run. Daughter Gina had been waiting tables
and supervising for over two decades. She still wore the obligatory
Hawaiian shirt and jeans, never seeming to age. On occasion, her
brother, Tom Senior, tended bar. But these days it was more often his
son, Tommy, serving the drinks. Gina's oldest brother, Sam, ran the
kitchen with an iron hand. He prepared unaltered family recipes in the
time-honored way. Papa Sal was at least eighty now – and customers
rarely saw him anymore. Gina said the old man came in just often
enough to keep the new help on their toes – and his long-suffering
offspring pissed off.

Sal's seafood and pasta were terrific. Their steaks were carefully
selected prime cuts, prepared to perfection. They offered a selection of
mouthwatering homemade sauces... no extra charge. But, the *piece de
resistance* was their heavenly burger. Ordered medium rare by San
Diego aficionados, it was unfussy pure beef on a bun, impeccably
prepared. The 'half-pounder' was a meal in itself. It really required
nothing more than a side salad and maybe a healthy slab of Cheddar or
Swiss. Regulars knew that while Sal's chips were homemade and

delicious, their huge baked potatoes, topped with garlic butter or sour cream, were the sublime complement to any main course.

Vince and Dan walked through to their booth after ordering another Dos Equis and Corona to go with their cheeseburgers and Caesar Salads. Gina didn't even offer menus… she knew the drill.

Vince took a pull on the remains of his first beer and slouched back in his seat. "First, let's get the formalities out of the way. Are you going to be our softball 'ringer' again this year? Playing for the Feds must be the highlight of your pathetic existence, dude – particularly since I'll have to wangle you another coveted 'Federal Subcontractor' ID card."

"Sure man, count me in. If I didn't play shortstop for you guys, every soft grounder would dribble through your porous infield for an automatic hit. I'm getting old, but I can still cover some ground!"

With the mundane business out of the way, Dan pulled out his notepad, hoping to get through their true primary dinner topic before the food arrived. "Come up with anything on our pal, Manny Tejada?"

"Nothing in *our* files Dan. But the Border Patrol and Customs guys know this asshole pretty well. He's sure as shit dirty, but they've never caught him with his hand in the cookie jar." Vince pulled his own notebook from a coat pocket and flipped back a page or two. "Here's the paltry scoop so far: Tejada's office is at 4700 Camino del Rio North. He lives in a pricey stucco pile on Hacienda Heights – a swanky cul-de-sac in Mission Hills – number 5020 to be exact. He's lived there two years… quietly. There's no previous address on file. That's everything so far. Fuck-all, I'm afraid."

Dan shook his head and took a long pull on his Dos Equis. "Nonsense Vince. It's useful just to confirm that Tejada seems to maintain a low profile – and to finally learn *exactly* where he lives and works. My other sources hadn't even come up with that much yet. He's been courting one red-hot little stripper from The Pink Lady, but even she didn't seem to know his home or business addresses – or at least she wouldn't share them. Probably he keeps his playmates clear of his turf."

"What's his connection with Benny's murder?"

"Let's keep this between us for now, okay? Tejada's a known associate of Benito Rosado. I don't mean *Benny* by the way; Benito's his rat-ass cousin, who's seemingly taken a powder since the murder. There may be no connection between the button men and Tejada's crew, but Benny's family think the timing of Cousin Benito's disappearance is peculiar. And he's the only person in the Rosado clan who habitually attracts lowlifes like flies on shit."

"So, you think that Benny might just have been in the wrong place at the wrong time, caught up in some sort of vendetta aimed at his lowlife cousin? I think I'll run a background check on Benito Rosado as well."

"Thanks Vince. It could be something like you're describing. Benny was almost assuredly tailed to the Chula Vista job site where the hit went down... so he didn't exactly walk into this by pure chance. It's possible he may have been *mistakenly* fingered for the hit at some earlier point – and Manny Tejada may just know how the wrong Rosado cousin bought the farm."

Vince nodded and suggested a transparently self-serving course of action. "Brenda may uncover something I can't find on Benito or Tejada. Let's get together later in the week and we can all compare notes."

Gina arrived with their burgers; right on cue it seemed, as they'd covered everything on Manny and Cousin Benito. "Okay Vince, I'll set something up. I'm sure Brenda will be happy to meet up with us – and then I can make a hasty exit after we compare notes on these two bums; but only if that suits you, Mr Romeo."

"What do you mean, man?" Vince tried to put on an incredulous look after Dan's insensitive remark concerning his theoretical wish that 'the old third wheel' might leave two very professional law enforcement colleagues on their own.

Dan had to smile. "I *mean* that this is a perfectly legitimate reason for Brenda, you and me to get together. And if the two of you linger over a drink after I take off, so be it. I can't understand why you're getting so upset!"

Dan could swear, even in Sal's subdued lighting, that Vince had gone a little red. "Fuck you Paige – just for that, I'm *definitely* making you pay for tonight's meal."

Dan chuckled. "No biggie dickhead, you knew I was going to anyway."

They both laughed and their conversation drifted back to baseball... the upcoming (probably dismal) season for the Padres and the prospects for Vince's *'Federales'* fast-pitch softball team – Civil Servants' League Champions three years running.

Unwinding with Vince was easy and enjoyable... no need to fend off the sort of macho bullshit that emanated from Rod when they hung out. And they certainly weren't pestered by fans or hangers-on... a near certainty when he was out on the town with Derrick. They took their time and finished off with an Irish Coffee in the bar, listening to The

Talking Heads and watching the end of another pre-season ball game (sound muted) on the TV behind the bar.

Dan arrived home at eleven and put in a late-night call to Sophie. It wasn't unusual for the two of them to have a short chat before heading off to bed. In fact, she seemed to worry if he *didn't* call her most nights. Dan hoped that he'd be seeing her soon. "Can you have dinner with me tomorrow night, Sophs? I could really use some relaxation time with you. This case seems to be all dead ends."

Sophie seemed to pause ever so slightly before answering tentatively, "I'm going out tomorrow night with the kids to the new Thai restaurant in Encinitas... want to join us?"

Dan was so desperate to see her that he almost agreed, before thinking better of it. "I'll take a rain check. Let's not push our luck on the Jason front right now. How about this weekend?"

Sophie giggled mischievously; there had to be something she was about to spring on him. "You're in luck there Dan. I've got great seats to the Symphony on Sunday evening if you'd like to go."

Obviously, this was some charity do... he could tell from her flippant tone. "Sounds great, I'd love it. How about an early meal in Horton Plaza and then on to the concert?"

Taken aback, Sophie answered, "It's a date then... try to push the boat out and wear your best suit and a nice tie." (Translated: "Wear something decent; we'll be chatting up the great and the good.")

"For you, anything! I'll even forego my favorite white socks and shine my only pair of lace-up shoes. Do you want me to buy you a corsage?"

Sophie had to laugh out loud; Dan was letting her know that he realized he was being roped into another formal – and undoubtedly stuffy – night with her charity friends and associates. She cooed, "Be still my heart! No white socks and loafers...this is beginning to sound like a bona fide heavy date!"

Dan hadn't worn white socks with a tie since the eighth grade. He knew that he could, in fact, scrub up pretty well when required to do so. "I love spending our quiet time together Sophs – just the two of us – but if you want to get out more often, nothing would please me more. It's an ego booster when envious onlookers wonder how a jerk like me ever managed to attract a hottie like you. You didn't insist, but I may even go whole hog on this occasion and wear my tux!"

Sophie laughed again down the line. "Goodnight charmer. Pick me up at six on Sunday, so that we can enjoy that relaxing meal in town. I'll make a pre-concert dinner reservation at The Renaissance. Don't be late."

Dan chuckled as he hung up. He considered trying to reach Brenda again, but decided against it. She'd be in the middle of a shift. And, she'd certainly get back to him quickly when and if she had something to share on Benny's hit or the mysterious Mr Tejada.

He turned on 'CNN Late Night' and caught up with the latest on the 'Governator's' newest tax initiatives for California, a state still careening on the brink of insolvency. What was this – Round Seven in the State Legislature's 'Imperative Initiatives' rollout? Everyone seemed to have an easy answer... and no one appeared to have a viable solution. Sometimes Dan felt like California was becoming his generation's newest and greatest albatross, replacing America's all-too-familiar burdens from 'The Old South'. What was it the majestic Neil Young had sung? *"You've got the rest of the Union to help you along..."* wasn't it? Go to the head of that illustrious class California!

Chapter 17

Friday

A new day

As he slowly rolled out of bed, Dan was certain a strenuous run would help clear his head. He needed milk anyway – and no doubt Mrs. Getz could use fresh provisions. If he didn't run the occasional errand for the old lady, she'd be perpetually pouring milk on her porridge that more closely resembled cottage cheese.

Twenty minutes later he trotted back, a plastic bag suspended from each hand. Equally weighted for balance, each bag held two tall cans of 'Kitty King Quality Feast' and a quart of milk, as well as canned soup and pasta for his cupboard. Luckily, the KwikMart was well stocked with the cat's preferred repast, Breast of Chicken. If Dan purchased another flavor (or, God forbid, settled for an alternative brand – even an equally expensive one) Pooky and Mrs. Getz were prone to throwing simultaneous hissy fits. He hoped, no doubt in vain, that little 'Pookums' would reward this timely breakfast delivery by *not* taking the usual smelly dump on his hesitant benefactor's doorstep.

After dropping off his neighbor's provisions and grabbing a shower, Dan sped through his phone calls. First up was Detective Lopez. The sole news was the coroner's relatively speedy release of Benny's body, as requested by the diocese and the family. The autopsy results were cut and dried. As suspected, the .22 slugs lodged in his frontal lobe had done their job very effectively. The bullets, vital evidence if a weapon was ever recovered, had been examined and logged. Dan was relieved Benny's funeral wouldn't be delayed... a blessing for Connie and the family. Gunnar had mentioned the back-up plan was a memorial service, followed by a small family funeral later on, if Benny's body couldn't be immediately released.

Dan moved on to his next call, a catch-up with Neil and Annie. She seemed to have everything under control now that Saturday's funeral was going ahead. She, Neil and the kids would meet Dan at the church that afternoon, just before Benny's three o'clock service. Dan would only have to swing by to pick up his own family and turn up on time.

When he phoned home, Mandy answered. She and Marty were all set to attend Benny's service, but Sally (no surprise) was bailing out... "Mom says she's too upset to make an appearance." Dan told Mandy to have Marty ready around two, hopefully appropriately dressed. That meant his *only* suit and a dark tie. Dan told her to remind Marty the funeral would begin at three sharp; the mourners certainly wouldn't wait if they were tardy! Mandy sighed, realizing she had her work cut out for her, and they said their goodbyes.

Next he got onto Rod, to confirm plans for Sunday's regatta. Rod sounded pretty jazzed; his big day was looming. "Neil's a no-show Dan – but Lightnin's confirmed that he's back on! And, he's bringing along some of his 'A-List' hotties to help us with the strenuous crewing. Notice I didn't say *'screwing'*, even if that's what was really on the tip of my tongue!" Rod cackled at his own little joke.

Dan let out an audible groan. He'd been looking forward to a little relaxation on the water, as well hoping to fish for information on his buddies' dubious trucking venture. Now their attention would be diverted by a bevy of bimbettes and the regatta could easily turn into one of those tiresome, unproductive mornings.

"I'll be there at nine, Rod, but I won't be entertaining any of your hot crew. As I mentioned before, I might even bring Sophie along if she can make it." On that note, Dan hung up. (The last statement had always been a pure fabrication. But the prospect of Sophie on board might reduce the 'bimbo headcount' and encourage Rod and Derrick to drag along ladies who possessed at least a scrap of decorum.)

Dan's last call was to Walt, up in LA. He tried to stick to work topics. "Everything copasetic at the coal face boss man? I can pop into the office if anything needs my attention."

"Everything's fine and dandy hombre. Don't sweat it. We finally got a full signed confession out of Bob Crossley, our budding thespian and Sea World's occasional whale trainer. His employer seems to be in the clear and not a participant in this little scam. Bob's been canned, of course – and he's filing for bankruptcy. Probably the ex-wife knew he was on the verge of rolling craps when she sent us the clipping. We're unlikely to see any of our money, even if we chase his ass for fraud. We got out pretty cheaply though... it was a very auspicious spot on your part, Dan."

"Well, the fact that I zeroed in on him was more down to his nasty ex-wife than to any perceptiveness on my part. We'd still be shelling out on his bogus claim without her 'good citizen's' tip-off. So, score one for the good guys! To change the subject, I'd like to take next week off as well, if that's okay, Walt. That'll just about run me out of vacation time."

"No problems. If you need some extra days off, just let me know. We're happy to help out any way we can on this one. How's the chase going? Trini told me you hadn't uncovered too much yet?"

"It's going okay, Walt. It's still early days, but I'm onto a couple of leads that could pay dividends. Thanks again for the flexibility on the time off."

"Don't mention it stud."

They hung up and Dan considered, yet again, how lucky he was to work for a guy like Walt. His boss managed to keep everything ship-shape in his Region, without hauling out the dreaded *'TriState Staff Guide'* at every turn. His firm hand on the tiller and easy demeanor produced better results than any asinine 'by the book' methods would ever achieve.

Five minutes later, as he rinsed out his cereal bowl, the phone rang. "Hey Dan, it's Eddie. Remember, you said to let you know *ASAP* if I dug up something interesting on Manny Tejada? Got a pencil and paper?"

Dan dried his hands on his shirt before grabbing the pad and pencil by the phone. "Hang on a second... okay, shoot."

"Tejada's got a trading company registered as 'SoCal Import and Export'. It's at 4700 Camino del Rio North, Suite 124. He lives in Mission Hills; at 5020 Hacienda Heights... he owns the place outright, no mortgage... ever. Here's an interesting tidbit. I found another dummy corporation where he's listed as a director – 'Overture Inc.' it's called. I checked it out and it looks suspiciously like a money laundering set-up... big cash money in and smaller, more frequent, batches of near-cash and pure cash out. And guess who else is listed as a director – from day one – of this outfit? Only San Diego's beloved *Ernest Kincaid, Esquire!*"

The first information was useful, in that it confirmed what Vince had already told him. But that last bit was *dynamite!*

Eddie's work habits were beyond thorough and he seldom forgot anything – or anyone – he'd researched. He'd run a superficial check on Ernest Kincaid for Dan the year before, when Melinda was considering partnering her mentor in a dodgy-sounding real estate enterprise. Dan had warned her that the ex-Mayor's son might not be as principled – or financially stable – as he professed to be. In fact, Eddie had uncovered some alarming warning signs in a straightforward credit check he'd run on Ernest. When Dan gave Melinda the grim news, she feigned offense at his unsolicited intrusion... but he never heard her speak again of the Escondido office development in which she'd been so eager to invest.

Dan didn't like the direction this investigation was taking, but he was pleased with one thing. Eddie's information might help him to finally shift Melinda out of Kincaid's sphere of influence. Why should he care though? He knew it wasn't jealousy or any lingering lust. He decided that he simply wished his ex well – and nothing would change that. Maybe he was growing up a little. An old flame could be a friend… that is, if that was okay with Sophie.

Dan's mind snapped back to the phone conversation. "Keep digging Eddie. That's all very interesting poop so far. If Tejada's dummy company's dealings are indeed grubby, some garbage is bound to rub of on our esteemed Mr. Kincaid. Sometimes I bemoan the fact that, for all its so-called 'cosmopolitan' aspirations, San Diego still suffers from a narrow-minded, small town mentality. When you turn over our city's rocks, the same greedy slime balls and influence peddlers seem to wriggle out. A respected name like 'Kincaid' helps an otherwise evident rogue to paper over a multitude of sins, hiding his true nature from the yokels."

This was the second bit of seemingly serendipitous information Eddie had uncovered in less than a week. First (and worst!), Rod and Derrick might tie into Oakridge's auto parts scamming. How deep had Oakridge, that chop shop lowlife, sunk his talons into his friends? Now, a slime trail appeared to connect Manny Tejada to the esteemed Ernest Kincaid. Dan asked himself, not for the first time: Am I simply a trouble magnet, attracting hassles like flies on crap? Or am I, in my dotage, finally recognizing the unholy amount of shit that generally floats around, even in my petty little world?

Eddie was still on the line, presently addressing Dan's point about San Diego's avariciousness and provincial mentality. His insight belied his tender years. "Well Dan, whether you see us as a biggish town or smallish city, San Diego attracts greedy bastards from both sides of the border. *Dollars* seem to be the common language and adults behave pretty badly when money's at stake. For people like Mr Kincaid, once they've lived the high life, they don't want to let go."

As Dan hung up, he contemplated yet again how invaluable this switched-on kid would be to any number of investigations or business negotiations. The boy had more brains and intuition that most cops Dan had come across. Downing his last sip of coffee, he referred to his case notes and decided to add a few entries. There was little in the way of *verifiable* new information, but he could pencil in a few thoughts, gleaned from his chats with Winter (who he still preferred to think of as the lovely, naïve Carrie), slippery Cousin Benito and, of course, the stellar Eddie.

Under **'MOTIVE'**, he added…

Mistaken identity angle… has this the ring of truth?

Cousin Benito in deep shit with some nasty enemies – drugs?

Linking Benny's murder to Benito wasn't a slam-dunk, but there was mileage in this line of enquiry. Benito's behavior was suspect and his known associates fit into Dan's sense of the direction this case was taking. He jotted down a few new comments...

COUSIN BENITO
Twitchy and distant – what's he got to hide?
Tied into Tejada – and they're not just importing ceramic pots and knick-knacks
Winter's probably not in the loop, but she's pollen to a pair of killer bees - Benito and Tejada

Dan jotted down a few more lines about Manny himself...

TEJADA

What's his scam? No doubt drugs involved – anything else?

Not _the man_, but significant – somewhere up the food chain in one of the major cartels?

He runs Benito, but on a loose lead

Why is Cousin Benito's tit in a wringer with Manny?

And as for Ernest Kincaid, what Eddie had discovered thus far was a *bit* surprising... even for this oily slice of old money...

ERNEST KINCAID ESQ
Can Melinda help me out here? Can she be trusted?

Do the dots really connect from Benito > to Tejada > to Kincaid?
Where and how do Kincaid's and Tejada's business interests intersect?

Reviewing his updated notes, Dan was certain he'd uncovered a few itchy scabs, ripe for the picking. Maybe something would break loose if he got in these guys' faces. As usual, his MO would include feigning greater knowledge with his suspects than he possessed. He'd start with the trio's common denominator – Manny Tejada. But, this lowlife was cagey, and a true unknown quantity. He'd no doubt been around long enough to know how to sustain a cool exterior and give little away. On second thought, it might initially pay dividends to burrow into Manny's connection to Kincaid – and start from the top. If the devious businessman knew *anything* about the murder, he could be an easier nut to crack.

But, in the end, Dan flip-flopped and decided that his first stop should be at Manny Tejada's office after all. If there *was* a connection between Benny's murder and Cousin Benito's timorous demeanor, the shifty importer was likely to be the hard man stirring this particular shit stick. Interrogating him was as good a place to start as any.

Down in the Valley

It was a short hop down to Mission Valley and Camino del Rio North. Dan walked up to Manny's reception desk just after eleven. A peroxide blonde, who obviously spent her free time basting her face and exquisite body in Hawaiian Tanning Oil, glanced up from a movie magazine to greet him. Her silk blouse looked expensive enough; but, probably intentionally, a tad undersized for her ample bosom. She'd been totally immersed in a gossip columnist's finely tuned assessment of George Clooney's latest squeeze, so she was ill-prepared for the interruption. But, she put on a welcoming smile after scoping out her dishy visitor.

"Good morning sir. And just how can I help *you* today?"

Dan switched on his highest megawatt babe-melting grin. "And good morning to you, young lady! I have an appointment with Mr Tejada concerning some computer components he's exporting for us. Would you announce me please? My name is Henry Hudson."

A puzzled look came over the receptionist's china doll face. "I'm so sorry Mr Hudson, but Mr Tejada isn't expected back until late this afternoon." She clicked the diary icon on her screen and confirmed to herself that there were no 'meeting' entries for prospective customers, including a 'Henry Hudson'. "I don't seem to see your appointment here. I'm so sorry."

In spite of himself, Dan was rather enjoying the view down the front of her overburdened blouse. "Oh? Well, I phoned late the other evening and he answered himself. We agreed to meet this morning. He must have neglected to enter it in the office diary."

The blonde cracked a broad smile, displaying a hint of crimson lipstick on a highly whitened front tooth. "Can I have your card Mr

Hudson? I'll tell Mr Tejada that you stopped by and he can phone you to rearrange your meeting."

"No need, doll. I'm down from Santa Barbara for the next few days and he'll be unable to reach me at my office until the middle of next week. I'll give you my cell number though." Dan proceeded to spit out a convincing series of random digits – and the blonde dutifully bent towards her notepad to write the number down, exhibiting an even more enticing view of lacy bra and bodacious cleavage.

"If you're going to be in town tonight anyway Mr Hudson, you might check back around five. Mr Tejada often turns up just before closing time. I think it's a good bet he'll pop by tonight, because he's meant to be away on vacation all next week. And if he doesn't turn up, it needn't be a *complete* waste of your time. I'll be happy to be your host and guide for an evening here in San Diego. I'll take you to a great spot where the happy hour drinks are scrummy and *potent* – and the food isn't at all bad either. It's no fun being stuck on your own on a business trip. If you can make it, I'm Bonnie, by the way."

"Hey, Bonnie's a really nice, old-fashioned name. I'll probably take you up on that offer Bonnie! It sounds like a solid plan, whether Mr Tejada returns or not. And by the way, call me Hank... my dad was called Henry or Mr Hudson, not me! Maybe you can help me out a bit here, doll. I've never dealt with Mr Tejada before, but he comes highly recommended. Where are his main trading markets? Is most of his business up and down from Mexico, or do you trade in the Far East as well?"

"I'm kinda' new here, Hank, but it seems that most deliveries are back and forth to TJ or Mexicali. And he sells stuff to a couple of regulars up in LA too, so it's not all exports. Many of our transactions involve electronics, so I'm sure we can handle your requirements."

Dan felt he'd squeezed everything he could out of the luscious, and oh-so-cooperative, Bonnie. "Well, thanks for the tip doll. I'll stop by around five then. Don't tell Mr Tejada I popped in, if you speak to him before then. To tell you the truth, I'd rather catch him off guard for our initial negotiations anyway – an element of surprise usually gives me a modest edge. I'll let you in on a little secret Bonnie. I told him I'd stop by this week, but I didn't exactly have an appointment for this *specific* time. And now that we're better acquainted, I'm sure you're right; stopping by this evening won't be a wasted trip, regardless!"

As he crossed the parking lot, Dan wondered whether Bonnie would tell Tejada he'd popped in if he did come back to his office. Even if she spilled the beans, he was pretty sure Manny wouldn't connect some prospective customer called Henry Hudson with a still low-key murder investigation.

Dan knew one thing for sure… an initial interrogation couldn't wait if Manny was going on a week's vacation. Anyway, it might be more effective to catch him off guard at home over the weekend – say, late tomorrow evening, after Benny's funeral. At worst, he'd nose around Tejada's house and neighborhood. And, with luck, he might even get past the door and extract some unguarded answers from the shady exporter. He could spin some bullshit about how he was assisting a worried Rosado clan in their search for Benito – and someone had loosely connected Manny to the missing man. He might fluster the low-life and prod him into a mistake. It would all depend on just how tough – and alert – Winter's secret boyfriend would be on his home turf… that is, if he were even home and receiving visitors.

So, now he'd head into TriState for a pit stop and then head home to unwind before tomorrow's dreaded funeral. He wished he'd be seeing Sophie on Saturday night, rather than making a long-shot house call on Manny Tejada. Sunday evening seemed an eternity away.

Chapter 18

Saturday

A poignant morning

Dan and his siblings arrived at National City's Catholic Church in good time, parking across the street in front of some shabby duplexes. Dan spotted Gunnar Morales stationed on the church's steps, acknowledging mourners as they arrived. Benny's boys would no doubt arrive a bit later, accompanying their mother and their *mama grande*, Hortensia.

The church's lawn was home to a celebrated San Diego landmark. A ten-foot plaster statue of a beneficent Jesus, freshly whitewashed and standing on a faux-marble plinth, greeted worshippers as they arrived. His arms were outstretched, in welcome and benediction – but his hands were missing. They'd been lopped off years before by a gang of vandals, who'd never been apprehended. A wise parish priest elected to turn the other cheek and convey a profound Christian moral in this senseless act. He declared that Christ's hands would not be repaired or replaced. Instead, a message was engraved into the plinth. It simply stated to all who approached: *"The only hands I have are yours."*

This clear-cut illustration of hope and forgiveness made the national news. It ushered in a renaissance for this struggling parish in a gang-infested neighborhood – and, miraculously, local kids began to display a new respect for the church and its parishioners. Nowadays, Father Riordan was the beneficiary of his predecessor's wise decision. His well-honed sermons – buttressed by a plaster Savior with severed limbs and a passionate choir – attracted 'standing room only' attendances at most Sunday Masses.

As he and his siblings walked opposite the church, Dan noticed an outlandish purple low-rider parked on their side of the street. It was facing in the wrong direction and encroaching into the crosswalk. The aging rust-bucket sported gaudy green racing stripes. The two men slouched in the car weren't mourners. They were dressed casually and looking ill at ease. The driver was porky and unkempt, a cigarette dangling from his mouth.

These goons had apparently turned up early to commandeer this prominent viewing spot. Leaning back, eyes half closed, both were attempting to feign disinterest. But, Dan could see that they were intent on watching everyone arrive. He quickly memorized the Pontiac's plate number; a skill retained from his past life.

140

He'd love to roust these turkeys, but this obviously wasn't the time or place. Brenda would run the plate number for him later. And as there wasn't a snowball's chance that this worthless heap of shit was stolen, he might even catch a break on an owner's name and address. Anyway, Gunnar might be able to put names to these assholes right away – or Benito might do it later. The flogged Firebird was a true one-off.

Across the street, Annie, Neil and the kids were rounding the corner and approaching the front steps of the church. As Dan, Mandy and Marty crossed at the corner, he heard Gunnar telling them that Connie seemed to be in fair shape; the boys were dutifully looking after her. Gunnar hadn't seen Hortensia yet... apparently she'd only come up from Tijuana that morning, accompanied by some of her other grandchildren.

Gunnar waved to Dan and pulled him over for a quiet word. "Run across Benito yet Dan? I know Hortensia hopes he'll turn up today, but I doubt he'll show his face."

Although he felt a pang of guilt, Dan kept his promise to Cousin Benito. "I'm looking for him Gunnar – and I have a couple of leads. By the way, do you recognize those two greasers across the street in the low-rider?"

Gunnar gave the beat-up Pontiac a long stare. "No Dan, but they're certainly weird looking shitbirds to be hanging out in front of a funeral service. I'll ask the boys about them when I see them."

"Thanks Gunnar. I'll call you tomorrow." They left Gunnar to his duties and entered the church. The three Paiges sat in the back, in space created as the earlier arrivals squeezed along. Obviously, the service would be full to overflowing. Dan was grateful that no TV crews were hovering out front. Obviously, the news vultures had moved on to another unsolved murder or political scandal.

Meanwhile, across the street, Jesus gripped the steering wheel and lifted one cheek off the driver's seat, cutting loose a resounding fart. He grunted with pleasure. Flaco lit a match and disgustedly blew it out, inhaling the resulting smoke. A pile of spent matchsticks grew exponentially at his feet. "Cut that out you fuckin' *chavalita*... I'm tellin' you for the last time! And keep your eyes peeled for Benito. Mr Tejada said he's almost certain to show – and today we can't afford to lose him! This time, that little shit's going to be in our sights to become dead meat soon after we catch up to him."

Jesus irritably screwed his gloved fist into the palm of his left hand and then pushed his grimy straw hat to the back of his head. "I ain't no brain Flaco, but that don't give you the right to call me pussy names out loud. But, think about it... even *I* wouldn't turn up at no funeral if hard-asses like us was on my tail. Benito's long gone, man – and we're screwed and tattooed with that asshole Tejada. I think if we vamoose for El Paso *before* the boss runs out of patience, we'd be makin' a righteous move."

Flaco gave his partner a sideways glance. "Stay cool *carnal* – there's every chance Benito ain't even made the connection between his cousin's hit and our *jefe*. Tejada's giving us a second chance, so keep your fuckin' eye on the ball!"

Jesus leaned back in the driver's seat, undid his belt buckle and zipped the fly on his worn leather trousers halfway down. A layer of loose flab erupted into the exposed area. "Look man, we tried that cantina down in TJ again – no luck. And he's steering clear of The Pink Lady. At least Enrique will reimburse us for the dough we spread around at the strip club... not our worst assignment ever. Benito's either gone, *muchacho* – or he's lying very low."

Flaco turned and hissed, "The cash we blew was supposed to be spread around *all* the strippers and the sad-assed customers hanging out at that pussy bar! Your share was gone in ten minutes, wasted on two bitches who wouldn't recognize Benito if they were gyratin' their muffs in his face while you were speakin' to them!"

Jesus reached into his unzipped trousers with his gloveless hand and gave his *cajones* a generous scratching. "This stakeout's a real waste of time. Everyone's gone in and they won't be back out for an hour. I'm hungry *vato*. Can we go get us some lunch?"

"I just told you to keep an eye peeled for Benito idiot! He's likely to arrive *late*, if he turns up at all. We ain't wastin' time if we're doin' the work we're told to. Besides, every day we keep our noses clean is another day for Tejada to put our embarrassin' little fuck-up further out of mind." The smaller man sat back, silent for a minute or two before he spoke again. "But, there's no denying it. I'm hungry too, amigo. Run down to that corner shop and buy us some sandwiches and a six-pack. But make it snappy, okay?"

Jesus started to straighten up, but stopped short. "Hold it! Check out the fucker in the shiny black suit slidin' into the church with the old lady."

Flaco turned his head and stared at the entrance. "Good spottin' bro, but that guy's too young to be Benito – and he must be over six feet. There's a shitload of beaners and family gonna' turn up just before the service starts. There's bound to be a 'Benito lookie-likie' or two. Takin' out the wrong dude is how our tits ended up in Tejada's wicked wringer in the first place, so I'm makin' sure we zero in on the right hombre this time."

142

"Right *carnal*, so what kind of sandwich do you want?" Jesus flipped his cigarette butt out of the window, opened the door and gestured to Flaco to hand over some lunch money as he zipped up his fly.

So long, Benny

Hortensia was indeed last to arrive, accompanied by one of her many grandsons. The pair walked to the front row and found seats with the family just as Father Riordan began to lead the congregation in prayer. The church was overrun with flowers – including wreaths and arrangements from a number of Benny's long-time customers. Many featured the subtle desert blooms Benny himself had favored in his work.

Family members sat close to Benny's ornate open coffin. Dan hadn't viewed the body, but he knew that cosmeticians could work wonders with entry wounds, as long as they hadn't been produced by large caliber weapons or hollow point rounds. Benny Rosado would probably go to his grave resembling an eerie waxworks double of himself... almost as if a mannequin had been assigned to take this final journey in his stead.

Dan had never seen so many tiny, wizened old ladies in one place, all covered head to toe in black. The prayer ended and the assemblage went quiet. Muffled sobs emanated from many of the women sitting near Hortensia. Connie sat dry-eyed – her elder sons to her left and Greg and Gunnar on her right. The altar shimmered with a forest of burning tapers... more than Dan would ever have imagined the space could accommodate. He reflected on the possible fire hazard, but obviously the church had this part of the ritual down to a science.

While Dan listened intermittently, Father Riordan tried to pay justice to the exceptional man they were mourning. No one else rose to speak. After what seemed like an eternity – actually forty minutes or so – Gunnar led the pallbearers over to the polished ebony coffin and closed the lid. Eight men, including Victor and Omar, slowly carried Benny through the double front doors and down the front stairway, sliding the coffin into the back of a waiting hearse. Gregorio accompanied Connie and his grandmother outside, while Father Riordan thanked those in attendance and requested that they honor the family's wishes to limit the service at the cemetery to close family.

As Dan emerged with his sister and brother, he spotted the garish low-rider, still parked across the street. Both men had tossed their cellophane sandwich wrappers on the dash and were staring intently, foregoing any attempt at disinterest, as Benny's mourners exited.

Even Marty noticed that the incongruous duo in the old junker hadn't moved on. He whispered to Dan, "Hey bro, those dudes are still up to no good. They're sticking out like that proverbial turd in the punchbowl."

"Yeah bro, I've got them spotted. As I said, I've memorized their plate and I'll be onto Brenda. In fact, if you guys'll wait here a minute, I'm going to stir them up a bit."

Dan strode across the street, sauntered up to the passenger window and leaned into the car. He noisily cleared his throat and asked, "Hey boys, can I help you with something? Do you know you're parked half-way into the crosswalk?"

The passenger – maybe a bit of a Steve Tyler double, but with darker skin and shorter hair than the craggy rocker – just grinned and stared. "Thanks for pointing that out man. We're just finishing our lunch break and we're about to leave." As the last of the mourners filed out, the Firebird's engine coughed and turned over. They swung into oncoming traffic as they crossed to the proper side of the road, ran the prominent stop sign and rolled straight into the busy intersection. They accelerated noisily away – in full view of the idling hearse and a number of bemused mourners.

When Dan returned to his siblings, Mandy clearly remained uneasy. "Who were those two morons, Dan?"

"I don't know hon. But, I'll tell you one thing, they weren't even *trying* to blend in. Either they're genuinely unconnected to Benny or Benito – or they're the most clueless stake-out artists I've ever come across." He pulled out his cell phone and tried Brenda. She didn't reply, but he left a message with the plate number and told his old partner to try to reach him after she'd had a chance to run it.

Neil and Annie finished chatting with other parishioners and strolled over. Annie looked as drawn and exhausted as Dan had ever seen her. And, low and behold, strolling just behind them, accompanying their kids, was Melinda. Dan hadn't noticed his ex in the church. He stifled a malicious and admittedly unwarranted notion about Melinda exploiting *any* opportunity to hand out her business cards and thought to himself that she undoubtedly possessed a barely detectable lovable side, visible if you searched intently.

Neil grabbed Dan's elbow. "Some of us are going over to Connie's around six. I think Gunnar and the boys would particularly appreciate seeing you there. Can you make it?"

"Sure, I'll drop off Mandy and Marty in OB and meet you guys down there."

Melinda spoke for the first time. "That's okay Dan. I can drop them off on my way home. It saves you the trip up to Ocean Beach and back... you go straight to Neil and Annie's place and rest up a bit."

Mandy smiled and stepped towards Melinda. "That's very kind of you. It's not too far out of your way is it?"

"Not at all Mandy. I'm dropping into my La Jolla office on the way home anyway, so I'll just take the scenic beach route up to there. It'll be nice." It was all settled – and Dan could look forward to a little respite.

When they arrived at Neil's, Annie put Carol King's 'Tapestry' on their old Dual turntable. She still preferred preserved vinyl and gigantic speakers, but on this occasion, she dampened the volume. Neil made a pot of coffee. Dan used the quiet time to catch up with them. Brenda hadn't phoned, but that wasn't surprising. It could take time check out a license number, even in this day of computers – and there was a chance this particular license plate would be on a stolen list, belonging to a different car.

Just after six, the three of them headed out in two cars. Dan still intended to visit Manny at his Mission Hills home later that evening – or to at least familiarize himself with the lay of the land. He'd be leaving Connie's place well before Neil and Annie.

Gunnar took Dan aside as soon as they arrived. "Dan, no offense, but can you give me a quick and dirty rundown and then head out? I don't want the boys getting riled and bouncing any half-assed ideas off you this evening. It's better if they stay cool and help Hortensia and Connie get through the rest of this miserable day."

Dan nodded his agreement. "No offense taken man. I was pretty much on that very wavelength myself. Annie will be a help here, but I'm happy to say my hellos, offer my commiserations and beat a hasty retreat."

Dan pulled his case notes from his pocket and methodically ran through the sparse facts he could share with Gunnar. "I've got a lead on a guy named Manny Tejada who runs a so-called import/export business – and he smells as dirty as they come. Ever heard of him?"

Gunnar thought for a second before replying, "No Dan. How does he tie in?"

"Well, he's a KA – sorry, that's a 'known associate' – of Benito's. And I've tentatively tied his activities into another 'silent partner' and moneyman, a guy who's fairly prominent locally. I've got to keep that name on ice, even from you, for now. He may be a blind alley, but

Tejada's the best suspect I've uncovered so far, for what can best be described as a poorly planned and executed murder."

Gunnar leaned in and whispered, "This will flip you out Dan. Guess who slipped over the back fence forty-five minutes ago – in his sharpest suit and tie? *Benito*, in the flesh! He paid his condolences to Connie and spent a few minutes with Hortensia. I had a hard time keeping Omar and Vic away. I managed by promising them that I'd get his address, so *you* could follow up with him. By the time I turned around from my chat with the boys though, Benito had already high-tailed it back over the fence. Slick on his part – and ballsy, I'd say."

"Did he say anything interesting to the ladies?" Dan was yet again tempted to tell Gunnar where Benito was hiding, but thought better of it. Benny's boys were loose cannons and withholding this morsel from them might sorely test Gunnar's usually solid resolve.

"He told Connie he'd no idea why his cousin should end up in harm's way and promised her he was doing his best to look into it. He emphasized that the hit most assuredly had *nothing* to do with him – and his clandestine investigations were turning into a full-time thing; hence, his recent low profile. When we noticed he'd taken off, the boys ran around to the next street, intent on grabbing him. But he was long gone."

Dan frowned and shook his head before returning to the subject of their strange gawkers at the funeral. "Did you ask the boys about those greasers in the low-rider across from the church?"

"Yeah, I did Dan. They got a good look at the pair, but they didn't recognize them either. I think they're probably fairly new blood around here – and, definitely, not on the up and up."

"Okay Gunnar, I'll get back to you tomorrow morning. Then I'll be taking a couple of hours off to do some sailing with Rod Grissom. Remember him? After that, I'll be chasing down some possible leads on Manny's unnamed silent partner. The guy's probably a dead end though, particularly since he's sure to have played his cards very close to his chest. He may be dirty – and he may bear some share of the blame. But, unlike Tejada, this particular businessman probably wouldn't have a clue on how to seek out and hire serious button men."

With that, Dan waved across the room to Neil and beat that hasty retreat. His abrupt leave taking would no doubt appear rude to some of the mourners, but he was sure Gunnar would invent a palatable excuse that would at least placate Connie and the boys. Besides, the family surely had more significant things to worry about than the suitability of Dan's flying visit.

Chapter 19

A disagreeable evening in old Mission Hills

After changing out of his suit, Dan heated a can of corned beef hash, toasted and buttered some stale bread and half-watched a couple of atrocious prospective 'entertainers' on a schlocky show called 'America's Brightest New Stars'. He'd selected a dark outfit suited to a bit of low key snooping – slacks, a windbreaker and a new pair of black leather Converse All Stars. Once he'd arrived at Tejada's, he could switch to his trusty old Harris Tweed sportcoat if he felt okay about boldly walking up and ringing the bell.

Dan washed the dishes that had been lying in the sink for a couple of days and headed out, tiptoeing by Mrs Getz's door. Her living room light was still on and he wasn't in the mood for inane conversations or last-minute shopping requests.

Around nine-thirty, he pulled up near the end of Manny's dead-end street in Mission Hills. Thirties-style stucco piles dominated the neighborhood, with a couple of newer builds mixed in for good measure. The street's occupants were no doubt loaded... nearly every house featured a gate and security fence. Aptly named 'Hacienda Heights', the diminutive avenue's parking strips had long ago been planted with rows of eucalyptus trees. The potent, medicinal smell of their foliage permeated the evening air.

He quietly closed his car door and ambled towards the end of the cul-de-sac, casually reading the house numbers painted on the curb as he went. When he reached the street's semicircular turnaround, the second number into it was Tejada's. With his gaze diverted to curb level, he practically bumped into an object that came as little surprise. The distinctive purple Firebird he couldn't fail to recognize was parked near Manny's front gate!

Well, I'll be damned, he thought, as he felt the Pontiac's hood to see if the engine was still warm. *Manny's* greaseballs were checking out Benny's funeral today – and I'll bet fifty grand that they're reporting in at this very minute! There's no chance of him inviting me in for a quiet chat tonight.

As usual, the excrement appeared to be flowing as one would predict: inexorably *downhill*... from Manny to the two stooges in the Pontiac – and probably even further down the slippery slope to the Rosado cousins. It was all too cozy to put down to coincidence. He might be on track and starting to connect the right dots – and the picture was unmistakably turning into a sloppy murder botched by a pair of inept button men. He'd have a theory to share with Lopez and Knowles in the morning.

The wrought iron gate to Manny's driveway was locked. A small security camera, set unobtrusively into the top of its adjoining brick fence, swiveled to cover the entire area. Perhaps Manny's security had already picked up his dark-clad presence on the sidewalk. Dan decided to take a calculated risk. Rather than buzzing the bell in the gate and cooking up some cock and bull story about why he was dropping by on a Saturday evening, he'd first settle for a bit of clandestine poking around. He could sneak onto the grounds, grab a peak inside the house and be back out front in a few minutes. He'd announce himself at the gate *only* when and if the two goons left. His sportcoat would stay in the car for now.

He crouched and hugged the perimeter of the fence, moving along the cul-de-sac to the darkest corner of Manny's front garden. He stopped momentarily and listened before tossing a smallish stone over the six-foot wall. *Silence.* He gripped the fence-top railings and quietly pulled himself up. From this vantage point he looked down into a well-manicured yard, which contained few trees or bushes for cover. The front of the house remained dark. He hoisted himself over and jumped down as silently as he could. He was still pretty light on his feet for an old dude, thanks in part to the Converse sneakers, as well as his surfing prowess.

"Oh shit!" he gasped out loud, not five seconds later. Intense panting and pounding paws were fast approaching from his left. These dogs had the run of the yard – or he'd set off some silent alarm and the fast approaching Dobermans had been instantly set loose to respond. The pair had rounded the corner from the back yard almost before he'd taken a step backwards. One dog snarled, stopping three feet short of him. The other shot by, spinning around to cover his back. He could just make out the vicious canine facing him... all teeth, lean and muscular, standing stock-still with the hair on his back rising menacingly.

A powerful flashlight rounded the corner from the direction the dogs had just taken. An indistinct figure behind the beam spoke slowly and deliberately. "Don't move – or I'll give the boys an attack command!"

Dan fought to suppress a basic flight instinct. Instead he attempted a casual pose, hands upturned. "Hello there! I've been invited to a surprise party for my workmate Kyle – and I seem to have popped into the wrong yard. I'm really sorry... I'll just be on my way, okay?"

"Not so fast asshole. Now raise your hands further, so I can see them clearly, and don't move a muscle! I have a gun trained on your forehead and I'll use it!"

Dan thought again of making a break for the fence... for about a millisecond. He raised his hands higher, as instructed – and the dogs were commanded to retreat to the back yard.

Still frozen to the spot, Dan heard more footsteps behind him. The new person grabbed his raised arms, wrenching them painfully behind his back. He was cuffed – far too tightly – and pushed towards the rear of the house. As they moved off, Dan sensed yet another set of footsteps pacing behind him – a third captor. As the group passed by the gruff sentry holding the flashlight, the man stepped off the paved walk and fell in with the others. At this point, Dan could feel a handgun's muzzle being pressed into his back.

They passed a curtained window just prior to rounding the house's back corner. As they stepped into a larger area, Dan noticed a pocket-sized swimming pool sunk into the well-manicured lawn, ten feet to his left. A few more paces brought them to three stone steps leading to open French doors. Dan stumbled on the last step as he was prodded into Manny Tejada's cavernous living room. There were few surprises here... the décor consisted of bulky, rough-hewn wooden furniture and garish oils on velvet. The look was meant to capture 'hacienda chic', but it came off looking cheap and tacky.

As his captors manhandled him into the room, Dan's eyes fixed on a stocky, pockmarked Latino, decked out in what could only be described as a 'vintage' green dressing gown. Dan couldn't help himself... he felt like an overmatched film noire Bogart. Manny Tejada stood behind a large desk near the French doors. Probably in his early fifties, the man's once-fit body was going to fat. Smiling malevolently, he spoke to one of the captors. "Good work Enrique. Frisk him, so we can discover who's dropping in at this unsociable hour." Then he ordered the others, "You two, keep a tight grip on those cuffs. Don't allow our guest any wriggling room!"

Dan still couldn't catch a glimpse of the men behind him, but he assumed that they were the muscleheads he'd confronted at the funeral. Enrique, facing Dan as he searched his pockets, was decked out in some sort of unfashionable, make-do servant's get-up. He quickly extracted Dan's billfold from his trouser pocket, along with the ID wallet and keys from his windbreaker. The peculiar looking manservant handed the items to Tejada, who intently peered at Dan's shield and ID.

"So, Señor Paige, what can I do for you? It's truly a bit late for a social call. By the way, your police ID's long expired. Should you really be carrying around an invalid ID and badge?"

A reedy voice, with a distinct Mexican accent, piped up from behind him. One of Manny's two toadies could actually speak! "He was at the funeral today Mr Tejada. He's the guy that we told you came over and hassled us as everybody was leavin'."

A high-pitched, nearly effeminate, voice chimed in, "Yeah, he wouldn't leave us the fuck alone! He had to tell us how we was parked all wrong. What an asshole!"

While these two losers remained out of view, Dan caught a strong whiff of at least one of them. This dude certainly didn't smell fresh, undoubtedly having given soap and water a body swerve for far too long. Tejada probably kept a fairly loose grip on these underlings – Dan couldn't imagine them coming around his upmarket neighborhood too often.

Manny frowned and again looked past Dan towards his roughhewn subordinates. "Well, Mr Paige's curiosity has certainly gotten the better of him this time boys – and he's landed right in our laps! I'm afraid that now he's become yet another tiresome thread worked loose by your untidy work habits."

Dan decided it would be wise to at least take a shot at calming things down. "I think we've got something to clear up here, Mr Tejada. Truthfully, I'm here because my associates and I were hoping that you could answer a few simple questions concerning Benny Rosado's untimely death. Benny's friends asked me to look at a few people who've been recently connected to his close friend and cousin, Benito Rosado. Your name, amongst others, popped up. So, my pals on the force would like to quickly eliminate you from their lengthy list of suspects – and I was sent around, sort of 'off the record', to have a quiet word in your ear."

Manny shook his head slowly and fixed a stern gaze on his captive. "Mr Paige, minutes ago these boys were telling me, in regard to another matter *entirely*, that they were innocently parked near a funeral service today. So I'm sure you did, indeed, bump into them there. But, I'm in the dark concerning the unfortunate demise of this funeral's primary participant. I'd be interested to know why you, the cops or even Benito Rosado's so-called 'friends' think they want to speak to *me*. I'm sure I don't know how I fit into all of this."

Dan decided to stir the shit by throwing in some fresh – and very thought provoking – *misinformation*. "I also came here looking for Benito Rosado, Mr Tejada. Someone at the funeral told us he'd

150

probably be staying with you." This grasping at straws was all he could come up with on short notice – it would have to do.

"I can only surmise that my supposed 'connection' to him is based entirely on a case of mistaken identity Mr Paige. I'm sure I don't know this 'Benito' person very well, if at all. And, I'm certainly not familiar with his dead cousin. Perhaps I could enquire, who is assisting you in any sort of *official capacity* in what appears to be a very *private* fishing expedition?"

Dan smiled and tried to look at ease. "You're right in one regard, Mr Tejada. It's not an official investigation… yet. The Rosados are simply concerned, because they haven't seen their cousin Benito since before the shooting and a few people have tied him to you. Truthfully, the police would like to speak with *him* more than you. I'm simply trying to get in touch with a cousin who's close to the deceased. He might even be in Benny's will."

Manny Tejada sat behind his bulky mahogany desk and coyly rested his chin on his fists. A quality 'Victorian Reproduction' with an inlaid leather top, it was the only piece of furniture in the room that hadn't been fabricated in Baja. It stood out like a sore thumb, albeit a halfway classy one, in the room's gaudy surroundings.

Dan incongruously pondered why, when he was up to his eyeballs in ominous shit, he was so intrigued with Tejada's taste in furnishings. Perhaps it was because the damned desk *was* so out of place, surrounded by trashy décor that would be better suited to a B-movie soundstage. The out of place mahogany desk reminded him that he *too* was loitering on unfamiliar turf. The surroundings undoubtedly provided insight into the man. Get a grip, he thought. Keep your wits about you.

Tejada pretended to browse momentarily through some papers on his desk before responding to Dan's lame cover story. Then he coolly ordered, "Enrique, please take Mr Paige into the front office. I want to have a word with these two gentlemen. I believe that Mr Paige has shared all that he is going to tell us for the time being."

The malevolent manservant circled behind Dan. The still unseen hand released its grip on the handcuffs and Enrique's free hand immediately replaced it. Dan got his first clear view of the room's other occupants as the pair crossed over to sit across from Tejada. It confirmed what already he knew… these were indeed the geeks he'd seen that very afternoon in the low-rider across from the church.

Dan felt the muzzle of Enrique's pistol press into his backbone. Tejada's bizarre manservant proceeded to roughly guide him down a narrow hallway into a modest studio office near the front entrance, turning on the overhead light as they entered. The room was fitted out with cheap, gray office furniture and a pair of old file cabinets.

Tejada's assistant was a large man – and he knew how to handle a gun. Dan held no illusions that the unconventional Enrique was some sort of amateur. Keeping his gun pointed directly at Dan's torso, the manservant pointed his captive to a straightback office chair before settling himself on the edge of a small leatherette couch a few feet away. His aim never wavered.

Meanwhile, in the living room, Jesus and Flaco sat attentively across from Manny. He rested his arms on the desktop and glowered at them. "Now can you see where your fuck-up's led us? There's no way of knowing who Paige has taken into his confidence – or how much these other people know. This guy's got to take a little trip – and never return! Take him out to Torrey Pines, to that hang-gliding area we and our business associates sometimes use for late-night meets. He's going to take a solo flight off the top of those impressive cliffs... short of a bit of vital aviation equipment. At least make it look like it *might* have been an accidental fall, okay? Here's his stuff." Manny tossed everything he'd taken from Dan across the desk.

"Put his wiped-down wallet and ID back in his inside jacket pocket when you get there. Leave his ride in the car park, unlocked, with the keys in the ignition. And don't forget; wipe his keys off once you have gloves on – and thoroughly rub down everything inside and outside of his car *again*, just before you leave Torrey Pines. *He was never here...* got it?" With that, Manny motioned to Flaco to pick up Dan's belongings, quietly ordering, "Now, get on with it!"

Flaco pocketed Dan's billfold, keys and ID wallet. He rubbed his chin, shifted in his seat and peered earnestly into Manny's eyes. "We'll take care of it Mr Tejada."

Manny's expression remained frozen. "And one more thing, morons... whoever drives Paige's car – *wear your fuckin' gloves the whole time you're in it!* We don't want prints or DNA leading back to us, okay? When you're finished, come back here and tell me *personally* that you've finally done one fuckin' thing right, okay?"

"Consider this job done – and completed A-okay, Mr Tejada," Flaco uttered as he rose to leave. Then, he paused before even straightening up – tension on his face. "You mentioned gloves *jefe*. Got any we can borrow?"

It was some comfort to Manny to learn that Flaco had at least taken his instructions on board. He opened a desk drawer, withdrew a fresh roll of duct tape and handed it to Flaco. "Tell Enrique to dig out some unused gardening gloves in the garage, along with a clean plastic sheet.

Tape up Paige's feet, mouth and eyes and roll him up in the plastic tarp before dumping him in *his* trunk – not yours. It's bound to be cleaner than your heap and it won't contain awkward fibers or foreign substances that would interest overly conscientious investigators. Remember, cut him a bit of breathing space through the plastic once he's trussed up in the tarp – we don't want him to appear to have been suffocated."

Jesus, who'd managed to remain lurking and silent up to this point, chimed in, "Should we plug up his ears too Mr Tejada?"

"Wrap the duct tape around his eyes *and* his ears... better safe than sorry. And, listen you two... don't forget to remove every scrap of tape – *and the cuffs* – before you heave him over the cliff. And, make sure his billfold and ID are on him, stowed in his inside pocket. Remember, we want it to play out like it just *might* have been an accident – or even a suicide, brought on by the death of one of his dear friends. Bring all of the used tape, the plastic tarp and cuffs back here when you report in, okay?" (Manny knew better than to leave the disposal of such damning evidence to these morons.) He gave the pair a backhanded wave and they beat a hasty retreat down the hallway.

Curiously, the normally taciturn Jesus felt compelled to convey a few final encouraging words to their agitated boss as they hurried into the hall. He turned and pointed at Manny, still seated behind his desk, "You can count on us *patrón*... job done!"

Manny Tejada winced, knowing full well that the chances of Paige's demise being written off as an accident or suicide were almost nil. But, if Dan had kept mum about where he was headed on this fateful evening, there was a better than even chance a cold trail wouldn't lead anyone back to Hacienda Heights. And, if the cops turned up, he'd just have to brazen it out. Manny's biggest loose end remained that damned missing underling, Benito Rosado. He had to find the little shit and *eliminate* him, with prejudice, before the stupid turd made a silly mistake or spilled his guts to the wrong people

Meanwhile, Dan sat stock-still in the small study. The two henchmen darted in and practically blundered through Enrique's sightline to his captive. The manservant didn't move a muscle, but barked, "Back off a bit you morons. What do you want?"

Flaco held up the roll of duct tape. "The boss says you can get us some new gardening gloves and a clean plastic tarp from the garage. In the meantime, we're supposed to tape this dude up – nice and tight, but breathing."

Enrique gingerly handed his gun to Flaco. He knew better than to trust the diminutive man's slow-witted partner with the weapon. "Keep him covered – and you, greaseball, handle the taping duties while I'm gone. I'll be back in a couple of minutes."

Dan struggled briefly as Jesus did as he was told. But the burly man was simply too strong to resist... and the guy covering him looked like he wasn't afraid to use the weapon. Jesus wrapped four or five revolutions of the durable tape around Dan's feet and cut it with his pocketknife. He then added two layers around his mouth. Next, he wound the tape over Dan's ears with one quick revolution and moved up, to finish with two layers over his eyes. Dan could breathe, but only through a mashed nose and his exposed nostrils – and he could barely move a muscle. He was well and truly hog-tied; any chance of escape had slipped away in the past few minutes.

Dan's sense of hearing wasn't totally erased... if he focused intently. He sensed, as much as heard, Enrique return five minutes later and picked up on the sound of something cumbersome (the plastic tarp?) hitting the floor next to him.

The manservant barked out a new order: "Don't leave *anything* at the scene Flaco, wherever you're taking him. All of this shit comes back with you, got it? Got your own gun, by the way?"

"Sure man," Flaco answered, "We've got us a gun in the car – and Mr Tejada has already given us clear instructions. We know exactly what to do."

Enrique ordered Jesus to pick up the tarp and wrap up their captive. Dan was slung off the straightback chair onto the floor and felt himself being rotated like a crocodile's prey inside of the heavy plastic. His pulse pounded in his temples. He'd run out of options... and, strangely, all he could think about was how hard this would be on Sophie! She'd already lost one man she'd counted on – and it seemed she was about to roll craps again.

The heat inside the tarp was stifling. Dan was already soaking in sweat and he felt both ends of the wrapping tighten, as tape was added to secure him inside this plastic egg roll. Only his bound feet were sticking out of one end. Thankfully, the burly dude cut a fairly generous air hole near his nose. "Okay, let's roll," Enrique barked and Dan felt himself being lifted and slung over the big guy's shoulder. His securely wrapped head banged the doorframe as he was bundled into the hallway.

In seconds, the air in his makeshift breathing hole grew cooler and he thought he heard the little guy say, "His wheels are parked over there." He'd obviously recognized Dan's crappy company ride from that afternoon encounter at the church. A few strides later, Dan heard the creak of an opening trunk lid.

"Sling him in, man. Don't ding the fucker up too much. We'll leave the real bruising for his unfortunate fall. And, when you've stepped away, don't touch this car again until we reach our destination and your gloves are on. They're still in your pocket, right?"

Dan landed in a heap in the trunk and the lid slammed down. He could barely move. He felt the Chevy rock slightly as someone slipped behind the wheel. Hog-tied and entombed in the cramped trunk space, he had no chance of making out any more of his captors' conversation. He felt the car move off and wondered if he'd ever again see the light of day.

Dan felt his metal toolbox digging into his back. Now he was absolutely certain he was in his Chevy. He concentrated with all of his might on the direction the car was taking. He sensed the turn at the end of Manny's street and knew that they were heading downhill, towards I-5 and the beaches. He knew San Diego's roads well. It was a long shot, but he prayed he'd gain a slight edge if he figured out where they were taking him. If he conserved his energy, he just might be able to make some half-assed move at their ultimate destination. It was a snowball's chance in Hell, but he was seriously low on options.

Chapter 20

Adios, Paige

Dan felt the Malibu come to a stop after what seemed like an eternity – but it was probably no more than thirty minutes. He'd lost all sense of where they'd headed. There'd been too many twists and turns. His wrappings barely allowed a breath, let alone a chance to shift about in the trunk. Worse yet, the handcuffs severely restricted his circulation, leaving his hands numb and useless. The final insult was that his legs were fast asleep from being wedged in an awkward position. He feared that the rest of his body would shortly be as dead to the world as his limbs already were.

He was lying directly over his holstered .38, still stowed under the spare. During the journey, he'd made a futile attempt to loosen his arms so that he could undo the tarp and reach the gun – but he'd gotten nowhere. Now he'd just have to suck it up and play things by ear.

He lay in silence for a few moments. Then the Chevy rocked slightly as the driver disembarked. The trunk lid opened and two sets of arms unceremoniously hauled him into the damp night air, standing him upright. Dan felt loose gravel under his shoe's soles, rather than grass or concrete. He could barely hear his captors, now speaking Spanish. But even though he understood a bit of their native tongue, he couldn't make out these dudes.

The men poked and prodded him, checking out the state of their groaning cargo, before Flaco fell into his normal role... taking charge. "Go ahead; unwrap Paige and toss the tape and plastic in our car." Jesus quickly did as he was told, being careful to keep Dan on his feet as he unwound the tape from the tarp.

When Jesus eventually finished and returned from the Firebird, Flaco issued new orders in a near-whisper. "Remove the rest of the tape, but be careful. Don't leave any stray bits; that'd be a dead giveaway when the body's discovered. Set your gloves on the ground by mine; and then don't touch his car again. We'll need a decent bare-hand grip on this dude for the next few minutes."

Dan felt a sharp pain as the last of the tape was ripped from his face and hair. It was dark in this place, but his eyes began to adjust. He gulped in damp, fresh air... *sea air*! The atmosphere had a clean, briny smell – a welcome relief from the dank clamminess of the Chevy's trunk. It felt like some hair had been pulled out by the roots, even though the big guy had been fairly careful. Dan imagined he wouldn't be looking his finest at the moment.

Flaco continued speaking in Spanish. "I've got him covered. Leave the cuffs on for now." He reached into his pocket and handed his partner Dan's wallet and ID. "Wipe these things off and put them deep into his inside jacket pocket; we wouldn't want them to fall out mid-flight, would we?" Then the little man switched to English. "Let's go for a short walk Mr Paige. Don't try nothin' funny now."

Jesus unwound the last loop of tape from Dan's ankles and roughly gripped his left arm with hands that felt like meat hooks. Out of the corner of his eye, Dan could see a short length of used tape trailing from the big guy's sleeve. Without dwelling on it, Dan noticed again that the big dude didn't smell too sweet up close, even in the cool night air.

Dan considered making a run for it, but the little guy still stood in front of him, with a shiny pistol pointed squarely at his chest. It wouldn't be smart to try to make a dash when they stood motionless... best to hope for these halfwits to make a mistake when they were on the move.

He was obviously facing out to sea, but he could see only moonlit clouds on the horizon – no sand, no beach. A glance to both sides revealed scrub bushes and stunted pines. *Of course!* They were standing in the parking lot at Torrey Pines Cliffs, near the take-off platform used by San Diego's barmy hang-gliders. A nightmarish picture of his imminent execution came clearly into focus.

Dan had visited this very spot a few weeks before with Sophie and her kids. They'd watched as a few brave souls leapt into the ozone, catching updrafts that bore them north to Del Mar or south, as far as La Jolla. He wasn't sure if Jason had been on the level when he'd proclaimed he was considering taking this hobby up. Sophie winced and wisely informed him he'd have to save up his own money for the gear.

So far, Dan's captors hadn't begun the short walk towards the edge of the platform. Finally, the little guy shoved his gun into his trouser pocket and stepped in. He joined his smelly partner; tightly latching onto Dan's other arm. The trio began to stroll slowly – and the gravel underfoot soon gave way to the landward edge of the concrete take-off slab. Dan had to make his move, even if it was a long shot. He was out of options.

Ducking as low as he could, he spun and slammed his head into the gut of the beefier honcho. In the same instant, he felt the little guy tighten his grip on his right arm. His strength was surprising! Flaco spun Dan to again face the cliff's edge as Jesus recovered his balance and wrapped his torso and arms in a suffocating bear hug. Dan's feet lost contact with the ground. Before he knew it, the little guy had removed the handcuffs. As a last resort, Dan let his legs go slack, hoping to sink to his knees and roll. But no dice. The big guy simply *carried* him, legs kicking and toes scraping the concrete, towards his certain doom.

Jesus hesitated momentarily to establish his footing as the trio reached the far edge of the platform. Dan attempted, yet again, to drop into a judo crouch – and to lock a now unbound arm under the big boy. At least he might take the smelly dude with him. But at that moment, the large man loosened his iron grip and Dan felt one last well-placed shove from his second captor. He hurtled – solo – into oblivion.

Standing near the precipice, Jesus panted from the effort. Flaco retrieved the gun from his pocket and issued a final order. "Okay man, let's go. Make sure you retrieve any loose tape. I've got the cuffs. Unless Paige is Superman, *San Pedro* already greets him at the Pearly Gates. There's going to be another funeral this week, amigo!"

They headed for the parking lot and Flaco gave Dan's car a last thorough inspection. Playing it safe, he used the canvas gloves on the ground to thoroughly wipe down the Chevy's interior and exterior one final time – not forgetting to rub down Dan's keys, still in the ignition. Everything seemed to be in order. Perhaps some clumsy driver *had* simply fallen off the cliff during a late night stroll – stranger things had happened. They jumped into the Pontiac and drove away, heading back to Manny's Mission Hills hacienda.

Freefallin'

Sunset Cliffs Park offered stunning sea views. One end of the recreational area provided a vantage point renowned for unobstructed views of San Diego's infamous Black's Beach, a stretch of judiciously policed sand where nude sunbathing was allowed. On most weekends, at least a dozen off-duty servicemen threw Frisbees around on Black's for every female naturist willing to brave the hordes. A few steep pathways wound from the apex of the cliff to the beach, but there were no trails carved out of the near vertical incline below the hang gliding area. At this end of the park, the beach was inaccessible to all but expert climbers.

Dan didn't qualify as a mountaineer at the best of times. Presently, he was wildly ricocheting off jagged protruding rocks, tumbling towards what could only be an inevitable agonizing demise.

But, miraculously, on his third or fourth bone-jarring collision with the rock face he landed in a heap on a minuscule ledge and made a desperate grab for a handhold. Unfortunately, this outcropping offered no viable grips – and the ledge tilted ominously down towards the awaiting abyss. He started to slide and then fell *again...* now it was all over!

The tiny rock shelf had, however, taken the velocity out of his fall and, unbelievably, he tumbled only a few more feet before crashing in a heap on a more generous outcrop. Here he managed to stick fast. Lying face down, his hand felt a branch – little more than a twig – protruding from the rock face. He clung to it with all of his remaining strength.

Dan couldn't determine how long he sprawled there, stunned and aching. Eventually he calmed himself and felt all over, searching for critical damage. He found no obvious broken bones or ruptured organs, but he'd certainly suffered, at the very least, minor sprains and contusions. Of course, he was running on pure adrenaline. In his past life, he'd seen guys who'd sustained compound leg fractures get up and run from the cops, passing out from the intense pain only after being locked in the back of a black and white. He knew his adrenaline high wouldn't last.

His fingers explored the edge of the welcome outcropping. He quickly confirmed the miraculous nature of his death-defying escape. This insignificant ledge, covered in bird droppings, could barely accommodate a creature of his size. And if he'd fallen two feet to the left or right, he'd certainly have missed this unlikely sanctuary altogether. His final resting place would have been the intended boulders at the base of the cliff.

Turning on his side, he scanned the little he could make out of the massive cliff face; first looking down, and then up. Retracing his journey back *up* the face, in spite of the inevitable scarcity of handgrips, looked like a better bet. The cliff below his vantage point became markedly more vertical beyond the next few feet... far too steep for a descent. Besides, it was twice as far to climb *down* as up.

"Well, I guess there's nothing for it but to get started," he said to two docile gulls resting nearby. They nonchalantly stared at him and continued grooming themselves. He needed to begin his ascent before the pain and stiffness worsened. He tightened and retied his All Stars' shoelaces – a solid toe grip in the rock face would be essential. Rubbing his hands together to enhance his circulation, Dan began the suicidal climb.

Twenty minutes later – to Dan, a seeming eternity – he was hoisting himself over the front edge of the concrete platform. He lay panting, thanking his lucky stars for the few nearly imperceptible hand and toeholds he'd managed to discover on his way up. It had been an incredibly tough ascent, but his tedious running regime had undoubtedly paid dividends this time. He slowly got to his feet and dusted himself down. Looking inland towards the main road, he saw that the Chevy was still right where his captors had left it – parked in the darkest corner of the gravel lot. It was unlikely that any passers-by had pulled in and discovered the abandoned car at this late hour.

He limped over and tried the driver's door. It wasn't locked… and his keys were right there in the ignition. They're not as stupid as they look, Dan thought. This car looks like it was stolen and dumped, pointing the finger at dim teenagers. Or it might even have been discovered in this quiet spot by morons who'd drive it away, leaving incriminating prints or DNA when they abandoned it. When caseloads are heavy, cops go for undemanding solutions – or buy into manifestly ridiculous scenarios that quickly close problematic files.

Dan reached into his glove compartment for a soothing CD, but the jackass who'd driven the car over from Mission Hills had obviously lifted his discs, along with some battered maps. They were, however, smart enough to leave his phone untouched. After all, it could be easily traced. He tuned in a 'Soft Rock' FM station for the background noise, fired up the Chevy and headed into the night.

Arriving home, Dan parked one street over, just to be safe. Who knew, they might check up to be *certain* he hadn't returned. He grabbed his sportscoat off of the back seat, where it was still lying, and his gun from under the spare before approaching his building from the alley. He remained alert for signs of unwelcome guests. As tired as he was, a final concern niggled at him… if Tejada was clever, he'd order a break-in to see if incriminating files or notes had been left lying around.

But there were no signs of intruders. Tejada probably felt that he'd have sufficient time to construct an airtight alibi for this evening – and for the Benny Rosado fiasco as well – if any of Dan's friends eventually came sniffing around. Why tempt fate by sending his half-assed lackeys on another relatively dangerous assignment?

Once inside, Dan closed his curtains, foregoing the lights and TV. He sat stiffly at his kitchen bar and slowly downed a cold Dos Equis. The deadbolt was set and his gun was on the counter, near his right hand. He knew that these precautions were probably unwarranted. Perhaps (although this was a long shot) Tejada hadn't even bothered to write down or memorize his home address before handing the billfold and ID over to his minions. At least, Dan was fairly certain these dimwits wouldn't break in and search the place without *explicit* instructions from Manny.

His adrenaline high had long worn off and Dan was feeling the after-effects of his unscheduled solo flight. He went to his bathroom cabinet and popped a couple of Tramadol tablets, washing them down with a second beer. They were the strongest pain relievers he had to hand. His ribs ached, but past experiences on the football field told him they were probably only badly bruised and not broken.

Before heading to bed, Dan threw his torn, dirty clothes in an old dry cleaning bag, attaching a note for Bren and Vince about how and where they'd been damaged. It would be useful evidence down the line, if things took a bad turn. He took a long shower and changed into old sweat bottoms and a baggy Chargers jersey. He sat in his easy chair and pondered his future tactics, taking into account the fact that he was now only an unpleasant memory to Manny's crew. Since they'd unceremoniously slung him off the cliff, the gloves were well and truly off. And he'd exploit an advantage... he was now a ghost, a man who could make critical moves with virtual invisibility. Dan certainly knew how to play hardball; but he was in new territory, stepping further outside the law than he'd ever treaded before.

Dan realized he was probably past the need to make notes to flesh out his thinking, but a brief 'case history' left in the apartment could be invaluable to Brenda and Vince if things turned sour. He added a few hard-earned annotations; namely...

Tejada and his goons are involved up to their necks in Benny's murder... his reaction to my visit seals it!

The <u>two Mexicans</u> in the Firebird are prime suspects for Benny's shooters – deadly, but a bit dim.

<u>Physical Descriptions</u>:
1.   5' 6", wiry, but tough. He's the boss man of the two. Looks like a Mex Steve Tyler – or a little like Ron Wood?
2.   6' 1", flabby, but strong as hell. Long, stringy hair. High-pitched voice. Tight leather pants and dirty cowboy shirt. Smells like an abandoned shitpile .

Bren's already checking the plate number of their beat-up, purple Pontiac low-rider.

<u>I'm a dead man</u> to them – I'm going to use it!

A little description of tonight's saga is attached to the dry cleaning bag in the bedroom.

Keep Gene and Melinda in the dark – she could inconveniently spill the beans to Ernest.

Was it time to telephone Brenda and Vince to let them in on everything he'd discovered – and on what he now surmised? He trusted them implicitly, but they might feel bound by the cop's unwritten code to put their partners and trusted colleagues in the picture. Too many lawmen in the loop could create havoc if he was inclined to bend the rules. These two could be brought in when it was closer to the time to grab up the bad guys. In the meantime he'd maintain the tight inner circle– just Gunnar and himself. And maybe Benny's boys, if reliable muscle was called for.

As he slipped out of his clothes and fell into the sack, Dan considered how he'd handle his next interrogation of slippery Cousin Benito. Another chat with the unctuous little prick would probably provide further insight into what Manny Tejada and his associates were up to. Dan ardently desired another imminent sparring round with his dim Mexican captors, Frick and Frack, as well. These two goons were due some serious payback. He also hoped that when he put the screws to Manny Tejada, he might just crack and give up Ernest Kincaid – and even some higher-ups. The exporter and the slimy businessman should indeed be the catalysts in the downward spiral that ultimately led to Benny's death. Cousin Benito would get a call first thing in the morning.

Chapter 21

Sunday

A new dawn

He was dreaming, but Dan's semi-conscious brain told him he was proactively creating these familiar surroundings. He was out in Ocean Beach's breakers, once more riding the gnarly old board he'd treasured as a teenager. On this hazy morning however, his dad – a customary spectator in this recurring nightmare – was nowhere to be seen. The same stray mutts meandered up the beach, but this time they paid him no heed. Instead, they dug at the weeds spreading beyond the sand to the parking strip and a rusty VW Campervan.

He paddled furiously out, plowing under the curls to overtake his little brother, Marty – twelve or thirteen and paddling impetuously away, intending to be first to ride a monster into shore. The surf was *fantastic*, but that only made Dan more apprehensive. These waves were too fierce for a boy like Marty. When Dan rolled over the crest of the next incoming swell and peered out to sea, his little brother had disappeared. Dan felt panic growing in his chest... where was the little shit?

He shouted to Marty and the sound of his own voice, booming out in the bedroom, stirred him out of his half-sleep. He opened his eyes and rolled towards his alarm clock. "Christ, it's past nine and I've got to call Benito and the girls!"

Springing out of bed, he was immediately reminded of his fatigued and bruised limbs. In fact, his entire body felt like sadists had pounded on it with two-by-fours, connecting soundly with every nook and cranny. This was no doubt the closest he'd ever get to the agony experienced by boxers who'd survived a few rounds with Tyson in his prime.

Dan stumbled into the kitchen to make some instant coffee. His *Bob's Big Boy* mug spun in the microwave, the image of Big Boy repeatedly waving at Dan as the cup revolved. Retrieving Lila's number from his notes, he sat with his mug of black tar and dialed. After three rings, he heard: "Hi, this is Lila! Me and Winter are out doin' our thing, but you can leave a message. No heavy breathing now, or we may not call back. Bye."

Dan responded impatiently, "Come on guys, pick up. I know you're there. It's Dan Paige and I need to speak to Benito... right now! Inform your honored guest that I had an unintended run-in with Manny Tejada and his nasty underlings – and Benito may find himself mired even deeper in this messy shitpile in the near future if we don't meet up."

Lila promptly came on the line and cooed, "Hey sweetie, simmer down. Benito and Winter drove up to Laguna Beach early this morning for a little richly deserved R&R. Benito said they'd be safe from Manny and his goons up there. Our boy was going stir crazy, honey. For sure, Winter won't be answering her phone, but I'll text her and forward your message."

This unplanned trip was *not* what Dan wanted to deal with. "Do text her, hon. Tell her that I need to see Benito later today *for sure* – I've plenty to fill him in on. Tell them to be back at your place at four, okay?"

"Sure Dan, they intended to be back pretty early anyway. Should I tell Benito anything else when I text them?"

"No Lila, just make sure he turns up... for the sake of his own greasy neck."

"Consider it done, sport. Benito knows he's running out of friends – and options – while Manny and his boys are hunting for him. Me and Winter don't know exactly what's going down, but Benito is in over his head; even I can tell that."

Dan hung up and dialed Gunnar. He caught Benny's trusted foreman at his own place, just as he was heading out to pick up Greg for a 'cash-only' Sunday job. The boy had been obliged to promise Consuela he'd turn up at a later Mass if he missed their regular Sunday morning service – and to attend with Gunnar in tow.

Needless to say, Dan's impromptu rock climb piqued Gunnar's interest. The little man was pissed off and willing – in fact, downright *anxious* – to play a key role in Dan's new scheme to lure Manny Tejada and his cohorts into their web.

It didn't take much persuading to convince Gunnar that Manny, while no doubt a key participant in Benny' murder, didn't rest atop the decision-making pyramid. Gunnar vowed that he wouldn't rest until they nailed the higher ups. Dan, however, was a realist. He realized – but didn't articulate – that even if they ultimately exposed Ernest Kincaid as a drug financier, the true kingpins would skate. They'd simply congregate at some fortress in Baja to anoint Ernest's replacement from a lengthy list of greedy candidates. They'd have their new Americano front man in situ before Kincaid went to trial.

Dan intimated that he was chasing a solid lead on Benito's whereabouts, but apologized and said he couldn't elaborate. After comparing notes, the skeleton of a plan for taking down Manny Tejada took shape. They agreed to speak again that afternoon, hopefully after

Dan had run Benito down. Gunnar was on board... anxious to do his bit to carry out their still sketchy strategy.

Next up was an afternoon of crewing for Rod Grissom. He'd decided to carry on with his pal's regatta. A morning on the bay would keep him out of harm's way – and help to relax his exhausted mind and body until his appointment with Benito and the girls. His pleasurable plans for the evening – the dinner and concert with Sophie – needn't be put on ice either.

Dan's mind drifted to the prospective roles for his law enforcement 'partners in crime' in his budding strategy. He was convinced of the rectitude of keeping Vince and Brenda in the dark for the time being. The cartel was still hot on grabbing up Benito, so Manny would be hanging around San Diego. Reeling in his disloyal subordinate had to remain his priority – and Dan and Gunnar would be using that fact to their advantage. In all honesty, it was clear to Dan his future tactics might not attract the unreserved backing of his law enforcement buddies. But, if all went well, they'd be in line to garner the lion's share of credit for some major collars. Vince and Bren didn't need to know *exactly* how the impending sting was being laid out.

After another curative shower and some welcome painkillers, Dan felt ready to face the world. Sure, he'd seen better days, but he was good to go. A hearty breakfast at Lenny's beckoned, followed by a few low-key hours on the bay with Rod and, most probably, First-Mate Derrick. He hoped that the inevitable on-board 'bimbo brigade' would be few in numbers and well behaved... he was in no mood to entertain them. He was due at the jetty around eleven. An earlier arrival would simply necessitate a larger dose of 'pre-sail' socializing. He'd arrive at quarter past, leaving little time for idle chitchat.

On a clear day

Dan used his whole wheat toast to mop up a dollop of egg yolk. Stan the Man was in high gear, sharing his engineering insights with a dapper new 'Senior Menu' customer further down the counter... "I'm telling you, the so-called 'benefits' of sending breathing jet jockeys into the cosmos add up to nothin' but a pile of shit!"

Jerry had obviously already borne too much of this one-sided debate – or heard this particular tune before. He'd finished his breakfast and escaped. His plate, mug and dollar tip rested next to Stan, who continued in exceptional solo form. Maybe he was back sampling the sauce, who knew?

The cranky engineer continued, "My old employer's designing the proposed propulsion system for the Shuttle replacement. I've *personally* been at the heart of most everything that's hit the skies in the past forty years. And I'll sure as shit tell you somethin' for nothin': We're beatin' our heads against the wall sending men – and, God forbid, nowadays *women* as well – into space. They aren't doing anything up there that a robot or camera couldn't do better!"

The imprudent stranger, unaware of the perils associated with challenging the all-knowing Stan Crawford, enquired, "Where's your sense of adventure? Remember how Kennedy challenged our generation to reach the moon – and then explore the universe? And just think of the technological benefits we've all enjoyed thanks to NASA."

This well-worn argument played like a red rag waved at a cantankerous bull – Stan redoubled his rant. "What the hell are you blabbering about? I just *told* you we could send up robots, computerized docking arms, telescopes and cameras. We'd retrieve better data and suffer fewer fuck-ups. Those 'astronits' are useless, fragile cargo."

But the plucky gentleman was finding his voice… he wasn't going to give in. "What if we'd just sent robots and cameras into the Old West? You might be interested to know that I'm a retired history professor. I've learned that leaps of progress often come serendipitously; sometimes accompanied by temporary setbacks. But in the main, setting out on our great adventures has been worthwhile. If we hadn't explored, fulfilling our so-called *Manifest Destiny*, you and I wouldn't be sitting here right now."

Stan's face took on a look of utter disdain. "Yeah buddy – what a loss it would be for the western edge of this vast continent if our ancestors had stayed put in the East… or, better yet, remained in Europe! I bet the vanishing Native Americans – and our near-extinct bears and bison – would be *thrilled* if the white man had never come along." Stan wasn't stopping for breath. "And, it'll be the same shitty outcome if our pitiful race ever staggers into the cosmos. Sooner or later, some slimy-assed aliens will drop down and land in Arizona, sticking whatever serves as their noggins out of the saucer. They'll warn us to quit littering the heavens and killin' each other. And to mind our own fuckin' business… or else!"

The dapper man turned away and appeared to stare into the bottom of his mug, obviously hoping that breaking eye contact would end the onslaught. But, against his better judgment, he couldn't resist attempting to inject one last, rational thought. "It's man's nature to push on, to make new discoveries."

166

"Well, you're damned right there Prof, and I say let's concentrate on our real challenges here on Earth... vital breakthroughs; like effective antacid tablets or a Constitutional Amendment that would reserve 'public service' for at least half-honest politicians."

Dan set six dollars on the counter and waved to Rosie as he attempted to slip out. This conversation could play and play – and he, like Jerry before him, had heard enough. He pondered, not for the first time, if Stan and Jerry's meager, but regular contributions to Lenny's profit margin would ever compensate for the business Stan drove away.

Dan arrived at the marina and relaxed in the car for a moment before strolling down to the yacht. Rod, and hopefully Derrick, would already be aboard, probably champing at the bit. As he approached, Rod waved from the stern of the 'Moll Flanders', flashing a broad grin. "Hey man, we weren't sure you'd show! How's the investigation going? Any news?"

Dan managed a wan smile and waved back. "Things are going okay dude, but I'm a bit worse for wear this morning. Where's Derrick?"

"He's below man, brewin' some badly needed tar. And now for the *bad* news... the girls couldn't make it this morning, but they'll still be turning up to cheer us onto dry land after my splendid victory. I'm afraid it'll just be the three of us out on the bay, *kimosabe*."

Not even attempting to mask his delight at this auspicious news, Dan's face broke into a real grin. A relaxing sail, accompanied by Derrick and Rod *only* – and a fresh pot of coffee – was precisely what the doctor ordered. "Pipe me aboard then Captain; I'm at your command. By the way, Sophie won't be making it either."

He shouted below decks as he gingerly hauled himself over the railing, "Bring me a mug of that mud you're brewing Lightnin'. Surprisingly, I feel brave enough to face even your shitty coffee this morning." Derrick's lame attempt at coffee would be useful for washing down two more painkillers.

Over the next couple of hours Rod would no doubt demonstrate his remarkable knack for tactical sailing. A strong wind was blowing and if the three of them worked in tandem, Rod would probably make good on his nautical boasting. Dan knew he'd still be able to master the simple tasks, regardless of his aches and pains, while Derrick carried out the heavy lifting. Their main adversary was a renowned, if aging, local yachtsman who'd crewed ably for Dennis Conner in a couple of America's Cups. The challenge was revving up Rod's competitive juices.

On the longer tacks, when everything was ship-shape, the boys gave Dan the lowdown on the lovely ladies who'd turn up later... a quartet of beauty consultants from a posh Fashion Valley emporium. The girls had thrown themselves at Derrick a couple of weeks before at Pussies – and proved to be excellent company after Rod bought them drinks and dinner. Dan quickly formed a picture of their new companions in his mind's eye... eye candy and lots of laughs, but emphatically not 'partnership material' for the long pull.

After contributing to Rod's graphic description of the ladies' assets, Derrick's conversation took a more significant turn. When Rod went forward to adjust the spinnaker, Lightnin' whispered he'd appreciate a quiet word. He was just beginning to furtively describe Rod's latest "sure-fire business venture" when the man himself returned to the wheel.

"Are you telling Dan about our new commercial opportunity Lightnin'?"

Looking a bit sheepish, Derrick replied, "I was about to fill him in, Rod. Do you mind?"

"Hell no. If you're smart Dan, you'll want a little piece of this action yourself. Here's how it goes down: It's incredibly easy to export cars and auto parts to Mexico. They aren't too picky about paperwork and there's no such thing as a product liability lawsuit if the odd item isn't up to scratch. Deals are 'ask no questions'... and strictly cash."

Dan could feel himself wincing. "Yeah Rod, it's all so easy. And none of the shit going over the border is *hot*, right?"

Rod attempted to put on his most convincing wounded expression. "We buy from legit auto breakers and auction houses *only*, my man. If our chosen vendors tell me the parts and cars are kosher, then I can assure you that they are!"

Rod turned slightly and made eye contact with Derrick. His new partner felt obliged to jump in. "Look Dan, even the Mexican cops aren't too picky about car imports! Lots of them drive a BMW, Audi or Lexus with the serial numbers filed off. But we're not in that market. We insist that our cars have legitimate IDs and service histories – and Rod assures me that our parts come from legitimate breaking yards. Our products will stand up to rigorous inspection... they're on the up and up."

Dan hesitated and tried to make eye contact with Lightnin' before replying. "How many fly-by-night car dealers and chop shops do you think the police and insurance companies put out of business every year? And don't think that we don't chase down the money behind these scammers! We rarely recover a car from Mexico, but I take great pleasure in chasing down small-time car crooks and their oily investors.

I'll introduce you to a few of them when they eventually get out of the slammer."

Derrick looked a bit squeamish and Rod stepped in to deflect their pal. He knew when to quit pitching to the holier-than-thou Dan, who was becoming evermore chickenshit as the years passed. Roping in an unneeded minor partner was a hiding to nothing, particularly if he was flirting with losing a principal investor like Lightnin'. As far as Rod was concerned, Dan could go piss up a rope! He shrugged his shoulders and put on a winning smile. "Hey crew, time to come about. All hands to their stations and make it snappy!"

As Dan cranked the mainsail winch, he couldn't help but dwell on Eddie's timely unearthing of Rod's latest 'start-up venture'. These two were already inundated in the muck – buried up to their exceedingly exposed necks. Was Rod ready to sacrifice his already shaky reputation as a legitimate financial advisor – as well as Derrick's friendship and good name – for the lure of this supposed easy money? The guy must be desperate... other 'sweet deals' and 'fail-safe tax write-offs' were no doubt turning sour on him and his clients. Dan knew that he'd have to corner Derrick when Rod wasn't around. Old Rodney could be in too deep, but he might be able to attract gullible seed money elsewhere – and hopefully Derrick could quickly resign his directorship in this dubious venture!

Captain Rod managed to tack away from the touchy topic as quickly as he'd altered the sailboat's course. When they all resettled on the aft deck, he and Derrick returned to their favorite topic: updating their ratings for the contemporary crop at Pussies. They quickly agreed that the bar's current lovelies came in at around an aggregate 7.5 on their 'Official Horndog's Scale'. Of course, Rod was convinced that his inimitable blend of savoir-faire, sexual allure and *cash* still made him a surefire prospect for snaring the vast majority of those vixens who scored above their prerequisite entry level.

Rod had become evermore full of himself (some would say *delusional*) as his years of perfecting a 'single man about town' persona turned into decades. Incredibly, he'd tried to convince Lightnin' that his celebrity status was on the wane – and it was his own blend of Grissom patter and charm (*easy money?*) that attracted the ladies these days. Recently he'd told Dan, in confidence of course, "Man, I even have to explain to most of today's hardbodies who Lightnin' Jackson used to be!"

Dan had snorted derisively at this piece of news. "Sure thing, Rod-O! Your inimitable sense of style and savoir-faire leave your pals fightin' for the rejects. You haven't lost an ounce of that potent animal magnetism... and, consequently, poor old Lightnin' is left to bask in your reflected glory." (Rod might not recognize his diminishing ability to pull the foxes; but, in truth, his sailing skills hadn't deserted him. At this very moment, they were fighting hard for the lead in this very competitive regatta.)

As Dan tied off a slack sheet, he butted into his buddies' ongoing conversation about the quality of their playmates... commenting on their puerile 'rating' of the ladies' relative charms. He concluded, "I sure as hell can't figure what you two find to *talk* about with your top-quartile bimbos after you finish the inevitable horizontal mambo sessions!"

Rod smirked and lifted an eyebrow. "Talk about? Well, usually I'm lovingly whispering to them to watch out for the tips of their noses as I'm zipping up! Dan, I haven't bought cleaning rags for this tub in years. I wipe her down with the bikinis and lingerie you'll find in plentitude in my 'lost and found' bin."

Dan laughed out loud and told himself, yet again, that he was exceedingly thankful to have left behind this infantile scene. But, as they approached the dock, he felt more relaxed than he had in many days. Without Rod's half-hearted and delusional pitch for an investment in his budding export business, the day would have been truly enjoyable. And, true to his host's promise as they'd sailed off, a couple of luscious bunnies awaited them on the pier as the Moll Flanders backed into her slip.

The young ladies waved a greeting. "Hi Rod! Sorry, but Bree and Randi got called into work, so it's just the two of us I'm afraid. Hey Derrick, how'd you guys do?" The girl calling up to them was a goddess – dark brown, curvaceous and approaching six feet. She wore a lacy dusty rose beach top over her tiny ivory bikini.

"We were robbed ladies," Rod shouted down, before Lightnin' could reply. "We were forced off course and into second after the supposed 'winners' blatantly cut us off at the last buoy. I'm thinking of lodging a formal protest. Come aboard mates – Lightnin's dropping a ladder over the stern. Watch your step!"

The girls climbed up daintily and Derrick effortlessly lifted them over the railing. He smiled broadly and spoke for the first time. "This here's our friend Dan, ladies. I'm afraid he's in a bit of a hurry; he's got places to go. So, say hello and goodbye!"

The black goddess approached and put out a hand, treating Dan to an expansive smile. "Hi Dan, I'm Tania and this is Lori." Her friend was blonde and petite, but possessed of a pair of boobs that had cost a

170

pretty penny. She wore a gauzy floral print beach top, open down the front, exposing an electrifying hot pink bikini.

Dan shook Tania's hand and nodded towards the lovely Lori, already perched on Derrick's knee as he relaxed on the aft bench. They held brimming champagne flutes and Lightnin' was helping her out of her flimsy beach top. It was time to beat a hasty retreat.

"It was lovely to meet you ladies, but as Derrick says, I'm on a tight schedule. I'm sure we'll meet again though. Have a lovely evening – and, remember shipmates, don't let the old Cap'n here talk you into any heavy lifting... even if he threatens to keelhaul you!" (He hoped his parting remark was witty enough to help buoy up the party mood for his horny pals.)

And, his attempt at humor must have worked. Both girls were giggling as he slowly exited over the stern rail. Rod's arms already enveloped Tania the Amazon in a tight bear hug from behind, one hand 'inadvertently' cupping a lovely breast.

Halfway down the dock he heard more raucous laughter behind him. He looked back and wasn't surprised to note that Tania's ivory bikini top was already being smartly run up the Moll Flanders' mast.

Reaching the car, he threw his windbreaker on the passenger seat and grabbed his phone out of the still near-empty glove compartment. Time to check in with Lila. It was only three, but Marty's girlfriend was able to confirm that her roommate had checked in after she'd sent the text message. Winter and Benito were well down the road, returning from Laguna.

He phoned Gunnar, who was still working at his weekend jobsite with Gregorio. The news from his partner in crime was promising. "It's all set Dan. Marta's pal will cover her cleaning duties and she's taking a three-day weekend off. I've got her key. She won't return 'til noon on Tuesday. Call me back tonight if you want, but if I don't hear from you again, we'll be at her cabin well before ten on Monday night. Consider *'Phase I'* of our little campaign well and truly underway!"

171

Chapter 22

A sharp-dressed man

Dan arrived at the Point Loma apartment at four on the dot, dressed to kill for the day's final event, the charity concert. He'd have plenty of time to grill Benito, drive up to Del Mar for Sophie and return downtown for their special evening.

Lila opened the door in a pair of tiny cut-offs and a fishnet orange tank top – and let out a long, low wolf whistle. "You didn't have to throw on that wicked tux for little ol' me stud... but I'm sure glad you did!"

Dan wanted to smile, but he thought he'd better not offer any encouragement to his little brother's main squeeze. "I'm headed to a Charity Gala with my girlfriend after this detour, I'm afraid. It's an early evening thing. Hope you don't mind that I turned up here in my formal duds."

"Do I mind? I just wish a bit of your refinement would rub off on your brother! Marty could at least show me he *owns* a clean shirt and tie. Come on in Mr Paige."

She led Dan to the kitchen table where Carrie/Winter and Benito were seated, looking slightly apprehensive. Dan discreetly checked the proffered chair for grease spots or spills before sitting down in his dress trousers. Lila smiled, turned and headed for her bedroom, providing them with a bit of privacy.

Dan knew that it had to be now or never... it was well past time to loosen up Cousin Benito's tongue. He'd play his weak hand to the hilt and do a bit of fishing, hopefully putting the little shit on his back foot. "Benito, I've had a chat with Manny Tejada and he says you're into the organization *big time*, due to some half-baked scam that's gone down the tubes. He didn't come right out and spill the beans, but he insinuated that his goons might have been hunting for *you* when they latched onto Benny – an innocent bystander if there ever was one. Of course, Tejada wouldn't confess to ordering the hit. He didn't want Benny's friends and family to come after him. But, I got the drift... and it's bad news for you, I'm afraid."

Benito leaned back in his spindly dining chair; so far that it appeared that the back legs might actually slide out from under him. He couldn't distance himself from Dan's bad news any further without literally standing up and walking away. "It's all bullshit Dan. I barely know this Tejada guy – and I'm *not* into any major deals with him or his fuckin' associates. And anyway, Manny and his goons would never have put

172

the two of us cousins together as family… or mistaken one of us for the other. As anyone will tell you, me and Benny didn't exactly run in the same circles."

Dan frowned and leaned forward, cutting the space between him and Benito. It was Carrie's turn to wince and lean away; she was obviously wishing she could be anywhere else. Dan looked deep into Benito's eyes and said, "Let's cut the crap dude. You can tell me everything *right now* – and perhaps I can help you to extract yourself from this shit. Or, you can go another way. Think about it… the cops – or Manny's associates – could discover your current whereabouts at any moment and your slime trail would heat up exponentially. First and foremost, it means you'd be friendless and back on the run. And this wouldn't bode well for your innocent girlfriends here, either. It's your choice. You can start playing ball with one of the few friends you have left – or attempt to disappear for good!"

The dapper Chicano began to fidget even more visibly. And a glance towards his lovely Winter offered no reassurances. Her countenance unmistakably communicated that she was already taking an even *dimmer* view of a soon-to-be 'former lover', if such a thing was possible. Benito sat in silence, realizing that there'd be fences to mend after Dan left, regardless of the outcome of this conversation. He didn't know what to say.

"Well Benito, *talk to the man*," the previously mute Carrie hissed. Her expression reminded him of that unforgettable evening when they'd strolled along the Mission Beach Promenade at sunset. They'd had a terrific afternoon; they were content and laughing… that is, until Winter stopped dead in her tracks and stared with revulsion at a dollop of runny dog crap oozing over the toe of her expensive sandal. Somehow, she'd implied that *he* was at fault for the ugly incident… much as the current situation was proving to be all his doing as well.

Benito reddened as he tried to face up to Dan. Being chastised by his woman in front of a potential adversary was simply not acceptable in his world. He decided to play along to a degree, at least for the time being – and attempted to placate his stern interrogator. "Man, as I told you before, any beef Tejada has with me is pretty damned insignificant. We're barely more than business acquaintances whose dealings occasionally cross paths. Any differences we've had don't merit a contract hit! I'm sure he implied as much when you spoke to him."

Dan's jab had elicited a reaction. It was time to turn the thumbscrews. "Contrary to your opinion, Benito, Tejada and his friends seem *extremely* anxious to get in touch with you… they're even offering a reward. Now I'm going to describe two of Manny's Latino-looking associates and hopefully you can put names to faces, okay? One guy is beefy, unbelievably grubby and covered in tattoos. His hair's greasy and long and he smells like a junkyard dog. He dress taste sucks... bursting out of dirty leather trousers and sporting a single fingerless glove. The other guy's a spindly little shit, more dapper than his pal. He's sort of Indian-looking. He does all the talking. They drive around in a crappy old Firebird – metal-flake purple. Surely, these two doghumps ring some bells, huh?"

Benito realized that his best strategy was to at least *appear* to be playing ball with Dan, particularly if he wished to maintain some semblance of a relationship with his magnificent girlfriend. "I think I can help you on those dudes man! Honestly, I don't know their names, but I've seen them hangin' with Manny. They're not regular soldiers – more like cheap muscle brought in on occasion, usually for sortin' out bad debts. I'm told they roam both sides of the border, doin' freelance donkey work for a few dudes who aren't that particular about maintaining a law-abiding image."

Dan leaned even closer into the table. "I need *names*, I said... and a lead on where I'll find them!"

Benito's eyes went big as he replied. "I don't know their names man, *I swear*! But if I were you, I'd be looking for them near my family's neighborhood down in Tijuana. If they're your button men and they've figured out that Benny was the wrong target, they'll surely be workin' on mending fences with Tejada. And any 'do-over' could easily start with them back down in Tijuana, trying to hook up with me again. This whole scenario is a big stretch for me though. Totally straight man... I'm fucked if I can figure out *why* they'd be lookin' to harm a guy like me in the first place!"

"So, you think someone may have put them onto Benny – mistakenly or intentionally – when they were down asking questions about you in your old neighborhood?" Dan could see that this line of questioning might be going someplace... Benito was finally giving up some useful information – in spite of himself.

Benito knew he had to remain on the balls of his feet. His mouth was definitely running ahead of his brain and Dan was too clever take the bait on some half-assed misdirection that didn't ring true. "Honestly, here's the last thing I know about these assholes: I'm pretty sure that the last time I saw them, they were in our neighborhood cantina with their rear-ends parked at the bar. But, I have no idea *why* they were there – and, as I had no business with them, I gave them a wide berth, man. If these are the guys you're looking for, I can assure

174

you they're bad news. I ducked out the back and I'm sure that they never even noticed me."

Dan realized he'd never get the complete and unvarnished truth out of a weasel like Benito Rosado. He decided to draw a line under his interrogation of the devious little shit. Besides, he needed to have a word with Carrie on her own... her alter ego, Winter, had a small role to play in his plan to reel in Manny Tejada.

"Benito, I suggest that you don't set foot outside this apartment unless it's being strafed by gunfire or burning down. And keep the curtains drawn. I've got a few more angles to check out, but for now, it's a safe assumption that Tejada and his crew are most assuredly still hunting for you. Now, give Winter and me a minute here."

Benito left the kitchen and trotted towards the bathroom. As soon as he was out of earshot, Dan turned to Carrie. "I need a little assist on a sting for flushing out your secret Sugar Daddy, the charming Manny Tejada. Don't worry; you won't have to go anywhere near the douche bag. I'll come by the club tonight at eleven... alone. Meet me at the back door – you won't even have to miss a shift. Your contribution will only take five minutes. It'll be a simple play-acting job on audio tape, okay?"

Carrie seemed a bit calmer with Benito out of earshot. "I'll help if I can Dan, you know that. I feel bummed about Benny's murder and I hope that Manny lands in the deep stuff for being behind such a terrible thing. I'll be at the stage door at eleven sharp." She got up from the table, lit a cigarette and called to the back of the apartment for her roommate to return to the living room.

Lila sashayed down the hallway and escorted Dan to the door. As she opened it for him, her ample breasts, barely supported by her tank top's skinny straps, 'accidentally' brushed the front of his tux. "God, I wish that a bit of your style would rub off on Marty. I can't help feeling that you inherited all your family's charm genes and your little brother was born to be a loveable goofball."

Dan backed out the door and, rather than letting his irritation at her ill-mannered remark show, he unhurriedly adjusted his tie. "Cut him some slack, darlin'. He's a bit of a slow learner, but there's a quality lover and strong dude bursting to escape from just below that somewhat scrappy exterior."

As he retraced his route past the pool area, Dan scoped out a bevy of luscious coeds coolly reclining on their chaise longues. Many were as attractive as Marty's paramour Lila... perhaps only lacking her obvious surgical enhancements. He wondered why he'd felt obliged to defend his brother after Lila's thoughtless remark. After all, she was simply a slightly shopworn stripper, whose claim to fame was her 'film career' – actually, a couple of walk-ons in long-forgotten sitcoms. Well, he'd wasted his time with a couple of less appealing femme fatales in his heyday. And she seemed to make Marty happy... at least for now.

Setting the hook

The charity evening was sublime, principally because he was escorting the most enchanting woman in the concert hall. Sophie was stunning, as usual. She wore a black cocktail dress with her hair gathered, exposing her exquisite neck. A simple mother of pearl clasp secured her locks. She was elegance personified. All in all, his partner seemed worlds apart from the exotic 'ladies' he'd visited in Point Loma that afternoon.

He'd swapped over TriState's Chevy for his old Fiat 124 Spider at Sophie's place. It was a perfect evening for a drive in his prized possession, even if he'd be leaving the top up, to protect her hair-do. He still felt a stabbing pain or two and stiffness as he slid into the cramped bucket seat, but he valiantly tried to conceal any signs of wear from his lovely date. Indeed, there were few *visible* signs of damage to give the game away, but nothing got by Sophie. As she'd walked him out to the garage, she'd immediately detected a nearly imperceptible limp – and so began the third degree. Dan chose not to elaborate; simply telling her he'd run into a bit of difficulty... nothing he couldn't handle. Sophie knew that sporadic run-ins were an inherent part of Dan's world and wisely elected not to belabor the subject.

Time was tight if they were going to fit in Sophie's required pre-concert socializing, so they'd opted for a quick bite in her kitchen, rather than dinner out. A Caesar Salad with a dry white wine fit the bill perfectly. Dan apologized again for his slightly tardy arrival. Sophie just smiled. "Nonsense Dan. I'm dragging you to a stuffy charity event that starts far too early in the evening. If you're still peckish by the way, there'll no doubt be some pretty yummy finger food at the intermission."

When they arrived downtown, they skipped their pre-concert drink, opting instead for a leisurely walk from the parking garage to the auditorium. Window-shopping as they strolled, Sophie evaded the chill by wrapping up in her favorite black cashmere stole. Unlike many of her socialite friends, she didn't own a fur. Dan wondered to himself as they walked if there were *any* items in the windows worthy of this goddess. He realized that he'd been late to learn what epitomized style and value, even though an example of true class – Neal and Dawn's solid marriage – stood squarely in front of his eyes for years.

The evening passed all too quickly. Dan even enjoyed the music. And fortunately, he managed to carry off the dreaded pre-concert banter with Sophie's sometimes stuffy associates. The Fiat arrived back in her garage around ten and he went in for a quick coffee only, confessing he had one task to complete before turning in for the night. She didn't pry; she knew that the trail to Benny's killers was going colder by the hour. She worried, but she knew that Dan, the consummate professional, would be taking every precaution to protect the Rosado family and himself.

Dan drove his Malibu into the night, already missing Sophie. He turned his mind back to the investigation and found himself hoping, not for the first time, that he and Gunnar would get to the bottom of Benny's brutal killing quickly, for everyone's sake.

Dan easily arrived at the strip club's parking lot before eleven and found a corner space, shying away from the overhead lighting. The lot was only half full. A carload of college kids arrived and took a space near him just as he phoned Gunnar. His partner in crime answered on the first ring.

Gunnar sounded calm and focused on the task at hand. "It's all go, Dan. We've got Marta's place all tied up for tomorrow night. I've told Omar and Vic only what they *need* to know – and firmly reminded them of how they're expected to behave. I could have chosen other volunteers from any of Benny's crews – all of them would be proud to help us exact our revenge. But the boys would never forgive me if we left them on the sidelines when that sweet-assed hammer falls."

It was clear that Gunnar had chosen to include Benny's boys in spite of his and Dan's grave misgivings. Could they be relied upon if the shit hit the fan? Gunnar seemed to be reading Dan's mind: "They've both sworn to do *exactly* as they're told... they know you're in charge. They won't fuck it up, Dan. We'll see you tomorrow night, bro'. Stay cool."

At eleven sharp, Dan got out of the Chevy and grabbed his old audiocassette recorder out of the trunk. Technologically primeval, it still served its purpose in straightforward claims interviews. He darted to the stage door entrance and knocked softly, positioning himself where he'd be easily recognized through the peephole.

As promised, Carrie opened the reinforced steel door immediately. He slipped by her and entered a dimly lit corridor. She hastily led him into a combined storeroom and spare office just to their left, switched on the overhead light and closed the door behind them. They were standing by an old table which served as the only 'desk' in this office, but they didn't bother to sit down on the wooden chairs beside it.

She'd obviously just come off the runway. She'd thrown on a faded terrycloth robe, belt missing. It gaped to expose an eyeful of superlative cleavage. This wasn't 'Carrie' standing next to him... inhabiting her 'Winter Fox' working persona, the girl was clearly at ease in her sequined G-string, mini-bra and stilettos. This sex goddess was more hard-boiled and self-assured than her alter ego, the fretful and overmatched Midwesterner.

He could just make out a hard-hitting Joe Cocker tune accompanying the club's current featured dancer... base beat thumping and the incomparable Joe rasping, *"You can leave your hat on!"* But, in spite of the background disturbance, they didn't need to raise their voices at this far end of the building.

"Okay Carrie, here's the deal." Dan intentionally used her real name; it might help to summon back the troubled girl who'd have a better handle on the critical matters at hand. "I need to create a little breathing space between Manny Tejada and his army of stooges, so that I can have a private 'heart to heart' with him. You're the honey that'll lure him into my lair – and no harm will come to you, I promise."

A dark look came over Carrie's face and she unconsciously drew her shabby bathrobe around her. "You mean I'm the bait? I'm not sure if that's a good idea. I've sworn off that asshole permanently, Dan. He's bad news – and to me, he's already become *old* news."

"I promise you, you won't even have to see him Carrie. And if you help us, he won't be turning up on *anyone's* doorstep and causing trouble for a very long time. Everybody wins... you'd be helping yourself and Lila, as well as Benito and the entire Rosado clan. Are you in?"

Dan could come off pretty convincing when he put his heart into it. She seemed to visibly relax a little. "What the hell... okay, I'll trust you. I guess I'd never forgive myself if I didn't help catch Benny's killers. Besides, I'm thinking of moving back home to put a little distance between myself and all of this bullshit. There are tons of dancing gigs in Minneapolis or St Paul – and most of the clubs back there are a cut or two above this cheesy joint. I have to face it... my acting career out here is dead in the water, unless I'm up for making a porn flick. And I'm really not into that."

"Good girl. And you know, you could find more satisfying work than bare-assed gyrating back in Minnesota." (That came out a bit too preachy!) "Sorry to come on a bit strong; please don't take offence at my big brother routine." Dan just couldn't lay off of Carrie concerning her current gig, even if he felt she'd be insulted and defensive. The truth was, deep down she had to realize that she'd been pretty lucky so far. An overdue bill inevitably arrives when a girl settles for the easy, sordid rewards on offer in the world of sleaze.

"Here's the deal, Carrie. A 'friend of a friend' is the housekeeper for those tourist cabins scattered along the Pacific Beach Pier. She's allowed to live in the maid's unit at the end of the boardwalk. Conveniently for us, she's away tomorrow night. And, your love-starved Manny would without doubt *cream* himself for the chance of a sexy tryst in a cozy cabin over the crashing waves. You can tell him you're house-sitting this funky love nest for a girlfriend... and he's in for a special treat if he drops by to keep you snug and warm. Sell it big time girl! We need to lure him into our trap for that all important one-on-one chat."

"I'll give it a try Dan, but he's only ever picked me up here at the club and taken me back to his place – or, in the beginning, to some 'no-tell motel'. I can't see him biting for a frolic in an unfamiliar love nest."

"Make it sound real special! Tell him you're taking a night off to create a tryst beyond compare... a love-in just for him. He'll take the bait, hon. Leisurely lovemaking with the woman of your dreams, at the end of a pier with the surf crashing below... no man could resist. We need him to arrive at eleven tomorrow night – horny and *alone*. All you have to do is convince him to turn up and your job's done. You won't even be anywhere near the place."

Carrie nodded and a look of resolve came over her face. "What the shit, let's go for it. He can only say no to my sexy invitation, right? If he gets suspicious though, Lila and me will need a safe place to stay. I don't want Manny or any of his bad-ass buddies turning up on our doorstep."

"That won't happen, Carrie. But if you get spooked, we'll see to it that you and Lila are well out of harm's way. And if all goes down as planned, I'll personally send you girls – and Benito too, if you'd like – on a two week vacation to a nice resort in Tahoe. Or, I'll lay out the cash for your plane fare back to Minneapolis, if that's more appealing. No matter what, you'll be the first to know what goes down with Manny tomorrow night – and you can fill in the clueless Benito when and only *if* it suits you. Deal?"

Carrie unconsciously pulled the robe tighter around herself... a gesture that reminded Dan that a simple Midwestern girl was hiding under the terrycloth. "Dan, a plane ticket to Minneapolis sounds like a winner to me right about now. A fresh start surrounded by old friends couldn't be all bad, right? So, tell me. What's my role in this little production?"

Dan handed her a slip of paper which contained a few 'stage directions' and a couple of suggested lines she could try on Manny. It also listed Marta's cabin number for her supposed lover, set out instructions for parking his car down by reception (a spot Gunnar would keep clear) and confirmed the required meeting time. Dan was leaving little to chance.

Carrie took the note and Dan's phone and circled behind the table. After taking a deep breath, her face took on a frigid expression and *Winter* dialed Manny's home number, to be immediately greeted by the ubiquitous manservant, Enrique. Within a few seconds she'd been put through to the man himself. "Hey lover, it's your pussydoll. I've been planning a wild thank-you surprise for you. You're going to be in heaven! Remember that cozy cabin on the PB Pier that I described as the setting for one of my wildest sex fantasies?"

A short pause followed, while Manny obviously searched his memory. Then she purred again. "You *must* remember me whispering in your ear about this little love nest, big guy! My girlfriend who rents the place swears the whispering surf and the sea winds' sighs are fantastic aphrodisiacs! I've always pictured it as our own cozy 'From Here to Eternity' setting, only without annoying seawater and sand washing up our thankfully warm and dry butt cracks! Well, tomorrow's set to be your night of nights, Sugar Daddy. You'll be Burt Lancaster and I'll be Deborah Kerr! Your baby's got exclusive use of the cabin 'til morning – and I'm even bringing along a few of your favorite sex toys. But I know you! Don't even *think* of taping this little romp, okay? This will be a very special memory – just for us, Sweetmeat... forever!"

Dan was witnessing an extremely enticing offer from an immensely sexy vixen. Carrie had to be a terrific actress to play her alter ego's part so convincingly. And imagine someone from her generation even knowing about Burt and Deborah's torrid clinch in the waves! Manny just had to bite for this once in a lifetime offer of a true sex fantasy. Carrie paused again, listening to his reply, and then picked up where she'd left off.

"You won't be sorry, daddy. Your little Winter knows you've got a lot on your plate, but it can't be nothin' as delicious as this offer, believe me. I'll be the hors d'oeuvres, main course and dessert on your dream menu! Turn up just before eleven and park in the private bay by the office at the foot of the pier. My friend asked the manager to save that very secure and special space for you. I'll be hot, wet and panting at *eleven precisely*, in the last cabin on the left at the pier's end – remember, it's spicy Number 17. Just bring yourself – and a Viagra tablet or two if you're up for a *truly* memorable night! I'll uncork the bubbly, break out our toys and then you can unpeel what little I'll be wearing. I can't wait! See you then baby."

Dan grinned as she hung up. "Carrie, you're definitely a better actress than I anticipated. Maybe you should stick it out in California a bit longer if that audition piece is anything to go by. No! I take that back. I'm sure that Minnesota has its share of decent local theater if you still have the acting bug."

Carrie smiled more broadly than Dan had ever witnessed. "Thanks Dan. I have a talent for coaxing what I want out of horny men. It's been my most convincing acting role – and I get to play it so often! Manny's no exception; he's an ardent audience. But, I can't keep him on a lead indefinitely. So, if he had anything to do with Benny's killing, you'd better nail him and his buddies – and do it quickly! And, will you do me one favor?"

"If I can Carrie; name it."

"If you find out Benito's been bullshitting me and had something to do with his cousin's death, will you tell *me* first, before you confront him? I won't want him hiding behind me if he's involved in murdering an innocent guy from his own family."

Dan's level of respect for this girl went up another notch or two. "I'll do my best to tell you the score early on. Benito could be the innocent pawn he claims to be – or he may be in this shit up to his neck. And, of course, there's a massive gray gulf between those two extremes. Whatever the outcome, I'll definitely put you in the picture first, if that's possible. But you can't act on any information I might share without sounding me out. That could be counterproductive – and dangerous for you and Lila. Now, there's one last thing I need from you…"

Dan set his cassette recorder on the desk in front of Carrie and pointed out the small hand mike. "Just speak clearly into this, saying something sexy like, "Come on in lover. The bed's warm and I'm ready and waiting for you!"

Carrie adlibbed her lines – in her best 'Winter' persona – all in one convincing take. And then they were finished. They stepped back into the club's hallway and Dan opened the back door. He thanked her, kissed her cheek and told her not to worry. He sincerely hoped she'd soon have nothing more to worry about – from either Manny Tejada or Benito Rosado.

The heat is on

Forty minutes later, Dan was home and dry, settled into his easy chair. He popped two more painkillers – the last he intended to take. And then he reminded himself to take care... the gloves were now well and truly off. He was certain that Manny and his goons had been major players in Benny's murder. These days, even devoted cartel soldiers didn't readily throw curious outsiders off of cliffs just for nosing around some *jefe's* house on the US side of the border. Dan was getting warm... and the die had already been cast. The bad guys had decided that an irritating, prying bastard had to be taken out – and *for good*! He was certainly glad that he was already a ghost to them!

But the list of suspects in Benny's murder didn't end with Manny Tejada. This small-time hood liked to play the role of a big hitter, but Dan had been around the block. It didn't add up. There was plenty more juice behind this thug... people who believed that they could have *any* of their enemies wiped off the face of the earth with impunity. These despicable bastards – high-level gangsters who called the shots while remaining above the fray – invariably played the most lucrative and safest hands. But not this time. Dan wouldn't let this case rest until some of the prized bigger fish were well and truly fried.

When he'd arrived home, Dan had spent five minutes catching up with Gunnar. A few points needed going over – and Dan also felt the need to reiterate that they'd all be severely bending the rules to catch Benny's killers. Dan trusted Gunnar implicitly, but he wanted to make sure that his partner in crime was taking every precaution to shelter Connie's boys from the worst of the impending fireworks.

It all seemed to be coming together. Gunnar and Dan had reserved the dirtiest and most challenging jobs for themselves. Brenda and Vince would be close by for the final clean-up. Dan hoped that Bren would get sole credit for the police collars, so that she'd have a shot at moving on from her current assignment in the crappy world of the San Diego Vice Detail.

Gunnar had been key in creating some of the cleverer tactics for luring Tejada into their hands, well away from his slimy cohorts. He'd found Winter's out of the way 'love nest', an undisturbed place where they could interrogate their adversary at their leisure. When Dan explained that they could pull no punches with Manny, the little man hadn't flinched. In fact, that piece of news excited him. His devotion to Benny meant that he was even more anxious than Dan to play it rough if the occasion called for it.

Marta, the maid who'd be absent from her Crystal Pier cabin, was an old flame of Gunnar's. Obviously, they remained on good terms. She'd agreed to let him use her cabin, no questions asked. Gunnar said she could be trusted; she'd cover for them, no matter what.

Dan figured that the odds of overwhelming and detaining Tejada at Marta's quiet end of the pier were excellent – two against one in their favor inside the cabin, with Omar and Victor watching their backs outside. There were risks – and Consuela would undoubtedly be irate if she ever discovered that they'd included her boys in the scam.

Gunnar felt that Vic and Omar would handle themselves well, regardless of the circumstances. They were handy with their fists – and Dan was pretty certain that any back-ups or bodyguards that Tejada brought to the pier wouldn't hang around and risk arrest if they felt they were losing control and the shit was hitting the fan. Just in case though, the boys would be armed as they hid in the shadows. Dan prayed that this was the right decision – and that they wouldn't need to play a major role in the festivities.

On a more personal level, Gunnar felt it was only fair – or as he'd put it, "justice in action" – to allow Victor and Omar in on the sting. They had a son's right to help avenge the death of their father. And, Gunnar had repeatedly reminded the boys that Manny wouldn't be the end of this trail. So, if they made a false move, screwed up or went solo, the bigger fish might just swim away.

Earlier that day, Gunnar had completed a final reconnaissance of Marta's cabin. He confirmed to himself that there was plenty of room between her pier-end unit and her nearest neighbors. They'd have the time – and privacy – required to crack Manny Tejada once they had him securely ensconced inside.

There was nothing left to do but rest up for the big push. Dan slid into bed, punched his pillow into shape and curled into a ball. It had been a long day and, seemingly ages ago, he'd been very regretful to leave Sophie's place. But, things were coming together quickly in his unauthorized investigation. He was smack in the middle of a very decent run of luck – and he hoped it would long continue.

Manny Tejada, his butler Enrique and the two goons who'd heaved him off Sunset Cliffs would be surprised indeed when they again met up with their pesky adversary. Maybe even the oily Ernest Kincaid was securely in the loop with this crew – and had already been informed that Dan Paige was resting comfortably on a cold slab in the morgue. Their relentless hunter was literally going to be resurrected from the dead! Tomorrow would be the beginning of the end for some very wicked characters.

Chapter 23

Monday

The Snowbirds keep flocking

Dan jumped out of bed too quickly; his Torrey Pines aches were lingering. Maybe there *was* something in this 'aging' concept – something he'd adamantly argued was a youth-created fabrication. He decided a piping hot shower might hasten his recovery. Later, after coffee, he threw on jeans, Dockers and an old polo shirt. He headed out the door, grabbing his khaki windbreaker, bogus cop's ID and holstered .38. He could only just recall where he'd stowed the Chevy, well away from the apartment. When he arrived at the spot, he was relieved it hadn't been vandalized or stripped. The old neighborhood was apparently hanging in there! He stashed the shield and revolver in their customary hiding spot under the spare, tossed the windbreaker on the passenger seat and drove away.

A hearty breakfast was top of the agenda. When he arrived at Lenny's, the ubiquitous Stan and Jerry were in mid-flow, sorting out which more deserving US metropolis could soon take on the mantle of 'America's Favorite Hotspot' now that their city was, in Jerry's pithy words, "over-ripe to the point of imminent rot!"

The advertising guru moved the discussion onto his personal action plan, should the situation worsen. "If any more addled Snowbirds land here, I'm headin' for Corpus Christi. Shit, it'll take hours in traffic just to clear El Cajon headin' east. From there though, it's clear sailing all the way to Texas. Rent's cheap, their mature broads are charmers – *Southern Belles* – and gas costs less. What more does anyone need?"

Against his better judgment, Dan focused, if only momentarily, on this inane conversation. "Neither of you will *ever* depart San Diego until his smoky remains drift up the well-used stack at the Lemon Grove Crematorium. No doubt I'll join the remaining member of your little debating society at the first man's funeral – and I'll be the *only* mourner at the survivor's service." Rosie refilled their mugs, starched hanky jutting jauntily from her apron pocket as her inexpertly made-up face hovered above the coffee jug. Dan nodded towards the craggy waitress and added, "And, she won't attend *either* burial service unless you two loosen up on the tips. Rosie's due a helluva lot more cash for the hours she wastes serving you two. It sidetracks her from more amenable and *generous* customers."

Stan was poised to inject the last word as Dan downed his coffee and rose to leave. "You'll miss the scintillating banter when we skip town, amigo. And don't expect any postcards from *my* new digs, wherever I end up! I might even join Jerry on the Gulf Coast, even though I despise their odious mosquitoes and hurricanes. Wherever I go though, I'll be hunkering down at a pleasant, sparkling clean counter in some new diner... and swigging better coffee than this sewage plant serves up!"

Dan hit the parking lot, slid into his Chevy and dialed the strippers' apartment; hoping to confirm that Benito remained in situ. 'Old Mr Charm' himself answered on the first ring, attempting to camouflage his identity with a pitiful 'Italian' accent. Identifying Dan, Benito dropped the vocal trickery and informed his irritated caller that he was watching a terrific show called *'Christ's Pulpit in the New Jerusalem'* on an obscure cable channel. He told Dan that he was getting seriously into earning his long overdue redemption. The down-home philosophy of the Most Reverend Bobby Joe Hibbert seemed to strike some long forgotten chord with the recently reformed drug dealer. "What's your take on the power of Our Lord and Savior, Dan? It can't do no harm to have a lovin' Jesus firmly in your corner, right? I'm givin' prayer a shot – seeking salvation for me and my poor cousin, Benny. From now on, it's good deeds, Sunday TV services and a shitload of love for my fellow man. You know, Dan, it's never too late to book that business-class ticket to the Promised Land!"

Dan barely stifled a cackle. "Pray away Benito. But remember, a sinner's final judgment will focus on *deeds* more than words. The Almighty Himself probably invented that old adage, 'Talk is cheap'... He's been privy to rosy promises and acts of contrition from countless lost souls over the course of history. So, by all means, *do* concentrate on turning your life around – and let's hope your actions from this day forward can buy you a great measure of sweet forgiveness!"

Benito went quiet... perhaps he found difficulty in taking in the magnitude of Dan's words? Finally, he went on to say that the girls were still sleeping – and Dan satisfied himself that Carrie, the soon to be *ex*-Winter, hadn't spilled any details of their imminent sting to this unreliable little turd. He told Benito to return to his television sermon, wondering if Reverend Bobby Joe's new convert had been inspired enough to send away the "token $10 offering" solicited repeatedly by the unctuous preacher and his slick acolytes.

Sweating it off

As Dan checked in with Benito and his roommates, Flaco and Jesus were reclining on thick towels in The Agua Caliente Club's ancient, but still sumptuous, steam room. Situated along the far straight of Tijuana's infamous racetrack, the club's recently renovated, ornate Spanish edifice had become the 'hangout of choice' for many *trafficantes de drogas.* "Full membership privileges and the connections are worth the price – and, what the fuck, we've earned it," Flaco had explained to his overawed partner when they'd recently joined.

Their conversation had drifted onto the merits of permanent residence in California versus staying in Mexico… particularly in light of the spending power of their burgeoning ill-gotten gains. Flaco shared his clear-cut views on the subject. "Listen, soon we'll be living like kings in Tijuana or Ensenada – or I may even retire and buy me a fuckin' estate on the outskirts of Méjico City. Our women are *primoroso* – and obedient. A California *puta* – even a *Chicana* – spends money like water. And, behind your back she'll screw the first hot and horny hombre who's buyin' the drinks."

Jesus reclined on the topmost bench; eyes clenched tight, with sweat pouring from his body. Steaming was the only activity that put this grimy bear in the proximity of a shower stall, as Flaco had known only too well when he'd urged the big man to join the club. Unfortunately, Jesus' badly needed scrub-downs came at the *end* of their roasting sessions, so the odor emitted by his still-rancid pores was now saturating the steam room. His sweat even overpowered the pleasantly primeval, slightly musty smell still emanating from the spa's recently re-plastered walls.

Jesus grunted, warming to the topic of the ladies they'd soon attract. He responded to his partner's musings in his high-pitched voice, for some reason (perhaps excitement?) opting to practically shout in their quiet surroundings. "You don't know shit man! Baja women are Madonnas or *putas* from birth – and I don't wanna' end up with either type helpin' herself to my fuckin' money. And I didn't work my *cajones* off to support some greedy bitch's fat mama… who, by the way, is no doubt sleepin' in my fuckin' spare room and ridin' my ass every chance she gets. At least in California you get what you *pay* for and you're a helluva lot less likely to be burdened with hidden extras!"

Flaco considered this line of reasoning and decided the usually dim Jesus might have stumbled onto something. "You have a point man. Gringos don't seem to be swimming or tunneling into Méjico in the dead of the night… the grass probably *is* greener up north. And, sure as shit, some very tasty women up there will be ours for the taking! When we've built up our stake, we could head for Arizona. Money goes further there; we can each buy a big condo next to a swimming pool overflowing with *putas* – and take up golf!"

Jesus rolled off the top bench and began his slow climb down to the wet floor. Stretching and toweling off a layer of steam and sweat, he opted for a new topic: "I thought we had a coupla' days off comin'. We handled that nosey cop, so why does Tejada need us tonight?"

"He didn't give me no reason, man. It's just, "Turn up at my place at nine-thirty." That's all I know. He's meeting somebody somewhere in town and he wants us to cover his back. There's extra cash in it, so let's just go with the *jefe's* flow, okay? It'll pay to cooperate, even on the crap jobs, until we're permanently off his shit list."

Jesus padded through the steam room's ancient cedar doors into the adjoining changing area. He slipped into his flip-flops, which he'd left outside the door, and threw his damp towel over his shoulder. Flaco followed, towel modestly surrounding his waist. As they showered in adjoining stalls, Jesus began crooning an old folk song in his eerie contralto.

Flaco interrupted the burly man's dire performance by injecting a final remark concerning their imminent 'bodyguard' assignment. "We'll turn up and take Tejada's money, right? Then he can find other suckers for his next knee-cappin' or hit. I'm thinkin' we'll lie low, particularly up north– at least for a little while."

The calm before the storm

As Dan headed down Sunset Cliffs Boulevard towards his mom's, he noted the tranquil ocean waters… too calm for decent surfing. When he arrived, Mandy was studying at the kitchen table and Sally was in the back yard, hanging out the washing. As expected, Marty was still zonked out. Most days, the lazy little turkey surfaced around one, ready for the hearty brunch he expected his mother or sis to prepare.

Dan rousted Marty and they switched on the TV, sipping mugs of strong black coffee that Mandy prepared for them. *Sports Extra* was showing a re-run of ladies' beach volleyball in Puerto Rico… scintillating stuff! Dan paid scant attention, but Marty provided a lewd running commentary, focusing on the four girls' golden glow and toned bodies.

During a commercial break, Marty decided to 'subtly' pump his big brother for an update on Benito's troubles. Dan shared some inconsequential details and managed to quickly close down the

187

interrogation. He turned the conversation onto his brother's hot and prickly relationship with the delightful, if slightly dangerous, Lila Blue.

"Bro', I know you're pretty passionate for Lila – and that you care about her pal Winter too. But you must realize that the closer you gravitate towards this pair's dubious circle, the more loose and nasty shit might ricochet in your direction. They invariably attract trouble – and they're in no position to deflect hazardous vibes while they're working professionally as bona fide 'loser bait'. Can't you see that?"

"Yeah bro', you may be right. But Lila's had more than her share of tough breaks – and she's prepared to walk away from strippin'. Once we've settled into steady jobs, we'll move in together. Winter's boyfriend, Benito, even said he'd help me to catch on as a foreman with a decent contractor. He's tight with a few builders up in North County. Anyway, me and Lila will work it out. We're in love, man; that's what matters – and we're goin' to keep on keepin' on! You've gotta be cool with it... I'm a lucky dude."

"It all sounds terrific Marty, but I wouldn't count on Benito's help. And, exactly what sort of 'nine-to-five' job is Lila qualified for? Can you really see her happy in the 'straight' working gal's world, taking home chump change compared to an exotic dancer's earnings?"

"Sure, I can see it man! She's even talking about going to SDSU and earning a degree in Physiology, so she can work with handicapped kids. Believe it or not, she's already got some credits under her cute little belt from a few years back. She's got a big heart – and she absolutely loves rugrats and strays."

Dan couldn't believe his ears. Marty obviously wasn't perceptive enough to understand that his reference to Lila's "love of strays" was right on the money in respect of his *own* budding relationship with this beguiling girl. Dan could only hope that Lila's delusional aspirations would soon crash and burn of their own accord, thereby presenting his little brother with his first genuine reality check in years.

There was no point in pricking his brother's balloon at this point in time. "Going back to school could be a smart move for her, Marty – and after she's finished a couple of years at college and settled on a major, you could move in together. At that point, if you're 'on plan', you'll already be established in that foreman's job up in North County, right?"

Dan knew when to quit. If he kept grilling his little brother, he'd dig in his heels. And soon Marty would create some lame opening gambit to tap his big brother for seed money for yet another 'can't miss' venture – probably involving the brilliant Lila. This scenario was all too familiar. Dan couldn't help but wonder if Marty had even bothered to phone about Lightnin's Night Manager's opening in La Mesa.

Sally returned from the yard and saw that her boys were deep in conversation. She picked up the TV remote and flipped through the channels... the volleyball was winding up anyway. An ancient black and white film popped up. She smiled and sat down with her clothesbasket on her knee. "Look boys, it's *Gilda*! Check out that slinky dress and how Rita's hips sway as she dances for those gawking men. People told me I looked like Rita Hayworth when I was in my prime. Remember when I had long hair like that Dan?"

"I sure do mom. You were the original stone fox! Still are!"

On TV, Glenn Ford, attempting to maintain his machismo, utterly turned to mush as Rita/Gilda finished her number, sashayed down the stage steps and sat at his table. Occasionally, a snatch or two of *film noir* hit close to home with Dan. All too often, his life seemed to take on the tone of a pulp novel. It was time to grow up and stick to the straight and narrow – in other words, to clamp down on the drama. Maybe Sophie would be his last, best opportunity to 'roll over' for the right woman... and *stay* rolled over!

They sat together and watched Rita spin her magic until the film ended. Even Mandy set her books aside, joining them when she overheard her mom reminiscing. Later, Dan treated them all to an enormous brunch and a pitcher of Margaritas at the beach. As they sat in their favorite window booth at the Quad Tavern, he realized they needed to do this more often. Sally surely deserved every opportunity to enjoy some easy laughs with her kids.

They took a leisurely walk along OB's promenade and watched a group of small boys playing softball on the sand. The afternoon was ending; sun hovering on the horizon. But he'd be leaving them on a high note. And, as they walked up the hill, it struck him – perhaps belatedly – that 'family life' was a dichotomy... grave responsibilities interwoven with enormous blessings.

Back at his mom's, Dan thought about his sweet sister and how she'd unconsciously become this family's glue. When Mandy was in their midst, hassles and conflicts vanished. After what seemed like a fleeting visit, it was pitch dark and approaching nine-thirty. Dan said his goodbyes and drove up the coast towards Pacific Beach, where Gunnar and Benny's boys would be awaiting his arrival at Marta's cabin.

The honey trap

Dan parked off Garnet, two streets up from the famous Mission Beach Pier. Even though his Chevy resembled a thousand other company rides, there was no point in tempting fate by parking too close to his destination… Manny Tejada might recognize it. He opened the trunk and retrieved his shield and holstered gun. He also grabbed his battered cassette recorder from a cardboard box stuffed with office kit. Finally, Dan strapped on the shoulder holster under his windbreaker, pocketed his ID and headed to the beach.

As he approached Marta's tiny cabin at the end of the pier, Dan was reminded that Gunnar's chosen love nest was near perfect. The aged wooden bungalows were situated a good fifteen feet above the high-water line, suspended over one of the city's busiest daytime beaches. But the ocean's roar, sparse late-night foot traffic and a fairly generous spacing between cabins made Winter's proposed rendezvous spot a judicious choice.

Each cabin had a single parking space, marked on the boardwalk outside the door. Most units seemed to be unoccupied at this hour. The tenants, typically tourists, were no doubt still out on the town. The cabins were painted a garish robin's egg blue, with faded green shingle roofs. Personally, he couldn't warm to this scruffy motel's supposed attractions, especially considering the shocking rates the rooms commanded. Their 'Thirties California Ambiance' was no doubt better left to the imagination than experienced first-hand. But inland dwellers, particularly the Arizona crowd, couldn't resist the cabins' proximity to the ocean and the somewhat threadbare appeal of an old-fashioned 'beach weekend' on the ageing pier.

A faint glow shone through the curtains of the marginally smaller cabin at the end of the boardwalk. This unit alone lacked a parking space… the end of the pier was left open and uncluttered, an attraction for guests and paying fishermen. Thankfully, this public area appeared to be deserted.

Cabin 16 was the nearest 'guest-occupied' unit, opposite the maid's quarters and a good few yards down the boardwalk. It was hard to fathom why they'd situated the lone staff unit at the pier's far end back in the thirties. A guest cabin on this prized spot could've featured a picture window facing out to sea, thus commanding a premium. Dan figured that the current owners were just too lazy to undertake the obviously attractive remodel.

The staggered bungalows meant that no window looked directly into the opposing neighbors'. Unit 16 was *clearly* occupied; Dan could hear loud music, laughter and high-pitched shrieks… probably kids enjoying the dying throes of a three-day weekend bash. Hopefully, the party's Monday evening stragglers would be oblivious to any commotion in Marta's cabin. They'd 'party on' and remain none the wiser, as long as Dan and Gunnar kept any racket down to a dull roar.

As Dan surveyed the scene, two young revelers emerged and wandered towards the pier's end, lighting cigarettes as they passed. Both wore SDSU sweatshirts, nylon baggies and flip-flops. Sniggering and whispering, they seemed to be concentrating on clever strategies to entice their dates to suck up at least one more potent cocktail before their weekend of wooing and partying wound down.

Dan, indulging in a little pre-emptive 'damage control', wandered over to the railing and nodding a greeting. "Hey guys, sounds like you're having a great time!" With that, he pulled out his shield and flashed it at them.

The less lubricated young stud submissively raised his hands to shoulder level before replying. "I'm sorry about the noise, sir. We'll keep it down – we don't want any trouble. And by the way, no one is underage in there, sir."

"I'm not trying to hassle you son. In fact, my associates and I are working undercover here and I hope you'll just forget you've seen us and continue to 'party hearty', okay? But steer clear of this end of the pier if you don't mind. If you hear *anything* going down, you and your crew should concentrate on your festivities and keep your heads down; got it?"

"Fine sir. If we get too rowdy though, just let us know. This party should break up around midnight – only one or two of us may be hanging in later; and then only if we kinda' 'get lucky'. Anyway, we read you loud and clear. We're to butt out and give you room to work. You can count on our discretion."

"Thanks dudes. If all goes to plan, your guests don't even need to know we're over here, right?" Dan attempted to finish on a light note. "And, don't do anything with those fine ladies that I wouldn't have done at your age, okay?"

The boys tossed their cigarettes into the sea and hightailed it back to their room. As perfect as this spot was for taking in Tejada, this little frat party was a bit of a bummer. Dan knew the boys wouldn't be able to pass up the chance to tell their exciting new story to the girls, in spite of his warnings. He hoped the kids wouldn't get too curious. Oh well, too late to switch tactics now! He turned and walked to Marta's door, knocking lightly.

Gunnar opened the door immediately. "Hey amigo, how goes the wars? I saw you scaring off those kids." He turned and said, "Vic, Omar – Dan's here and he's got a few instructions for you." Benny's boys were sitting on Marta's sofa, watching television.

Dan grabbed a kitchen chair and sat down facing the boys. "Listen up. Gunnar says you're anxious to provide back-up for this little caper. I won't go over the finer details – I know Gunnar's already done that. But I do want to reiterate one important point. You'll be outside when Tejada shows up. If we're lucky, he'll arrive solo. But he could bring back-up – and we've got to be ready for unexpected guests. I'd wager his boys *will* accompany him when he comes down the pier from his car and then quietly retreat when he knocks and comes inside. But, if they stick around or try to join our little party, you're to signal us with a loud whistle, okay? Remember, *be cool*. Stay out of sight and leave his bodyguards alone. They'll surely be armed – and you won't."

Vic spoke for both boys. "Don't worry Dan. We know the plan and our part in it. We're convinced, as you and Gunnar've told us, there are some major turds resting higher on the shitpile... guys that only Manny Tejada will lead us to. We won't screw up – we want justice for our family. You can count on us."

"Okay then, relax for now and you can get set up down the pier just before eleven." Dan walked across Marta's tiny room and set his cassette player on the kitchen table. He turned the volume knob to full and motioned Gunnar over. "I'm going to stand outside the door and knock once. Then I want you to play Winter's recording, as a test."

A minute later, as Dan stood outside Marta's door, Winter's seductive invitation emerged loud and clear. A quick rewind and it would be ready for rebroadcast.

Further preparations were superfluous. Gunnar would hold his nerve; Dan knew he'd be reliability itself in a tight spot. The boys would be in position for Manny's arrival – no doubt feeling the chill, but suitably hidden and hopefully not over-eager. The plotters sat on Marta's worn couch and killed time, catching the end of a lame *Magnum PI* escapade before settling in for a more satisfying *Rockford Files* rerun.

After Jim Rockford nailed the slippery culprits, Gunnar turned off the TV and walked over to the cabin's entrance to switch off the overhead light. The boys slipped out to take their positions on the pier. As in many motel rooms, the 'on/off' for Marta's bedside lamp was also connected to its own switch by the entrance. Gunnar turned on the small lamp, creating a soft glow that would emanate through the closed curtains. The cabin would look inviting for Winter's avid suitor. Both men sat facing the entrance on the straightback kitchen chairs. They were ready, come what may.

Chapter 24

Springing the tender trap

At one minute past eleven, Manny Tejada drove under the arched electric sign at the pier's ancient entrance. He parked his black Chrysler, as instructed, in the 'Manager's Space' just beyond the office, which exhibited two wooden signs. A permanent outside sign informed potential guests that this was, indeed, the *'Office'* and a small plank hanging inside the window stated there were currently *'No Vacancies'*. The office and its adjoining parking space were deserted, just as Winter had promised. Manny had to snicker… if late-arriving guests wanted any assistance or wished to check in, it was just tough shit!

He lowered his window and inhaled the sea air. Glancing over his shoulder, he whispered to Jesus and Flaco, who were hunched below window level in the back seat. "Okay you two, I'm getting out. Slip out between the car and the office and stay in the shadows. Remember, you're here to *cover my ass*. So, stay alert and do your damnedest to remain inconspicuous. Follow on after me when I'm around twenty paces down the pier. Try to look casual, like you're heading to your own cabin, got it?"

"No sweat *jefe*," Flaco replied. "If we detect any funny business you don't pick up on, we'll let out a loud whistle, just like you've told us to – and we can all beat it back to the car. Barring that, when you're inside we'll wait for the 'all clear' signal with the curtains or shades and catch a cab. Piece of cake!"

Manny was decked out in his finest… a mauve silk shirt, black lightweight wool slacks and expensive alligator loafers in dark oxblood. His favorite 'protector', a silver-plated .22 Special, rested in the right-hand outside pocket of his burgundy blazer. As he closed his door, he paused to make sure his minders had slipped unobtrusively into the shadows. Satisfied, he hit the central locking button on his key fob and sauntered down the boardwalk.

Meeting up with some bitch on unfamiliar territory was no doubt a foolhardy move. But the bottom line was, Manny trusted Winter… mainly because she was too fuckin' frightened of him to try anything funny. But with that little shit Benito Rosado on the loose, there was no point in taking chances. If that son of a *puta* lurked in the shadows, Jesus and Flaco would get the drop on him. Benito wasn't clever enough to outfox the likes of Manny Tejada – and the little asshole lacked guts at the best of times.

194

As Manny approached the end bungalow – slightly smaller than the others, just as Winter had described it – he paused. He detected a dim light through the curtains, but no sound escaped the cabin. He knocked lightly and waited.

Winter's sublime, husky voice beckoned from beyond the closed door. "Come on in Sweetmeat! Your baby's all wet where it counts and excited beyond belief – and so *tired* of waiting for you!"

Manny's heart was pounding. He felt a rush of anticipation flowing from the top of his ribcage to his groin. He turned the knob and stepped into the dimly lit room. He glanced with bated breath towards a bed he could just make out in the corner. But it was empty... his sex goddess was *not* draped across it! Instead, two guys stood by a wooden table, weapons drawn.

"Welcome, Mr Tejada," chortled Dan. "Surprised to see me resurrected from the dead? Don't make any sudden moves." Dan glanced quickly towards Gunnar, "Frisk him partner and then we'll all settle in for a friendly chat."

Gunnar moved swiftly around their guest and locked the door. Then he cautiously approached Manny from behind, poised to frisk him. Their captive didn't move a muscle, obviously still in shock. Dan was certain that Tejada recognized him, even in the dim light, but he was probably still coming to terms with the 'ghost' facing him.

As Gunnar stepped forward to begin frisking their captive, Dan heard a loud whistle from down the boardwalk. In the next instant, the door behind Gunnar burst open, its frame shattering. Feisty little Flaco flew headlong into the room, executing an astonishingly athletic shoulder roll, pistol drawn. Barely managing to avoid Gunnar and the still-frozen Manny, the tiny man rose, preparing to fire towards Dan, standing open mouthed by the kitchen table.

The quick-thinking Gunnar instantly sprang to life; stepping back to flip the door's switch that extinguished the bedside lamp. The room went pitch black, undoubtedly saving Dan's life. Although he had been painfully slow to react, the alert Gunnar had given him a second chance – and Dan used it to dive out of Flaco's line of fire.

Manny had been in tight spots before and he wasn't about to panic in this one. A finely-honed instinct for self-preservation kicked in. He dropped to his right, lighting on one knee as he grabbed the shiny .22 from his blazer pocket. He too began firing at the spot where Dan stood microseconds before.

Muzzle flashes strobe-lit the room. But, initially, no shots struck home. In the ensuing wild seconds, the blinding light from handgun barrels was the only means of spotting erratic and fast-moving targets.

Dan's third round, fired from the prone position, finally found its mark. Manny's nimble little bodyguard groaned and Dan heard a dull thud as his elusive target hit the floor. An instant later, he heard Gunnar snarl, "Don't move Tejada – drop your weapon or I'll blow a hole clean through you." A gun clattered to the floor. Dan rose up and carefully made his way over to the door, switching all the lights on.

Tejada had managed to maneuver well away from the entrance towards the empty bed, but Gunnar had crouched low and almost instinctively stuck to him, tracking Manny's muzzle flashes to his new position. He'd cleverly finished up directly behind his intended target, pistol pressed into the center seam of Manny's sporty blazer.

Momentarily, no one moved or spoke. Dan carefully reassessed the situation. Was Manny expecting more cavalrymen to come to his rescue... or was the gunplay over?

There was a soft knock. Although the frame was shattered near the lock, the door had swung nearly closed in the melee. Gunnar nodded towards Dan, his weapon still aimed squarely at Manny's spine. Dan pointed his gun at the entrance and took a step back. "Come in... but slowly!"

The door swung slowly open and, mercifully, it was Omar Rosado who entered. A clearly agitated Victor stood just outside, with a gun resting squarely in the back of a huge, scruffy brute. The large man stepped forward, hands clasped above his head – and Benny's oldest son slipped in behind him. Dan retreated into the center of the room, trained his own weapon back on Tejada, and signaled to Omar to close the door.

Obviously, the boys had managed to signal with that loud whistle, but only at the last instant. The little guy had been wily and quick, eluding the brothers. *And where had Vic's gun come from?* It was apparent they hadn't exactly followed Gunnar's orders concerning 'no weapons' – much to Dan's relief now. Vic had no doubt stashed his revolver somewhere outside the cabin earlier in the evening, fetching it when they went to their positions.

True to form, the ineffectual Jesus hesitated on the boardwalk when the shit hit the fan. He'd never even managed to draw his weapon – it still protruded from the waistband of his filthy leather trousers. Dan spotted the gun and spat out two quick commands. "Keep that fat asshole covered Vic! And Omar, see Tejada's gun on the floor? Kick it towards me." They did as they were told and Dan inched forward, using his left hand to delicately extract the bulky automatic jammed into Jesus' beltline. Gunnar still had Tejada covered, so he'd retrained his weapon on the big man. He'd not hesitate to shoot the bastard, even if Vic might.

Did this idiot even have the safety on? As he stepped back, Dan checked Jesus' gun for himself. Sure enough, the cretin had carelessly shoved an old Army .45 into his groin with the safety off! Dan reset the safety before bending down and picking up Manny's shiny little pistol. He laid both weapons on the kitchen table.

Dan had immediately recognized Vic and Omar's burly captive. He was the dirtbag who'd been most instrumental in flinging him off the Torrey Pines cliffs, no doubt about it. With Manny and the Big Bear covered, he turned his attention to the third intruder; the little guy still lying motionless, face down on the floor.

He knelt and felt Flaco's scrawny neck for a pulse. There was none. When Dan turned him over, the reason was apparent. His shirt bore a neat new hole – a bloody ring the size of a quarter in the center of his chest. The bullet had pierced his heart and lodged in his spine or shoulder blade on its upward trajectory from Dan's crouched position. There had been no sign of an exit wound when the little man was lying face down... because none existed.

Dan recognized this tough little hombre as the big guy's partner. Belatedly he noticed that the corpse still clung to his gun... Dan had committed yet another rookie mistake by not kicking the weapon away from the prostrate body first thing! "Gunnar, pick up the stiff's weapon and stow it, along with the others, in the kitchen cupboard. Then you can sit our two still-breathing guests at the kitchen table. I'm going outside to check on our neighbors. Hopefully we haven't disturbed their party."

Dan strolled ten yards down the pier and saw Cabin 16's curtains flutter. A boy peered out momentarily, trying to appear nonchalant. He recognized Dan and simply waved to him and disappeared. Dan was pretty certain these kids would maintain a low profile.

Re-entering Marta's cabin, Dan found the big man already trussed up, gagged and perched on a poky kitchen chair. Manny sat quietly opposite him, with Vic and Omar behind, awaiting further orders. Dan was happy to oblige. "Finish tying up Mr Tejada as well boys and toss his carcass on the bed." He glanced in Gunnar's direction and then turned back to address their honored guest. "Well, Manny, you came here to test out that very mattress... so here's your chance!"

The boys went to work on Manny; Vic covering him while Omar stripped off his blazer and roughly trussed him up. Dan turned his attention back to the unfortunate Flaco, now lying face-up, staring vacantly at the ceiling. Luckily, Marta's floorboards were bare and the little guy hadn't bled profusely. The clean-up wouldn't be too bad; they'd be able to mop up any blood traces if they weren't allowed to dry in.

Manny was quickly shifted to the bed, hog-tied and face down. Omar had retrieved a wicked looking flick knife from his inside blazer pocket. Victor found a phone and keys in his trousers – as well as a fat money clip. The boys set Manny's possessions on the side table by the sofa.

Dan and Gunnar certainly weren't going to summon the law at this point... even those few cops they felt they could actually trust. The corpse on the floor was a casualty of war, lost in an unfortunate skirmish. There'd be much ground to cover with Tejada before end game... and it would be judicious for them to forego any bothersome legalities in the meantime. Of course, Dan couldn't move to *permanently* eliminate even a scumbag like Manny without feeling some remorse, but memories of Benny's murder – and his own cliff-diving episode – were fresh and raw. Recent history made it a helluva lot easier to operate outside the law.

Dan lifted Flaco by his feet and dragged the scrawny corpse to the door. Then he grabbed a dishtowel and some liquid detergent from under Marta's sink and set about wiping up the small pool of blood seeping into floor. "Make sure you throw in a nice set of dishtowels when you take you-know-who out for her thank-you dinner, Gunnar. Flowers would go a long way too. That – plus the agreed cash – should keep her sweet, eh?"

"Sure," Gunnar replied. But you know, we really don't need to give her *nothin'* pard. My occasional sweet lovin's all she craves... I'm still her *amante numero uno.*"

"Humor me anyway, Gunnar. Go that extra mile for your old flame! It looks like Manny'll be springing for her bonus anyway, from the looks of that money clip."

Vic dampened a second towel and gave the spot Dan had just swabbed another thorough scrub. There'd be no visible stain when the floorboards dried. Omar was putting the finishing touches on their guest of honor – he was bound tightly, with a red bandana stuffed in his mouth. Gunnar gave Tejada's bindings one last tug and grinned at Dan. "I do believe that Manny's ready for your chat now."

Omar gave Manny a short punch in the gut for good measure and Gunnar pistol-whipped the side of his scalp – but not too viciously – to get his undivided attention. Dan stepped in and quietly issued instructions, attempting to calm things a trifle. "Vic, go get your truck and pull it up flush with the doorway. I hope you remembered blankets.

198

We can wrap up the stiff – and then you guys can haul both of Manny's sidekicks away." Vic nodded and immediately headed out the door.

Dan felt another pang of guilt about their somewhat rash decision to involve Connie's boys. They'd performed admirably, aside from ignoring Gunnar's instruction to carry no weapons. But there was no denying that they had become willing accessories to some very significant felonies. And, there was the potential for further exposure to danger when the boys disposed of Manny's henchmen.

The team sat in silence, guns to hand, for the five minutes it took Victor to retrieve the truck. When he pulled up outside, Dan peered from the curtains. They'd brought an old 'long-body' van, with no signage. Omar mentioned they'd 'found' some plates to slap on for the evening's work. The truck wouldn't be easily connected to Rosado & Sons.

Obviously, the boys were likely to be a bit itchy... running on adrenaline. Dan couldn't start interrogating Tejada until they were out of the way. He and Gunnar had to handle the grilling carefully or their investigation into the cartel's hidden hierarchy could unceremoniously end at Manny's relatively low level, allowing the *real* brains and power behind Benny's murder to escape justice. At least they had a shot at grabbing up any of the more accessible slimebags who resided in San Diego. They might be in for a long night.

Chapter 25

Manny spills his guts

Omar and Vic were outside, already tightening Jesus' gag and hefting his weighty carcass onto the cab's passenger seat. In seconds they had him securely bound to the headrest. Omar returned to Marta's cabin with a large tarpaulin. He rolled Flaco's spindly body into it, tying off both ends with heavy cord. He slung the puny carcass over his shoulder and hustled it out, tossing his consignment through the van's side-loading door. With the truck secured, the boys returned for their final orders.

Vic was carrying a bulky burlap sack, which he handed to Gunnar. "It's the stuff you asked for. Everything's there; I double-checked."

Gunnar threw the sack on the sofa and turned to face the boys. "You did great amigos. I can't say your dad would've approved of our undertaking; he was too much of a damned pacifist. But *I'm* sure as hell proud – you behaved like real men!" He removed a leather tool belt from the sack, strapped it around his waist and said, "Back in a minute. I need a coupla' more things from the truck."

He returned, carrying a couple of narrow strips of wood and a sturdy slide lock. Benny's vans always carried odds and ends that came in handy at job sites. Gunnar had what he needed to repair Marta's door. He set the wood and lock next to the burlap bag on the sofa and said, "That's me finished in the truck boys. You're done here – as soon as you hand that gun over to me, Vic." The boy grimaced, but did as he was told.

Gunnar's eyes told Dan to remain silent as he gave the boys their final instructions. "Take these assholes into the scrub east of San Ysidro. Dig the bullet out of the stiff and dispose of the slug later... carefully. Bury the dead *puto* in a shallow grave near the border fence. If he's ever found, he'll appear to be an unlucky wetback who got rolled by some loco illegal or border bandit. There won't be much of an investigation. Untruss the big turd and let him go... *and make sure he heads south, through the fence.* You can bet your ass we won't hear from him again. He won't want to get tangled up in Tejada's impending problems with the cartel's big fish, let alone talk to any San Diego cops. Now, get going!"

With that, Victor and Omar each gave Gunnar a high five and headed out to the truck. Dan heard it fire up and head sedately down the pier. Although he didn't wish to go there, his mind's eye shot ahead an hour or so. He could visualize Flaco's burial spot; near the border fence, east of Otay Mesa. He queried Gunnar, "Do you really think they'll let the big fuck-up go scot-free at the border?"

"Who the fuck knows Dan? What I *do* know is, I'll never ask them about this night again. And they'll tell me nothin'. Whatever goes down between that big asshole and Benny's boys, it's only justice served in my book. Their dad was the best man I ever knew – and his sons have earned the right to wreak justice on his killers, *mano a mano*."

So, Dan thought, it had come down to this. Their plan was working tolerably well... except for the two fine kids they'd involved in a foolhardy shoot-out, as well as a probable revenge execution. It wasn't his finest moment... maybe he was getting too old – and a tad too slipshod – to indulge in this kind of shit!

As Dan's mind drifted, Gunnar busied himself repairing Marta's door. He had it looking almost as good as new in ten minutes, patching the frame with the scrap wood. He both cemented and screwed the replacement strips of wood into the remains of the existing frame, setting the original lock plate neatly back into place. He added the sturdy slide lock to Marta's door for good measure... now it was more secure than ever. He stepped back and admired his work and said, "It looks okay, but I guess I'll just have to come back later in the week to paint these repairs. I'm sure finishing the job properly will put Marta in a very thankful – and *receptive* – frame of mind!" Then he let out a dirty laugh and set about tending to Manny, still bound and gagged on Marta's bed. Satisfying himself that their captive couldn't work his bindings loose, Gunnar crossed the room and replaced the tool belt, minus a pair of pliers he'd pocketed, in the burlap bag. He then made a big show of removing a small ball of baling wire from the bag.

Gunnar walked to the bed and slipped off Manny's immaculate loafers. He wrapped two loops of the stout wire around Tejada's already bound ankles and wrists, using the pliers to tighten both. The now-panicking Mexican emitted a dreadful groan under his gag. Gunnar removed a piece of strong cord from his pocket and looped it through the wire on Manny's wrists and ankles, cinching it until his hands and feet nearly touched in the small of his back. Manny moaned again. Dan thought Tejada's shoulders might easily pop from their sockets.

In the meantime, Dan had tossed Marta's bloodstained kitchen towels into the burlap bag and carried a kitchen chair over to the bed. Poking their panicking captive in the ribs, Dan whispered, "First, Manny, I'd like to say thanks for that rock climbing expedition you arranged for me the other night. Now, I have a few surprises lined up for you in return."

Gunnar pulled up another chair at the base of the bed. Unbelievably, he attempted to tighten Manny's bindings even more... and nearly succeeded. The Mexican let out a muffled yelp and tried to turn his face away from his interrogators.

Dan leaned in closer and said, "Okay Gunnar, let's loosen Mr Tejada's gag and see if he's willing to chat. If he yells out – or, worse yet, decides to clam up – have a serious go at *really* cutting off his circulation!"

Gunnar removed the gag – and Manny cut loose a piercing scream. Gunnar instantly shoved the gag half-way down their captive's throat and gave his partner a nod. Dan sauntered over to the burlap bag and returned with an eighteen-inch length of wicked, gleaming *barbed* wire. He handed it gingerly to Gunnar, who'd already retrieved the pliers from his back pocket.

Leaning close into Manny's ear, the little Mexican-Scandinavian grinned malevolently and whispered, "I'm going to have to *assist* you in droppin' trou' here amigo. We're about to treat your puny *John Henry* to its own little crown of thorns – and your cooperation will dictate just how snug your pecker and balls are gonna' feel in our makeshift tiara. I'd suggest that you start telling my friend here what he needs to know, okay?"

Gunnar removed a pair of gardening gloves from his back pocket – and Manny's immaculate slacks and silk boxers were soon resting below his knees. The little man wrapped the length of barbed wire loosely around Tejada's exposed privates and gave the ends an initial 'attention-getting' twist. "Hey Dan, the boys brought way too much wire. We only need a smidgen for these pathetic *cajones* and that shriveled excuse for a pecker."

Dan saw that Manny was sweating even more profusely now – and the frightened man's eyes were as big as saucers. He began by whispering, "Now, where were we? Oh yeah, I was asking if you'd be cool if we removed the gag. Let's try it again. Give me a nod if you mean to play ball this time, okay?"

Manny stared intently into Dan's eyes before attempting to turn away; he obviously wanted to believe his quizmasters weren't nasty enough to mean business with the barbed wire. Gunnar obviously picked up on this ill-considered display of machismo. He grabbed his pliers and gave the barbed wire a hearty twist. Tejada immediately refocused... big time! He nodded vigorously – and did indeed remain quiet when Gunnar removed the gag.

Manny's face was ashen. It was clear he was ready to strike a bargain. "What do you want to know man? I can't even figure why you're talkin' to *me*. I'm just here to meet a lady friend. There's nothing else in it. Let me go and I'll forget all about running into you two – and I'll pretend I never knew those assholes you dragged out of here. This misunderstanding can go away, believe me."

Gunnar's hand tensed on the pliers. Dan shook his head in consternation and gave Tejada an exaggerated eye-roll. His voice rose from affected whisper to agitated growl. "Forget those dudes who escorted your buddies out of here Manny. As far as you're concerned, they're *Frick and Frack* – and they've merely taken your associates on a sightseeing tour. Now, let's move onto the vital part of this quiz – and pay attention; *we'd better like your answers!*"

Dan leaned back and stared at the ceiling, breaking eye contact with Tejada. "As you know, our dear friend, Benny Rosado, was brutally murdered. Your just departed buddies were seen loitering outside of his funeral. And, when I came nosing around your place, you didn't hesitate to send me with them on that Torrey Pines excursion. This adds up to one conclusion Manny... *you're in this shit up to your grubby neck!* But me and my friend here might be persuaded that you're *not* the brains behind this fiasco. If you can convince us, I'll make sure you beat a murder rap."

Manny tried to convey sincerity and innocence with a lame attempt at a 'put-upon' expression. "Honestly, I don't know what you're on about. What *little* I heard about Benny Rosado was all good. What sort of monster would order a hit on a stand-up guy like him?"

Gunnar gave the pliers another vicious twist – and this time Manny couldn't help himself; he screamed out in pain. The little man released the pressure and nodded to Dan.

Dan shook his head and continued, "Please curb the noise Manny. We don't want to disturb the neighbors do we? And, kindly *cut the crap...* do you think we're unaware of Cousin Benito Rosado's unseemly dealings with you? *He* was your target, but those recently departed fucknuts botched the job, didn't they?"

"Honestly, I know nothing about Benny's murder. Jesus and Flaco *did* act as my bodyguards tonight, but they're just cheap muscle I've been using for a couple of weeks while my regular guys are out of town. I admit I instructed them to cart you away and scare you a little the other night, but it wasn't supposed to turn life-threatening. I did *not* give them permission to seriously harm you Mr Paige, that's the truth."

Dan frowned and nodded to Gunnar, who again twisted the pliers. Manny cried out in agony. Dan could literally see tears rolling down his cheeks. He sensed that Gunnar's not-so-subtle tactics were taking their hostage near his breaking point.

"Last chance; it's time to cut the bullshit, buddy. You're a key drug wholesaler for a major Mexican family, but you're not their biggest bulk supplier or primary banker. Big money's behind this cartel – and the family's head honcho or a major deputy *must* have ordered the hit on Benito, right? Come on, we can sell the cops on you as 'an unwilling accessory' and you can save your own neck! You wouldn't be San Diego's first and only candidate for the Federal Protected Witness Program. Be smart man!"

Dan made eye contact with Gunnar, signaling him to loosen up a bit on the barbed wire. Manny's eyelids were trembling and he appeared to be earnestly contemplating his next move. Dan nodded and his partner put even more slack on the coils. Manny sighed, his eyes opened and he vigorously nodded to his captors. He'd reached an epiphany... *"Ever heard of Ernest Kincaid?"*

Holy shit! In spite of himself, Dan was stunned to find that Melinda's beloved mentor was being dangled before him as a major local drug player. The mayor's son was a no-account, slimy turd; that was a given. And, it wasn't a major leap to deduce that what remained of his inheritance wouldn't fund Ernest's current lavish lifestyle. So, now the do-do was about to really hit the fan... Melinda's lunch partner would soon find himself mired up to his nostrils in an inescapable, self-made shit swamp!

Dan made furtive eye contact with Gunnar, but he was certain his cunning partner wouldn't panic and inadvertently fold their strong hand too early in the game. Gunnar's face registered nothing – his grip remained firm on the still-poised pliers. The little man knew there was more to be pried out of their anxious captive before Dan finished the interrogation.

Dan rose and strolled over to the kitchen table, returning with his cassette recorder. Rewinding it and hitting 'Record', he asked in a clear voice, "Tell us about Ernest Kincaid, Mr Tejada. Why was he after Benito Rosado – or *Benny* Rosado, for that matter?"

Manny cleared his throat. "That slimy bastard Benito Rosado got too smart for his own good, okay? Everybody skims a little; that's expected. But it doesn't pay to get too greedy. The organization suspected him of flogging competitors' dope on the side – in our exclusive territory. *Kincaid* ordered me, in no uncertain terms, to make an example of him. I had to act or I'd be suspected of being in on it, see? Ernest Kincaid's the guy you want. He gave the order. I just mistakenly picked those two idiots to be Kincaid's button men."

Dan raised his eyebrows. "Are you telling me that Kincaid *himself* instigated the hit order on Benito Rosado?"

"Absolutely. I didn't even know about the fuck-up with Benito's hit until I heard about Benny Rosado's death on the news and put 'two and two' together. I've been mixed up in drugs...that I'll admit. But I've never ordered a hit on anyone. And those stupid button men don't work *directly* for me – they're some sort of squirrely foot soldiers in Kincaid's organization and once in a while I've been stuck with supervising them."

"Hold on here Manny. In case you've forgotten it, you ordered those same douche bags to kill *me* the other night. And I'm not buying into any bullshit about those dimwits taking it upon themselves to heave me off of that cliff. If you want to save your ass, I *might* be able to forgive you and that demented butler of yours. But, you'd better be ready to redeem your sorry asses by generating some *major* busts for the San Diego cops. You'll have to give up some boss men further up the food chain than the gutless Ernest Kincaid. He may be a player in your organization, but he's not a kingpin – or even a serious power behind the throne."

Manny replied with obvious resignation, tinged with palpable fear. "What do you expect me to say? I'm just a foot soldier, Mr Paige. I don't know the names of the bigger fish south of the border... they only deal with *Kincaid*, not me."

Dan stopped the recorder for a moment. "Listen, I can't make any guarantees, but I'll see to it that you're handed over to some very influential DEA-types who'd shit themselves to grab up a couple of major California players. They're trying to connect the dots down to Mexico and even on to Colombia... and anyone who helps them could no doubt earn an air-tight disappearing act. On the other hand, if I hand you to the local cops, they'll congratulate themselves on slapping a *'Solved'* sticker on a high-profile murder file. You'd never see the outside of a cell until your dying day, amigo... and trying to survive without protection in the slammer, that dying day might come real soon."

Dan's 'Lay of the Land' spiel appeared to have grabbed Manny's undivided attention. "Okay! Okay! I can help the Feds out man. I'll give up some solid leads – maybe even connect the DEA with a guy who'll help them nail a couple of big players over the border. If they arrange a new identity for me and get me well away from here, I'll become a real asset! I've already given you Ernest Kincaid – and once he's in your grasp, more big names will follow, I guarantee it."

Dan switched the tape back on, but five minutes later his interrogation hadn't really progressed. Manny was breathing heavily, nearly hyperventilating, but telling them nothing new. Clearly, he'd been willing to trade a soft target like Ernest for the possibility of a more propitious incarceration, but he was loathe to rat out any of the more menacing Mexicans... at least until he was well away from San Diego. It was certainly true that even if he ended up in DEA custody, ratting out the top bosses could easily lead to a death sentence. The organization's tentacles reached deep into the penal system, far into government agencies and throughout the so-called 'safe world' of new identities. They had the capability to hunt him down well beyond the confines of Southern California.

Dan would be pleased if he could help his pal Brenda reel in Ernest Kincaid. A bust like that – the collar of a local bigwig who'd been flying under the radar – would impress both her colleagues and superiors. And Dan had been straight with Manny about Vince's DEA buddies relishing a fresh connection to a potential bust of a couple of cartel kingpins – achieved through a 'joint operation' with their Mexican colleagues of course. The Feds, who were in a position to throw some attractive bargaining chips on the table, would get more out of Manny than he and Gunnar ever could... even if they were tempted to employ even more primitive tools of torture. The promise of witness protection and a fresh identity would no doubt trump their crude tactics with the desperate mid-level gangster.

Dan switched off the recorder for the last time and nodded to Gunnar to remove their captive's 'tackle trappings'. "Let's all get some sleep. We'll phone Kincaid in the morning and I'm sure that Manny here will help us by spinning a *convincing* yarn – a story that should help us to net San Diego's esteemed former 'Businessman of the Year'."

Gunnar unwound the barbed wire and yanked Manny's trousers back up, even loosening the whimpering man's other bindings slightly. Their prisoner could recline in relative comfort on Marta's single bed until morning. The gag was, however, reapplied. Manny could prove to be a slippery customer, right up to the point when they turned him over to Vince – and they didn't want to hear a sound out of him for the rest of this eventful night.

Dan and Gunnar decided on two-hour guard shifts, with Dan taking the first. Gunnar slipped out of his shoes and curled up on the sofa, almost immediately drifting into a light slumber. Surprisingly, Tejada soon followed suit, muffled snoring escaping from under his gag. Perhaps the crook knew when he was well and truly beaten – and felt that conserving his energy for whatever came next was his best bet.

A final resting place

Victor drove the unmarked van down the quiet freeway towards San Diego's South Bay and the Mexican border. Taking the final exit on the US side, they headed east, skirting the ancient Brown Field Airstrip. In five minutes, the truck left the road and headed south on a rutted gravel trail into the desert scrub. They halted within view of the towering fence separating the US from her neighbor to the south.

Victor remained seated for a moment, looking about and listening for unwelcome engine noises. At this point, the greatest chance for a screw-up would no doubt involve an encounter with the Border Patrol on a routine run. Detecting no signs of life, he restarted the engine and drove a hundred yards off the trail. They halted again near dense undergrowth on the far side of a small rise that concealed their activities from anyone using the gravel track.

Omar, crouched behind the driver's seat, crawled across the truckbed and opened the side-loading door. Getting out, he looked around to ensure they hadn't attracted undue attention and then disappeared back inside. Seconds later, the rolled-up tarp flew out and Victor, standing nearby, quickly opened it. Flaco's body lay face down on the canvas. Next, Omar dragged Jesus out of the cab. Still bound head to foot, hands behind him, the burly man fell in a heap at Vic's feet. Vic pulled the gag from his mouth and set him on his knees.

The terrified Jesus knew it was time to start begging for his life. At the same time, he began to work at loosening his bindings. He managed to pry off his fingerless glove before imploring, "Hey amigos, I won't say nuthin'. Just untie me and drive away. I'll be under that fence and out of your lives in two minutes. You'll never hear from me again! I barely know that puto lying over there. I'll have forgotten all about him – and all the shit that's gone down tonight – by the time I've walked into TJ."

Vic grabbed Jesus by the throat and said, "So, answer a coupla' questions for us – no bullshit – and you just may get your wish *charro*. Did you shoot our dad, or was it your partner over there who did the deed?"

"It wasn't either of us amigo, I swear! We weren't anywhere near him when he got it. I'm certain that it was Manny and his bad-ass butler who whacked him and we're being framed for a job we didn't do!"

Omar slipped away and retrieved a thick leather tool-belt from the truck. Victor retreated a few feet from Jesus and nodded towards his returning brother. Omar unfastened a pair of hardened steel pruning shears from one of the belt's side loops and showed them to Jesus.

207

Vic leaned towards the petrified man and whispered, "My brother here is eager to cut off your fingers... one at a time. So, I'm asking again... was it you, or that little shit over there, who shot our father?"

A trickle of warm urine flowed down the inseam of Jesus' already damp leather trousers, making a small puddle in the dirt. He swayed and Victor moved in, physically holding him up. Jesus whined, "That little fucker over there did all the shootin' man. It blew me away. He told me we was just goin' to *scare* Benito, not kill him! It was only later we actually found out Flaco had whacked the wrong dude. Manny admitted he fingered an innocent guy."

Vic's eyes caught Omar's and his brother backed into the shadows. Then, the elder son turned his attention back to Jesus, almost staring a hole through him. "You know man, I believe that story. A musclehead like you is only up to being the back-up, not the shooter."

Jesus, still kneeling, looked imploringly at Victor. He obviously figured he'd come close enough to the truth and had talked his way out of a tight spot. He smiled as he heard Omar stroll up behind him and held his bound wrists away from his spine so that his captor could cut through the wraps.

A single blow from the well-worn, but razor-sharp, machete on Omar's tool belt all but decapitated the huge Mexican. Jesus fell forward soundlessly, hitting the dirt with a thud. A fleeting gurgle emanated from his severed windpipe. Victor watched in silence, his face registering neither distress nor surprise.

Vic paced back over to Flaco's prostrate body. "That's truly pathetic man. The fat fucker really thought we were cuttin' him loose." He rolled Flaco over with his foot, extracted a switchblade and small plastic bag from his pocket, opened the knife and dug deep into the lifeless torso. He twisted the blade in the little man's chest cavity and soon extracted Dan's slug, still lodged there. He cleaned his knife blade on the ground and dropped it, along with the spent round, into the bag. The evidence went into his pocket; he'd carefully dispose of it later.

They returned to their truck and retrieved shovels and a couple of ten-gallon watering cans. Victor rinsed his bloodstained hands and thoroughly washed Omar's machete.

As experienced landscapers, digging came naturally... and they'd brought first-rate tools. They'd soon hollowed out a bathtub-sized hole in the hardpan and both bodies were quickly thrown in and covered over. As they scattered loose dirt and brush on the unmarked grave, Omar felt compelled to ask... "Did you believe him bro' – did the little guy do the shooting?"

Victor continued smoothing over the gravesite as he answered. "It's probably true, man. Remember back at the cabin? The little guy showed *cajones* and knew how to handle himself. The big asshole was useless… obviously in over his head. But, it doesn't matter. Both were cold-blooded, murdering bastards as far as I'm concerned – and we've done the world a favor by exterminating these vermin."

Omar nodded. "We won't speak of this again, brother… and Greg need never know. Gunnar won't ever ask us about what happened to these two and I'm telling him nothing. If this righteous execution is a mortal sin, it's one I'd commit again for our family's honor – and so that our father can truly rest in peace."

Five minutes later they'd satisfied themselves that there were no signs of the unmarked grave. And, if the bodies were discovered later, there'd be scant evidence to connect these unidentified victims to Dan, Gunnar or the Rosados.

The boys returned to the truck and used the remnants in the water cans to scrub their tarp and shovels. They'd discreetly toss the canvas sheet into a bonfire at some construction site. Finally, they rechecked the gravesite, scattering a bit more loose brush over it. It had been a long and eventful day. It was time to head home, wash up and get to bed.

Chapter 26

Tuesday

Breakfast at Marta's

Dan slowly came to life, aware of the aroma of frying bacon. He glanced at his watch; it was just past eight. His trusty partner had allowed him to sleep straight through to the morning after taking over for the second watch. It didn't surprise him – Gunnar would feel that bit more secure keeping an eye on Tejada *personally*.

Gunnar sat at the table, holding a plate under Manny's chin while spoon-feeding him. Tejada's hands were secured to the chair back, but the remainder of his bindings had been removed. Gunnar seemed to conclude that their guest had finished eating when he made a face like a child and turned his head away. He retied the gag over Tejada's mouth and bound his ankles to the chair's legs. Now he and Dan could linger over their own meal. It was too early to begin the next stage of their scheme.

As Dan scraped up the last of his eggs, Gunnar switched on Marta's television. Dan moved to the sofa to watch it as his partner examined Marta's ceiling and walls, looking for bullet holes. Last evening's stray rounds had, for the most part, sliced clean through the cabin's thin siding, flying harmlessly out to sea. The fact that the cabin was at pier's end was a huge plus – and, luckily, no combatant had been crouching by the wall nearest the next door cabin. Gunnar dug wood filler out of their handy burlap bag and repaired the holes – both inside and outside the cabin. He'd paint over the repairs later.

The morning news made no mention of a dead illegal found near the border. This was no surprise. Crimes involving wetbacks seldom made the TV or radio news. A *'Juan Doe'* might merit a couple of column inches in the Union-Trib, but then again, probably not. Hopefully, Jesus and Flaco were out of their lives forever; disappearing without a trace.

At nine-fifteen it was time to make their move. Gunnar whispered to Dan, "I actually hope the fucker tries something. A few bitch slaps couldn't do the asshole any harm – and the exercise would give me immense satisfaction."

Dan cleared his throat to get Tejada's attention. "We'll use your phone to give Kincaid a call now. I've written a little script for you; no adlibbing required. Let's go over it a couple of times first, so that you'll sound that bit more convincing. Here's the scoop: don't change *anything* – and keep Ernest on topic. Listen man, you're just about over

210

the hump! If you help us, I'll see that you get a fair shake with the Feds, okay?"

Manny rehearsed for a few minutes and actually put a bit of effort into memorizing his lines. In truth, the man was a quick study. A born bullshitter, he was able to inject just the right tone of urgency and realism into his delivery.

Dan decided that it was now or never... it was time to lure Ernest Kincaid into the snare. He took out Manny's cellphone and remarked, "I see Kincaid isn't in your quick-dial. Remember his private number by any chance?"

Manny had no trouble reciting the number off the top of his head. He either possessed an excellent memory or he'd dialed it on more than a few occasions. Their quarry answered on the second ring. "This is Ernest Kincaid, how may I help you?"

Dan immediately recognized Ernest's crisp diction and mellifluous tones. Kincaid had a unique way of projecting power and influence. Dan put on a preposterous Latino accent, slurring, "Please hold for Mr Tejada." He held the cellphone up to Manny's face, sharing the earpiece.

"Mr Kincaid, I'm afraid it's me, Manuel Tejada. I apologize for phoning you at this early hour, but we've run into a bit of a crisis. Could I implore you to please listen to our friend here for a moment? It will undoubtedly ease a sticky situation... for both of us."

A pretty fair delivery Dan thought. Manny had woven in the right amount of urgency, without conveying utter panic. Dan murmured into the receiver, "Please hold on for one moment, señor..." and then fell silent. He signaled Gunnar to put Manny's gag back on and drag him back over to the bed. Their hostage's job was done.

Then, Dan returned to the script. He put on a *different* Latino accent to readdress his prey; subtler than the first... a voice the businessman would never associate with Melinda's ex-husband. "Listen carefully Mr Kincaid. My amigos are keeping your partner on ice. He's filled us in on your shady import deals. And, depending on what you do in the next few moments, he may – or may not – have to repeat his wicked tales to the *policia*. Of course, we hope that this can work out to everyone's advantage. I'm afraid the bad news is you'll have to *buy* him – and your own precious skin, Mr Kincaid – out of this dreadful situation."

As Dan suspected, Ernest was far too clever to strike at this first cast from an unknown adversary. "I don't know what Mr Tejada has been telling you, but we've only had a few dealings, concerning some very minor exports to Mexico and South America... nothing illegal – and no *imports* of any kind, I can assure you."

211

Dan cut in quickly. It was time to add that extra smidgen of pizzazz and urgency to his spiel. "Listen closely *tonto*! Save us time and cut the crap. Tejada has shown us convincing written evidence of your involvement in drug dealings – and I've already confirmed many particulars with associates on both sides of the border. Ever heard of 'the ring of truth'? That's exactly what Tejada's story has – *in spades*. You already know that you're in shit up to your *cajones*, but what you don't realize is that you've run into a bit of truly good fortune! We're not going to be greedy. Half a mil will buy back Tejada's sorry ass – and all of his written records – for you and your superiors. We'll virtually hand him to you on a plate. I'm sure your *Mejicano* partners will consider this money well spent."

Ernest didn't answer immediately. Dan could actually visualize him sitting at the ornate wrought-iron table on his balcony, pondering his next move while staring into his bone china cup of Kona coffee. One fine morning, many years previously, Dan and Melinda had enjoyed a pot of coffee with their host at the selfsame table. When the businessman finally replied, he did a poor job of masking his growing panic. "To whom do I have the pleasure of speaking, if I may ask? How do I know that you are genuine?"

"Call me 'Julio' if you wish, Mr Kincaid. You might wish to think of me as an old colleague of a certain Benito Rosado, a man whom I believe you still seek. We've been trying to flush out this *puto* ourselves – and your Mr Tejada has proved very helpful in that regard. Here's some crucial background information for you, Mr Kincaid. Rosado went missing with $500,000 of *our* heroin. That price is retail, by the way. So, as you can see, Tejada's ransom, paid by you and your friends, will simply reimburse us for the street price of our 'mislaid' goods. And, a substantial bonus for you, Mr Kincaid, is that Manny seems to know where Rosado and the missing smack are hidden at this very moment. But your partner is of the opinion that telling *us* would be to Rosado's detriment, whereas telling *you* – after we've returned him to you in exchange for the value of our lost merchandise – will work out very well indeed. So you see, it's a 'win-win', Mr Kincaid. You'll get Tejada back and your chatty partner can, in turn, put you onto Benito and our missing heroin. And here's the beauty of my offer – you'll already have *paid us* for the drugs, right? So they'd be yours to keep!"

Dan paused to let it all sink in. "So, let's recap your options here… if you reimburse us for our smack, you're onto a very attractive triple whammy. You'll have the slippery Benito Rosado in your grasp, as well as your talkative partner, Tejada – and, in short order, you'll be in possession of some high-grade goods that you can release into an out-of-state market. I must caution you of one thing… *don't even consider selling your newfound inventory in Southern California.* We don't want our dealers running into unwelcome competition. And, as it started out life as our product, we'd quickly be able to test it and surmise where these new supplies were coming from, wouldn't we?"

At this point Dan hesitated again, but Ernest didn't require more time to consider his options. "Your proposition sounds more than fair Mr Julio. I must apologize for the inconvenience that Rosado has put you and your friends through. And, I'm happy to reassure you that neither I nor my partners have *any* desire to encroach on your business dealings in California. It isn't our 'bag', as you'd put it."

Dan had to smile to himself. This was almost too easy. "You'll get Tejada himself – and access to his information – in exchange for a satchel filled with $500,000 worth of unmarked fifties and twenties. As you can see, we're not greedy. And, just in case your partner isn't anxious to share Rosado's whereabouts with you after he's been recovered, I believe we can even be of assistance to you there. All of the embarrassing business details he's shared with us will be neatly laid out in a typewritten note, signed by your friend and pinned to his inside coat pocket at the exchange. That piece of evidence – and, of course, your own supporting accusations – should ensure his full cooperation with your most daunting enforcers."

"That sounds more than fair Mr Julio. But, it will take me a bit of time to get the cash together, as I'm sure you'll understand."

Dan expected as much. "I'm going to be generous and give you an *entire* day. We don't mind hosting Mr Tejada for another twenty-four hours – and he assures us that Benito Rosado won't be going anywhere in the near future. I'll call this number at eight this evening with explicit instructions for our mutually beneficial exchange. And don't think of involving your business partners at this stage Mr Kincaid. If all doesn't go to plan, Manny's typewritten and signed meanderings – along with some interesting videotapes we'll keep on file permanently – will no doubt be of great interest to the *policia*. Let's call these items our little insurance policy. His story is, without a shadow of doubt, spicy enough to earn you a very long stretch… long that is, if your good fortune holds out while you're behind bars."

With that, Dan abruptly disconnected and smiled broadly at Gunnar. "He's hooked. We just need to keep Shithead here on ice until the meet. If everything goes to plan, Kincaid will be a cooked goose and Melinda will be in for the surprise of her life! Vince will get a heavyweight witness in our Mr Tejada – and Brenda will get credit for one of the biggest recent collars in San Diego County, an ex-Mayor's wayward son. Plenty of glory to go around… except for you and me pard. We'll just ride off into the sunset."

Gunnar grinned back at Dan. "I don't give a shit about the laurels Dan. I just want to be able to tell Connie that Benny's killers have paid the price, big time!"

Dan turned to face the petrified Manny Tejada. "And hey man, if you play your cards right with the DEA, you just might see daylight as a free man before you're senile!"

Gunnar walked to Marta's door and turned back into the room as he opened it. "I'm going to bring Manny's car down from the other end of the pier. He and I can veg out at my place until the meet. I'll be back in a minute."

In next to no time, Gunnar was making a slow turnaround at Marta's cabin and parking the Chrysler. They grabbed Manny under his armpits and trundled him outside, throwing him bound and gagged onto his own back seat. Gunnar jumped into the black sedan, gave Dan a short wave and sedately headed down the pier.

Alone in Marta's cabin, Dan washed and dried the breakfast dishes and gave the place a final thorough check. Any blood traces on the wooden floor were invisible to the naked eye. He put an extra $50 under an ashtray (even though Gunnar would undoubtedly pay Marta generously) and, locking the door behind him, dropped her key through the mail slot.

As he ambled down the pier, Dan glanced at the cabin across the way. If any of the partying youngsters were still there, the sounds of their celebrations had evaporated into the morning mist. Maybe the boys didn't 'get lucky' after all. What the hell, whether the kids were still in residence or not, he felt pretty certain they'd create no hassles for him or his partners in crime.

Chapter 27

Resting up

The haze had practically dissipated by the time Dan arrived back at his Chevy. He was still deep in thought... a recurring doubt nagging at him. Try as he might, he'd never be able to rationalize involving Benny's sons in this elaborate scheme. He felt another stab of guilt. Connie's boys were fine young men. Benny and Gunnar had shielded them from the worst of Southeast San Diego's gang activities, pushing them into sports and taking them on family camping trips into Baja. But now, thanks to Dan and Gunnar, Benny's older boys had been tested and forged in the city's tough underbelly. Helping them to wreak retribution on their father's killers by allowing them to virtually take the law into their own hands signaled a grave change in their lives. Gunnar, however, had convinced Dan that a 'Chicano ethos' dictated the boys' inclusion. These young men were exercising a long-established birthright.

In every major US city, 'subcultures' and ethnic groups impose their local conventions – and law enforcement agencies often tacitly choose to remain spectators. Dan recalled his early patrolman's education concerning 'street justice'. Most minorities believe that *'the letter of the law'* – invariably alluded to by a dwindling white majority – delivers little justice. San Diego's inner city dwellers are pragmatic. Local residents do what they can to stifle gang activity and staunch the flow of affordable street drugs. The police, in turn, tend to focus on drive-by shootings and 'serious' violence. Thus, 'The Rule of Law' pragmatically ignores evermore significant 'petty crimes and misdemeanors'.

Early in their discussions, Gunnar had explained to Dan that Connie, and perhaps even Greg, wouldn't condone a code of honor which decreed that sons should seek personal retribution for a father's murder. Gunnar understood that Benny's sweet wife lived in relative tranquility on the periphery of Southeast San Diego's war zone – and Greg was fortunate to move in different circles.

Dan simply had to resolve these conflicts as straightforwardly as he could. The truth was, the boys would return to their day-to-day lives, satisfied that they'd achieved a measure of justice for their father. Doing 'the honorable thing' left scant room for remorse over the fate of sociopaths like Jesus and Flaco. These low-lifes had simply played out a bad hand... and received a just punishment.

As Dan left the beach, he refocused on the unfolding plan. Up to now, he'd rate their progress as 'so far, so good'. Kincaid had been levered into motion; he was falling inexorably into their web. The businessman's self-satisfied existence – living large, cosseted in La Jolla's opulence – was soon to be shattered. His luck was running out.

There was little left to do until 'Mr Julio' telephoned Ernest at eight. He was dog-tired, but he wouldn't relax just yet. He'd head to the office and touch base with his caseload. Who knew... maybe Trini, 'The World's Most Seductive Receptionist', could even regale him with her latest dating tribulations. He'd also check in with Sophie, before calling Brenda and Vince to arrange their contributions to the unfolding escapade.

He popped *'Pearl'* into his CD player. Janis Joplin's searing, soulful voice might help to sooth his sagging spirits. Maybe he should feel elated... they'd caught up with Benny's killers – and certainly sooner than expected. One murderer (and, alas, maybe *two*) had paid the ultimate price for playing a part in Benny's death. San Diego would soon be rid of a significant drug dealer and his silent partner. And Brenda and Vince were in line for the accolades associated with some significant arrests. But none of this would bring Benny back. Dan realized that San Diego would never again be the sun-soaked, carefree paradise of his youth... the city was changing and so was he. The past few days had made him even *more* jaded, if that was possible. He'd crossed a line.

'The Bartender's Bank of National City'

Ernest Kincaid finished a second cup of coffee before telephoning his office to say he'd be taking the day off. Then he sat back to focus his exceptional – and devious – mind. His servants would assume that he was lingering over his newspaper, as he often did. Actually, he needed to think things through, to avoid making any foolish moves.

Was there a way to cut Tejada loose from his unknown captors without coughing up that excruciating ransom? A few long-shot possibilities came to mind, but each option had its own very unappetizing downside. In the end, the other unsavory alternatives were even more perilous than paying Mr Julio off and attempting to recoup the organization's losses with the man's suggested one-off foray into out-of-state heroin dealing.

Yes... paying these villains, thereby taking Manny (and, more importantly, himself) out of harm's way – *while also recovering the elusive Benito Rosado* – seemed to be the only smart play. By God

216

though, this would be costly. And there certainly were no assurances that he'd ever see any of his hard-earned money again. After all, what did he know about dealing smack in some distant market? That would require the talents of his Mexican bosses, of that there was no doubt. And they'd probably just cut him out of the profits after *his* ransom payment financed their acquisition of a large quantity of illicit product.

He'd certainly have to turn Tejada over to his bosses post-haste. The moron had surely outlived his usefulness to the organization by spilling his guts to dangerous competitors. The cartel's view would be that, under pressure, the stupid ass would behave similarly again. Manny had to be silenced, *permanently*... but preferably only after leading the cartel to Benito Rosado and that attractive cache of stolen heroin.

Explaining to the Mexicans how a significant competitor had boldly grabbed up Manny in the first place – and then squeezed so much sensitive information out of him – would be no walk in the park. But it had to be done. Clearly, involving his powerful partners presented the most viable opportunity to deal with this mess quickly and efficiently. And, there was one positive in all of this: it could turn out to be a real coup – he might just salvage and enhance his own position in the organization if all went well. He wasn't certain if the slippery Mr Julio's story about their missing heroin rang true. But he could only hope it was on the level. If ransoming Manny for $500,000 ultimately generated substantial saleable product for his demanding bosses, he might even salvage some of his cash!

In the end, Ernest could be certain of one thing. Manny's taped revelations with his captors must never see the light of day. Surely, Mr Julio's people would also keep a copy of the signed notes they promised to return. In reality, there could be no assurances that Manny's ramblings wouldn't turn up to haunt him later.

Finally, he settled on the only logical conclusion... involving his Mexican colleagues and handing them the whereabouts of Rosado and any windfall heroin was his safest bet. They'd be keen to recover *every* copy of Manny's taped interrogation and written notes for their own peace of mind. And, he knew they could be resourceful when it came to self-preservation. They might even be able to shut down Mr Julio and his unknown associates... permanently.

Ernest set his newspaper aside. He'd pay the revolting Mr Julio the $500,000. And, he'd present Manny Tejada to his Mexican superiors on a plate – along with the incriminating signed note, as promised by Mr Julio. The unfortunate Tejada would be forced to spill Benny's whereabouts to his bosses – and that could conceivably lead the cartel to a cheap new dope supply. This strategy would cut into the ransom he'd *personally* recover, but it would go a long way towards demonstrating his loyalty. He'd concentrate on this best-case scenario... he'd get back to his cosseted life and continue to generate a generous illicit income. But, unfortunately, he'd be out a tidy sum. The loss would be an unexpected overhead in his illicit dealings – and, sadly, not even a tax write-off!

Then, in a flash, a cunning idea popped into Ernest's head. He knew where he could lay his hands on the requisite $500,000 – and perhaps even more. And, truth be told, half of the cash would actually be *Manny's*, not his. If the cartel cut him in on their ultimate out-of-state heroin profits, he could be out from under this mess with little or no net outlay!

An hour later, dressed in casual slacks and a navy cashmere sweater, he headed down the corridor to his four-car garage. He was toting a large vinyl gym bag he'd dug out of the attic. Feeling unexpectedly jaunty, he stepped into his spacious garage, beeped open the outside door and selected his silver Mustang convertible for a drive down to National City. No need for the Jag today... a bit too ostentatious for a blue-collar district.

The Mainsail Tavern was situated on National City Boulevard in South Bay, near an I-5 exit ramp. The ramshackle bar was another of Manny's 'legitimate' businesses. His cousin Gloria managed it. The bar's patrons were horny sailors, blue-collar workers and a regular crew of seasoned hookers, all attracted by cheap beer and a decent pool table. In truth, the place just about broke even after providing Gloria's meager living. But it offered other, less obvious, attractions to Manny... and to Ernest as well.

First, a bit of drug money could be laundered through the bar. And, more importantly, the back office provided an undisturbed venue for meetings Manny preferred to keep 'off the radar'. Ernest's infrequent visits to the dingy bar were the only occasions when the two men were in each other's company – and only Gloria had even peripherally witnessed their clandestine get-togethers, always held after dark. They arrived and left through a locked rear door, which led directly into the back office. Each man had a key. No one would suspect that the shabby office harbored a high-tech floor safe. The bar didn't merit such a strongbox. A worn linoleum tile under the nondescript desk concealed the safe's steel door and robust combination lock. This inconspicuous vault held most of the cartel's liquid US working capital, as well as Ernest's and Manny's 'slush fund'. In point of fact, their fund represented nearly all of the money in the safe these days. And the way this fiasco was playing out, Manny might not need his share of the cash in the foreseeable future.

Even if by some miracle Tejada survived this scrape, he couldn't begrudge Ernest using this capital to ransom his life, could he? And, the cash was so easy to access. Gloria seldom used the office; she'd been told to conduct day-to-day dealings with suppliers out front. A corner booth was her de facto office. She almost certainly knew of the safe, but she'd have no idea of its contents. And, she was genuinely – and justifiably – in fear of her cousin. My God, thought Ernest, what if Manny had cleaned the safe out? But why would he have done such a foolish thing? Barring unforeseen complications, their little stash would be intact, ready to extract him from this sordid dilemma.

Ernest pulled into The Mainsail's rear lot and parked the Mustang two spaces down from the only other car, a rusty blue Neon. He grabbed the sports bag off the seat and locked the convertible. He hated parking in this low-rent neighborhood... he imagined that bums and assorted ne'er-do-wells lurked behind every dumpster and telephone pole. He sprinted to the door, slipped his key in the lock and hurried inside. It was the first time he'd ever visited The Mainsail in daylight. The bass boom of some dreadful pop anthem thudded through the walls from the jukebox out front, but there was no sign of the apathetic Gloria.

Ernest switched on the overhead light and settled into the ramshackle chair at the dusty desk. He slid back a few inches, bent down and used the door key to pry at a barely perceptible slot in the edge of a worn linoleum tile. The large tile and its plywood backing lifted, exposing a shiny combination dial on a dull-gray steel door. The combination was simplicity itself to recall. It was the four digits of his street address, followed by Manny's four digits... dialed as a series of two-digit numbers.

He swiveled the sturdy door open and gazed into the safe. The money was there all right... plenty of cash to help make this unpleasantness go away! He quickly removed all of the bundled notes. The stacks made an impressive pile on the desktop. Suddenly he realized how sloppy he was being. He went to the office door and used the chain to secure the entrance from the bar... something Manny always did upon arrival. He returned to the desk and counted out $500,000 in banded stacks... luckily almost all in Mr Julio's preferred twenties and fifties. The cash was almost assuredly unmarked, being the proceeds of myriad deals with assorted retailers. He took the $500,000 and arranged it carefully in his gym bag.

This 'unanticipated withdrawal' put a huge dent in their slush fund, but their cash was by no means wiped out. Mr Julio's ransom demand could have stretched to another $150,000 or so if Manny's captors had known how much they'd set by. He could even get greedy and grab the remaining $75,000 or so that unequivocally belonged to the cartel, but that would make sense only if he were going on the run. Common sense told him to leave that amount right where it was, in its own small cash box inside the safe.

Ernest stared at the surplus $150,000 belonging to Tejada and him, hesitated for split second and came to a decision. What the hell... he'd take the lot. He tucked the balance of their cash – even some loose tens – into his bag and zipped it tight. Seconds later the safe was closed, the tile replaced and the door into the bar unchained. Ernest left as he'd come, having never even acknowledged his presence to Gloria.

As he fired up the Mustang, Ernest quickly reviewed his situation. Many would consider the cash in the gym bag a fortune. It *was* a decent amount, but definitely *not* a life-changing figure in Ernest's eyes. He'd play it straight with Mr Julio and use the bulk of the cash to ensure his own future and Manny's release. He wouldn't consider undertaking untoward risks to recover the ransom from Manny's captors. 'Discretion was the better part of valor', as the saying went – and he was no doubt dealing with some very nasty men.

A little niggle rattled around in his overtaxed mind, however. If real dangers were imminent, this sum could finance a clean getaway to a new life in Belize. His villa was bought and paid for... 'off the books' so to speak and totally under the radar of his illegitimate associates. $650,000 would last a lifetime down there, if he exercised a modicum of self-discipline. Perhaps he might even be able to trust Melinda Jeffries to surreptitiously exercise that Power of Attorney he'd had drawn up (so that she might quietly assist him in some 'low-key' property transactions). He'd have to dangle the right 'commission' to purchase her silence, but eventually she could unload some holdings and wire the proceeds to his numbered account in the Caymans. Too bad the economy had gone so sour... currently he had so little mad money in that offshore account!

He was halfway home before he'd categorically rejected the 'flight option'. He needed to snap out of it! He had more than enough cash to spring Manny and hand his grubby little ass over to the organization – along with any information the little prick had on Benito. The Mexicans stood to recover Rosado – and a half million in new dope. These were significant trump cards for the undeniably awkward negotiations he'd soon be experiencing. Finally, if Tejada bowed out of the picture *permanently*, no one need be the wiser about the spare $150,000 from the slush fund. In all probability, Manny would never again visit The Mainsail to check out their assets after the Mexicans finished with him.

The gathering clouds held another silver lining. Ernest had learned some difficult lessons, albeit the hard way. Never again would he trust a 'partner' like Manny Tejada, who could finger him to the law or undermine him with the cartel... particularly if said cohort's IQ had difficulty approaching triple digits. And, he realized that he'd soon have to part company with the testy Mexicans as well. It was time to ease out of the drug trade. He'd had enough. It might mean curtailing his lifestyle a bit, but the acquisition of 'easy money' no longer seemed so effortless or palatable.

Chapter 28

Let's make a deal...

TriState seemed a haven of tranquility when Dan stopped by after leaving Marta's cabin. Disappointingly, Trini's weekend antics with a *single one* of her assorted 'main squeezes' proved to be relatively tame. Hanging with just the one guy for an *entire* weekend probably constituted the Holy Grail for her... perhaps the girl was finally slowing down.

Dan hunkered in his cubicle and quietly reviewed his caseload. As expected, Walt had things shipshape. He soon reverted to the investigation and phoned the Point Loma apartment, waking up Carrie. As promised, he shared the bare bones of the previous evening's proceedings – leaving out the incriminating details – before reconfirming her vital role for the upcoming evening. The important point to share was that they had Manny Tejada in custody, thanks to her critical assistance. And, her ex-lover was most assuredly in no position to take out his fury concerning his unexpected incarceration on her.

Next, Dan dug into his Rolodex to retrieve the number of a specialist car rental firm near Mission Bay. He phoned to reserve a suitable ride for their rendezvous with Ernest. A black Lincoln Town Car was available. He also phoned Gunnar to tell him they'd meet up at the rental agency and then head out... he'd change into his 'Mr Julio, Drug Soldier' get-up on their way to the meet.

An hour later, after checking in with Sophie, Dan left Trini working on her lonesome and headed home. He parked in his usual spot, expecting scant trouble from Manny's remaining sidekicks. He knocked on Mrs Getz's door to see if she needed provisions ... he'd be going out for cereal, milk and a six-pack of Henry's anyway. Mrs Getz was only too pleased to hand over a fairly skimpy shopping list.

Upon returning, it was obvious his chatty neighbor would not be averse to popping over for a chin-wag. He managed to give her a semi-polite body swerve and settled down in front of the TV for the balance of the afternoon. As he scrolled through the listings, he was reminded of that old song... tons of channels, but, in truth, nothin' was on. He settled on a Bogart movie, *Key Largo*. It depicted (in dreamy black and white) a tropical paradise that was undoubtedly mythical even when the film was made – swaying palms, single-lane Florida 'highways' and weather-beaten cabanas set back from deserted beaches.

Film Noir was nourished by the stuff of dreams... no different than Midwesterners' naïve present-day take on the allure of San Diego.

'Sun, sand, surf and bliss' was an image the city's PR honchos meticulously attempted to evoke, but the reality was a hodgepodge of freeways, rush-hours and boxy condos cascading down coastal canyon walls. Dan's mind wandered, not for the first time, to an imaginary ranch house near Billings… a couple of laid-back neighbors residing (not too) nearby, with his and Sophie's names painted on a roadside metal mailbox. A nice dream, but he'd never have the guts to turn it into reality.

Just before eight, he retraced his steps to the convenience store. He needed to use their payphone, so that the caller's number couldn't be traced back. Everyone had a cell these days; functioning payphones in San Diego's neighborhoods were a rarity. But he'd checked this one earlier. It was in working order – and vandals seldom loitered outside this well managed local store in an old-timers' neighborhood. He dialed Ernest's number from memory and the officious businessman answered on the second ring.

"Ernest Kincaid, how may I help you?"

Dan slipped into his barely passable 'Latino' accent. "Well, Señor Kincaid, you can make my day by telling me our money is to hand and you're ready for an exchange."

"I'm resigned to paying for Tejada's release, Mr Julio. I've secured the $500,000 in unmarked bills – almost all fifties and twenties, with a few hundreds thrown in. I hope that this suffices. May I have your further instructions please?"

Great! No hiccups and Ernest was behaving himself. "My instructions, amigo, are for you to meet me at eleven tonight – *entirely alone* if you please – bringing the ransom money in an unmarked and 'bug-free' hold-all. I'll hand over your pal and his undersigned interview notes, as promised. If you're in luck, Rosado will still be holding our missing heroin… dope that becomes *yours* as soon as you're onto him. We'll part friends and put this unpleasantness behind us, all right?"

"That sounds more than acceptable Mr Julio. Where will this meeting take place?"

"Drive to the northeast corner of the Sports Arena's vast parking lot – Area 'C1' to be precise. Stand outside your car, with the bag at your feet, *at precisely eleven*. If I get the 'all clear', I'll approach you to complete the transaction. Naturally, you fear that I'm a man of little honor Mr Kincaid, but please be assured of my goodwill. My colleagues' principal desire is to be reimbursed the fair market value of their missing merchandise… and you can help us achieve that. Benito ripped us off Mr Kincaid, but we're certain your friends will deal with

223

him. And, as we obviously have no further use for your friend, Manny Tejada, I'm sure you'll agree that this ends well for all parties. One last warning… remember, you and your organization would be wise to stay out of the heroin trade here in California. But, this is surely already your most assiduous intention, not so?"

With that, Dan hung up the receiver and strode briskly away from the mini-mart. The hook was well and truly set!

You can't tell the players without a program!

Dan walked into his apartment and headed for the phone. No messages. He dialed Brenda at work and reached her as she headed out on shift. "Hey Dan, what's going down?"

"I know you're busy keepin' a lid on San Diego's vice trade, but I'm betting you'd enjoy a short break in the parking lot near The Pink Lady's stage door just after eleven tonight. Keep an eye out for a shifty Latino accompanied by a prominent businessman… a bigwig you'll no doubt recognize. Sit tight as they head inside. A few minutes later the selfsame businessman and a *different* 'associate' should head out. If you grab these two up and bark out something about questioning them as material witnesses in the murder of Benny Rosado, the businessman's new pal should immediately become cooperative. He'll pretty much tell you *anything and everything* to distance himself from his overmatched companion."

There was a slight delay before Brenda's reply. She was obviously jotting down his instructions. Finally she enquired, "What the hell is this shit, partner? This little scenario sounds more than a bit dubious – even by your deranged standards."

"It *is* a tad shaky, but trust me. You'll be in for one of the year's biggest busts if you and Frank just play this hand out. I'd fill you in on more if I could, but the gory details could put some innocent people, including *yours truly*, in harm's way. You'll have to trust me."

"I trust you Dan. Now, listen to this playback." She read out her brief notes, to confirm she'd clearly understood his instructions.

As usual, she'd taken everything down straight and true. Dan confirmed, "Check pard, you've got it covered."

"Okay then, Frank and I'll swing by, but if it's all the same to you, I won't go out on a limb and thank you yet for a 'major bust'. I've got to go. Take care of yourself."

"I'll keep a low profile Bren. And, by the way, if you see our playmate Parelli hanging out around The Pink Lady, don't run him off.

The Feds won't filch your bust; Vince'll be off duty, but he can be handy when the shit hits the fan... and he could be invaluable tonight."

Dan hung up, leaving Brenda to gauge the depth of the quagmire into which she and partner Frank were being lured. Next, he phoned Vince and caught him at home. The FBI man was happy to provide 'unofficial' back-up for Brenda and Frank after Dan put him in the picture. Dan shared more background with Vince than he'd dared tell Brenda. Contrary to common belief, Feds could be less fussy than the locals about 'procedure' when seriously bad guys were in play. They had the means to make the occasional mix-up disappear.

After his calls, Dan settled back with a soothing Marvin Gaye CD. He mentally replayed his last conversation with Gunnar. Were there any obvious loose ends? He took time to reflect on the substance of their lengthy discussion...

This plan is too intricate for my liking Gunnar. But, if it comes off, the Rosados will at least gain some closure on Benny's murder– and some major bad guys will finally pay for their sins. But I'm worried if we've covered all the bases.

Gunnar had hesitated before replying. I hope we're squared away Dan. The boys turned up an hour or so ago to help me baby-sit Tejada. His associates were deposited, per our instructions, somewhere out in the back and beyond of Otay Mesa. Both boys insist the fat fart was alive and kicking when they cut him loose. I'm 'good to go' with that probable piece of fiction if you are. Manny's still cuffed and gagged, by the way. He ate tortillas and sipped some water. We allow him a piss, but we don't even un-cuff him or loosen his bindings for that little excursion. We unzip his fly, lean him forward and Omar aims his puny pecker at the bog using my old salad tongs.

Dan had to chuckle at that delightful mental image before returning to more serious business. We're agreed then that the plan's on track? The boys will take Manny to The Pink Lady around 10:30. When it's all clear, Carrie will let them in the back door and the boys can bundle our blindfolded hostage into the storeroom by the back entrance. Omar will stand guard while Vic jogs over to the Sports Arena, to help you provide cover at our meet. You two'll follow Ernest and me to the club after I've grabbed our pigeon up. We'll take his car; you two'll follow in the rented Lincoln.

Be sure to keep an eye out for Brenda and her partner Frank lurking somewhere in the lot – and you might even spot Vince Parelli loitering in the background. Remember, everyone lies low until Tejada and Ernest re-emerge into the parking area. Tejada won't cause any trouble. He'll be exhausted and hoping to book that long-term stay at

'Chez Fed'. Ratting out Kincaid – and God knows who else – means his ass won't be worth bugshit in non-Federal custody. Make sure Manny's grabbed up quick... preferably by Vince. In the meantime, Ernest should be pissing himself... a straightforward collar for Brenda and Frank. Stay out of sight. If all goes to plan, all of us'll simply disappear in the rental car.

So Gunnar, you and the boys should just stay cool. By tomorrow morning, Vince will have Manny in protective custody somewhere in the bowels of the Federal Building. And, Mr Ernest Kincaid will have been charged with drug dealing – and hopefully, as an accessory to Benny's murder – by San Diego's finest. I'd love to see Melinda's face and hear Gene squealing when they spot her esteemed mentor on tomorrow's newscast.

Gunnar had laughed and replied, I'd like to see that too Dan, but I'd gladly trade that picture for the privilege of informing Connie and Greg about the arrests – omitting the contributions of her older boys, of course.

Okay then Gunnar. I'll see you at ten at the rental agency. Wear dark clothes and remember to bring your license. You'll be doing most of the driving.

Their rendezvous point with Ernest had been carefully chosen, as had the quiet lair at The Pink Lady for stowing Manny Tejada until his release. The Sports Arena's parking lot would be deserted... and hopefully Ernest would be out of his element; on his back foot. And, the close proximity of these two locations suited their planning.

Winter and Lila would keep Manny's holding pen at the back of the club under the radar with their co-workers. Few people other than the cleaners used the office/storeroom anyway. If their sting played out to plan, the takedown could conceivably even provide Cousin Benito with an undeserved *'Get out of Jail Free'* card. If Benny's grubby relative did the smart thing and split from San Diego, Carrie/Winter would have the little shit – *and* the evil Manny Tejada – out of her life forever. She'd get a fresh shot at becoming just 'Carrie' again, wherever she decided to go.

As Marvin Gaye finished his silky crooning, Dan switched on the television and half-watched a *Nash Bridges* rerun, attempting to relax until he'd pack up his 'Latino tough guy' garb and hit the road. He'd take his gun of course. In fact, a bulge under his armpit would no doubt add credence to his half-baked 'underworld' characterization. In his get-up, with a wide-brimmed hat low over his eyes, Ernest would almost assuredly fail to recognize him.

Chapter 29

The meet...

Dan stood in the shadows, just outside the murky orange beam emanating from an overhead light. Ernest Kincaid was driving into the Sports Arena parking lot bang on eleven. He steered his Jaguar to Mr Julio's designated section – C1. Emerging from the car, he placed the large gym bag by his feet on the asphalt.

Dan tried to instill a note of calm in his voice. "Señor Kincaid, please take three generous steps backwards."

Ernest didn't respond to the order from the shadowy form straight away. He obviously wasn't anxious to separate himself from such a substantial amount of money until he felt he might establish a modicum of control.

"First, may I ask where you're keeping our friend Manny Tejada, Mr Julio?"

Dan added more resolve to his tenor. "Relax! He remains nearby, out of harm's way – and he'll be handed over soon after we inspect the cash. Remember, no need for weapons, Mr Kincaid. My nervous associates are observing us." With that, Kincaid did as instructed and stepped backwards. Dan slipped into the light and bent to unzip the nylon bag, making sure to obscure his face from Ernest's gaze. Sure enough, the bundled bills were neatly stacked, filling the bag more than half-way. Dan zipped the bag, left it on the asphalt and ambled over to Ernest's sleek Jaguar. He opened the door and slid into the passenger seat, tilted his slouched hat towards the driver's side and motioned Ernest to join him; which he did.

"Now you must yet again demonstrate some trust in us, Mr Kincaid. The money will remain here for my friends to collect and count. You and I will drive to a nearby location so that you may retrieve your colleague. Don't eyeball me during the drive, if you please. My associates would be forced to take distasteful measures against you if they believed you could identify me to your esteemed partners."

Kincaid gripped the wheel and grimaced. Dan could sense the difficulty the businessman was experiencing in retaining his fragile composure. Ernest replied softly, "I'll abide by your every instruction Mr Julio. Forgive me, but as you'll no doubt understand, my so-called colleagues and I are in no position to trust you unreservedly. However, I've convinced my associates to play by your rules. And, I'm reasonably certain of one thing… you're telling me the truth about that scoundrel Rosado absconding with your heroin. Whatever the outcome this evening, you'll appreciate that I've made *every effort* to see that your organization has been suitably reimbursed for his greed and misdeeds."

"You take a very pragmatic approach Mr Kincaid. I can assure you we will not hold you to account for Benito's – or Manny Tejada's – rash choices. I'm a man of my word, so if you'd be so kind as to take a short drive with me, you'll soon be enjoying your reunion with Manny… and I'm sure he'll very submissively lead you to Benito Rosado as well."

Ernest stared straight ahead and turned over the Jag. Dan was relieved to see that he kept his eyes fixed on the road as they exited the vast parking lot. He turned left onto Sports Arena Boulevard, as instructed. Glancing furtively over his shoulder, Dan caught sight of their rental Lincoln pulling up next to the abandoned gym bag. The driver's door opened and an arm reached down to scoop up the holdall. Then, Dan could just make out Victor trotting out of the shadows and jumping into the Lincoln on the passenger side.

Both cars covered the quarter mile to The Pink Lady in short order. Dan saw the rental sedan park in a dark corner of the club's lot shortly after he'd hustled Kincaid out of the Jag. He stood directly behind Ernest, who knocked, as ordered, on the backstage door. It opened and there stood the gorgeous Winter in full stage make-up, wrapped in a drab green bathrobe.

A fair exchange?

Dan pushed Ernest through the entry and caught a fleeting glimpse of the leggy blonde fleeing down the corridor. She made a sharp right at the end of the hallway, entering what was no doubt the *artistes'* main dressing room. He stepped into the brightness and put a hand on Ernest's shoulder. "Please hold up here, Mr Kincaid. See the door directly to your left? You may open it and slowly enter. We'll conclude our business in privacy."

Ernest opened the door into the storeroom, an unlit area that smelled of disinfectant and floor polish. As their eyes began to adjust to the darkness, Dan was certain that Kincaid would sense someone – undoubtedly the hostage, Manny Tejada – bound to a chair in the center of the room. Dan remained just outside the doorway, waiting for Ernest to advance into the room. No sense in crowding their pigeon.

Ernest slowly approached the gagged and bound Manny Tejada, glancing surreptitiously to his left and right. Suddenly, he froze. He turned more sharply to his right and stared intently at a spot just behind the door – the dark corner meant to conceal Manny's silent sentry! Omar's back was pressed firmly against the shelves behind the open door, but even the murkier edges of the room were evermore visible to Dan – and most assuredly the inadequately hidden Omar was coming into focus for Ernest as well.

"Christ," Kincaid hissed, "You've set me up!"

In a flash, everything was turning to shit! Dan could only surmise it was dawning on Ernest that this con job tied even more directly than he'd expected into Benny's unfortunate murder. At this moment, he'd be assuming he was being scammed for a cool half million by a vengeful Rosado clan – and that his charmed existence was truly over and he had little in the way of 'wriggling room'.

An amazed Dan saw Ernest reach into his trouser pocket. What the hell, this pompous asshole had unexpected grit… was he going for a gun? Damn, why hadn't he frisked this seemingly innocuous sap at the Sports Arena?

A nine-millimeter emerged in what seemed like slow motion. And, Dan's *own* hand felt like it was moving through treacle. He plainly couldn't draw his weapon with any agility from under his ridiculous trench coat. He changed tack instantly and launched himself with all of his might into Ernest's back… but, a few milliseconds too late. Kincaid had already squeezed off two shots – and his initial target, Manny Tejada, slumped forward as the two rounds tore into his chest. Ernest fell in a heap under Dan's tackle, but the astonishingly agile man managed to instinctively roll away from the collision. Omar was recovering from his own shock and hastily ran towards the men on the floor… but Ernest Kincaid wasn't finished! He continued turning and rose onto a knee, steadying himself and pointing his weapon at Omar's torso. Omar saw or sensed the gun trained on him… he practically stopped on a dime.

Encumbered by his 'Mexican Mafioso' garb, Dan *still* hadn't managed to draw his own pistol as he rose from his ill-timed tackle. Kincaid seemed to have the drop on them – again! Ernest spat out a warning laden with startling authority for a so-called 'lightweight' businessman… "Don't make any sudden moves Mr Julio. I have this young man in my sights and I won't hesitate to shoot him. And, I must inform you… I'm an *expert* marksman."

Dan and Omar remained stock-still. How would this mind-blowing debacle play out?

The answer came in an instant. A muzzle flash exploded from the hallway and a tiny crimson rose blossomed on Ernest Kincaid's expansive forehead. Dan's remarkable adversary dropped in a heap, precisely where he'd been kneeling only an instant before.

A bulky silhouette dashed through the entrance and their unknown savior barked out an order. "Don't anyone move! I'm turning the light on."

The illumination revealed FBI Agent Vincent Parelli, standing just behind the still immobile Omar, gun drawn and smoking. Dan was startled – and immensely relieved. "What in hell are you doing here? I told you to wait outside with Bren and Frank."

"I know what you *told* me to do dick-wad, but I figured we'd all be better off if I covered the potential secondary exit at the end of the hallway. I hid in the girls' dressing room ... clever huh? The ladies have been great company! San Diego's Finest are more than capable of covering the stage door exit... and, although you'd probably never admit it amigo, you were undeniably in need of more effective back-up than Bren and Frank sitting on their butts in the parking lot! By the way, that take-out shot in Ernest Asshole's forehead was just dumb luck. Even I'm not *that* skilled at hitting the bull's-eye in a dim interior!"

Unsurprisingly, by this time the aforementioned Brenda and Frank were poised in the hallway. Weapons drawn, they pushed back bystanders, reassuring themselves the gunplay had ceased. Omar knelt over Manny Tejada, feeling for a pulse, as Brenda shouted into the storeroom, "All clear? Any good guys down?"

It was Vince who replied, as he was clearly in charge. "It's all clear in here Brenda... one perp definitely dead and another down, but maybe not out! Good guys okay. Call for an ambulance and back-up." The FBI Agent turned back to Dan and whispered, "I'd say that you were pretty damned lucky I *was* lurking inside when the shit hit the fan. That worn out piece of shit over there definitely got the drop on you two, Ace."

"Jesus, you're right there Vince. And neglecting to pat down *any* adversary prior to a clandestine tête-à-tête is a rookie mistake I thought I'd never make. Now I *know* I'm going senile. This shit just confirms it. I'm glad I'm slurpin' coffee in an insurance office and off the streets... forever! Nice shooting anyway, dude. Don't sell your skills short."

"As I said, more luck than skill, man. I had to take that shot past Omar's inert torso and over your shoulder as you were hunching down. As my intended target was kneeling and partially obscured, I could only take the head shot. I take it the stiff over there *is* Kincaid – and his friend Tejada is that other bundle being tended to by the Rosado kid?"

Before Dan could reply, Manny, still bound to his overturned chair, emitted a low moan. Blood oozed from his left shoulder and also trickled sideways down his chest from just below his right collarbone. But, luckily, he was alive... and, at least for the moment, conscious.

Dan managed to shake off the remaining fog... time to focus on business. He kicked Ernest's gun away from his prostrate body and felt for a pulse on the businessman's neck. This confirmed the obvious. Ernest was *quite* dead, as Vince had surmised.

Brenda stepped into the room and grabbed her FBI counterpart for a quiet word in the corner. Her partner Frank was already on his cell, summoning the paramedics and a shitload of back-up uniforms.

As Dan emerged into the hallway, chaos reigned up and down the corridor, with onlookers collecting down by the dancers' dressing room. Assorted strippers, some scantily clad and others in modest robes, milled about under the watchful eyes of a burly bouncer, as well as Gunnar and Victor. Omar joined Dan and whispered, "Sorry man. Me and Vic decided not to remind Gunnar our crews had done some tidy-ups at a few of Kincaid's properties last year. Melinda kindly recommended us to him. Neither of us *ever* spoke with old Ernest himself, but he must have noticed me at a job site and remembered my face tonight. If we'd told you about our past business association with Kincaid, you'd have cut us out of tonight's action. We couldn't risk that."

Dan, still lightheaded, hissed, "Well, that's real nice work kid! You and Victor took it upon yourselves to take a risk that cost at least one life tonight – and perhaps another man won't see morning as well. Shit man, we're just damned lucky to have escaped with our *own* lives! For now, just keep your head down, your mouth shut and go join Gunnar and Vic down at the other end of the hallway."

Carrie swept by the bystanders, still in her dog-eared bathrobe, and pushed her head through the storeroom door. Eyes wide, she asked, "Hey, why doesn't someone untie Manny? I don't think he's going anywhere in that condition!"

Brenda turned from Vince and began to loosen the gunshot victim's now irrelevant bindings. Amazingly, the paramedics arrived moments later. (Most nights, it seemed as if at least *one* ambulance team camped out in this seamy neighborhood.) Two attendants took over as Brenda undid the last of the ropes. As they wheeled Manny out of the room, Vince flashed his Government ID at them. "I'm riding with you on this one. He's going to the County ER and my boys will be waiting there

231

for us. He's now officially a Federally Protected Witness... and we desperately need to pull his ass through, got it?"

"Right sir," the efficient woman at the front of the wheeled stretcher replied. "He's lost a lot of blood. We'll pump some plasma into him on the way downtown. At least no arteries appear to be spurters!" With that, Vince followed the unconscious Manny's stretcher and the paramedics out of the room and into the night, nodding to Dan and Brenda as he went.

A 'mover and shaker' no more

Brenda turned her attention to the body sprawled on the floor. Dan walked over and joined her. Frank shouted that a second stretcher was on its way from the parking lot to scoop up the victim. Brenda lifted one eyebrow and enquired, "Was this turkey going to be our career-enhancing bust, Dan?" She knelt down for a closer look and barely managed to stifle a gasp. "For Christ's sake, isn't this Ernest Kincaid? Don't tell me this old dude was involved in Benny Rosado's hit!"

"Not *directly* in the hit, in all probability... but he was involved in the big picture up to those ugly crinkles in his wizened neck. I guess that being sole heir to our beloved ex-mayor didn't guarantee him a feeding spot high enough up on the proverbial San Diego hog. I'm fairly certain Ernest *was* a financier for the scum who put out the contract. I've got Cousin Benito tucked away, by the way... I'll scoop him up in the morning and bring him 'round to you when things quiet down. If Tejada pulls through, he'll be singing like a bird for the Feds. And Benito will sing harmony for you on many of those tunes if you cut him a halfway attractive deal. If you're clever enough – and I *know* you are – Benito should be the first of many collars coming to you and Frank as this crappy scenario plays out."

Brenda hesitated before asking, "Do you really see Benito Rosado cooperating with us Dan? Won't he clam up?"

"That depends on how much juicy gossip and hard evidence Vince can squeeze out of his pal Tejada – and on the slack your team is willing to cut him, Bren. I'll simply hand the little shit over to you. And then you, Frank and the DA can decide if he's best used as bait for further busts or if it's more advantageous to toss him into the system. I did, however, sort of promise you'd cut him some slack if he chose to cooperate."

"If Benito rats out a prize fish or two, I'm sure we'll arrange a soft landing for him, Dan. Do you suppose he's repentant – and truly convinced that his *only* chance of freedom in the next few decades hinges on playing ball with us?"

"I'm fairly certain he's aware he's best served by becoming a team player Bren. But, on the other hand, he was never a paid-up member of *any* brain trust. Initially, he'll probably attempt to tough things out – and he may even take a shot at 'lawyering up'. You'll have to *quickly* cut through the usual crap, before some 'People's Champion' asshole in the DA's office or a publicity-seeking defense lawyer cuts you out of the action."

Brenda turned just as Gunnar, Vic and Omar passed in the corridor. Thankfully, her partner Frank chose to ignore them and instead concentrated on keeping a new rush of curious onlookers at bay. Brenda whispered a quick final word to Dan. "It's time your pals were heading out Dan. It's lucky we didn't see them here, huh?"

Dan stepped over and waved as the trio approached the rear exit. He didn't need to pass on Brenda's suggestion about making a hasty move to them. They were outside and in the rented Lincoln before a second wave of noisy black and whites arrived.

Dan and Brenda quickly re-examined the crime scene... everything must point to a 'good shoot' for Vince. "Thanks for letting Gunnar and the boys head out, Bren. It wouldn't look good for the Rosados – or for myself, for that matter – if Omar was placed in this room at the time of the shooting. I know Vince won't admit to seeing anyone in here but me and Manny when he took out Kincaid."

The back exit had now been jammed open and a phalanx of gawkers stood outside in a tight circle, attempting to peer into the club's interior. An unmarked police sedan squealed to a halt beyond the mounting rank of squad cars. Moments later, Detective Lieutenant Gene Jeffries, accompanied by one of his mustachioed drones, strutted into the crowded hallway.

Lieutenant Gene peered into the storeroom and immediately spotted Dan and Brenda. "Well, if it isn't *Mister* Paige – and what a coincidence, it's his favorite little ex-partner too! Love the gangsta' outfit, Dan. What are you up to in your spare time? Workin' as an extra in some Tarantino flick?" He glanced over at the lifeless corpse and the paramedics who were about to load it on a stretcher. "Who's the stiff?"

Even if the evening hadn't gone *precisely* to plan, Dan couldn't have anticipated this splendid windfall; he'd secured himself a ringside seat for Gene's imminent very unpleasant discovery. Melinda's mentor was still lying motionless on the storeroom floor, with a startled look frozen on his chalky, upturned face and a dark crimson 'third eye' in the center of his forehead.

233

Gene knelt down to take a closer look. He visibly blanched as his brain took in the enormity of the corpse's identity. "Holy shit! It's Ernest Kincaid." He took a few seconds to regain his composure before turning to his mustachioed underling to bark an order. "Cuff this bastard, Curt," he instructed, pointing an accusing finger at Dan. "And, you've got some explaining to do, Brenda my sweet."

Brenda stepped between the befuddled Curt and her old partner and stared directly at Gene. "Not so fast, detective. First, let's do a more thorough crime scene run-through. I think you'll discover that the bullet that killed your pal Ernest is a 'clean shot through the brain cavity', with the slug lodged somewhere in the back wall. Kincaid will be sporting a nasty exit wound in the back of his skull, as the pool of blood under his noggin readily indicates. And, I think you'll *eventually* find that the slug was fired by a weapon registered to a highly-placed FBI Agent. Your deceased buddy's weapon has been fired as well, Lieutenant. It's lying over there in the corner. We haven't touched it. Vincent Parelli, of the FBI's Organized Crime Task Force, is presently on his way to the County ER, accompanying Mr Kincaid's unfortunate shooting victim."

Dan took the opportunity to interject. "Gene, Melinda's dear friend here, Mr Kincaid, happened to be wallowing in slime well above his nut-sack... enjoying ill-gotten gains generated by dealings with San Diego's drug underworld. Shocking, huh?"

Gene attempted to lay a convincing sneer on Dan, but his shoulders visibly lowered. "Do you expect me to believe this implausible bullshit, Paige?"

Dan stared at his old adversary, barely able to conceal a smirk before replying. "Not only do I expect you to *believe* me Gene, but I'm afraid I'm duty-bound to inform the DA's office that they'd best hook up with Internal Affairs to check on your ongoing knowledge of Kincaid's misdeeds – or even, God forbid, your direct involvement!"

Of course, this spiteful threat was pure bluff. But, it triggered the outraged, red-faced reply that Dan was anticipating. "*Fuck you, Paige!* This whole thing stinks... start to finish. And you're in this crap-pile up to your ears; I know it! I'll see you in my office first thing in the morning – and you can bring along your legal representative if you wish."

"I don't think I'll be popping by Gene. You can clear up your Crime Scene Report, if you're harebrained enough to prepare one, by reading Brenda and Frank's case notes. I think that for the foreseeable future, she and her partner will be seconded to a fresh *City/County Drugs Task Force*, working alongside our esteemed DA, the DEA and FBI."

Once again the agitated Gene flushed a glowing red before turning on his heel and storming out of the storeroom. His sidekick followed, visibly stifling a grin.

Dan didn't take time to gloat. "Wait here a second, Bren. I want to have a word with one of the *artistes* before she heads out." With that, he exited the dingy room and headed down the corridor.

A make-up-free Carrie paced the changing room, already in her street clothes. Her 'Winter' garb and the old bathrobe hung on a rail, near a brightly lit mirror. She was now clearly anxious to beat a hasty retreat. But she threw her shoulder bag aside and sat down when Dan entered. He grabbed the chair by her makeup station, pushing aside an open jar of glittery body powder. "You did great kid, but you and Lila should get out of here, pronto. The club will be closed for the duration of this evening anyway. Give me five minutes to set up your 'free pass' and then tell the cops at the door that the female detective and her partner have interviewed both of you and have your home address. She's my old partner and she'll back up your exit story if they ask questions."

"Thanks Dan. Is Manny going to be okay?"

"Honestly, I'm not sure honey. The doctors and Vince will take good care of him – and if he's lucky, he'll live to tell the Feds some spellbinding tales. I don't expect you'll be seeing much of him around here, though. As of now, he's officially on the Feds' 'Low-profile Witness' list. Now, I've got one more extremely important favor to ask of you. When you get home tonight, *don't tell Benito what's gone down!* Make up some story. Maybe a fracas between the sailors and locals getting the joint closed down for the evening? I'd be most obliged if he's none the wiser until I'm ready to deal with him." Dan took Carrie by the shoulders and repeated, "Not a word to him, okay?"

"Tomorrow morning, quite early, I'll drop by. It's for his own good. If I were to take him in tonight, I couldn't guarantee he'll be handed over to Brenda and Frank – their hands will be full for the rest of the evening. Just so you know, they're the only cops that I *know* Benito can trust. I've already had a chat with Bren – and there's a strong chance that if he plays ball, he'll walk free in no time. In any event, he'll want to be well out of harm's way when some heavy shit hits the fan in San Diego. The DA will be able to get him to safety, and a new life – if he proves to be useful."

Carrie appeared to be having difficulty in taking it all in. "I'd feel like a shit if I steered Benito towards a major fall, Dan. Can't you just help him to *disappear* tonight, before the cops are hot on his trail?"

"Yeah kid, I could manage that. But I don't think his relentless Mexican colleagues would be down with that turn of events at all. Remember, he was due for a hit *before* this evening's fiasco. After these events, he'll be *numero uno* on their shit list, wherever he goes. He needs a few powerful allies, whether he's smart enough to realize it or not. I'll pick him up in the morning and take him to see my old partner. She can keep Benito far away and out of harm's way... but only if he's willing to cooperate."

"All right Dan. I can see his options are either piss-poor or non-existent – and your cop buddies are undoubtedly providing a lifeboat. I'll keep quiet about your visit tomorrow morning. And, me and Lila won't talk about what went down tonight around him."

"Thanks doll – and feel free to give Lila a rundown on *why* you're keeping mum with Benito, okay? It may help."

Two minutes later, Dan returned to his old partner, still occupied in the storeroom. The stretcher was finally leaving with the lifeless Ernest Kincaid, his body covered to thwart the gawkers and any curious press. She joined him in the hallway.

"Bren, if you don't need me, I'm out of here. You can reach me at home – and I'll bring Benito Rosado in to you, hopefully in a cooperative mood, first thing tomorrow morning. Looks like you and Frank may be here a while. Crime scenes like this have a way of cutting into your beauty sleep, huh? By the way, a luscious blonde called Winter and a dark beauty named Lila need a free pass out of here tonight. They're on our side and still have a bit of work to do keeping Benito Rosado happy, so you'll get first crack at them in your own time. In the meantime, it's best that they're not given the third degree by anyone else. I told them to tell anyone stopping them that you and Frank had already interviewed them and you've cleared them to split. Can you put Frank in the picture, so that the girls can be out of here in a couple of minutes?"

"Consider it done, Dan. So you know, I'll be at my desk in Vice from eight-thirty tomorrow morning. We'll swing by County Hospital after clearing this crime scene, to get an update on Tejada. I'll fill you in on his condition in the morning."

"Of course you realize Bren, if Vince is able to crack Manny Tejada and you're credited with the collar on his pal Benito, the two of you will undoubtedly have to work *very* closely together in the coming months. I know that's a sacrifice for you... Vince Parelli can be a real pig to deal with."

Brenda visibly blushed. "Shut up Dan. You seem to think that goofball's got some *personal* interest in me, but I know better."

"Maybe you're a worse cop than I thought Bren! I'm usually not much of a matchmaker, but this fucked-up case has thrown you two 'Dating Game' contestants together in the weirdest way I've ever come across! I'm pretty sure Vince will finally try to make his move this time. I've got to get some sleep... see you just after nine."

Brenda shook her head and tried to focus on the business at hand. "Might as well make it ten, Dan. We'll have a load of paperwork to catch up on and you'll no doubt benefit from that bit of extra beauty sleep before grabbing up Benito. And bring the bagels... remember, Frank and I don't like raisin."

Dan was home and in bed thirty minutes later, mulling over his eventful evening. Their basic strategy had turned sour during the tortuous 'rollout phase', but that was par for the course when rash tactics were ineffectually executed. Most importantly, their luck had held... and a number of exceedingly bad guys would soon be swallowed up in the system.

Of course, more than a handful of the more odious Mexican scumbags would avoid the closing police net in the US. And counting on the Mexican authorities to arrest them was a long shot, at best. The big fish swim higher up the food chain, cleverly distancing themselves from life's temporary setbacks. The cartel would soon recruit willing aspirants to run the San Diego action. The underworld's 'Shit-creation Gauge' might hover at *Low* temporarily... but it would never remain there for long.

He'd phone Gunnar and Vince in the morning, before heading out to the girls' place to grab up Benito. For now though, he was looking forward to some hard-earned sack time – and, hopefully, a sound and dreamless snooze. As keyed up as he was, Dan felt that exhaustion would probably trump exhilaration... at least for the next few hours.

Chapter 30

Wednesday

Clearing the air

Dan awoke earlier than he'd have preferred and decided to clear his head with a run. Today's activities might be arduous – he'd best face them on his toes. He set a decent pace, surprised by the energy he retained after the previous night's commotion. His brief slumber had undoubtedly enhanced his spirits. A heavy rain began to fall just as he headed down into Mission Valley. The radio's earlier 'gray skies, intermittent showers and afternoon partial clearing' forecast would be right on the money for the next few days.

Screw it, Dan thought. It's warm enough – and the last time I checked, I'm not yet over the hill. A bit of a soaking shouldn't slow me up! When he'd jogged half-way into the canyon the transitory downpour abated as quickly as it had begun. He was left with San Diego's glorious damp earth aroma filling his nostrils.

At quarter to eight, shaved and showered, Dan relaxed in his underwear with a mug of strong coffee and a heaping bowl of corn flakes. *All-News Radio* briefly mentioned a late-night shooting at The Pink Lady, but a distinct lack of detail implied that they were covering it as yet another bust-up between 'regular patrons' (read: 'sleazy scumbags and drug-addled sex addicts').

Tossing his mug, bowl and spoon into the sink, Dan got on the phone to Gunnar. He wanted to bring their versions of the previous evening's disturbance into line before heading out. This hour of the morning would normally constitute a tardy start for Gunnar and the boys, but Dan reasoned they'd no doubt headed home exhausted – and almost certainly would have opted for that rare opportunity to sleep in.

Gunnar answered on the second ring. He reassured Dan that he'd cautioned the boys to say *nothing* to their mother – or to their brother for that matter. He'd handle any details or loose ends with the Rosado clan when the time was right. And, he'd reminded Vic and Omar yet again that the less Greg *ever* knew about their role in any of the recent events, the better.

In the light of day, Gunnar had scant fresh insights. His pragmatic take on the previous evening could be summed up as: "Three out of four very bad guys permanently out of the loop ain't too shabby, amigo. Those two pig-ignorant greasers and that slimy Kincaid are *history* – and I hope that Manny follows them on his *own* painful journey to hell in the near future! As for Cousin Benito, if he manages to slide, it'll be an injustice; but for the family's sake, it'll be okay by me."

Dan had little to add. He thanked Gunnar again and apologized for things not proceeding precisely to plan. He didn't mention Ernest's gym bag – he knew Gunnar would hide the cash safely and find a good use for it. Finally, he reiterated the absolute necessity of keeping the boys on a tight lead. (He knew it went without saying!) They'd talk again later in the day.

Dan caught Vince in his office. He'd slept there, after confirming Tejada had been taken off the critical list. His prized stoolie was doped up and under heavy guard at the hospital, but Manny – and a handpicked medical team – would no doubt be ensconced in the Federal Building before the day was out. "My guys'll give the deeper investigation into Kincaid's involvement a body swerve for now – except, of course, to confirm with the locals on why my shooting was righteous. We'll liaise with Brenda's team on his actual role in this fiasco later. Both teams will undoubtedly write you up as a bystander who simply adores hanging out in one of San Diego's finer establishments. And it transpired you were innocently doing *just that* when you heard a shot in back. And, if we're ever asked, none of us will remember seeing any Rosados on the premises. I'm betting a fair number of arrests will soon come Brenda's way; but you already know that."

As Dan assumed, Vince was falling into line. "Keeping me well away from this shitty situation suits me to the ground, bro'. And, thanks for suggesting that Gunnar, Vic and Omar were never at the scene. It's up to you though. If it means nailing another of the slimeballs behind Benny's murder, I'm sure that Gunnar, in particular, can be counted on to step up."

"Get some rest Dan. I'm not only going to keep all of you out of this, but I'm sure I can convince Manny that it's in his best interest to suffer 'amnesia' on how he happened to end up in that storeroom last night. He'll swear that he never recognized his kidnappers."

Fantastic... one more loose thread *almost* woven into place! Hopefully, late arrival Dean and his stooges hadn't noticed the Rosados leaving the scene. If that was the case, Gunnar and the boys were probably home scot-free. "I was counting on your persuasive skills for keeping a gag on Manny Tejada, Vince. Do your best on squeezing more useful shit out of Manny, for the sake of the Rosados, okay?"

"Gotta go, Dan. The boss just walked by my desk. It's time to put him and the rest of the suits in the picture – *sort of.*"

Adios amigo

Dan pulled up in front of the apartment complex, intent on separating the shifty Benito from his long-suffering roommates. He realized he'd taken a big risk by allowing the little turd his freedom for so long. Now he'd grab up Benito and get him to Brenda and Frank before the unreliable greaseball reassessed the state of play and devised some loopy escape plan for himself – that maybe included Carrie as well.

Carrie answered the door at Dan's first knock. Her blush spoke volumes. Even with her near-opaque complexion, Dan was convinced that few things would make her go red... she'd seen and experienced so much in her young life. But the glow undoubtedly extended to her toes. Dan instantly understood her discomfort... the final piece in this puzzle was long gone!

"So, where's Benito this morning Carrie?"

"Come in and have some coffee Dan. He left you a note. God, he must have had a strong hunch that something big was in the wind... I just *knew* he'd fixed his mind on splitting the last day or two. When we came home last night, even *I* couldn't coax him that things were okay – and I tried my hardest."

Dan let Carrie's comments pass concerning Benito's fortuitous premonitions. But face it; the guy wasn't *that* intuitive. He'd been told *something* that set him running. Dan sat on the couch and picked up the sealed envelope on the coffee table. Carrie left him to his reading, going into the kitchen to make mugs of instant coffee.

Benito's note was brief and to the point...

Hey Dan, when you read this I'll be off to find a better life. Don't blame Winter. She kept me in the dark as good as she could, but I could always make her share thoughts and secrets with me. It's getting too hot around here, so I'll take my chances down the road. Don't press the girls on this. They don't have no clue where I'm headed.

Sorry I sort of let you down. I do know one thing though – you'll get to the bottom of this stupid mess soon enough, even without my help. And when you do, you'll understand why I had to put some very real space between me and a bunch of ruthless assholes. Take care – and please go easy on Winter.

Your friend, B

There was no point in interrogating Carrie, though it was clear she'd helped her ex-boyfriend to plan his getaway – and perhaps in penning his *almost* poignant farewell missive as well. Benito was clever enough, but his opportune departure pointed to a well-meaning friend dropping

240

some less than subtle hints. She brought through the coffee and sat by Dan, seemingly reading his mind. "I told him nothin' Dan, I swear."

"It's okay Carrie. Beating a hasty exit might be his safest option, even though it's the coward's way out in respect of his family obligations. I do think though, that it's about time you kissed off your life as the lovely 'Winter' and headed up the road yourself. Honestly, I don't see much of a future for you – or your sexy alter ego – here in San Diego."

Carrie flashed Dan a smile, clearly relieved that he was letting her off the hook so easily. "Thanks Dan. I know where you're coming from and I'd be grateful for some solid advice on that score."

Tying up loose ends

Dan drove down to SDPD's central headquarters after leaving the girls. Brenda and Frank would no doubt have come in straight off shift and headed to their desks to write up their reports on the previous night's activities. He drove into the municipal underground lot – marked *'Police and City Staff Only'* – and the security guard casually waved him through. His reputation as a stand-up ex-cop did have its residual benefits.

Five minutes later he sat opposite Brenda at her squad room desk. She looked exhausted, but elated. "Hey Dan, come in to get our stories straight?"

"Fuckin' A, Bren. As you know, a lot of the extraneous shit should stay buried, but you can count on Vince to provide some essentials to help close your case – and to pass along any appropriate new suspects as and when the Feds uncover them for you. Enough people saw me at The Pink Lady that it's best if I just give you a statement along the lines of: *'I was sitting out front, enjoying a quiet drink, and suddenly I heard a commotion backstage. When I ran back, San Diego's Finest had everything under control. I chatted with a few of my old colleagues and then went home.'* Does that sound okay?"

It took Dan and Brenda the best part of a quarter of an hour to iron out details and synchronize their stories, go over his recent conversation with Vince, review her own early-morning hospital visit to check on Tejada and, most importantly, to commiserate over Benito's inopportune disappearance. Then Dan typed and signed his short statement, confirming his 'peripheral involvement' in the previous night's events.

Frank strolled in, looking tired, with a mug in his hand. Bren promptly put him in the picture. He swiftly took it all in and asked only one question. "Will Vince work with us?" Of course, what he was implying was: *Can Vince see past the suspicions and competitiveness that poison the well whenever the Feds and local police are asked to work together? Can we trust him to give us top-notch support?*

"You can count on Vince, Frank," Dan replied. "The deal is, the FBI, DEA and Mexican authorities are getting a crack at Manny Tejada... and all of the Mexicans and out-of-staters he'll hopefully rat out. You'll collar the locals who're subject to state charges, including any surviving accomplices in Benny Rosado's murder. Tejada's slimy assistant, Enrique, comes to mind in this latter category. Unfortunately, as Benito's flown the coop, your most straightforward bust, as well as your prime source for scooping up local shitbags, is in the wind. But, I'm betting there'll be plenty of arrests for everyone, regardless of who ultimately gets jurisdiction in each case."

Brenda got up and went out to refill her coffee. Frank took the opportunity to lean in and whisper, "If this case gets me and Bren out of Vice, it'll be a godsend Dan. The hours are shitty, the perps and players are *major* scumbags and the duty's fuckin' hard on my marriage. Who'd ever believe that working on a special assignment like a 'DEA / Police Criminal Task Force' would feel like a leg up out of the muck, huh?"

Dan slouched in his chair and rubbed his face. "If Vince has the luck with Tejada that I think he will Frank, I'd say both you and your partner will be in line for promotions and pretty much a choice of duty assignments in the not-too-distant future. He should be in touch with you later today, to get things rolling."

Just as Dan straightened up, his old nemesis, Gene Jeffries, sauntered into the squad room and grabbed a chair from across the aisle. He sat down, legs straddling the chair's back, inches from Dan's face. He'd obviously regained some composure, following his abrupt departure from the strip joint. He smirked and literally spat out, "Well, if it isn't *'Mr Dodgy Claims Adjustor'*! Come to square up bullshit stories with our Vice Squad pin-ups? Here's a little warning dimwit... a shitload of dubious detail will come to light in the coming days, so you'd better come clean about your involvement in Kincaid's suspicious shooting while you still can. And, if I were you, I'd be contacting a good criminal lawyer."

Dan laughed and leaned back in his chair, increasing the distance between himself and the smug lieutenant's dodgy breath. "I don't know where you're coming from, Gene. I was out front in the club last night, enjoying the show, when the shit hit the fan. I was just telling Frank here that you and Melinda were *extremely* tight with poor Ernest. Just

242

last week, she was bragging to me about some 'secret deals' he was cutting you two in on. I wasn't simply pulling your chain last night when I mentioned your cozy relationship with the deceased, pal. I think the new DEA Task Force and your Internal Affairs Division will be fascinated with my story, when and if Frank here decides to pursue it."

The smirk left Gene's face, replaced in a flash by a look of utter disdain. "What are you driving at Paige? You know damned well that Melinda isn't mixed up in Kincaid's dirty laundry!" And, as his anger visibly turned to bewilderment, he softly added, "And, even if she *is* involved, it's certainly without *my* knowledge or consent."

Dan placed his head in his hands and momentarily closed his tired eyes. "That's a very chivalrous and revealing observation Gene. I'll leave the substance of your individual relationships with Ernest Kincaid for you lovebirds to sort out – and eventually, when you're on the same page, you can each touch base with Brenda and Frank. I'm sure they'll know which, if any, of my insinuations deserve a follow-up with the Task Force... or perhaps with Internal Affairs. I wish you the best of luck." (He actually meant that in Melinda's case. His fervent hope was that any wild hair up Gene's ass would go away of its own accord.)

With that, Dan stood and stared down at his dejected adversary. Lieutenant Gene looked thunderstruck – and, for once, the clueless windbag was lost for words. Brenda walked up with her coffee and grinned, obviously sensing the vibes. She sat on the corner of her desk and waved to Dan as he turned to leave. "Later, partner."

Dan allowed himself a hint of a smile as he walked down the corridor, passing a bevy of patrolmen and women heading out on their shifts. "Well..." he addressed himself out loud, "Thank you Lone Ranger!" Hopefully, this reluctant hero's work was done... and he could ride off into the sunset.

Now, where might he find some congenial company for the remainder of this fine morning? Should he head into the office for the latest steamy rundown on Trini's love life? Or, would he rather plow into eggs, toast and a pile of greasy hash browns with the boys at Lenny's?

No rest for the wicked.

Epilogue

One month later...

Benito lounged on his Cozumel balcony and downed his first Dos Equis Amber of the morning. He was already fed up with this purported paradise – and besides, it was far too close to his old cartel's stomping grounds. He pondered, yet again, if plastic surgery was his best bet for keeping a step ahead of his pursuers. But the dodgy surgeons who catered for criminal types would no doubt be early ports of call for his persistent former colleagues. It was time to move on... preferably far away from Méjico!

He recalled his last night in San Diego. Winter had come home all wound up. Attempting to give him a wide berth, she'd immediately locked herself in the bathroom. Eventually he coaxed her out and quizzed her about why she and Lila were home so early. Both girls broke down in tears and ran into Lila's room. Soon, after a little added pressure, Winter spilled her guts. Benito immediately resolved to make a run for it – sadly, on his own, without a gorgeous, but fussy, *gringa* in tow.

His border crossing was uneventful – and *Mama Grande* Hortensia brooded silently as he climbed into her loft to retrieve his old suitcase. The emergency stash wasn't a fortune, but it would last a decent period somewhere below the border. Benito had no qualms about fleeing. How could Paige – or his 'trustworthy' cop buddies – protect an expendable soldier like himself from the organization's brutal tentacles? He was sorry about his late cousin's fate, but as it was time to move on, there was no sense in crying over spilled milk.

Carlita sauntered onto the balcony. She was naturally slender and fairly light skinned for a rural *puta*, but no way was she in Winter's league! She raised her arms over her head and stretched like a cat before settling into the empty chaise lounge to file her nails. She removed her bikini top to cultivate that all-over 'golden glow', which she insisted enhanced her silicon-inflated rack. This slut believed her long, well-manicured nails were deep into him... and was certain she'd found herself a *primero* sugar daddy. Benito paid the sulky bitch no heed as he reclined and contemplated his next move. He had to disappear for good!

· · · · ·

Dan popped into the internet café to touch base with Eddie Kane. The boy peered intently into his screen in the quiet far corner. A few days ago, Dan had instructed him to dig deeper into Zenith Transport, Rod and Lightnin's dubious trucking company; but Eddie didn't have much to report yet. He couldn't uncover any data to tie Derrick into the day-to-day operations of the firm, but Rod's 'electronic fingerprints' were scattered over a fair number of e-mails and transactions. Dan was far from thrilled with this not unexpected development.

When Dan had last seen the boy, Ernest Kincaid's death had just hit the news and he'd given Eddie a $100 bonus. Eddie objected, but Dan insisted he take it... and told him it should have been a helluva lot more.

On today's visit Dan's tone became very serious and he spoke to the boy in a more personal manner than ever before. "Listen kid, I still have a few connections at San Diego State. If you apply yourself and do well on your SAT's, I'm sure you can get admitted to one of California's better Computer Sciences programs. You might even earn a scholarship – and I can help out with odd jobs and a bit of tuition."

Eddie pushed himself away from his computer and grinned. "Hey man, it's a thought. Hanging out here's fun – and easy money... but I know I can't be doing this freelance crap when I'm thirty and over the hill!" The boy undoubtedly recognized that a diploma was little more than a piece of paper, but unless he could emulate 'super-dropout' Bill Gates, it would do no harm to hold that ticket to future employment in reserve. Dan was pointing him in a new direction – and he could sense the boy was taking it all in, to mull over in his own time.

· · · · ·

Melinda and Gene were partaking of a rare lunch together, occupying an inconspicuous back corner booth at Winston's Jazz Cafe in the downtown Gaslamp District. It was one of those faux-thirties hangouts frequented by undemanding tourists in baggy shorts and tee shirts... ugh! But it served up huge portions of Gene's favorite grub: barbequed ribs, baked beans and steaming hot corn on the cob. Melinda could only *pray* that no friends or business associates would spot her lingering in this hideous establishment.

She sipped her giant goblet of overly perfumed Chardonnay and whispered, "I'm still in shock over Ernest's apparent double life Gene. You should have been onto him and in a position to warn me, you know. Haven't you ever heard how 'guilt by association' can ruin a fabulous career? The fact that I was chummy with him hasn't gone down well with La Jolla's more conservative movers and shakers. Was it asking too much to expect that you'd do your bit to safeguard our income and social position from this all too foreseeable catastrophe?"

245

Gene picked a bit of corn out of his teeth before replying. "Listen Melinda, I tried to warn you off of that creep, okay? I didn't know anything about his involvement in the drug trade... shit, who did? Suffice to say, *you* chose to get tight with a slimebag and it's come back to bite *both* of us in the ass. Lesson learned, honey? Your taste in business associates, old boyfriends and ex-husbands – categorically including Ernest Kincaid *and* that putz Paige – leaves a lot to be desired. Let's both of us try to keep a lower profile, okay?"

With that, Gene used his checkered napkin to wipe a large dollop of barbecue sauce from his chin. Then he piled dark, sauce-laden beans onto his knife blade. Disgusted, Melinda took a long pull of her tepid wine and eyed him as if he'd just hung his bare, bony ass into the narrow aisle and set a match to a loud, lingering fart.

· · · · ·

Marty and Lila sprawled lazily on chaise longues beside her pool. Marty turned and cooed, "Man, that nasty afternoon session's left me limp... in more ways than one, if you know what I mean! Heard from Winter again, Tasty?"

"Yeah, as a matter of fact I did. She phoned yesterday. I told you that she's 'Carrie' now, okay? She seems to be getting on better than expected with her mom – and she's enrolled next semester at a local JC. In the meantime, she's waitressing at some Thai restaurant in the mall. God, it all sounds so boring!"

Marty rubbed some more Hawaiian Tanning Oil on his chest. "Yeah, it sure does babe. Had any luck getting one of the new girls to move into our spare bedroom?" Marty had wasted little time moving in when Winter left – after all, Benito had set a very useful precedent. And now he saw no reason to forego a three-way rent split if the opportunity of a foxy female roommate presented itself.

"I'll ask Roxanne again, but only on one condition Marty. I don't *ever* want to hear any crap about how fun a threesome might be, got it?"

Marty gave Lila what he was sure passed as his most sincere smile. "No probs, babe! You're more woman than I can handle. Hangin' with you is just too fantastic to fuck up for some short-term side action. You can count on my best behavior."

The dark temptress turned her back on Marty and returned to a favorite recurring daydream: she was handcuffed naked to her bed, making prolonged, passionate love to his big brother. Dan Paige was a *keeper*... a stud more than worthy of her considerable charms. Oh well,

Marty was paying his way – so far. And it did mean she could keep closer tabs on his sexy brother for the foreseeable future.

· · · · ·

Neil and Dan strolled up a rocky trail in the afternoon sun. Annie and Sophie were lost in their own conversation twenty yards behind. The couples had driven north for a few days, renting cabins in the San Bernardino Mountains. It was wonderful to get away together. Sophie's stepdaughter, Alicia, was staying with Neil and Annie's kids, even though Annie realized they were just about old enough to look after themselves.

Annie was filling Sophie in on the latest with Connie and the boys. "They're doing pretty well, Sophie. Of course, Gunnar looks after all of them. And the fact that the police investigation indisputably pointed the finger at Ernest Kincaid and Manny Tejada for Benny's murder gives the family some 'sense of closure'... whatever that psycho-babble means. Gunnar reassured Connie and Hortensia that Manny Tejada will never see the light of day outside of federal prison – whether that's true or not! I guess they'll never know who did the actual shooting, but Gunnar and the boys seem to be putting that thorny issue behind them."

In turn, Sophie shared a little of what she knew about the case with Annie, although Dan had told her slightly more than she was now letting on. She could disclose that Manny had sung his head off to the DEA and there was still some way to go before his future – be it imprisonment or witness relocation – could be ascertained. But, she agreed with Annie that Connie would feel safer in future believing that Manny Tejada was behind bars, rather than running some dry cleaning business in Toledo.

Further up the hill, Neil and Dan were also discussing the case. "Ever hear where Benito ran off to Dan?"

"No, Neil – and I felt bad about letting Brenda and Frank down on what should have been a major bust. But it's working out okay. Vince still has Manny stashed somewhere. He's ratted out a few big fish already. Brenda's been credited with the collar on that slimy 'Enrique' character, Manny's so-called valet. Now, Enrique and Manny should be competing to see who can score more 'get out of jail free' points with their respective captors... so, more arrests will undoubtedly follow."

Neil chuckled. "Yeah, Annie informs me that Brenda and Vince are working quite closely on this case. Is my wife just trying to inject a little old-fashioned romance into the mix, or is there a chance of a bit of *real fire* lurking under this smoke?"

Dan smiled and gave his old pal a knowing wink. "Well Neil, you can ask Brenda and Vince about that yourself, if you and Annie want to join the four of us for dinner at Tio Jorge's next weekend."

· · · · ·

Late that same evening, four weary Mexicans stealthily made their way over the border, burrowing under the fence and scampering into the scrubland east of Otay Mesa. The full moon helped them to find their way – but it also made it easier for US Immigration to spot their quarry. Each illegal carried a note in his pocket, spelling out in coded Spanish who his 'safe contact' would be at his ultimate destination. The men were heading towards their initial US meeting point, marked by an 'X' on an old road map. From there, they'd be picked up and trucked to a house situated to the north and inland, near Escondido.

In California, a number of Chicano's garages are permanently fitted out as temporary sleeping quarters for friends, family and paying guests... illegals aiming for new lives in the fabled 'Land of Opportunity'. These four travelers carried their scant belongings in burlap bags. Three of the exhausted Mexicans knew that their wives and children were counting on them to make their way in this new land before sending for them as well. The fourth man – really just a boy – was too young to head his own family.

The men stayed low; bending at the waist, keeping an eye out for the dreaded Border Patrol. The youngster looked down and spotted a weather-beaten, fingerless leather glove in the dust at his feet. He smiled, picked it up and slipped it onto his hand. He whispered to the others in Spanish, "Hey amigos, I'm keeping this... it gives me an edgy look."

The oldest Mexican, obviously their leader, gave the boy a terse sideways glance. "Throw that stupid glove away man. It makes you look like a greasy *zonzo*. Besides, we're lookin' for decent *jobs*, not new troubles, when we all reach our destinations!"

The four walked on, oblivious to a barely discernible mound, covered in loose dirt and scrub, a few feet to their left. All they desired was a chance at a better future. And good things were bound to happen in the USA!

The End

Acknowledgements

I'd like to express my sincere gratitude to John Hudspith, my UK editor. His comments and suggestions were invaluable. John is a pro... his unstinting advice added valued focus to the story's pacing and point of view.

Thanks also to a fine illustrator, Jane Dixon-Smith, for creating a cover that perfectly captures the spirit and ambiance of the book.

I would also like to thank a great friend (and published author), Anne Stormant, for her advice and encouragement. Without her guidance, it's hard to tell if I would've managed to navigate from 'there to here'.

Al Daniels

Al Daniels was born and raised in Seattle, Washington. After graduating from the University of Washington, he spent three years in Germany, serving in the US Armed Forces. He returned to the US with his Scottish wife, Jennifer, and for the next ten years they lived in San Diego, California.

For the past twenty-nine years, Al and Jennifer have resided in Edinburgh, Scotland, her city of birth. Thanks to Jennifer's undiminished sense of adventure, they have traveled the world. *'Tequila Shooters'* is Al's first novel.